Robert Michael Ballantyne

Post Haste

A Tale of Her Majesty's Mails

Robert Michael Ballantyne

Post Haste
A Tale of Her Majesty's Mails

ISBN/EAN: 9783337088484

Printed in Europe, USA, Canada, Australia, Japan

Cover: Foto ©Andreas Hilbeck / pixelio.de

More available books at **www.hansebooks.com**

POST HASTE

A TALE OF HER MAJESTY'S MAILS.

BY R. M. BALLANTYNE,

AUTHOR OF "THE LONELY ISLAND;" "IN THE TRACK OF THE TROOPS;" "THE
SETTLER AND THE SAVAGE;" "UNDER THE WAVES;" "RIVERS OF ICE;" "BLACK
IVORY;" "THE PIRATE CITY;" "ERLING THE BOLD;" "THE NORSEMEN
IN THE WEST;" "THE IRON HORSE;" "FIGHTING THE FLAMES;"
"THE FLOATING LIGHT;" "SHIFTING WINDS;" "DEEP
DOWN" "THE LIGHTHOUSE;" "THE LIFEBOAT;"
"GASCOYNE;" "THE GOLDEN DREAM," ETC.

With Illustrations.

THIRTEENTH THOUSAND.

LONDON:
JAMES NISBET & CO., 21 BERNERS STREET.

CONTENTS.

vi

CONTENTS.

LIST OF ILLUSTRATIONS.

CHAPTER I.

ONCE upon a time—only once, observe, she did not do it twice—a widow of the name of Maylands went, in a fit of moderate insanity, and took up her abode in a lonely, tumble-down cottage in the west of Ireland.

Mrs. Maylands was very poor. She was the widow of an English clergyman, who had left her with a small family and the smallest income that was compatible with that family's maintenance. Hence the migration to Ireland, where she had been born, and where she hoped to live economically.

The tumble-down cottage was near the sea, not far from a little bay named Howlin Cove. Though little it was a tremendous bay, with mighty cliffs landward, and jutting ledges on either side, and forbidding rocks at the entrance, which waged continual warfare with the great Atlantic billows that rolled into it. The whole place suggested shipwreck and smugglers.

A

The small family of Mrs. Maylands consisted of three babes—so their mother styled them. The eldest babe, Mary—better known as May—was seventeen years of age, and dwelt in London, to which great city she had been tempted by an elderly English cousin, Miss Sarah Lillycrop, who held out as baits a possible situation and a hearty welcome.

The second babe, Philip, was verging on fifteen. Having kicked, crashed, and smashed his way through an uproarious infancy and a stormy childhood, he had become a sedate, earnest, energetic boy, with a slight dash of humour in his spirit, and more than a dash of determination.

The third babe was still a baby. As it plays little or no part in our tale we dismiss it with the remark that it was of the male sex, and was at once the hope, fear, joy and anxiety of its distracted mother. So, too, we may dismiss Miss Madge Stevens, a poor relation, who was worth her weight in gold to the widow, inasmuch as she acted the part of general servant, nurse, mender of the household garments, and recipient of joys and sorrows, all of which duties she fulfilled for love, and for just shelter and sustenance sufficient to keep her affectionate spirit within her rather thin but well-favoured body.

Phil Maylands was a hero-worshipper. At the time when our tale opens he worshipped a youth—

the son of a retired naval officer,—who possessed at
least some of the qualities that are occasionally found
in a hero.   George Aspel was daring, genial, enthusiastic, tall, broad-shouldered, active, and young—
about twenty.   But George had a tendency to dissipation.

His father, who had recently died, had been
addicted to what he styled good-fellowship and
joy.   Knowing his so-called weakness, Captain
Aspel had sent his boy to be brought up in the
family of the Rev. James Maylands, but some time
before the death of that gentleman he had called
him home to help to manage the small farm with
which he amused his declining years.   George and
his father amused themselves with it to such an extent that they became bankrupt about the time of
the father's death, and thus the son was left with
the world before him and nothing whatever in his
pocket except a tobacco-pipe and a corkscrew.

One day Phil met George Aspel taking a ramble
and joined him.   These two lived near to each
other.   Indeed, Mrs. Maylands had been partly
influenced in her choice of a residence by her desire
to be near George.

It was a bitterly cold December afternoon.   As
the friends reached the summit of the grey cliffs,
a squall, fresh from the Arctic regions, came sweeping over the angry sea, cutting the foam in flecks

from the waves, and whistling, as if in baffled fury, among the opposing crags.

"Isn't it a grand sight?" said Phil, as they sought shelter under the lee of a projecting rock.

"Glorious! I never look upon that sight," said Aspel, with flashing eyes, "without wishing that I had lived in the days of the old Vikings."

The youth traced his descent from the sea-kings of Norway—those tremendous fellows who were wont in days of yore to ravage the shores of the known and unknown world, east and west, north and south, leaving their indelible mark alike on the hot sands of Africa and the icebound rocks of Greenland. As Phil Maylands knew nothing of his own lineage further back than his grandfather, he was free to admire the immense antiquity of his friend's genealogical tree. Phil was not, however, so completely under the fascination of his hero as to be utterly blind to his faults; but he loved him, and that sufficed to cover them up.

"Sure, they were a wild lot, after all?" he said in a questioning tone, as he looked up at the glowing countenance of his friend, who, with his bold mien, bulky frame, blue eyes, and fair curls, would have made a very creditable Viking indeed, had he lived in the tenth century.

"Of course they were, Phil," he replied, looking down at his admirer with a smile. "Men could not

well be otherwise than wild and warlike in those
days ; but it was not all ravage and plundei with
them.   Why, it is to them and to their wise laws
that we owe much of the freedom, coupled with the
order, that prevails in our happy land ; and didn't
they cross the Atlantic Ocean in things little better
than herring-boats, without chart or compass, and
discover America long before Columbus was born ?"

"You don't mean that ?" said Phil, with increased
admiration ; for the boy was not only smitten by his
friend's physical powers, but by his supposed in-
tellectual attainments.

"Yes, I do mean that," returned Aspel.   "If the
Norsemen of old did mischief, as no one can deny,
they were undoubtedly grand old scoundrels, and it
is certain that they did much good to the world,
whether they meant it or not."

Phil Maylands made no reply, but continued to
look meditatively at his friend, until the latter
laughed, and asked what he was thinking about.

"It's thinking I am, what I wouldn't give if my
legs were only as long as yours, George."

"That they will soon be," returned George, "if
they go on at the rate they've been growing of
late."

"That's a true word, anyhow ; but as men's legs
don't go on growing at the same rate for ever, it's
not much hope I have of mine.   No, George, it's

kind of you to encourage me, but the Maylands have ever been a short-legged and long-bodied race. So it's said. However, it's some comfort to know that short men are often long-headed, and that many of them get on in the world pretty well."

"Of course they do," returned Aspel, "and though they can't grow long, they never stop short in the race of life. Why, look at Nelson—he was short; and Wellington wasn't long, and Bonny himself was small in every way except in his intellect—who's that coming up the hill?"

"It's Mike Kenny, the postman, I think. I wonder if he has brought a letter from sister May. Mother expects one, I know."

The man who had attracted their attention was ascending towards them with the slow, steady gait of a practised mountaineer. He was the post-runner of the district. Being a thinly-peopled and remote region, the "runner's walk" was a pretty extensive one, embracing many a mile of moorland, vale and mountain. He had completed most of his walk at that time, having only one mountain shoulder now between him and the little village of Howlin Cove, where his labours were to terminate for that day.

"Good-evening, Mike," said George Aspel, as the man approached. "Any letters for me to-night?"

"No, sur, not wan," answered Mike, with some-

thing of a twinkle in his eye; "but I've left wan at
Rocky Cottage," he added, turning to Philip Maylands.

"Was it May's handwriting?" asked the boy
eagerly.

"Sure I don't know for sartin whose hand it is i'
the inside, but it's not Miss May's on the cover.
Niver a wan in these parts could write like her—
copperplate, no less."

"Come, George, let's go back," said Phil, quickly,
"we've been looking out for a letter for some days
past."

"It's not exactly a letter, Master Phil," said the
post-runner slowly.

"Ah, then, she'd never put us off with a newspaper," said Phil.

"No, it's a telegram," returned Mike.

Phil Maylands looked thoughtfully at the ground.
"A telegram," he said, "that's strange. Are ye
sure, Mike?"

"Troth am I."

Without another word the boy started off at a
quick walk, followed by his friend and the post-
runner. The latter had to diverge at that place to
leave a letter at the house of a man named Patrick
Grady. Hence, for a short distance, they followed
the same road.

Young Maylands would have passed the house,

but as Grady was an intimate friend of George Aspel, he agreed to stop just to shake hands.

Patrick Grady was the soul of hospitality. He was not to be put off with a mere shake of the hand, not he—telegrams meant nothing now-a-days, he said, everybody sent them. No cause for alarm. They must stop and have a glass of mountain dew.

Aspel was resolute, however; he would not sit down, though he had no objection to the mountain dew. Accordingly, the bottle was produced, and a full glass was poured out for Aspel, who quaffed off the pure spirit with a free-and-easy toss and smack of the lips, that might have rendered one of the beery old sea-kings envious.

"No, sur, I thank ye," said Mike, when a similar glass was offered to him.

"What! ye haven't taken the pledge, have ye?" said Grady.

"No, sur; but I've had three glasses already on me walk, an' that's as much as I can rightly carry."

"Nonsense, Mike. You've a stiff climb before you—here, take it off."

The facile postman did take it off without further remonstrance.

"Have a dhrop, Phil?'

"No, thank ee," said Phil, firmly, but without giving a reason for declining.

Being a boy, he was not pressed to drink, and the

party left the house. A short distance farther on the road forked, and here the post-runner turned off to the right, taking the path which led towards ˎ. the hill whose rugged shoulder he had yet to scale.

Mike Kenny breasted it not only with the energy of youth and strength, but with the additional and artificial energy infused by the spirits, so that, much to his own surprise, his powers began to fail prematurely. Just then a storm of wind and sleet came down from the heights above, and broke with bitter fury in his face. He struggled against it vigorously for a time till he gained a point whence he saw the dark blue sea lashing on the cliffs below. He looked up at the pass which was almost hid by the driving sleet. A feeling of regret and self-condemnation at having so readily given in to Grady was mingled with a strong sense of the duty that he had to discharge as he once more breasted the steep. The bitter cold began to tell on his exhausted frame. In such circumstances a small matter causes a man to stumble. Kenny's foot caught on something—a root it might be—and he fell headlong into a ditch and was stunned. The cold did its work, and from that ditch he never rose again.

Meanwhile Mr. Grady looked out from the window of his cottage upon the gathering storm, expressed some satisfaction that it did not fall to his lot to climb hills on such a day, and comforted himself—though he did not appear to stand in need of special comfort—with another glass of whisky.

George Aspel and Philip Maylands, with their backs to the storm, hurried homewards; the former exulting in the grand—though somewhat disconnected—thoughts infused into his fiery soul by the fire-water he had imbibed, and dreaming of what he would have dared and done had he only been a sea-king of the olden time; the latter meditating somewhat anxiously on the probable nature of his sister's telegram.

CHAPTER II.

TELLS OF WOMAN'S WORK AND SOME OF WOMAN'S WAYS.

MANY, and varied, and strange, are the duties which woman has to perform in this life—especially in that wonderful and gigantic phase of this life which is comprehended in the word London.

One chill December afternoon there sat in front of a strange-looking instrument a woman—at least she was as nearly a woman as is compatible with the age of seventeen. She was also pretty —not beautiful, observe, but pretty—sparklingly pretty; dark, dimpled, demure and delightful in every way; with a turn-up nose, a laughing eye, and a kindly look.

Her chief duty, from morning to night, consisted in playing with her pretty little fingers on three white pianoforte keys. There were no other keys —black or white—in connection with these three. They stood alone and had no music whatever in them —nothing but a click. Nevertheless this young woman, whose name was May Maylands, played on them with a constancy and a deft rapidity worthy of a great, if not a musical, cause. From dawn to dusk, and day by day, did she keep those three keys clicking and clittering, as if her life depended on the result; and so in truth it did, to some extent, for her bread and butter depended on her performances on that very meagre piano.

Although an artless and innocent young girl, fresh from the western shores of Erin, May had a peculiar, and, in one of her age and sex, almost pert way of putting questions, to which she often received quaint and curious replies.

For instance one afternoon she addressed to a learned doctor the following query :—

" Can you send copy last prescription ? Lost it. Face red as a carrot. In agonies ! What shall I do ? Help !"

To which the learned doctor gave the matter-of-fact but inelegant reply :—

"Stick your feet in hot water. Go to bed at once. Prescription sent by post. Take it every hour."

But May Maylands did not stick her feet in hot water; neither did she go to bed, or take any physic. Indeed there was no occasion to do so, for a clear complexion and pink cheeks told of robust health.

On another occasion she asked an Irish farmer if

he could send her twenty casks of finest butter to cost not more than 6d. per lb.

To which the farmer was rude enough to answer —"Not by no manner of means."

In short May's conduct was such that we must hasten to free her from premature condemnation by explaining that she was a female telegraphist in what we may call the literary lungs of London— the General Post-Office at St. Martin's-le-Grand.

On that chill December afternoon, during a brief lull in her portion of the telegraphic communication of the kingdom, May leaned her little head on her hand, and sent her mind to the little cottage by the sea, already described as lying on the west coast of Ireland, with greater speed than ever she flashed those electric sparks which it was her business to scatter broadcast over the land. The hamlet, near which the cottage stood, nestled under the shelter of a cliff as if in expectation and dread of being riven from its foundations by the howling winds, or whelmed in the surging waves. The cottage itself was on the outskirts of the hamlet, farther to the south. The mind of May entered through its closed door,—for mind, like electricity, laughs at bolts and bars.

There was a buzz of subdued sound from more than twelve hundred telegraphists, male and female, in that mighty telegraph-hall of St. Martin's-le-Grand, but May heard it not. Dozens upon dozens of tables, each with its busy occupants— tables to right of her, tables to left of her, tables in rear of her, tables in front of her,—swept away from her in bewildering perspective, but May saw them not. The clicking of six or seven hundred instruments broke upon her ear as they flashed the news of the world over the length and breadth of the land, pulsating joy and sorrow, surprise, fear, hope, despair, and gladness to thousands of anxious hearts, but May regarded it not. She heard only the booming of the great sea, and saw her mother seated by the fire darning socks, with Madge engaged in household work, and Phil tumbling with baby-brother on the floor, making new holes and rents for fresh darns and patches.

Mrs. Maylands was a student and lover of the Bible. Her children, though a good deal wilder, were sweet-tempered like herself. It is needless to add that in spite of adverse circumstances they were all moderately happy. The fair telegraphist smiled, almost laughed, as her mind hovered over the home circle.

From the contemplation of this pleasant and romantic picture she was roused by a familiar rustle at her elbow. Recalling her mind from the west of Ireland, she fixed it on a mass of telegrams which had just arrived from various parts of the city.

They had been sucked through several pneumatic tubes—varying from a few yards to two miles in length—had been checked, assorted, registered, and distributed by boys to the various telegraphists to whose lot they fell. May Maylands chanced, by a strange coincidence, to command the instrument in direct connection with Cork. The telegrams just laid beside her were those destined for that city, and the regions to which it was a centre of redistribution. Among others her own village was in connection with it, and many a time had she yearned to touch her keys with a message of love to her mother, but the rules of the office sternly forbade this. The communicative touch which she dispensed so freely to others was forbidden to herself. If she, or any other telegraphist in St. Martin's-le-Grand, wished to send a private message, it became necessary to step out of the office, go to the appointed place, pay her shilling, and become one of the public for the occasion. Every one can see the necessity for such a rule in the circumstances.

May's three-keyed machine, by the way, did not actually send forth the electricity. It only punched holes in a long tape of white paper, which holes, according to their relative arrangement, represented the alphabet. Having punched a message by playing on the keys, she transferred her tape to the electric machine at her elbow and passed it through.

This transmitting machine was automatic or self-acting. It required only to be fed with perforated tapes. In Ireland the receiving-machine presented its messages in the form of dots and dashes, which, according to arrangement, became alphabetic. You don't understand this, reader, eh? It would be surprising if you did! A treatise on electric telegraphy would be required to make it clear—supposing you to have a mechanical turn of mind. Suffice it to say that the Wheatstone telegraph instrument tapes off its messages at the rate of 100 words a minute.

But to return—

With a sigh May Maylands cast her eyes on the uppermost telegram. It ran thus :—

"Buy the horse at any price. He's a spanker. Let the pigs go for what they'll fetch."

This was enough. Romance, domesticity, and home disappeared, probably with the message along the wire, and the spirit of business descended on the little woman as she applied herself once more to the matter-of-fact manipulation of the keys.

That evening as May left the post-office and turned sharply into the dark street she came into collision with a letter-carrier.

"Oh! Miss," he exclaimed with polite anxiety, "I beg your pardon. The sleet drivin' in my face prevented my seeing you. You're not hurt I hope."

" No, Mr. Flint, you haven't hurt me," said May, laughing, as she recognised the voice of her own landlord.

" Why, it's you, Miss May ! Now isn't that good luck, my turnin' up just in the nick o' time to see you home? Here, catch hold of my arm. The wind's fit to tear the lamp-posts up by the roots."

" But this is not the way home," objected the girl.

" That's true, Miss May, it ain't, but I'm only goin' round a bit by St. Paul's Churchyard. There's a shop there where they sell the sausages my old 'ooman's so fond of. It don't add more than a few yards to the road home."

The old 'ooman to whom Solomon Flint referred was his grandmother. Flint himself had spent the greater part of his life in the service of the post-office, and was now a widower, well stricken in years. His grandmother was one of those almost indestructible specimens of humanity who live on until the visage becomes deeply corrugated, contemporaries have become extinct, and age has become a matter of uncertainty. Flint had always been a good grandson, but when his wife died the love he had borne to her seemed to have been transferred with additional vehemence to the "old 'ooman."

" There's a present for you, old 'ooman," said Flint, placing the paper of sausages on the table on

entering his humble abode, and proceeding to divest
himself of his waterproof cape ; "just let me catch
hold of a fryin'-pan and I'll give you to understand
what a blow-out means."

"You're a good laddie, Sol," said the old woman,
rousing herself and speaking in a voice that sounded
as if it had begun its career far back in the previous
century

Mrs. Flint was Scotch, and, although she had
lived from early womanhood in London, had retained something of the tone and much of the pro-
nunciation of the land o' cakes.

"Ye'll be wat, lassie," she said to May, who was
putting off her bonnet and shawl in a corner. "No,
Grannie," returned the girl, using a term which the
old woman had begged her to adopt, "I'm not wet,
only a little damp."

"Change your feet, lassie, direc'ly, or you'll tak'
cauld," said Mrs. Flint in a peremptory tone.

May laughed gently and retired to her private
boudoir to change her shoes. The boudoir was
not more than eight feet by ten in size, and very
poorly furnished, but its neat, methodical arrangements betokened in its owner a refined and orderly
mind.   There were a few books in a stand on the
table, and a flower-pot on the window-sill. Among
the pegs and garments on the walls was a square
piece of cardboard, on which was emblazoned in

scarlet silk, the text, "God is love." This hung at
the foot of the bed, so as to be the first object to
greet the girl's eyes on awaking each morning.
Below it hung a row of photographs, embracing the
late Rev. James Maylands, his widow, his son Philip,
his distant relative Madge, and the baby. These
were so arranged as to catch the faint gleam of
light that penetrated the window; but as there
was a twenty-foot brick wall in front of the window at a distance of two yards, the gleam, even
on a summer noon, was not intense. In winter
it was barely sufficient to render darkness visible.

Poor May Maylands! It was a tremendous change
to her from the free air and green fields of Ireland
to a small back street in the heart of London; but
necessity had required the change. Her mother's
income could not comfortably support the family.
Her own salary, besides supporting herself, was devoted to the enlargement of that income, and as it
amounted to only £50 a year, there was not much
left to pay for lodgings, etc. It is true Miss Lillycrop would have gladly furnished May with board
and lodging free, but her house was in the neighbourhood of Pimlico, and May's duties made it
necessary that she should live within a short distance of the General Post-Office. Miss Lillycrop
had heard of the Flints as being good-hearted and
trusty people, and advised her cousin to board with

them, at least until some better arrangement cou'ld
be made for her. Meanwhile May was to go and
spend part of every Sunday with Miss Lillycrop at
No. 9 Purr Street.

"Well, Grannie," said May, returning to the front
room, where the sausages were already hissing deli-
ciously, "what news have you for me to-night?"

She sat down beside the old woman, took her
hand and spoke in that cheery, cosy, confidential
way which renders some women so attractive.

"Deed, May, there's little but the auld story—
"Mercies, mornin', noon, and night. But, oo ay, I
was maist forgettin'; Miss Lillycrap was here, an'
left ye a message o' some sort."

"And what was the message, Grannie?"

"She's gone and forgot it," said Solomon Flint,
putting the sausages on the table, which had
already been spread for supper by a stout little girl
who was the sole domestic of the house and attendant on Mrs. Flint. "You've no chance of getting
it now, Miss May, for I've noticed that when the
old 'ooman once forgets a thing it don't come back
to her—except, p'r'aps, a week or two afterwards.
Come now, draw in and go to work. But, p'r'aps,
Dollops may have heard the message. Hallo!
Dollops! come here, and bring the kettle with you."

Dollops—the little girl above referred to—was
particularly small and shy, ineffably stupid, and

remarkably fat. It was the last quality which induced Solomon to call her Dollops. Her hair and
garments stuck out from her in wild dishevelment,
but she was not dirty. Nothing belonging to Mrs.
Flint was allowed to become dirty.

" Did you see Miss Lillycrop, Dollops?" asked
Solomon, as the child emerged from some sort of
back kitchen.

" Yes, sir, I did; I saw'd 'er a-goin' hout."

" Did you hear her leave a message ? "

" Yes, sir, I did. I 'eard 'er say to missis, ' Be
sure that you give May Maylands my love, an'
tell 'er wotever she do to keep 'er feet dry, an'
don't forgit the message, an' say I'm so glad about
it, though it's not much to speak of arter all !' "

"What was she so glad about?" demanded Solomon.

" I dun know, sir. She said no more in my
'earin than that. I only comed in w'en she was
agoin' hout. P'r'aps it was about the findin' of 'er
gloves in 'er pocket w'en she was a talkin' to
missis, which she thought she'd lost, though they
wasn't wuth pickin' up out of the ――"

" Pooh ! be off to your pots an' pans, child,"
said Flint, turning to his grandmother, who sat
staring at the sausages with a blank expression.
" You can't remember it, I s'pose, eh ? "

Mrs. Flint shook her head and began to eat.

" That's right, old 'ooman," said her grandson,

patting her shoulder; "heap up the coals, mayhap it'll revive the memory."

But Mrs. Flint's memory was not so easily revived. She became more abstracted than usual in her efforts to recover it. Supper passed and was cleared away. The old woman was placed in her easy-chair in front of the fire with the cat—her chief evening amusement—on her knee; the letter-carrier went out for his evening walk; Dollops proceeded miscellaneously to clean up and smash the crockery, and May sat down to indite an epistle to the inmates of Rocky Cottage.

Suddenly Mrs. Flint uttered an exclamation.

"May!" she cried, and hit the cat an involuntary slap on the face which sent it with a caterwaul of indignant surprise from her knee, "it wasn't a message, it was a letter!"

Having thus unburdened her mind the old woman relapsed into the previous century, from which she could not be recalled. May, therefore, made a diligent search for the letter, and found it at last under a cracked teapot on the mantelpiece, where Mrs. Flint had told Miss Lillycrop to place it for safety.

It was short but satisfactory, and ran thus :—

"DEAREST MAY,—I've been to see my friend in power,' and he says it's 'all right,' that you've only to get your brother over as soon as possible, and he'll see to getting him a situation. The enclosed paper is for his and your guidance. Excuse haste. —Your affect. coz., SARAH LILLYCROP."

It need hardly be said that May Maylands finished her letter with increased satisfaction, and posted it that night.

Next morning she wrote out a telegram as follows :—" Let Phil come here *at once*. The application has been successful. Never mind clothes. Everything arranged. Best love to all."

The last clause was added in order to get the full value for her money. She naturally underscored the words "at once,' forgetting for the moment that, in telegraphy, a word underlined counts as two words. She was therefore compelled to forego the emphasis.

This message she did not transmit through her own professional instrument, but gave it in at the nearest district office. It was at once shot bodily, with a bundle of other telegrams, through a pneumatic tube, and thus reached St. Martin's-le-Grand in one minute thirty-five seconds, or about twenty minutes before herself. Chancing to be the uppermost message, it was flashed off without delay, crossed the Irish Channel, and entered the office at Cork in about six minutes. Here there was a short delay of half-an-hour, owing to other telegrams which had prior claim to attention. Then it was flashed to the west coast, which it reached long

before the letter posted on the previous night, and
not long after May had seated herself at her own
three-keyed instrument.   But there, telegraphic
speed was thwarted by unavoidable circumstances,
the post-runner having already started on his morning rounds, and it was afternoon before the telegram
was delivered at Rocky Cottage.

This was the telegram which had caused Philip
Maylands so much anxiety.   He read it at last with
great relief, and at the same time with some degree
of sadness, when he thought of leaving his mother
" unprotected " in her lonely cottage by the sea.

CHAPTER III.

BRILLIANT PROSPECTS.

MADGE—whose proper name was Marjory Stevens —was absent when May's letter arrived the following day. On her return to the cottage she was taken into the committee which sat upon the subject of Phil's appointment.

"It's not a very grand appointment," said Mrs. Maylands, with a sigh.

"Sure it's not an appointment at all yet, mother," returned Phil, who held in his hand the paper of instructions enclosed in May's letter. "Beggars, you know, mustn't be choosers; an' if I'm not a beggar, it's next thing to it I am. Besides, if the position of a boy-telegraph-messenger isn't very exalted in itself, it's the first step to better things. Isn't the first round of a ladder connected with the top round?"

"That's true, Phil," said Madge; "there's nothing to prevent your becoming Postmaster-General in course of time."

"Nothing whatever, that I know of," returned Phil.

"Perhaps somebody else knows of something that may prevent it," said his mother with an amused smile.

"Perhaps!" exclaimed the boy, with a twinkle in his eye; "don't talk to me of perhapses, I'm not to be damped by such things. Now, just consider this," he continued, looking over the paper in his hand, "here we have it all in print. I must apply for the situation in writin' no less. Well, I can do it in copperplate, if they please. Then my age must be not less than fourteen, and not more than fifteen."

"That suits to a T," said Madge.

"Yes; and, but hallo! what have we here?" said Phil, with a look of dismay.

"What is it?" asked his mother and Madge in the same breath, with looks of real anxiety.

"Well, well, it's too bad," said Phil slowly, "it says here that I'm to have 'no claim on the superannuation fund.' Isn't that hard?"

A smile from Mrs. Maylands, and a laugh from Madge, greeted this. It was also received with an appalling yell from the baby, which caused mother and nurse to leap to the rescue. That sprout of mischief, in the course of an experimental tour of the premises, had climbed upon a side-table, had twisted his right foot into the loop of the window-curtains, had fallen back, and hung, head downwards, howling.

. Having been comforted with bread and treacle, and put to bed, the committee meeting was resumed.

"Well, then," said Phil, consulting his paper again, "I give up the superannuation advantages. Then, as to wages, seven shillings a week, rising to eight shillings after one year's service. Why, it's a fortune! Any man at my age can live on sixpence a day easy—that's three-and-six, leaving three-and-six a week clear for you, mother. Then there's a uniform; just think o' that!"

"I wonder what sort of uniform it is," said Madge.

"A red coat, Madge, and blue trousers with silver lace and a brass helmet, for certain—"

"Don't talk nonsense, boy," interrupted Mrs. Maylands, "but go on with the paper."

"Oh! there's nothing more worth mentioning," said Phil, folding the paper, "except that boy-messengers, if they behave themselves, have a chance of promotion to boy-sorterships, indoor-telegraph-messengerships, junior sorterships, and letter-carrierships, on their reaching the age of seventeen, and, I suppose, secretaryships, and postmaster-generalships, with a baronetcy, on their attaining the age of Methuselah. It's the very thing for me, mother, so I'll be off to-morrow if—"

Phil was cut short by the bursting open of the door and the sudden entrance of his friend George Aspel.

"Come, Phil," he cried, blazing with excitement, "there's a wreck in the bay. Quick! there's no time to lose."

The boy leaped up at once, and dashed out after his friend.

It was evening. The gale, which had blown for two days, was only beginning to abate. Dark clouds were split in the western sky by gleams of fiery light as the sun declined towards its troubled ocean-bed.

Hurrying over the fields, and bending low to the furious blast, Aspel and Philip made their way to the neighbouring cliffs. But before we follow them, reader, to the wave-lashed shore, it is necessary, for the satisfactory elucidation of our tale, that we should go backward a short way in time, and bound forward a long way into space.

CHAPTER IV.

THE ROYAL MAIL STEAMER.

OUT, far out on the mighty sea, a large vessel makes her way gallantly over the billows—homeward bound.

She is a Royal Mail steamer from the southern hemisphere—the *Trident*—and a right royal vessel she looks with her towering iron hull, and her taper masts, and her two thick funnels, and her trim rigging, and her clean decks—for she has an awning spread over them, to guard from smoke as well as from sun.

There is a large family on board of the *Trident*, and, like all other large families, its members display marked diversities of character. They also exhibit, like not a few large families, remarkable diversities of temper. Among them there are several human magnets with positive and negative poles, which naturally draw together. There are also human flints and steels which cannot come into contact without striking fire. .

When the *Trident* got up steam, and bade adieu to

the Southern Cross, there was no evidence whatever
of the varied explosives and combustibles which
she carried in her after-cabin. The fifty or sixty
passengers who waved kerchiefs, wiped their eyes,
and blew their noses, at friends on the receding
shore, were unknown to each other; they were
intent on their own affairs. When obliged to jostle
each other they were all politeness and urbanity.

After the land had sunk on the horizon the intro-
circumvolutions of a large family, or rather a little
world, began. There was a birth on board, an engagement, ay, and a death; yet neither the interest
of the first, nor the romance of the second, nor the
solemnity of the last, could check for more than a
few hours the steady development of the family
characteristics of love, modesty, hate, frivolity, wisdom, and silliness.

A proportion of the passengers were, of course,
nobodies, who aspired to nothing greater than to live
and let live, and who went on the even tenor of
their way, without much change, from first to last.
Some of them were somebodies who, after a short
time, began to expect the recognition of that fact.
There were ambitious-bodies who, in some cases,
aimed too high, and there were unpretending-bodies
who frequently aimed too low. There were also
selfish-bodies who, of course, thought only of themselves—with, perhaps, a slight passing reference to

those among the after-cabin passengers who could give them pleasure, and there were self-forgetting-bodies who turned their thoughts frequently on the ship, the crew, the sea, the solar system, the Maker of the universe. These also thought of their fellow-passengers in the fore-cabin, who of course had a little family or world of their own, with its similar joys, and sins, and sorrows, before the mast ; and there were uproarious-bodies who kept the little world lively—sometimes a little too lively.

As the Royal Mail steamer rushed out to sea and was tossed on the ocean's breast, these human elements began to mix and effervesce and amalgamate, or fizz, burst, and go off, like squibs and crackers.

There was a Mrs. Pods with three little girls, and a Mrs. Tods with two little boys, whose first casual glance at each other was transmuted into a glare of undying and unreasoning hate. These ladies were exceptions to the rule of general urbanity before mentioned. Both had fiery faces, and each read the other through and through at a glance. There was a Miss Bluestocking who charmed some people, irritated others, frightened a few, and caused many to sneer. Her chief friend among the males was a young man named Mr. Weakeyes, who had a small opinion of himself and a very receptive mind. Miss Troolove, among the ladies, was her chief friend. The strange misnomers which one meets with in

society were also found in the little world in tha
steamer—that Royal Mail steamer we should say—
for, while we turn aside for a brief period to con
descend upon these particulars, we would not hav
the reader forget that they have an indirect bearing
on the main thread of our tale.

One misnamed lady was a Miss Mist, who, instead
of being light, airy, and ethereal, as she ought to
have been, weighed at least twelve stone six.   But
she sang divinely, was a great favourite with the
young people on board, and would have been very
much missed indeed if she had not been there.
There was also a Mr. Stout, who was the tallest and
thinnest man in the ship.

On the other hand there were some whose names
had been obviously the result of a sense of propriety
in some one.   Among the men who were rabidly
set on distinguishing themselves in one way or
another was a Major Beak.   Now, why was it that
this Major's nose was an aquiline of the most out-
rageous dimensions?   Surely no one would argue
that the nose grew to accommodate the name.   Is
it not more probable—nay, certain—that the name
grew to accommodate the nose?   Of course when
Major Beak was born he was a minor, and his nose
must have been no better than a badly-shaped
button or piece of putty; but the Major's father
had owned a tremendous aquiline nose, which at

birth had also been a button, and so on we can
proceed backwards until we drive the Beaks into
that remote antiquity where historical fact begins
and mythological theory terminates—that period
when men were wont, it is supposed, to name each
other intelligently with reference to personal characteristic or occupation.

So, too, Mr. Bright—a hearty good-natured fellow, who drew powerfully to Major Beak and hated
Miss Bluestocking—possessed the vigorous frame,
animated air, and intelligent look which must have
originated his name. But why go on? Every
reader must be well acquainted with the characters
of Mr. Fiery and Mr. Stiff, and Mrs. Dashington,
and her niece Miss Squeaker, and Colonel Blare who
played the cornet, and Lieutenant Limp who sang
tenor, and Dr. Bassoon who roared bass, and Mrs.
Silky, who was all things to all men, besides being
everything by turns and nothing long; and Lady
Tower and Miss Gentle, and Mr. Blurt and Miss
Dumbbelle.

Suffice it to say that after a week or two the
effervescing began to systematise, and the family
became a living and complex electrical machine,
whose sympathetic poles drew and stuck together,
while the antagonistic poles kept up a steady discharge of sparks.

Then there arose a gale which quieted the

machine a little, and checked the sparkling flow
of wit and humour. When, during the course of
the gale, a toppling billow overbalanced itself and
fell inboard with a crash that nearly split the deck
open, sweeping two of the quarterboats away, Mr.
Blurt, sitting in the saloon, was heard to exclaim :—

" 'Pon my word, it's a terrible gale—enough
almost to make a fellow think of his sins."

To which Mrs. Tods, who sat beside him, replied,
with a serious shake of her head, that it was indeed
a very solemn occasion, and cast a look, not of
undying hate but of gentle appeal at Mrs. Pods,
who sat opposite to her. And that lady, so far
from resenting the look as an affront, met her in a
liberal spirit; not only admitted that what Mrs.
Tods had said was equally just and true, but even
turned her eyes upward with a look of resignation.

Well was it for Mrs. Pods that she did so, for
her resigned eyes beheld the globe of the cabin
lamp pitched off its perch by a violent lurch and
coming straight at her. Thus she had time to bow to
circumstances, and allow the missile to pass over her
head into the bosom of Lady Tower, where it was
broken to atoms. The effect of mutual concession
was so strong on Mrs. Pods and Mrs. Tods, that the
former secretly repented having wished that one of
Mrs. Tods' little sons might fall down the hatchway
and get maimed for life, while the latter silently

regretted having hoped that one of Mrs. Pods' little girls might fall overboard and be half-drowned.

But the storm passed away and the effervescence returned—though not, it is pleasing to add, with so much pungency as before.   Thus, night and day, the steamer sped on over the southern seas, across the mystic line, and into the northern hemisphere, with the written records, hopes, commands, and wishes of a continent in the mail-bags in her hold, and leaving a beautiful milky-way behind her.

But there were more than letters and papers in these mail-bags.   There were diamonds !   Not indeed those polished and glittering gems whose proper resting-place is the brow of beauty, but those uncut pebbles that are turned up at the mines, which the ignorant would fling away or give to their children as playthings, but for which merchants and experts would give hundreds and thousands of pounds.   A splendid prize that Royal Mail steamer would have been for the buccaneers of the olden time, but happily there are no buccaneers in these days—at least not in civilised waters.   A famous pirate had, however, set his heart on those diamonds—even old Neptune himself.

This is how it happened.

CHAPTER V.

WRECK AND RESCUE.

ONE evening Miss Gentle and rotund little Mr. Blurt were seated on two camp-stools near the stern, conversing occasionally and gazing in a dreamy frame of mind at the milky-way over which they appeared to travel.

"I wonder much, Miss Gentle," said Mr. Blurt, "that you were not more afraid during that gale we had just before crossing the line?"

"I was a good deal afraid, though perhaps I did not show it. Your remark," she added, with an arch glance at her companion, "induces me to express some surprise that you seemed so much afraid."

"Afraid!" echoed Mr. Blurt, with a smile; "why, I wasn't afraid—eh! was I?"

"I beg pardon," hastily explained Miss Gentle, "I don't mean frightened, of course; perhaps I should have said alarmed, or agitated—"

"Agitated!" cried Mr. Blurt, pulling off his hat, and rubbing his bald head—he was prematurely bald, being only forty, though he looked like fifty —"agitated! Well, Miss Gentle, if you had diamonds—"

He stopped short, and looked at his companion with a confused smile.

"Diamonds, Mr. Blurt," said Miss Gentle, slightly surprised; "what do you mean?"

"Well—ha! hem!" said the other, rubbing his forehead; "I see no reason why I should make a mystery of it. Since I have mentioned the thing, I may as well say that a man who happens to have a packet of diamonds in the mail-bags worth about twenty thousand pounds, may well be excused showing some little agitation lest the ship containing them should go to the bottom."

"I don't quite see that," returned Miss Gentle. "If the owner is on board, and goes to the bottom with his diamonds, it does not matter to *him*, does it?"

"Ah!" said Mr. Blurt, "it is the inconsiderateness of youth which prompts that speech (Miss Gentle looked about twenty, though she was in reality twenty-seven!) Do you think I have no anxiety for any one but myself? Suppose I have a wife and family in England who are dependent on these diamonds."

"Ah! that did not occur to me," returned the lady.

"Have you any objection to become a confidante?" asked Mr. Blurt.

"None whatever," replied Miss Gentle, laughing.

"Well, then, to let you understand my feelings, I shall explain. I have a brother—a dear little fellow like mys—ah, excuse me; I did not mean *dear* like myself, but *little*. Well, he is a naturalist. He lives in London, and is not a very successful naturalist; indeed, I may say that he is an unfortunate and poor naturalist. Last year he failed. I sent him a small sum of money. He failed again. I sent him more money. Being a successful diamond merchant, you see, I could afford to do so. We are both bachelors; my brother being much older than I am. At last I resolved to send home my whole fortune, and return to live with him, after winding up my affairs. I did so : made up my diamonds into a parcel, and sent it by mail as being the most secure method. Just after doing this, I got a letter informing me of my brother being dangerously ill, and begging me to come to England without delay. I packed up at once, left my partner to wind up the business, and so, here I am, on board the very steamer that carries my diamonds to England."

"How curious—and how interesting," said the sympathetic Miss Gentle.

Whatever more she intended to say was checked

by a large parti-coloured ball hitting her on the cheek, and falling into her lap. It was followed up and captured with a shriek by the two little Todses and the three little Podses. At the same moment the gong sounded for tea. Thus the conversation came to a close.

The voyage of the *Trident*—with the exception of the gale before referred to—was prosperous until her arrival in the waters of the northern hemisphere. By that time the passengers had crystallised into groups, the nobodies and self-forgetting-bodies fraternised, and became more and more friendly as time went on. The uproarious-bodies got up concerts and charades. The hatred of Pods for Tods intensified. The arrogance of Major Beak, and the good-natured modesty of Mr. Bright, increased. The noise of Dr. Bassoon made the manner of Mr. Silky quite agreeable by contrast, while the pride of Lady Tower and Mr. Stiff formed a fine, deep-shade to the neutral tint of Miss Gentle, and the high-light of Miss Squeaker.

Gradually, however, feelings began to modify. The squalls and breezes that ruffled the human breasts on board the *Trident* moderated in exact proportion as that vessel penetrated and experienced the storms of what should have been named the *in*-temperate zone.

At last they drew near to the shores of Old

England, and then there burst upon them a nor'-
wester, so violent that within the first hour the
close-reefed topsails were blown to ribbons, and
the foretopmast, with the jib-boom, was carried
away. Of course this was a comparatively small
matter in a steamer, but when it was afterwards
discovered that the vessel had sprung a leak, things
began to look more serious.

"It's only a trifle, Miss Gentle; don't alarm
yourself. We can put that to rights in a few
minutes," said Major Beak, with the confident air
of a man whose nautical education had begun with
Noah, and continued uninterruptedly down to the
present time.

"He's a hooked-nosed humbug, Miss Gentle,
an' knows nothing about it," growled the captain.

"Water rising rapidly in the hold, sir," said the
carpenter, coming aft and touching his cap.

"Rig the pumps," said the captain, and the pumps
were rigged. What is more to the purpose, they
were wrought with a will by the crew; but in spite
of their efforts the water continued to rise.

It might have done a student of human nature
good to have observed the effect of this information
on the passengers Regarded as a whole, the little
world became perceptibly paler in the cheeks, and
strikingly moderate in tone of voice and manner.
Major Beak, in particular, began to talk low, and

made no reference whatever to nautical matters, while Mrs. Pods looked amiably—almost affectionately—at Mrs. Tods.

Of course the passengers observed with breathless interest the action of the captain at this crisis. That important personage did his best to stop the leak, but only succeeded in checking it, and it required the constant exertions of the crew night and day at the pumps to reduce the water in the hold even by an inch. In these circumstances the young men among the passengers readily volunteered their services to assist the crew.

The gale continued and steadily increased. At night the ladies, and such of the passengers as were not employed at the pumps, retired to the cabin. Some of those who did not realise the danger of the situation went to bed. Others sat up in the saloon and consoled each other as best they might.

Morning came, but with it came no abatement of the storm. Water and sky seemed mingled together, and were of one uniform tone. It was obvious that the men at the pumps were utterly exhausted, and worst of all the water was beginning to gain slowly on them. The elderly men were now called on to help. It became necessary that all should work for their lives. Miss Bluestocking, who was muscular as well as masculine, rose to the occasion, and suggested that the ladies, so to speak.

should man the pumps. Her suggestion was not acted on.

At this point Mr. Bright, who had been toiling night and day like an inexhaustible giant, suggested that music might be called in to aid their flagging powers. It was well known that fatigued soldiers on a march are greatly re-invigorated by the band. Major Beak, soaking from head to foot with salt water, almost blind with fatigue and want of sleep, and with the perspiration dropping from the point of his enormous nose, plucked up heart to raise himself and assert that that was true. He further suggested that Colonel Blare might play to them on the cornet. But Colonel Blare was incapable by that time of playing even on a penny trumpet. Dr. Bassoon was reduced so low as to be obliged to half whisper his incapacity to sing bass, and as for the great tenor, Lieutenant Limp— a piece of tape was stiffer than his back-bone.

"Let the ladies sing to us," sighed Mr. Fiery, who was mere milk and water by that time. "I'm sure that Mrs. Tods and Mrs. Pods would be —"

A united shriek of protest from those ladies checked him.

"Or Miss Troolove," suggested Mr. Blurt, on whose stout person the labour told severely.

The lady appealed to, after a little hesitation, began a hymn, but the time was found to be too slow, while the voice, although sweet and true, was too weak.

"Come, let us have one of the Christy Minstrels'," cried Mr. Bright in a lively tone. "I'm certain Miss Mist can sing one."

Poor Miss Mist was almost hysterical with fear and prolonged anxiety, but she was an obliging creature. On being assured that the other ladies would support her, she struck up the "Land of Dixey," and was joined in the chorus with so much spirit that those who laboured at the pumps felt like giants refreshed. Explain it how we may, there can be no question that lively music has a wonderful power of sustaining the energies of mankind. With the return of cheerful sensations there revived in some of them the sense of the ludicrous, and it was all that they could do to refrain from laughter as they looked at the forlorn females huddled together, wrapped in rugs and cloaks, drenched to the skin, almost blown from their seats, ghastly with watching and fear, solemn-visaged in the last degree, and yet singing "Pop goes the weasel," and similar ditties, with all the energy of despair.

We paint no fanciful picture. We describe facts, and there is no saying how far the effect of that music might have helped in the saving of the ship, had not an event occurred which rendered further efforts unnecessary.

The captain, who had either lost his reckoning or his head, or both, was seen to apply himself too frequently to a case-bottle in the cabin, and much anxiety began to be felt as to his capacity to manage the vessel. Owing, also, to the length of time that thick weather had prevailed, no reliable observation had been obtained for several days. While the anxiety was at its height, there came a sudden and terrible shock, which caused the good ship to tremble. Then, for the first time, the roar of breakers was heard above the howling of the storm. As if to increase the horror of the scene, the fog lifted and revealed towering cliffs close a-head of them.

The transition from a comparatively hopeful state to one of absolute despair was overwhelming. The wild waves lifted the great hull of the vessel and let it down on the rocks with another crash, sending the masts over the side, while the passengers could only shriek in agony and cling to the wreck. Fortunately, in taking the ground, the vessel had kept straight, so that the forepart formed a comparative shelter from the waves that were fast breaking up the stern.

In the midst of all this confusion the first mate and Mr. Bright seemed to keep quite cool. Between them they loaded and fired the bow signal-guns several times, by which means they brought a few fishermen and coastguard-men to the scene of disaster. And among these, as we have seen, were our heroes, Philip Maylands and George Aspel.

On arriving, these two found that the rocket apparatus was being set up on the beach.

"Phil," said Aspel in a quick low voice, "they'll want the lifeboat, and the wind carries the sound of their guns in the wrong direction. Run round, lad, and give the alarm. There's not a moment to lose."

The boy turned to run without a word of reply, but he could not help observing, as he turned, the compressed lips, the expanding nostrils, and the blazing eyes of his friend, who almost quivered with suppressed excitement.

For some time George Aspel stood beside the men of the coastguard while they set up their apparatus and fired the rocket. To offer assistance, he knew, would only retard them. The first rocket was carried to the right of the vessel, which was now clearly visible. The second went to the other side. There was a reef of rocks on that side which lay a few yards farther out from the beach than the wreck. Over this reef the rocket-line fell and got entangled. Part of the shore-end of the apparatus also broke down. While the men were quickly repairing it Aspel said in a hurried manner :—"I'll clear the rocket-line," and away he darted like a greyhound.

"Hold ha-a-rd! foolish fellow, you'll be drownded," roared one of the men.

But Aspel heeded him not. Another minute and he was far away on the ledge of rock jutting out from a high cape—the point of which formed the outlying reef above referred to. He was soon at the extremity of the ledge beyond which nearly a hundred yards of seething foam heaved between him and the reef. In he plunged without a moment's halt. Going with the rush of the waves through the channel he struck diagonally across, and landed on the reef. Every billow swept over it, but not with sufficient force to prevent his struggling towards the rocket-line, which he eventually reached and cleared.

" Wasn't that nately done ! " cried an enthusiastic young fisherman on the beach ; " but, och ! what is he up to now ? "

A few seconds sufficed to give an answer to his question. Instead of letting go the line and returning, young Aspel tied it round his waist, and ran or waded to the extreme edge of the reef which was nearest to the wreck. The vessel lay partially to leeward of him now, with not much space between, but that space was a very whirlpool of tormented waves. Aspel gave no moment to thought. In his then state of mind he would have jumped down the throat of a cannon. Next instant he was battling

with the billows, and soon reached the ship ; but now
his danger was greatest, for the curling waves threw
him so violently against the side of the wreck that
he almost lost consciousness and missed the life-
buoy which, with a rope attached, had been thrown
to him by the anxious crew.

A great cry of anxiety arose at this, but Mr.
Bright had anticipated it, and the first mate was
ready to aid him. Leaping into the sea with a
rope round his waist, Mr. Bright caught Aspel as he
struggled past. The mate's powerful hands held
them both fast. Some of the crew lent a ready
hand, and in a few seconds George Aspel was hauled
on board. He had quite recovered. by that time,
and replied with a smile to the ringing cheer that
greeted him. The cheer was echoed again and again
by the men on shore. Major Beak attempted to
grasp his hand, but failed. Mr. Blurt, feeling an irresistible impulse, tried to embrace him, but was
thrust aside, fell, and rolled into the lee-scuppers.

Scattering the people aside Aspel sprang on the
bulwarks at the bow, and, snatching Mr. Stiff's
travelling-cap from his head, held it up as a signal
to the men on shore.

Well did the youth know what to do in the circumstances, for many a time had he talked it over
with the men of the coastguard in former days. On
receiving an answering signal from the shore he

began to haul on the rocket-line. The men in charge had fastened to it a block, or pulley, with two tails to it; a line was rove through this block. The instant the block reached his hands Aspel sprang with it to the stump of the foremast, and looking round cried, "Who'll lend a—"

"Here you are," said Mr. Bright, embracing the mast with both arms and stooping,—for Mr. Bright also knew well what to do.

George Aspel leaped on his shoulders and stood up. Mr. Bright then raised himself steadily, and thus the former was enabled to tie the block by its two tails to the mast at a height of about eleven feet. The line rove through the block was the "whip," which was to be manipulated by those on shore. It was a double, and, of course, an endless line.

Again the signal was given as before, and the line began to run. Very soon a stout hawser or cable was seen coming out to the wreck. Aspel fastened the end of this to the mast several feet below the pulley.

A third time the signal was given.

"Now then, ladies, stand by to go ashore, and let's have no hesitation. It's life or death with us all," said the mate in a voice so stern that the crowd of anxious and somewhat surprised females prepared to obey.

Presently a ring-shaped life-buoy, with something like a pair of short breeches dangling from it, came out from the shore, suspended to a block which traversed on the cable, and was hauled out by means of the whip.

. A seaman was ordered to get into it. Mrs. Tods, who stood beside the mate, eyeing the process somewhat curiously, felt herself firmly but gently seized.

" Come, Mrs. Tods, step into it. He'll take care of you—no fear."

" Never ! never ! without my two darlings," shrieked Mrs. Tods.

But Mrs. Tods was tenderly lifted over the side and placed in the powerful arms of the sailor. Her sons instantly set up a howl and rushed towards her. But Mr. Bright had anticipated this also, and, with the aid of a seaman, arrested them. Meanwhile, the signal having been given, the men on the land pulled in the cradle, and Mrs. Tods went shrieking over the hissing billows to the shore. A few minutes more and out came the cradle again.

" Now, then, for the two 'darlings,'" growled the mate.

They were forcibly put over the side and sent howling to their mother.

After them went Mrs. Pods, who, profiting by

the experience of her friend, made no resistance. This however, was more than counterbalanced by the struggles of *her* three treasures, who immediately followed.

But the shades of evening were now falling, and it was with an anxious feeling at his heart that the mate surveyed the cluster of human beings who had yet to be saved, while each roaring wave that struck the wreck seemed about to break it up.

Suddenly there arose a cry of joy, and, looking seaward, the bright white and blue form of the lifeboat was seen coming in like an angel of light on the crests of the foaming seas.

We may not stay to describe what followed in detail. The lifeboat's anchor was let go to windward of the wreck, and the cable paid out until the boat forged under the vessel's lee, where it heaved on the boiling foam so violently that it was difficult to prevent it being stove in, and still more difficult to get the women and children passed on board. Soon the lifeboat was full—as full as she could hold—and many passengers yet remained to be rescued.

The officer in charge of the mail-bags had got them up under the shelter of the companion-hatch ready to be put into the boat, but human life was of more value than letters—ay, even than diamonds.

" Now, then, one other lady. Only room for one,"
roared the mate, who stood with pistol in hand near
the gangway.

Miss Gentle tried to get to the front, but Lady
Tower stepped in before her.

" Never mind, little woman," said Mr. Bright, encouragingly, " the rocket apparatus is still at work,
and the wreck seems hard and fast on the reef.
You'll get off next trip."

" But I can't bear to think of going by that awful
thing," said Miss Gentle, shuddering and sheltering
herself from the blinding spray under the lee of
Bright's large and powerful body.

" Well, then," he returned, cheerfully, " the lifeboat will soon return ; you'll go ashore with the
mails."

Mr. Bright was right about the speedy return of
the lifeboat with her gallant crew, who seemed to
rejoice in danger as if in the presence of a familiar
friend, but he was wrong about the wreck being
hard and fast. The rising tide shifted her a little,
and drove her a few feet farther in. When the
other women and children were got into the boat,
Mr. Bright, who stood near the mail-bags looking
anxiously at them, left his position for a moment to
assist Miss Gentle to the gangway. She had just
been safely lowered when a tremendous wave lifted
the wreck and hurled it so far over the reef that the

fore part of the vessel was submerged in a pool of
deep water lying between it and the shore.

Mr. Bright looked back and saw the hatchway
disappearing. He made a desperate bound towards
it, but was met by the rush of the crew, who now
broke through the discipline that was no longer
needed, and jumped confusedly into the life-boat on
the sea, carrying Bright along with them. On recovering his feet he saw the ship make a final
plunge forward and sink to the bottom, so that
nothing was left above water but part of the two
funnels. The splendid lifeboat was partly drawn
down, but not upset. She rose again like a cork,
and in a few seconds freed herself from water
through the discharging tubes in her bottom. The
men struggling in the water were quickly rescued,
and the boat, having finished her noble work, made
for the shore amid cheers of triumph and joy.

Among all the passengers in that lifeboat there
was only one whose visage expressed nothing but
unutterable woe.

"Why, Mr. Bright," said Miss Gentle, who clung
to one of the thwarts beside him, and was struck by
his appearance, "you seem to have broken down all
at once. What has happened?"

"The mail-bags!" groaned Mr. Bright.

"Why do you take so deep an interest in the
mails?" asked Miss Gentle.

" Because I happen to be connected with the
post-office; and though I have no charge of them,
I can't bear to see them lost," said Mr. Bright with
another groan, as he turned his eyes wistfully—not
to the shore, at which all on board were eagerly
gazing—but towards the wreck of the Royal Mail
steamer *Trident*, the top of whose funnels rose black
and defiant in the midst of the raging waves.

CHAPTER VI.

TREATS OF POVERTY, PRIDE, AND FIDELITY.

BEHIND a very fashionable square in a very un-fashionable little street, in the west end of London, dwelt Miss Sarah Lillycrop.

That lady's portion in this life was a scanty wardrobe, a small apartment, a remarkably limited income, and a tender, religious spirit. From this it will be seen that she was rich as well as poor.

Her age was, by a curious coincidence, exactly proportioned to her income—the one being forty pounds, and the other forty years. She added to the former, with difficulty, by teaching, and to the latter, unavoidably, by living.

By means of a well-known quality styled economy, she more than doubled her income, and by uniting prayer with practice and a gracious mien she did good, as it were, at the rate of five hundred, or five thousand, a year.

It could not be said, however, that Miss Lillycrop lived well in the ordinary sense of that expression.

To those who knew her most intimately it seemed a species of standing miracle that she contrived to exist at all, for she fed chiefly on toast and tea. Her dietary resulted in an attenuated frame and a thread-paper constitution. Occasionally she indulged in an egg, sometimes even in a sausage. But, morally speaking, Miss Lillycrop lived well, because she lived for others. Of course we do not mean to imply that she had no regard for herself at all. On the contrary, she rejoiced in creature comforts when she had the chance, and laid in daily "one ha'p'orth of milk" all for herself. She paid for it, too, which is more than can be said of every one. She also indulged herself to some extent in the luxury of brown sugar at twopence-halfpenny a pound, and was absolutely extravagant in hot water, which she not only imbibed in the form of weak tea and *eau sucrée* hot, but actually took to bed with her every night in an india-rubber bottle. But with the exception of these excusable touches of selfishness, Miss Lillycrop ignored herself systematically, and devoted her time, talents, and means, to the welfare of mankind.

Beside a trim little tea-table set for three, she sat one evening with her hands folded on her lap, and her eyes fixed on the door as if she expected it

and unprovoked assault on her.

her expectations were almost

realised, for the door burst open and a boy burst into the room with—

" Here we are, Cousin Lillycrop."

" Phil, darling, at last !" exclaimed Cousin Lilly-crop, rising in haste.

Philip Maylands offered both hands, but Cousin Lillycrop declined them, seized him round the neck, kissed him on both cheeks, and thrust him down into an easy chair. Then she retired into her own easy chair and gloated over him.

" How much you 've grown—and so handsome, dear boy," murmured the little lady.

" Ah ! then, cousin, it 's the blarney stone you've been kissing since I saw you last !"

" No, Phil, I've kissed nothing but the cat since I saw you last. I kiss that delicious creature every night on the forehead before going to bed, but the undemonstrative thing does not seem to recipro-cate. However, I cannot help that."

Miss Lillycrop was right, she could not help it. She was overflowing with the milk of human kind-ness, and, rather than let any of that valuable liquid go to waste, she poured some of it, not inappro-priately, on the thankless cat.

" I 'm glad you arrived before your sister, Phil," said Miss Lillycrop. " Of course I asked her here to meet you. I am *so* sorry the dear girl cannot live with me : I had fully meant that she should, but my little rooms are so far from the Post-Office, where her work is, you know, that it could not be managed. However, we see each other as often as possible, and she visits sometimes with me in my district. What has made you so late, Phil?"

"I expected to have been here sooner, cousin," replied Phil, as he took off his greatcoat, "but was delayed by my friend, George Aspel, who has come to London with me to look after a situation that has been promised him by Sir James Clubley, M.P. for I forget where. He's coming here to-night."

"Who, Sir James Clubley?"

"No," returned the boy, laughing, "George Aspel. He went with Mr. Blurt to a hotel to see after a bed, and promised to come here to tea. I asked him, knowing that you'd be glad to receive any intimate friend of mine. Won't you, Coz?"

Miss Lillycrop expressed and felt great delight at the prospect of meeting Phil's friend, but the smallest possible shade of anxiety was mingled with the feeling as she glanced at her very small and not too heavily-loaded table.

"Besides," continued Phil, "George is such a splendid fellow, and, as maybe you remember, lived with us long ago. May will be glad to meet him; and he saved Mr. Blurt's life, so you see—"

"Saved Mr. Blurt's life!" interrupted Miss Lilly-crop.

"Yes, and he saved ever so many more people at the same time, who would likely have been all lost if he hadn't swum off to 'em with the rocket line, and while he was doing that I ran off to call out the lifeboat, an' didn't they get her out and launch her with a will—for you see I had to run three miles, and though I went like the wind they couldn't call out the men and launch her in a minute, you know; but there was no delay.   We were in good time, and saved the whole of 'em—passengers and crew."

"So, then, *you* had a hand in the saving of them," said Miss Lillycrop.

"Sure I had," said Phil with a flush of pleasure at the remembrance of his share in the good work; "but I'd never have thought of the lifeboat, I was so excited with what was going on, if George hadn't sent me off.   He was bursting with big thoughts, and as cool as a cucumber all the time.   I do hope he'll get a good situation here.   It's in a large East India house, I believe, with which Sir James Clubley is connected, and Sir James was an old friend of George's father, and was very kind to him in his last days, but they say he's a proud and touchy old fellow."

As Phil spoke, the door, which had a tendency to burst that evening, opened quickly, tho~ '
so violently as before, and ;
before them, radiant with a glo

Phil sprang to meet her. After the first effu-
sions were over, the brother and sister sat down to
chat of home in the Irish far-west, while Miss
Lillycrop retired to a small kitchen, there to hold
solemn converse with the smallest domestic that
ever handled broom or scrubbing-brush.

"Now, Tottie, you must run round to the baker
directly, and fetch another loaf."

"What! a whole one, ma'am?" asked the small
domestic—in comparison with whom Dollops was
a giantess.

"Yes, a whole one. You see there's a young
gentleman coming to tea whom I did not expect—
a grand tall gentleman too, and a hero, who has
saved people from wrecks, and swims in the sea in
storms like a duck, and all that sort of thing, so he's
sure to have a tremendous appetite. You will also
buy another pennyworth of brown sugar, and two
more pats of butter."

Tottie opened her large blue eyes in amazement
at the extent of what she deemed a reckless order,
but went off instantly to execute it, wondering that
any hero, however regardless of the sea or storms,
could induce her poor mistress to go in for such
extravagance, after having already provided a luxurious meal for three.

It might have seemed unfair to send such a child
even to bed without an attendant. To send her

into the crowded streets alone in the dusk of evening, burdened with a vast commission, and weighted
with coppers, appeared little short of inhumanity.
Nevertheless Miss Lillycrop did it with an air of
perfect confidence, and the result proved that her
trust was not misplaced.

Tottie had been gone only a few seconds when
George Aspel appeared at the door and was admitted by Miss Lillycrop, who apologised for the
absence of her maid.

Great was the surprise and not slight the embarrassment of May Maylands when young Aspel was
ushered into the little room, for Phil had not
recovered sufficiently from the first greetings to
mention him.   Perhaps greater was the surprise
of Miss Lillycrop when these two, whom she had
expected to meet as old playmates, shook hands
rather stiffly.

"Sure, I forgot, May, to tell you that George was
coming—"

"I am very glad to see him," interrupted May,
recovering herself, "though I confess to some surprise that he should have forsaken Ireland so soon,
after saying to me that it was a perfect paradise."

Aspel, whose curly flaxen hair almost brushed
the ceiling, brought himself down to a lower region
by taking a chair, while he said with a meaning
smile—

"Ah! Miss Maylands, the circumstances are entirely altered now—besides," he added with a sudden change of tone and manner, "that inexorable man-made demon, Business, calls me to London."

"I hope Business intends to keep you here," said Miss Lillycrop, busying herself at the tea-table

"That remains to be seen," returned Aspel. "If I find that—"

"The loaf and butter, ma'am," said Tottie, announcing these articles at the door as if they were visitors.

"Hush, child; leave them in the kitchen till I ask for them," said Miss Lillycrop with a quiet laugh. "My little maid is *such* an original, Mr. Aspel."

"She's a very beautiful, though perhaps somewhat dishevelled, original," returned Aspel, "of which one might be thankful to possess even an inferior copy."

"Indeed you are right," rejoined Miss Lillycrop with enthusiasm; "she's a perfect little angel—come, draw in your chairs; closer this way, Phil, so—a perfect little angel—you take sugar I think? Yes. Well, as I was saying, the strange thing about her was that she was born and bred—thus far—in one of the worst of the back slums of London, and her father is an idle drunkard; I fear, also, a criminal."

"How strange and sad," said Aspel, whose heart was easily touched and sympathies roused by tales of sorrow. "But how comes it that she has escaped contamination?"

"Because she has a good—by which I mean a Christian—mother. Ah! Mr. Aspel, you have no idea how many unknown and unnoticed gems there are half smothered in the moral mud and filth of London. It is a wonderful—a tremendous city;—tremendous because of the mighty influences for good as well as evil which are constantly at work in it. There is an army of moral navvies labouring here, who are continually unearthing these gems, and there are others who polish them. I have the honour to be a member of this army. Dear little Tottie is one of the gems, and I mean, with God's blessing, to polish her. Of course, I can't get her all to myself," continued Miss Lillycrop with a sigh, "for her mother, who is a washerwoman, won't part with her, but she has agreed to come and work for me every morning for a few hours, and I can get her now and then of an evening. My chief regret is that the poor thing has a long long way to walk from her miserable home to reach me. I don't know how she will stand it. She has been only a few days in my service."

As the unpolished diamond entered at this moment with a large plate of buttered toast, Miss

Lillycrop changed the subject abruptly by expressing a hope that May Maylands had not to .go on
late duty that evening.

"Oh, no ; it's not my turn for a week yet," said
May.

"It seems to me very hard that they should work
you night and day," said Phil, who had been quietly
drinking in new ideas with his tea while his cousin
discoursed.

"But they don't work us night and day, Phil,"
returned May, "it is only the telegraphs that do
that. We of the female staff work in relays. If
we commence at 8 A.M. we work till 4 P.M. If we
begin at nine we work till five, and so on—eight
P.M. being our latest hour. Night duty is performed
by men, who are divided into two sections, and it
is so arranged that each man has an alternate long
and short duty—working three hours one night and
thirteen hours the next. We are allowed half-an-
hour for dinner, which we eat in a dining-hall in the
place. Of course we dine in relays also, as there
are above twelve hundred of us, male and female."

"How many ?" asked George Aspel in surprise.

"Above twelve hundred."

"Why, that would make two pretty fair regiments of soldiers," said Aspel.

"No, George," said Phil, "it's two regiments of
pretty fair soldiers that they'd make."

"Can't you hold your tongue, man, an' let May talk?" retorted Aspel.

"So, you see," continued May, " that amongst us we manage to have the telegraphic communication of the kingdom well attended to."

"But tell me, May," said Phil, " do they really suck messages through tubes two miles long?"

"Indeed they do, Phil. You see, the General Post-Office in London is in direct communication with all the chief centres of the kingdom, such as Birmingham, Liverpool, Manchester, Edinburgh, Glasgow, Dublin, Cork, etc., so that all messages sent from London must pass through the great hall at St. Martin's-le-Grand. But there are many offices in London for receiving telegrams besides the General Post-Office. Suppose that one of these offices in the city receives numerous tele- grams every hour all day long,—instead of trans- mitting these by wire to the General Post-Office, to be re-distributed to their various destinations, they are collected and put bodily into cylindrical leather cases, which are inserted into pneumatic metal tubes. These extend to our central office, and through them the telegrams are sucked just as they are written. The longest tube, from the West Strand, is about two miles, and each bundle or cylinder of telegrams takes about three minutes to travel. There are upwards of thirty such tubes, and the suction business is

done by two enormous fifty-horse-power steam-
engines in the basement of our splendid building.
There is a third engine, which is kept ready to work
in case of a break-down, or while one of the others
is being repaired."

"Ah! May, wouldn't there be the grand blow-up
if you were to burst your boilers in the basement?"
said Phil.

"No doubt there would. But steam is not the
only terrible agent at work in that same basement.
If you only saw the electric batteries there that
generate the electricity which enables us up-stairs to
send our messages flying from London to the Land's
End or John o' Groat's, or the heart of Ireland! You
must know that a far stronger battery is required
to send messages a long way than a short. Our
battery-inspector told me the other day that he
could not tell exactly the power of all the batteries
united, but he had no doubt it was sufficient to blow
the entire building into the middle of next week.
Now you know, Phil, it would require a pretty
severe shock to do that, wouldn't it? Fortunately
the accidental union of all the batteries is impossible. But you 'll see it for yourself soon. And it
will make you open your eyes when you see a room
with three miles of shelving, on which are ranged
twenty-two thousand battery-jars."

"My dear," said Miss Lillycrop, with a mild smile,

E

"you will no doubt wonder at my ignorance, but I don't understand what you mean by a battery-jar."

"It is a jar, cousin, which contains the substances which produce electricity."

"Well, well," rejoined Miss Lillycrop, dipping the sugar-spoon into the slop-bowl in her abstraction, "this world and its affairs is to me a standing miracle. Of course I must believe that what you say is true, yet I can no more understand how electricity is made in a jar and sent flying along a wire for some hundreds of miles with messages to our friends than I can comprehend how a fly walks on the ceiling without tumbling off."

"I'm afraid," returned May, "that you would require to study a treatise on Telegraphy to comprehend that, but no doubt Phil will soon get it so clearly into his head as to be able to communicate it to you.—You'll go to the office with me on Monday, won't you, Phil?"

"Of course I will—only too glad to begin at once."

"My poor boy," said May, putting her hand on her brother's arm, "it's not a very great beginning of life to become a telegraph-messenger."

"Ah! now, May, that's not like yourself," said Phil, who unconsciously dropped—perhaps we should say rose—to a more decided brogue when he became tender or facetious. "Is it rousin' the pride of me you'd be afther? Don't they say that any ould fiddle is good enough to learn upon? Mustn't I put my foot on the first round o' the ladder if I want to go up higher? If I'm to be Postmaster-General mustn't I get a general knowledge of the post from the bottom to the top by goin' through it? It's only men like George there that can go slap over everything at a bound."

"Come, Phil, don't be impertinent," said George, "it's a bad sign in one so young. Will you convoy me a short way? I must go now."

He rose as he spoke and bade Miss Lillycrop good-evening. That lady expressed an earnest hope that he would come to see her frequently, and he promised to do so as often as he could find time. He also bade May good-evening because she was to spend the night with her cousin, but May parted from him with the same touch of reserve that marked their meeting. He resented this by drawing himself up and turning away somewhat coldly.

"Now, Phil," he said, almost sternly, on reaching the street, "here's a letter to Sir James Clubley which I want to read to you.—Listen."

By the light of a lamp he read :—

"DEAR SIR,—I appreciate your kindness in offering me the situation mentioned in your letter of the 4th, and especially your remarks in reference to my late father, who was indeed worthy of esteem.

I shall have pleasure in calling on you on hearing that you are satisfied with the testimonials herewith enclosed.—I am, etc."

" Now, Phil, will that do ?"

" Do ? of course it will.   Nothing could be better. Only—"

" Well, what ?"

" Don't you think that you might call without waiting to hear his opinion of your testimonials ?"

" No, Phil, I don't," replied the other in a slightly petulant tone ; " I don't feel quite sure of the spirit in which he referred to my dear father.   Of course it was kind and all that, but it was slightly patronising, and my father was an infinitely superior man to himself."

" Well, I don't know," said Phil ; " if you 're going to accept a favour of him you had better try to feel and act in a friendly way, but of course it would never do to encourage him in pride."

" Well then, I 'll send it," said Aspel, closing the letter ; " do you know where I can post it ?"

" Not I.   Never was here before.   I 've only a vague idea of how I got here, and mustn't go far with you lest I lose myself."

At that moment Miss Lillycrop's door opened and little Tottie issued forth.

" Ah ! she will help us.—D' you know where the Post-Office is, Tottie ?"

"Yes, sir, it's at the corner of the street, Miss Lillycrop says."

"Which direction?"

"That one, I think."

"Here, I'm going the other way: will you post this letter for me?"

"Yes, sir," said Tottie.

"That's a good girl; here's a penny for you."

"Please, sir, that's not a penny," said the child, holding out the half-crown which Aspel had put in her hand.

"Never mind; keep it."

Tottie stood bereft of speech at the youth's munificence, as he turned away from her with a laugh.

Now, when Tottie Bones said that she knew where the post was, she did so because her mistress had told her, among other pieces of local information, that the pillar letter-box stood at the corner of the street and was painted red; but as no occasion had occurred since her arrival for the posting of a letter, she had not yet seen the pillar with her own eyes. The corner of the street, however, was so plain a direction that no one except an idiot could fail to find it. Accordingly Tottie started off to execute her mission.

Unfortunately—or the reverse, as the case may be—streets have usually two corners. The child

went, almost as a matter of course, to the wrong
one, and there she found no pillar. But she was a
faithful messenger, and not to be easily balked.
She sought diligently at that corner until she really
did find a pillar, in a retired angle. Living, as she
did, chiefly in the back slums of London, where
literary correspondence is not much in vogue,
Tottie had never seen a pillar letter-box, or, if she
had, had not realised its nature. Miss Lillycrop
had told her it was red, with a slit in it. The
pillar she had found was red to some extent with
rust, and it unquestionably had a slit in it where, in
days gone by, a handle had projected. It also had
a spout in front. Tottie had some vague idea that
this letter-box must have been made in imitation
of a pump, and that the spout was a convenient
step to enable small people like herself to reach the
slit. Only, she thought it queer that they should
not have put the spout in front of the pillar under
the slit, instead of behind it. She was still more
impressed with this when, after having twice got on
the spout, she twice fell off in futile efforts to reach
round the pump with her small arms.

Baffled, but not defeated, Tottie waited till some
one should pass who could put the letter in for her,
but in that retired angle no one passed. Suddenly
her sharp eyes espied a brick-bat. She set it up
on end beside the pump, mounted it, stood on tip-

toe, and, stretching her little body to the very
uttermost, tipped the letter safely in. The brick-
bat tipped over at the same instant and sent he͏
headlong to the ground. But this was n͏
to Tottie.   Regardless of the fall. ͏
self up, and, with the ligʰ͏
gained a victory in ͏   . ͏an off
to her misᵉ͏·   ͏ıns.

CHAPTER VII.

PHIL BEGINS LIFE, AND MAKES A FRIEND.

SOME time after the small tea-party described in
our last chapter, Philip Maylands was invested
with all the dignity, privileges, and emoluments of
an "Out-door Boy Telegraph Messenger" in the
General Post-Office.   He rejoiced in the conscious
independence of one who earns his own livelihood,
is a burden to nobody, and has something to spare.
He enjoyed the privilege of wearing a grey uniform,
of sitting in a comfortable room with a huge fire
in the basement of the office, and of walking over
a portion of London as the bearer of urgent and
no doubt all-important news.   He also enjoyed a
salary of seven shillings sterling a week, and was
further buoyed up with the hope of an increase
to eight shillings at the end of a year.   His duties,
as a rule, began at eight each morning, and averaged
nine hours.

We have said that out of his vast income he had

something to spare. This, of course, was not much, but owing to the very moderate charge for lodging made by Solomon Flint—with whom and his sister he took up his abode—the sum was sufficient to enable him, after a few months, to send home part of his first year's earnings to his mother. He did this by means of that most valuable institution of modern days a post-office order, which enables one to send small sums of money, at a moderate charge, and with perfect security, not only all over the kingdom, but over the greater part of the known world.

It would have been interesting, had it been possible, to have entered into Phil's feelings on the occasion of his transacting this first piece of financial business. Being a country-bred boy, he was as bashful about it as if he had been only ten years old. He doubted, first, whether the clerk would believe him in earnest when he should demand the order. Then, when he received the form to fill up, he had considerable hesitation lest he should fill in the blanks erroneously, and when the clerk scanned the slip and frowned, he felt convinced that he had done so.

"You've put only Mrs. Maylands," said the clerk.

"*Only* Mrs Maylands!" thought Phil; "does the man want me to add 'widow of the Rev. James Maylands, and mother of all the little Maylands?'"

but he only said, "Sure, sir, it's to her I want to send the money."

"Put down her Christian name," said the clerk; "order can't be drawn without it."

Phil put down the required name, handed over the money, received back the change, inserted the order into a previously prepared letter, posted the same, and walked away from that office as tall as his friend George Aspel—if not taller—in sensation.

Let us now follow our hero to the boy-messengers' room in the basement of St. Martin's-le-Grand.

Entering one morning after the delivery of a telegram which had cost him a pretty long walk, Phil proceeded to the boys' hall, and took his seat at the end of the row of boys who were awaiting their turn to be called for mercurial duty. Observing a very small telegraph-boy in a scullery off the hall, engaged in some mysterious operations with a large saucepan, from which volumes of steam proceeded, he went towards him. By that time Phil had become pretty well acquainted with the faces of his comrades, but this boy he had not previously met with. The lad was stooping over a sink, and carefully holding in the contents of the pan with its lid, while he strained off the boiling water.

"Sure I've not seen *you* before?" remarked Phil.

The boy turned up a sharp-featured, but handsome and remarkably intelligent face, and, with a quick glance at Phil, said, "Well, now, any man might know you for an Irishman by your impudence, even if you hadn't the brogue."

"Why, what do you mean?" asked Phil, with an amused smile.

"Mean!" echoed the boy, with the most refined extract of insolence on his pretty little face; "I mean that small though I am, surely I'm big enough to be *seen*."

"Well," returned Phil, with a laugh, "you know what I mean—that I haven't seen you before to-day."

"Then w'y don't you say what you mean? How d'you suppose a man can understand you unless you speak in plain terms? You won't do for the G. P. O. if you can't speak the Queen's English. We want sharp fellows here, we do. So you'd better go back to Owld Ireland, avic cushla mavourneen—there, put that in your pipe and smoke it."

Whether it was the distraction of the boy's mind, or the potent working of his impertinence, we know not, but certain it is that his left hand slipped somehow, and a round ball, with a delicious smell, fell out of the pot. The boy half caught it, and wildly yet cleverly balanced it on the lid, but it would have rolled next moment into the sink, if Phil had not made a dart forward, caught it like a foot-ball, and bowled it back into the pot.

"Well done! splendidly done!" cried the boy, setting down his pot. "Arrah! Pat," he added, mocking Phil's brogue, and holding out his hand, "you're a man after my own heart; give me your flipper, and let us swear eternal friendship over this precious goblet."

Of course Phil cheerfully complied, and the friendship thus auspiciously begun afterwards became strong and lasting. So it is all through the course of life. At every turn we are liable to meet with those who shall thenceforth exercise a powerful influence on our characters, lives, and affections, and on whom our influence shall be strong for good or evil.

"What's your name?" asked Phil; "mine is Philip Maylands."

"Mine's Peter Pax," answered the small boy, returning to his goblet; "but I've no end of *aliases* —such as Mouse, Monkey, Spider, Snipe, Imp, and Little 'un. Call me what you please, it's all one to me, so as you don't call me too late for dinner."

"And what have you got there, Pax?" asked Phil, referring to the pot.

"A plum-pudding."

"Do two or three of you share it?"

"Certainly not," replied the boy.

"What! you don't mean to say you can eat it all yourself for dinner?"

FIRST MEETING OF PHIL AND PAX—PAGE 76.

"The extent of my ability in the disposal of wittles," answered Pax, " I have never fairly tested. I think I could eat this at one meal, though I ain't sure, but it's meant to serve me all day. You see I find a good, solid, well-made plum-pudding, with not too much suet, and a moderate allowance of currants and raisins, an admirable squencher of appetite.   It's portable too, and keeps well.   Besides, if I can't get through with it at supper, it fries up next mornin' splendidly.—Come, I'll let you taste a bit, an' that's a favour w'ich I wouldn't grant to every one."

" No, thank 'ee, Pax.   I'm already loaded and primed for the forenoon, but I'll sit by you while you eat, and chat."

" You're welcome," returned Pax, "only don't be cheeky, Philip, as I can't meet you on an equal footing ⌐ 'en I'm at grub."

"   careful, Pax; but don't call me Philip   ."

       ᴧhil ; come along, Phil ; ' Come fill up ᵧᵧ, come fill up my can '—that sort o' thing ᴧ understand, Phil, me darlint ?"

There was such a superhuman amount of knowing presumption in the look and air of Pax, as he poked Phil in the ribs and winked, that the latter burst into laughter, in which however he was not joined by his companion, who with the goblet in one hand and the other thrust into his pocket, stood regarding his new friend with a pitiful expression till he recovered, and then led him off to a confabulation which deepened their mutual esteem.

That same evening a gentleman called at the Post-Office, desiring to see Philip Maylands. It turned out to be George Aspel.

"Why, George, what brings you here?" said Phil in surprise.

"I chanced to be in the neighbourhood," answered Aspel, "and came to ask the address of that little creature who posted my letter the other night. I want to see her. She does not go to your cousin's, I know, till morning, and I must see her to-night, to make sure that she *did* post the letter, for, d'you know, I've had no reply from Sir James, and I can't rest until I ascertain whether my letter was posted. Can you tell me where she lives, Phil?"

At that moment Phil was summoned for duty. Giving his friend the address hastily, he left him.

George Aspel passed the front of the General Post-Office on his way to visit Tottie Bones, and, observing a considerable bustle going on there, he stopped to gaze, for George had an inquiring mind. Being fresh from the country, his progress through the streets of London, as may be well understood, was slow. It was also harassing to himself and the public, for when not actually standing entranced in front of shop-windows his irresistible tendency to look in while walking resulted in many collisions and numerous apologies. At the General Post-Office he avoided the stream of human beings by getting under the lee of one of the pillars of the colonnade, whence he could look on undisturbed.

Up to six o'clock letters are received in the letter-box at St. Martin's-le-Grand for the mails which leave London at eight each evening. The place for receiving book-parcels and newspapers, however, closes half-an-hour sooner. Before five a brass slit in the wall suffices for the public, but within a few minutes of the half-hour the steady run of men and boys towards it is so great that the slit becomes inadequate. A trap-door is therefore opened in the pavement, and a yawning abyss displayed which communicates by an inclined plane with the newspaper regions below. Into this abyss everything is hurled.

When Aspel took up his position people were hurrying towards the hole, some with single book-parcels, or a few newspapers, others with armfuls, and many with sackfuls. In a few minutes the rapid walk became a run. Men, boys, and girls sprang up the steps—occasionally tumbled up,— jostled each other in their eager haste, and tossed, dropped, hurled, or poured their contributions into

the receptacle, which was at last fed so hastily that
it choked once or twice, and a policeman, assisted
by an official, stuffed the literary matter down its
throat—with difficulty, however, owing to the ever-
increasing stream of contributors to the feast. The
trap-door, when open, formed a barrier to the hole,
which prevented the too eager public from being
posted headlong with their papers. One youth
staggered up the steps under a sack so large that
he could scarcely lift it over the edge of the barrier
without the policeman's aid. Him Aspel ques-
tioned, as he was leaving with the empty sack,
and found that he was the porter of one of the
large publishing firms of the city.

Others he found came from advertising agents
with sacks of circulars, etc.

Soon the minutes were reduced to seconds, and
the work became proportionally fast and furious;
sacks, baskets, hampers, trays of material were
emptied violently into that insatiable maw, and in
some cases the sacks went in along with their
contents. But owners' names being on these, they
were recoverable elsewhere.

Suddenly, yet slowly, the opening closed. The
monster was satisfied for that time; it would not
swallow another morsel, and one or two unfortunates
who came late with large bags of newspapers and
circulars had to resort to the comparatively slow

process of cramming their contents through the narrow slit above, with the comforting certainty that they had missed that post.

Turning from this point George Aspel observed that the box for letters—closing, as we have said, half an hour later than that for books and papers— was beginning to show symptoms of activity. At a quarter to six the long metal slit suddenly opened up like a gaping mouth, into which a harlequin could have leaped easily. Through it Aspel could look—over the heads of the public—and see the officials inside dragging away great baskets full of letters to be manipulated in the mysterious realms inside. At five minutes to six the rush towards this mouth was incessant, and the operations at the newspaper-tomb were pretty much repeated, though, of course, the contents of bags and baskets were not quite so ponderous. At one side of the mouth stood an official in a red coat, at the other a policeman. These assisted the public to empty their baskets and trays, gave information, sometimes ad- vice, and kept people moving on. Little boys there, as elsewhere, had a strong tendency to skylark and gaze at the busy officials inside, to the obstruction of the way. The policeman checked their propensities. A stout elderly female panted towards the mouth with a letter in one hand and a paper in the other. She had full two minutes and a half to spare, but felt convinced she was too late. The red-coated official posted her letter, and pointed out the proper place for the newspaper. At two minutes to six anxious people began to run while yet in the street. Cool personages, seeing the clock, and feeling safe, affected an easy nonchalance, but did not loiter. One minute to six—eager looks were on the faces of those who, from all sides, converged towards the great receiving-box. The active sprang up the wide stairs at a bound, heaved in their bundles, or packets, or single missives, and heaved sighs of relief after them; the timid stumbled on the stairs and blundered up to the mouth; while the hasty almost plunged into it bodily. Even at this critical moment there were lulls in the rush. Once there was almost a dead pause, and at that moment an exquisite sauntered towards the mouth, dropped a solitary little letter down the slope where whole cataracts had been flowing, and turned away. He was almost carried off his legs by two youths from a lawyer's office, who rushed up just as the first stroke of six o'clock rang out on the night air. Slowly and grandly it tolled from St. Paul's, whose mighty dome was visible above the house-tops from the colonnade. During these fleeting moments a few dozens of late ones posted some hundreds of letters. With kindly consideration the authorities of St. Martin's-le-Grand have set their timepieces one minute slow. Aware of this, a clerk, gasping and with a pen behind his ear, leaped up the steps at the last stroke, and hurled in a bundle of letters. Next moment, like inexorable fate, the mouth closed, and nothing short of the demolition of the British Constitution could have induced that mouth to convey another letter to the eight o'clock mails.

Hope, however, was not utterly removed. Those who chose to place an additional penny stamp on their letters could, by posting them in a separate box, have them taken in for that mail up to seven. Twopence secured their acceptance up to 7.15. Threepence up to 7.30, and sixpence up to 7.45, but all letters posted after six without the late fees were detained for the following mail.

"Sharp practice!" observed George Aspel to the red-coated official, who, after shutting the mouth, placed a ticket above it which told all comers that they were too late.

"Yes, sir, and pretty sharp work is needful when you consider that the mails we've got to send out daily from this office consist of over 5800 bags, weighing forty-three tons, while the mails received number more than 5500 bags. Speaks to a deal of correspondence that, don't it, sir?"

"What!—every day?" exclaimed Aspel in surprise.

"Every day," replied the official, with a good-

humoured smile and an emphatic nod. " Why, sir,"
he continued, in a leisurely way, "we 're somewhat
of a literary nation, we are. How many letters,
now, d' you think, pass through the Post-Office
altogether—counting England, Scotland, and Ireland ? "

" Haven't the remotest idea."

" Well, sir," continued the red-coated man, with
impressive solemnity, "we passes through our
hands in one year about one thousand and fifty-
seven million odd."

" I know enough of figures," said Aspel, with a
laugh, " to be aware that I cannot realise such
a number."

" Nevertheless, sir," continued the official, with a
patronising air, " you can realise something *about*
such a number. For instance, that sum gives thirty-
two letters per head to the population in the year ;
and, of course, as thousands of us can't write, and
thousands more don't write, it follows that the real
correspondents of the kingdom do some pretty stiff
work in the writing way. But these are only the
letters. If you include somewhere about four hundred and twenty million post-cards, newspapers,
book-packets, and circulars, you have a sum-total of
fourteen hundred and seventy-seven million odd
passing through our hands. Put that down in
figures, sir, w'en you git home—1,477,000,000—an'

p'r'aps it' ll open your eyes a bit. If you want 'em opened still wider, just try to find out how long it would take you to count that sum, at the rate of sixty to the minute, beginning one, two, three, and so on, workin' eight hours a day without takin' time for meals, but givin' you off sixty-five days each year for Sundays and holidays to recruit your wasted energies."

"How long *would* it take?" asked Aspel, with an amused but interested look.

"W'y, sir, it would take you just a little over one hundred and seventy years. The calculation ain't difficult; you can try it for yourself if you don't believe it.—Good-night, sir," added the red-coated official, with a pleasant nod, as he turned and entered the great building, where a huge proportion of this amazing work was being at that moment actively manipulated.

CHAPTER VIII.

DOWNWARD—DEEPER AND DEEPER.

As the great bell of St. Paul's struck the half-hour, George Aspel was reminded of the main object of his visit to that part of the City. Descending to the street, and pondering in silent wonder on the vast literary correspondence of the kingdom, he strode rapidly onward, his long legs enabling him to pass ahead of the stream of life that flowed with him, and causing him to jostle not a few members of the stream that opposed him.

"Hallo, sir!" "Look out!" "Mind your eye, stoopid!" "Now, then, you lamp-post, w'ere are you agoin' to?" "Wot asylum 'ave *you* escaped from?" were among the mildest remarks with which he was greeted.

But Aspel heeded them not. The vendors of penny marvels failed to attract him. Even the print-shop windows had lost their influence for a time; and as for monkeys, barrel-organs, and trained birds, they were as the dust under his feet, although at other times they formed a perpetual feast to his unsophisticated soul. "Letters, letters, letters!"

He could think of nothing else. " Fourteen hundred and seventy-seven millions of letters, etc., through the Post-Office in one year!" kept ringing through his brain ; only varied in its monotony by "that gives thirty-two letters per head to the entire population, and as lots of 'em can't write, of course it's much more for those who can! Take a man one hundred and seventy years to count 'em!"

At this point the brilliant glare of a gin-palace reminded him that he had walked far and long, and had for some time felt thirsty. Entering, he called for a pot of beer. It was not a huge draught for a man of his size. As he drained it the memory of grand old jovial sea-kings crossed his mind, and he called for another pot. As he was about to apply it to his lips, and shook back his flaxen curls, the remembrance of a Norse drinking-cup in his possession—an heirloom, which could not stand on its bottom, and had therefore to be emptied before being set down,—induced him to chuckle quietly before quaffing his beer.

On setting down the empty pot he observed a poor miserable-looking woman, with a black eye and a black bottle, gazing at him in undisguised admiration. Instantly he called for a third pot of beer. Being supplied by the wondering shop-boy, he handed it to the woman ; but she shook her head, and drew back with an air of decision.

"No, sir," she said, "but thank you kindly all the same, sir."

"Very well," returned the youth, putting the pot and a half-crown on the counter, "you may drink it or leave it as you please. I pay for it, and you may take the change—or leave that too if you like," he added, as he went out, somewhat displeased that his feeling of generosity had been snubbed.

After wandering a short distance he was involved in labyrinths of brick and mortar, and suddenly became convinced that he was lost. This was however a small matter. To find one's way by asking it is not difficult, even in London, if one possesses average intelligence.

The first man he stopped was a Scot. With characteristic caution that worthy cleared his throat, and with national deliberation repeated Aspel's query, after which, in a marked tone of regret, he said slowly, "Weel, sir, I really div not ken."

Aspel thanked him with a sarcastic smile and passed on. His next effort was with a countryman, who replied, "Troth, sur, that's more nor I can tell 'ee," and looked after his questioner kindly as he walked away. A policeman appearing was tried next. "First to the right, sir, third to the left, and ask again," was the sharp reply of that limb of the Executive, as he passed slowly on, stiff as a post, and stately as a law of fate.

Having taken the required turns our wanderer found himself in a peculiarly low, dirty, and disagreeable locality. The population was in keeping with it—so much so that Aspel looked round inquiringly before proceeding to "ask again." He had not quite made up his mind which of the tawdry, half-drunken creatures around him he would address, when a middle-aged man of respectable appearance, dressed in black, issued from one of the surrounding dens.

"A city missionary," thought George Aspel, as he approached, and asked for direction to the abode of a man named Abel Bones.

The missionary pointed out the entrance to the desired abode, and looked at his questioner with a glance which arrested the youth's attention.

"Excuse me, sir," he said, "but the man you name has a very bad character."

"Well, what then?" demanded Aspel sharply.

"Oh! nothing. I only meant to warn you, for he is a dangerous man."

The missionary was a thin but muscular man, with stern black eyes and a powerful nose, which might have rendered his face harsh if it had not been more than redeemed by a large firm mouth, round which played lines that told unmistakably of the milk of human kindness. He smiled as he spoke, and Aspel was disarmed.

"Thank you," he said; "I am well able to take care of myself."

Evidently the missionary thought so too, for, with a quiet bow, he turned and went his way.

At the end of a remarkably dark passage George Aspel ran his head against a beam and his knee against a door with considerable violence.

"Come in," said a very weak but sweet little voice, as though doors in that region were usually rapped at in that fashion.

Lifting the latch and entering, Aspel found himself confronted by Tottie Bones in her native home.

It was a very small, desolate, and dirty home, and barely rendered visible by a thin "dip" stuck into an empty pint-bottle.

Tottie opened her large eyes wide with astonishment, then laid one of her dirty little fingers on her rosy lips and looked imploringly at her visitor. Thus admonished, he spoke, without knowing why in a subdued voice.

"You are surprised to see me, Tottie?"

"I'm surprised at nothink, sir. 'Taint possible to surprise me with anythink in *this* life."

"D' you expect to be surprised by anything in any other life, Tottie?" asked Aspel, more amused by the air of the child than by her answer.

"P'r'aps. Don't much know, and don't much care," said Tottie.

"Well, I've come to ask something," said the youth, sitting down on a low box for the convenience of conversation, "and I hope, Tottie, that you'll tell me the truth. Here's a half-crown for you. The truth, mind, whether you think it will please me or not; I don't want to be pleased—I want the truth."

"I'd tell you the truth without *that*," said Tottie, eyeing the half-crown which Aspel still held between his fingers, "but hand it over. We want a good many o' these things here, bein' pretty hard up at times."

She spun the piece deftly in the air, caught it cleverly, and put it in her pocket.

"Well, tell me, now, did you post the letter I gave you the night I took tea with Miss Lillycrop?"

"Yes, I did," answered the child, with a nod of decision.

"You're telling the truth?"

"Yes; as sure as death."

Poor Tottie had made her strongest asseveration, but it did not convey to Aspel nearly so much assurance as did the earnest gaze of her bright and truthful eyes.

"You put it in the pillar?" he continued.

"Yes."

"At the end of the street?"

"Yes, at the end of the street; and oh, you've

no idea what an awful time I was about it; the slit was so high, an' I come down sitch a cropper w'en it was done!"

"But it went in all right?"

"Yes, all right."

George Aspel sat for some moments in gloomy silence. He now felt convinced of that which at first he had only suspected—namely, that his intending patron was offended because he had not at once called in person to thank him, instead of doing so by letter. Probably, also, he had been hurt by the expressions in the letter to which Philip Maylauds had objected when it was read to him.

"Well, well," he exclaimed, suddenly giving a severe slap to his unoffending thigh, "I'll have nothing to do with him. If he's so touchy as that comes to, the less that he and I have to say to each other the better."

"Oh! *please*, sir, hush!" exclaimed Tottie, pointing with a look of alarm to a bundle which lay in a dark corner, "you'll wake 'im."

"Wake who?"

"Father," whispered the child.

The visitor rose, took up the pint-bottle, and by the aid of its flaring candle beheld something that resembled a large man huddled together in a heap on a straw mattress, as he had last fallen down. His position, together with his torn and disarranged garments, had destroyed all semblance to human form save where a great limb protruded. His visage was terribly disfigured by the effects of drink, besides being partly concealed by his matted hair.

"What a wretched spectacle!" exclaimed the young man, touching the heap with his foot as he turned away in disgust.

Just then a woman with a black eye entered the room with a black bottle in her hand. She was the woman who had refused the beer from Aspel.

"Mother," said Tottie, running up to her, "here's the gent who—"

"'Av-'ee-go'-th'-gin?" growled a deep voice from the dark corner.

"Yes, Abel—"

"'Ave 'ee got th' gin, I say, Molly?" roared the voice in rising wrath.

"Yes, yes, Abel, here it is," exclaimed the woman, hastening towards the corner.

The savage who lay there was so eager to obtain the bottle that he made a snatch at it and let it slip on the stone floor, where it was broken to pieces.

"O don't, Abel dear, don't! I'll get another," pleaded the poor woman; but Abel's disappointment was too great for endurance; he managed to rise, and made a wild blow at the woman,—missed

her, and staggered into the middle of the room.
Here he encountered the stern glance of George
Aspel.   Being a dark, stern man himself, with a
bulky powerful frame, he rather rejoiced in the sight
of a man who seemed a worthy foe.

"What d'ee wan' here, you long-legged—hah !
would you ?" he added, on observing Aspel's face
flush and his fists close, " Take that !"

He struck out at his adversary's face with tremendous violence. Aspel parried the blow and
returned it with such good-will that Abel Bones
went headlong into the dark corner whence he had
risen,—and lay there.

"I'm *very* sorry," said the instantly-repentant
George, turning to Mrs. Bones, " but I couldn't
help it ; really, I— "

"There, there ; go away, sir, and thank you
kindly," said the unfortunate woman, urging—
almost pushing—her visitor towards the door.
"It'll do 'im good, p'r'aps. He don't get that every
day, an' it won't 'urt 'im."

Aspel found himself suddenly in the dark passage, and heard the door slammed. His first
impulse was to turn, dash in the door with his foot,
and take vengeance on Abel Bones, his next to
burst into a sardonic laugh. Thereafter he frowned
fiercely, and strode away. In doing so he drew
himself up with sea-king-like dignity and assaulted

a beam, which all but crushed his hat over his eyes. This did not improve his temper, but the beer had not yet robbed him of all self-control; he stooped to conquer and emerged into the street.

Well was it for George Aspel that his blow had been such an effective one, for if a riot with Bones had followed the blow, there were numerous kindred spirits there who would have been only too glad to aid their chum, and the intruder would have fared badly among them, despite his physical powers.   As it was, he soon regained a respectable thoroughfare, and hastened away in the direction of his lodgings.

But a dark frown clouded his brow, for as he went along his thoughts were busy with what he believed to be the insolent pride of Sir James Clubley.   He also thought of May Maylands, and the resolution with which she so firmly yet so gently repelled him.   The latter thought wounded his pride as well as his feelings deeply.   While in this mood the spirit of the sea-kings arose within him once again.   He entered a public-house and had another pot of beer.   It was very refreshing— remarkably so !   True, the tall and stalwart young frame of George Aspel needed no refreshment at the time, and he would have scorned the insinuation that he *required* anything to support him— but— but—it was decidedly refreshing !   There could be no doubt whatever about that, and it induced him

to take a more amiable view of men in general—of
"poor Abel Bones" in particular.   He even felt less
savagely disposed towards Sir James, though he by
no means forgave him, but made up his mind finally
to have nothing more to do with him, while as to
May—hope told him flattering tales.

At this point in his walk he was attracted by
one of those traps to catch the unwary, which are
so numerous in London—a music-hall.   George
knew not what it was, and cared not.   It was a
place of public entertainment : that was enough for
him.   He wanted entertainment, and in he went.

It is not our purpose to describe this place.
Enough is told when we have said that there were
dazzling lights and gorgeous scenes, and much
music, and many other things to amuse.   There
were also many gentlemen, but—no ladies.   There
was also much smoking and drinking.

Aspel soon observed that he was expected either
to drink or smoke.   He did not wish to do either,
but, disliking singularity, ordered a cigar and a
glass of brandy-and-water.   These were followed
by another cigar and another glass.   Towards midnight he had reached that condition when drink
stimulates the desire for more drink.   Being aware,
from former experience, of the danger of this condition, and being, as we have said, a man of some
strength of will, he rose to go.

At the moment a half-tipsy man at the little table next him carelessly flung the end of his cigar away. It alighted, probably by accident, on the top of Aspel's head.

"Hallo, sir!" shouted the enraged youth, starting up and seizing the man by his collar.

"Hallo, sir!" echoed the man, who had reached his pugnacious cups, "let go."

He struck out at the same moment. Aspel would have parried the blow, but his arm had been seized by one of the bystanders, and it took effect on his nose, which instantly sent a red stream over his mouth and down the front of his shirt.

Good-humour and kindliness usually served Aspel in the place of principle. Remove these qualities temporarily, and he became an unguarded savage—sometimes a roaring lion.

With a shout that suspended the entertainments and drew the attention of the whole house, he seized his adversary, lifted him in the air, and would infallibly have dashed him on the floor if he had not been caught in the arms of the crowd. As it was, the offender went down, carrying half-a-dozen friends and a couple of tables with their glasses along with him.

Aspel was prevented from doing more mischief by three powerful policemen, who seized him from behind and led him into the passage. There a

noisy explanation took place, which gave the offender time to cool and reflect on his madness.   On
his talking quietly to the policemen, and readily
paying for the damage he had done, he was allowed
to go free.   Descending the stair to the street,
where the glare of the entrance-lamps fell full upon
him, he felt a sudden sensation of faintness, caused
by the combination of cold air, excitement, drink,
and smoke.   Seizing the railings with one hand, he
stood for a moment with his eyes shut.

Re-opening them, and gazing stupidly before him,
he encountered the horrified gaze of May Maylands !
She had been spending the evening with Miss
Lillycrop, and was on her way home, escorted by
Solomon Flint.

"Come along, Miss May," said Solomon, "don't
be afraid of 'im.   He can't 'urt you—too far gone
for that, bless you.   Come on."

May yielded, and was out of sight in a moment.

Filled with horror, despair, madness, and self-
contempt, George Aspel stood holding on to the
railings and glaring into vacuity.   Recovering himself he staggered home and went to bed.

CHAPTER IX.

MR. BLURT AND GEORGE ASPEL IN PECULIAR CIRCUMSTANCES.

WHEN a man finds himself in a false position, out of which he sees no way of escape, he is apt to feel a depression of spirits which reveals itself in the expression of his countenance.

One morning Mr. Enoch Blurt sat on a high stool in his brother's shop, with his elbows on a screened desk, his chin in his hands, and a grim smile on his lips.

The shop was a peculiar one. It had somewhat the aspect of an old curiosity shop, but the predominance of stuffed birds gave it a distinctly ornithological flavour. Other stuffed creatures were there, however, such as lizards, frogs, monkeys, etc., all of which straddled in attitudes more or less unlike nature, while a few wore expressions of astonishment quite in keeping with their circumstances.

"Here am I," soliloquised Mr. Blurt with a touch of bitterness, "in the position of a shop-boy, in possession of a shop towards which I entertain feelings of repugnance, seeing that it has twice ruined my poor brother, and in regard to the details of which I know absolutely nothing. I had fancied I had reached the lowest depths of misfortune when I became a ruined diamond-merchant, but this is a profounder deep."

"Here's the doctor a-comin' down-stairs, sir," said an elderly female, protruding her head from the back shop, and speaking in a stage-whisper.

"Very well, Mrs. Murridge, let him come," said Mr. Blurt recklessly.

He descended from the stool, as the doctor entered the shop looking very grave. Every expression, save that of deep anxiety, vanished from Mr. Blurt's face.

"My brother is worse?" he said quickly.

"Not worse," replied the doctor, "but his case is critical. Everything will depend on his mind being kept at ease. He has taken it into his head that his business is going to wreck while he lies there unable to attend to it, and asked me earnestly if the shop had been opened. I told him I'd step down and inquire."

"Poor Fred!" murmured his brother sadly; "he has too good reason to fancy his business is going to wreck, with or without his attendance, for I find that very little is doing, and you can see that the entire stock isn't worth fifty pounds—if so much.

The worst of it is that his boy, who used to assist
him, absconded yesterday with the contents of the
till, and there is no one now to look after it."

" That's awkward. We must open the shop however, for it is all-important that his mind should
be kept quiet. Do you know how to open it, Mr.
Blurt ?"

Poor Mr. Blurt looked helplessly at the closed
shutters, through a hole in one of which the morning
sun was streaming. Turning round he encountered
the deeply solemn gaze of an owl which stood on a
shelf at his elbow.

" No, doctor, I know no more how to open it than
that idiot there," he said, pointing to the owl, " but
I'll make inquiries of Mrs. Murridge."

The domestic fortunately knew the mysterious
operations relative to the opening of a shop. With
her assistance Mr. Blurt took off the shutters,
stowed them away in their proper niche, and threw
open the door to the public with an air of invitation, if not hospitality, which deserved a better
return than it received. With this news the doctor
went back to the sick man.

" Mrs. Murridge," said Mr. Blurt, when the doctor had gone, " would you be so good as mind the
shop for a few minutes, while I go up-stairs ? If
any one should come in, just go to the foot of the
stair and give two coughs. I shall hear you."

On entering his brother's room, he found him raised on one elbow, with his eyes fixed wildly on the door.

"Dear Fred," he said tenderly, hurrying forward, "you must not give way to anxiety, there's a dear fellow. Lie down. The doctor says you'll get well if you only keep quiet."

"Ay, but I can't keep quiet," replied the poor old man tremulously, while he passed his hand over the few straggling white hairs that lay on but failed to cover his head. "How can you expect me to keep quiet, Enoch, when my business is all going to the dogs for want of attention? And that boy of mine is such a stupid fellow; he loses or mislays the letters somehow—I can't understand how. There's confusion too somewhere, because I have written several times of late to people who owe me money, and sometimes have got no answers, at other times been told that they *had* replied, and enclosed cheques, and—"

"Come now, dear Fred," said Enoch soothingly, while he arranged the pillows, "do give up thinking about these things just for a little while till you are better, and in the meantime I will look after—"

"And he's such a lazy boy too," interrupted the invalid,—"never gets up in time unless I rouse him. —Has the shop been opened, Enoch?"

"Yes, didn't the doctor tell you? I helped to

open it myself," returned Enoch, speaking rapidly
to prevent his brother, if possible, from asking after
the boy, about whose unfaithfulness he was still
ignorant. "And now, Fred, I insist on your hand-
ing the whole business over to me for a week or
two, just as it stands; if you don't I'll go back to
Africa. Why, you've no idea what a splendid
shopman I shall make. You seem to forget that
I have been a successful diamond-merchant."

"I don't see the connection, Enoch," returned the
other, with a faint smile.

"That's because you've never been out of London,
and can't believe in anybody who hasn't been born,
or at least bred, within the sound of Bow Bells.
Don't you know that diamond-merchants sometimes
keep stores, and that stores mean buying and sell-
ing, and corresponding, and all that sort of thing?
Come, dear Fred, trust me a little—only a little—
for a day or two, or rather, I should say, trust God,
and try to sleep. There's a dear fellow—come."

The sick man heaved a deep sigh, turned over on
his side, and dropped into a quiet slumber—whether
under the influence of a more trustful spirit or of
exhaustion we cannot say—probably both.

Returning to the shop, Mr. Blurt sat down in his
old position on the stool and began to meditate.
He was interrupted by the entrance of a woman
carrying a stuffed pheasant. She pointed out that

one of the glass eyes of the creature had got broken, and wished to know what it would cost to have a new one put in. Poor Mr. Blurt had not the faintest idea either as to the manufacture or cost of glass eyes. He wished most fervently that the woman had gone to some other shop. Becoming desperate, and being naturally irascible, as well as humorous, he took a grimly facetious course.

"My good woman," he said, with a bland smile, "I would recommend you to leave the bird as it is. A dead pheasant can see quite as well with one eye as with two, I assure you."

"La! sir, but it don't look so well," said the woman.

"O yes, it does; quite as well, if you turn its blind side to the wall."

"But we keeps it on a table, sir, an' w'en our friends walk round the table they can't 'elp seein' the broken eye."

"Well, then," persisted Mr. Blurt, "don't let your friends walk round the table. Shove the bird up against the wall; or tell your friends that it's a humorous bird, an' takes to winking when they go to that side."

The woman received this advice with a smile, but insisted nevertheless that a "noo *heye*" would be preferable, and wanted to know the price.

"Well, you know," said Mr. Blurt, "that depends

on the size and character of the eye, and the time required to insert it, for, you see, in our business everything depends on a life-like turn being given to an eye—or a beak—or a toe, and we don't like to put inferior work out of our hands. So you'd better leave the bird and call again."

"Very well, sir, w'en shall I call?"

"Say next week. I am very busy just now, you see—extremely busy, and cannot possibly give proper attention to your affair at present. Stay— give me your address."

The woman did so, and left the shop while Mr. Blurt looked about for a memorandum-book. Opening one, which was composite in its character— having been used indifferently as day-book, cash-book, and ledger—he headed a fresh page with the words "Memorandum of Transactions by Enoch Blurt," and made the following entry :—

"A woman—I should have said an idiot—came in and left a pheasant, *minus* an eye, to be repaired and called for next week."

"There!" exclaimed the unfortunate man, shutting the book with emphasis.

"Please, sir," said a very small sweet voice.

Mr. Blurt looked over the top of his desk in surprise, for the owner of the voice was not visible. Getting down from his stool, and coming out of his den, he observed the pretty face and dishevelled head of a little girl not much higher than the counter.

"Please, sir," she said, "can you change 'alf a sov.?"

"No, I can't," said Mr. Blurt, so gruffly that the small girl retired in haste.

"Stay! come here," cried the repentant shopman. The child returned with some hesitation.

"Who trusted you with half a sov.?"

"Miss Lillycrop, sir."

"And who's Miss Lillycrop?"

"My missis, sir."

"Does your missis think that I'm a banker?" demanded Mr. Blurt sternly.

"I dun know, sir."

"Then why did she send you here?"

"Please, sir, because the gentleman wot keeps this shop is a friend o' missis, an' always gives 'er change w'en she wants it. He stuffs her birds for her too, for nothink, an' once he stuffed a tom-cat for 'er, w'ich she was uncommon fond of, but he couldn't make much of a. job of it, 'cause it died through a kittle o' boilin' water tumblin' on its back, which took off most of the 'air."

While the child was speaking Mr. Blurt drew a handful of silver from his pocket, and counted out ten shillings.

"There," he said, putting the money into the child's hand, "and tell Miss Lillycrop, with my compliments—Mr. Enoch Blurt's compliments—that my brother has been very ill, but is a little—a very little—better; and see, there is a sixpence for yourself."

"Oh, *thank* you, sir!" exclaimed the child, opening her eyes with such a look of surprised joy that Mr. Blurt felt comforted in his difficulties, and resolved to face them like a man, do his duty, and take the consequences.

He was a good deal relieved, however, to find that no one else came into the shop during the remainder of that day. As he sat and watched the never-ceasing stream of people pass the windows, almost without casting a glance at the ornithological specimens that stood rampant there, he required no further evidence that the business had already gone to that figurative state of destruction styled "the dogs." The only human beings in London who took the smallest notice of him or his premises were the street boys, some of whom occasionally flattened their noses on a pane of glass, and returned looks of, if possible, exaggerated surprise at the owl, while others put their heads inside the door, yelled in derision, and went placidly away. Dogs also favoured him with a passing glance, and one or two, with sporting tendencies, seemed about to point at the game inside, but thought better of it, and went off.

At intervals the patient man called Mrs. Murridge
to mind the shop, while he went up-stairs. Sometimes he found the invalid dozing, sometimes fret-
ting at the thoughts of the confusion about his
letters.

"If they *all* went astray one could understand it,"
he would say, passing his hand wearily over his brow,
"because that would show that one cause went on
producing one result, but sometimes letters come
right, at other times they don't come at all."

"But how d' you find out about those that don't
come at all ?" asked his brother.

"By writing to know why letters have not been
replied to, and getting answers to say that they
have been replied to," said the invalid. "It's very
perplexing, Enoch, and I 've lost a deal of money
by it. I wouldn't mind so much if I was well,
but—"

"There, now, you 're getting excited again, Fred ;
you *must not* speak about business matters. Haven't
I promised to take it in hand ? and I 'll investigate
this matter to the bottom. I 'll write to the Secretary of the General Post-Office. I 'll go down to St.
Martin's-le-Grand and see him myself, and if he
don't clear it up I 'll write letters to the *Times*
until I bu'st up the British Post-Office altogether ;
so make your mind easy, Fred, else I 'll forsake
you and go right away back to Africa."

There was no resisting this. The poor invalid submitted with a faint smile, and his brother returned to the shop.

"It's unsatisfactory, to say the least of it," murmured Mr. Blurt as he relieved guard and sat down again on the high stool. "To solicit trade and to be unable to meet the demand when it comes is a very false position. Yet I begin to wish that somebody would come in for something—just for a change."

It seemed as if somebody had heard his wish expressed, for at that moment a man entered the shop. He was a tall, powerful man. Mr. Blurt had just begun to wonder what particular branch of the business he was going to be puzzled with, when he recognised the man as his friend George Aspel.

Leaping from his stool and seizing Aspel by the hand, Mr. Blurt gave him a greeting so hearty that two street boys who chanced to pass and saw the beginning of it exclaimed, "Go it, old 'un!" and waited for more. But Aspel shut the door in their faces, which induced them to deliver uncomplimentary remarks through the keyhole, and make unutterable eyes at the owl in the window ere they went the even tenor of their way.

Kind and hearty though the greeting was, it did not seem to put the youth quite at his ease, and there was a something in his air and manner which struck Mr. Blurt immediately.

"Why, you've hurt your face, Mr. Aspel," he exclaimed, turning his friend to the light. "And—and—you've had your coat torn and mended as if—"

"Yes, Mr. Blurt," said Aspel, suddenly recovering something of his wonted bold and hearty manner; "I have been in bad company, you see, and had to fight my way out of it. London is a more difficult and dangerous place to get on in than I had imagined at first."

"I suppose it is, though I can't speak from much experience," said Mr. Blurt. "But come, sit down. Here's a high stool for you. I'll sit on the counter. Now, let's hear about your adventures or misadventures. How did you come to grief?"

"Simply enough," replied Aspel, with an attempt to look indifferent and easy, in which he was only half-successful. "I went into a music-hall one night and got into a row with a drunk man who insulted me. That's how I came by my damaged face. Then about two weeks ago a fellow picked my pocket. I chased him down into one of his haunts, and caught him, but was set upon by half a dozen scoundrels who overpowered me. They will carry some of my marks, however, for many a day—perhaps to their graves; but I held on to the pickpocket in spite of them until the police rescued me. That's how my clothes got damaged.   The worst of it is, the rascals managed to make away with my purse."

" My dear fellow," said Mr. Blurt, laughing, " you have been unfortunate.   But most young men have to gather wisdom from experience.—And now, what of your prospects ?   Excuse me if I appear inquisitive, but one who is so deeply indebted to you as I am cannot help feeling interested in your success."

" I have no prospects," returned the youth, with a tone and look of bitterness that was not usual to him.

"What do you mean ? " asked his friend in surprise, " have you not seen Sir James Clubley ?"

" No, and I don't intend to see him until he has answered my letter.   Let me be plain with you, Mr. Blurt.   Sir James, I have heard from my father, is a proud man, and I don't half like the patronising way in which he offered to assist me. And his insolent procrastination in replying to my letter has determined me to have nothing more to do with him.   He'll find that I'm as proud as himself."

"My young friend," said Mr. Blurt, "I had imagined that a man of your good sense would have seen that to meet pride with pride is not wise ; besides, to do so is to lay yourself open to the very condemnation which you pronounce against Sir James. Still further, is it not possible that your letter to him may have miscarried? Letters will miscarry, you know, at times, even in such a well-regulated family as the Post-Office."

"Oh! as to that," returned Aspel quickly, "I've made particular inquiries, and have no doubt that he got my letter all right.—But the worst of it is," he continued, evidently wishing to change the subject, "that, having lost my purse, and having no account at a banker's, I find it absolutely necessary to work, and, strange to say, I cannot find work."

"Well, if you have been searching for work with a black eye and a torn coat, it is not surprising that you have failed to find it," said Mr. Blurt, with a laugh. "But, my dear young friend and preserver," he added earnestly, "I am glad you have come to me. Ah! if that ship had not gone down I might have—well, well, the proverb says it's of no use crying over spilt milk. I have still a little in my power. Moreover, it so happens that you have it in your power to serve me—that is to say, if you are not too proud to accept the work I have it in my power to offer."

"A beggar must not be a chooser," said Aspel, with a light laugh.

"Well, then, what say you to keeping a shop?"

" Keeping a shop !" repeated Aspel in surprise.

" Ay, keeping a shop—this shop," returned Mr. Blurt; " you once told me you were versed in natural history ; here is a field for you : a natural-historical shop, if I may say so."

" But, my dear sir, I know nothing whatever about the business, or about stuffing birds—and—and fishes." He looked round him in dismay. " But you are jesting !"

Mr. Blurt declared that he was very far from jesting, and then went on to explain the circumstances of the case. It is probable that George Aspel would have at once rejected his proposal if it had merely had reference to his own advantage, and that he would have preferred to apply for labour at the docks, as being more suitable work for a sea-king's descendant ; but the appeal to aid his friend in an emergency went home to him, and he agreed to undertake the work temporarily, with an expression of face that is common to men when forced to swallow bitter pills.

Thus George Aspel was regularly, though suddenly, installed. When evening approached Mrs. Murridge lighted the gas, and the new shopman set to work with energy to examine the stock and look over the books, in the hope of thereby obtaining at least a faint perception of the nature of the business in which he was embarked.

H

While thus engaged a woman entered hastily and demanded her pheasant.

" Your pheasant, my good woman ?"

" Yes, the one I left here to-day wi' the broken *h*eye. I don't want to 'ave it mended ; changed my mind. Will you please give it me back, sir ?"

" I must call the gentleman to whom you gave it," said Aspel, rather sharply, for he perceived the woman had been drinking.

" Oh ! you've no need, for there's the book he put my name down in, an' there's the bird a-standin' on the shelf just under the *h*owl."

Aspel turned up the book referred to, and found the page recently opened by Mr. Blurt. He had no difficulty in coming to a decision, for there was but one entry on the page.

" This is it, I suppose," he said. " ' A woman—I should say an idiot—left a pheasant, *minus*'—"

" No more a hidyot than yourself, young man, nor a minus neither," cried the woman, swelling with indignation, and red in the face.

Just then a lady entered the shop, and approached the counter hurriedly.

" Oh !" she exclaimed, almost in a shriek of astonishment, " Mr. Aspel !"

" Mr. Aspel, indeed," cried the woman, with in-effable scorn,—" Mr. Impudence, more like. Give me my bird, I say !"

The lady raised her veil, and displayed the amazed face of Miss Lillycrop.

"I came to inquire for my old friend—I'm *so* grieved; I was not aware—Mr. Aspel—"

"Give me my bird, I say!" demanded the virago.

"Step this way, madam," said Aspel, driven almost to distraction as he opened the door of the back shop. "Mrs. Murridge, show this lady up to Mr. Blurt's room.—Now then, woman, take your— your—brute, and be off."

He thrust the one-eyed pheasant into the customer's bosom with such vigour that, fearing a personal assault, she retreated to the door. There she came to a full stop, turned about, raised her right hand savagely, exclaimed "You're another!" let her fingers go off with the force of a pea-cracker, and, stumbling into the street, went her devious way.

CHAPTER X.

A MYSTERY CLEARED UP.

WHEN night had fairly hung its sable curtains over the great city, Mr. Blurt descended to the shop.

"Now, Mr. Aspel, I'll relieve you. The lady you sent up, Miss Lillycrop, is, it seems, an old friend of my brother, and she insists on acting the part of nurse to-night. I am all the better pleased, because I have business to attend to at the other end of the town. We will therefore close the shop, and you can go home. By the way, have you a home ?"

"O yes," said Aspel, with a laugh. "A poor enough one truly, off the Strand."

"Indeed ?—that reminds me : we always pay salaries in advance in this office. Here is a sovereign to account of your first quarter. We can settle the amount afterwards."

Aspel accepted the coin with a not particularly good grace.

" Now then, you had better—ha—excuse me—put up the shutters."

Instantly the youth pulled out the sovereign and laid it on the counter.

" No, sir," he said firmly ; " I am willing to aid you in your difficulties, but I am not willing to become a mere shop-boy—at least not while there is man's work to be had."

Mr. Blurt looked perplexed. " What are we to do ?" he asked.

" Hire a little boy," said Aspel.

" But there are no little boys about," he said, looking out into the street, where the wind was sending clouds of dust and bits of straw and paper into the air. " I would do it myself, but have not time ; I'm late as it is. Ah! I have it—Mrs. Murridge !"

Calling the faithful domestic, he asked if she knew how to put up the shutters, and would do it. She was quite willing, and set about it at once, while Mr. Blurt nodded good-night, and went away.

With very uncomfortable feelings George Aspel stood in the shop, his tall figure drawn up, his arms crossed on his broad breast, and his finely formed head bent slightly down as he sternly watched the operation.

Mrs. Murridge was a resolute woman. She put

up most of the shutters promptly in spite of the high wind, but just as she was fixing the last of them a blast caught it and almost swept it from her grasp. For two seconds there was a tough struggle between Boreas and the old woman. Gallantry forbade further inaction. Aspel rushed out just in time to catch Mrs. Murridge and the shutter in his strong arms as they were about to be swept into the kennel. He could do no more, however, than hold them there, the wind being too much even for him. While in this extremity he received timely aid from some one, whom the indistinct light revealed as a broad-shouldered little fellow in a grey uniform. With his assistance the shutter was affixed and secured.

"Thank you, friend, whoever you are," said Aspel heartily, as he turned and followed the panting Mrs. Murridge.

But the "friend," instead of replying, seized Aspel by the arm and walked with him into the shop.

"George Aspel!" he said.

George looked down and beheld the all but awe-stricken visage of Philip Maylands.

Without uttering a word the former sat down on the counter, and burst into a fit of half-savage laughter.

"Ah! then, you may laugh till you grow fat,"

said Phil, " but it's more than that you must do if
I'm to join you in the laugh."

" What more can I do, Phil ?" asked Aspel,
wiping his eyes.

" Sure, ye can explain," said Phil.

" Well, sit down on the counter, and I'll explain,"
returned Aspel, shutting and locking the door. Then,
mounting the stool, he entered into a minute explanation—not only in reference to his present
position and cicumstances but regarding his recent
misfortunes.

Phil's admiration and love for his friend were
intense, but that did not altogether blind him to
his faults. He listened attentively, sympathetically,
but gravely, and said little. He felt, somehow, that
London was a dangerous place compared with the
west of Ireland,—that his friend was in danger of
something vague and undefined,—that he himself
was in danger of—he knew not what. While the
two were conversing they heard a step in the now
quiet street. It advanced quickly, and stopped at
the door. There was a rustling sound ; something
fell on the floor, and the step passed on.

" It's only a few letters," said Aspel ; " Mr. Blurt
explained matters to me this morning. They seem
to have been a careless lot who have managed this
business hitherto. A slit was made in the door for
letters, but no box has ever been attached to the

slit. The letters put through it at night are just allowed to fall on the floor, as you see, and are picked up in the morning. As I am not yet fully initiated into my duties, and don't feel authorised to open these, we will let them lie.—Hallo! look there."

The last words were uttered in a low, soft tone. Phil Maylands glanced in his friend's face, and was directed by his eyes to a corner near the front door, where, from behind the shelter of an over-stuffed pelican of the wilderness, two intensely bright little eyes were seen glistening. The gradual advance of a sharp nose revealed the fact that their owner was a rat!

No Red Indian of the prairie ever sat with more statuesque rigidity, watching his foe, than did these two friends sit watching that rat. They were sportsmen, both by nature and practice, to the back-bone. The idiotic owl at their elbow was not more still than they—one point only excepted: Phil's right hand moved imperceptibly, like the hour-hand of a watch, towards a book which lay on the counter. Their patience was rewarded. Supposing, no doubt, that the youths had suddenly died to suit its convenience, the rat advanced a step or two, looked suspicious, became reassured, advanced a little farther and displayed its tail to full advantage. After smelling at various objects, with a view, no doubt, to supper, it finally came on the letters, appeared to read their addresses with some attention, and, seizing one by a corner, began apparently to open it.

At this point Phil Maylands' fingers, closing slowly but with the deadly precision of fate, grasped the book and hurled it at the foe, which was instantly swept off its legs. Either the blow or the fright caused the rat to fly wriggling into the air. With a shriek of agonised emotion, it vanished behind the pelican of the wilderness.

"Bravo, Phil! splendidly aimed, but rather low," cried Aspel, as he vaulted the counter and dislodged the pelican. Of course the rat was gone. After a little more conversation the two friends quitted the place and went to their respective homes.

"Very odd and absolutely unaccountable," observed Mr. Blurt, as he sat next morning perusing the letters above referred to, " here's the same thing occurred again. Brownlow writes that he sent a cheque a week ago, and no one has heard of it. That rascal who made off with the cash could not have stolen it, because he never stole cheques,—for fear, no doubt, of being caught,—and this was only for a small amount. Then, here is a cheque come all right from Thomson. Why should one appear and the other disappear?"

"Could the rats have made away with it?"

suggested Aspel, who had told his patron of the previous night's incident.

"Rats might destroy letters, but they could not eat them—at least, not during the few hours of the night that they lie on the floor. No; the thing is a mystery. I cannot help thinking that the Post-Office is to blame. I shall make inquiries. I am determined to get to the bottom of it."

So it ever is with mankind. People make mistakes, or are guilty of carelessness, and straightway they lay the blame—not only without but against reason—on broader shoulders than their own. That wonderful and almost perfect British Post-Office delivers quickly, safely, and in good condition above fourteen hundred millions of letters etc. in the year, but some half-dozen letters, addressed to Messrs. Blurt and Co., have gone amissing,—therefore the Post-Office is to blame !

Full of this idea Mr. Enoch Blurt put on his hat with an irascible fling and went off to the City. Arrived at St. Martin's-le-Grand he made for the principal entrance. At any other time he would have been struck with the grandeur of the buildings. He would have paused and admired the handsome colonnade of the old office and the fine front of the new buildings opposite, but Mr. Blurt could see nothing except missing letters. Architecture appealed to him in vain. Perhaps his state of irritability was increased by a vague suspicion that all Government officials were trained and almost bound to throw obstacles in the way of free inquiry.

"I want," said he, planting himself defiantly in front of an official who encountered him in the passage, "to see the—the—Secretary, the—the—Postmaster-General, the chief of the Post-Office, whoever he may be. There is my card."

"Certainly, sir, will you step this way?"

The official spoke with such civility, and led the way with such alacrity, that Mr. Blurt felt it necessary to think exclusively of his wrongs lest his indignation should cool too soon. Having shown him into a comfortable waiting-room, the official went off with his card. In a few minutes a gentleman entered, accosted Mr. Blurt with a polite bow, and asked what he could do for him.

"Sir," said Mr. Blurt, summoning to his aid the last rags of his indignation, "I come to make a complaint. Many of the letters addressed to our firm are missing—*have* been missing for some time past,—and from the inquiries I have made it seems evident to me that they must have been lost in passing through the Post-Office."

"I regret much to hear this," returned the gentleman, whom—as Mr. Blurt never ascertained who he was—we shall style the Secretary, at all events he represented that officer. "You may rely on our doing our utmost to clear up the matter. Will you be kind enough to give me the full particulars?"

The Secretary's urbanity gave the whole of Mr. Blurt's last rags of indignation to the winds. He detailed his case with his usual earnestness and good-nature.

The Secretary listened attentively to the close.

"Well, Mr. Blurt," he said, "we will investigate the matter without delay; but from what you have told me I think it probable that the blame does not lie with us. You would be surprised if you knew the number of complaints made to us, which, on investigation, turn out to be groundless. Allow me to cite one or two instances. In one case a missing letter having fallen from the letter-box of the person to whom it was addressed on to the hall-floor, was picked up by a dog and buried in some straw, where it was afterwards found. In another case, the missing letter was discovered sticking against the side of the private letter-box, where it had lain unobserved, and in another the letter had been placed between the leaves of a book as a mark and forgotten. Boys and others sent to post letters are also frequently unfaithful, and sometimes stupid. Many letters have been put into the receptacles for dust in our streets, under the impression that they were pillar letter-boxes, and on one occasion a letter-carrier found two letters forced behind the plate affixed to a pillar letter-box which indicates the hours of collection, obviously placed there by the ignorant sender under the impression that that was the proper way of posting them. Your mention of rats reminds me of several cases in which these animals have been the means of making away with letters. The fact that rats have been seen in your shop, and that your late letters drop on the floor and are left there till morning, inclines me to think that rats are at the bottom of it. I would advise you to make investigation without delay."

" I will, sir, I will," exclaimed Mr. Blurt, starting up with animation, "and I thank you heartily for the trouble you have taken with my case. Good-morning. I shall see to this at once."

And Mr. Blurt did see to it at once. He went straight back to his brother's house, and made preparation for a campaign against the rats, for, being a sanguine and impulsive man, he had now become firmly convinced that these animals were somehow at the bottom of the mystery. But he kept his thoughts and intentions to himself.

During the day George Aspel observed that his friend employed himself in making some unaccountable alterations in the arrangements of one part of the shop, and ventured to ask what he was about, but, receiving a vague reply, he said no more.

That night, after the shop was closed and Aspel had gone home, and Mr. Fred Blurt had gone to sleep, under the guardianship of the faithful Miss Lillycrop, and Mrs. Murridge had retired to the coal-hole—or something like it—which was her dormitory, Mr. Enoch Blurt entered the shop with a mysterious air, bearing two green table-cloths. These he hung like curtains at one corner of the room, and placed a chair behind them raised on two empty packing-boxes. Seating himself on this chair he opened the curtains just enough to enable him to peep through, and found that he could see the letter-slit in the door over the counter, but not the floor beneath it. He therefore elevated his throne by means of another packing-box. All being ready, he lowered the gas to something like a dim religious light, and began his watch. It bade fair to be a tedious watch, but Enoch Blurt had made up his mind to go through with it, and whatever Enoch made up his mind to do he did.

Suddenly he heard a scratching sound. This was encouraging. Another moment and a bright pair of miniature stars were seen to glitter behind the pelican of the wilderness. In his eagerness to see, Mr. Blurt made a slight noise and the stars went out—suddenly.

This was exceedingly vexatious. He blamed himself bitterly, resettled himself in his chair, rearranged the curtains, and glared intently. But although Mr. Blurt could fix his eyes he could not chain his thoughts. These unruly familiars ere long began to play havoc with their owner. They hurried him far away from rats and ornithological specimens, carried him over the Irish Channel, made him look sadly down on the funnels of the Royal Mail steamer, plunged him under the waves, and caused him to gaze in fond regret on his lost treasures. His thoughts carried him even further. They bore him over the sea to Africa, and set him down, once more, in his forsaken hut among the diamond-diggers. From this familiar retreat he was somewhat violently recalled by a scratching sound. He glared at the pelican of the wilderness. The little stars reappeared. They increased in size. They became unbearable suns. They suddenly approached. As suddenly Mr. Blurt rose to fight or fly—he could scarce tell which. It did not matter much, because, next instant, he fell headlong to the floor, dragging the curtains down, and forming a miscellaneous avalanche with the chair and packing boxes.

The unfortunate man had fallen asleep, and the rats, which had in truth ventured out, fled to their homes as a matter of course.

But Mr. Blurt had resolved to go through with it. Finding that he was unhurt, and that the household had not been disturbed, he rebuilt his erection and began his watch over again. The shock had thoroughly roused him. He did not sleep again. Fortunately London rats are not nervous. Being born and bred in the midst of war's alarms they soon get over a panic. The watcher had not sat more than a quarter of an hour when the stars appeared once again. The Pyramid of Cheops is not more immovably solid than was Mr. Blurt. A sharp nose advanced ; a head came out ; a body followed ; a tail brought up the rear, and the pelican of the wilderness looked with calm indifference on the scene.

The rat was an old grey one, and very large. It was followed by a brown one, nearly as large. There was an almost theatrical caution in their movements at first, but courage came with immunity from alarm. Six letters, that had been thrust through the slit by the evening postman, lay on the floor. To these the grey rat advanced, seized one in its teeth, and began to back out, dragging the letter after it. The brown rat followed the grey rat's example. While thus engaged, another brown rat appeared, and followed suit. Nothing could have been more fortunate. Mr. Blurt was charmed. He could afford to let the grey rat well out of sight, because the two brown rats, following in succession, would, when he sprang on them, leave a trail of letters to point the direction of their flight.

Just as the third rat dragged its missive behind the pelican of the wilderness the watcher leaped upon them, and in his haste consigned the pelican to all but irretrievable destruction ! The rats vanished, but left the tell-tale letters, the last two forming pointers to the first, which was already half dragged through a slit between the skirting and the wall. At the extremity of this slit yawned the gateway to the rats' palace.

Mr. Blurt rubbed his hands, chuckled, crowed internally, and, having rescued the letters, went to bed.

Next morning, he procured a crowbar, and, with the able assistance of George Aspel, tore off the skirting, uprooted a plank, and discovered a den in which were stored thirty-one letters, six post-cards, and three newspapers.[1]

The corners of the letters, bearing the stamps, were nibbled away, showing that gum—not money or curiosity—was the occasion of the theft.

As four of these letters contained cheques and money orders, their discovery afforded instant relief to the pressure which had been gradually bearing with intolerable weight on the affairs of Messrs. Blurt and Co.

[1] See Postmaster-General's Report for 1877, p. 13.

CHAPTER XI.

THE LETTER-CARRIER GOES HIS ROUNDS, AIDS A LITTLE GIRL,
AND OVERWHELMS A LADY STATISTICALLY.

SOLOMON FLINT, being a man of letters, was
naturally a hard-working man. By night and by day
did that faithful servant of his Queen and country
tramp through the streets of London with the letters
of the lieges in his care. The dim twilight of early
morning found him poking about, like a solitary
ghoul, disembowelling the pillar posts. The rising
sun sent a deflected ray from chimney-pot or steeple
to welcome him—when fog and smoke permitted.
The noon-tide beams broiled him in summer and
cheered him in winter on his benignant path of use-
fulness. The evening fogs and glimmering lamps
beheld him hard at work, and the nightly returning
stars winked at him with evident surprise when
they found him still fagging along through heat and
cold, rain and snow, with the sense of urgent duty
ever present in his breast, and part of the recorded

hopes, joys, fears, sorrows, loves, hates, business, and humbug of the world in his bag.

Besides being a hard-working man, Solomon Flint was a public man, and a man of note. In the district of London which he frequented, thousands of the public watched for him, wished for him, even longed for him, and received him gladly. Young eyes sometimes sparkled and old eyes sometimes brightened when his well-known uniform appeared. Footmen opened to him with good-will, and servant-girls with smiles. Even in the low neighbourhoods of his district—and he traversed several such—Solomon was regarded with favour. His person was as sacred as that of a detective or a city missionary. Men who scowled on the world at large gave a familiar nod to him, and women who sometimes desired to tear off people's scalps never displayed the slightest wish to damage a hair of the postman's head. He moved about, in fact, like a benign influence, distributing favours and doing good wherever he went. May it not be said truly that in the spiritual world we have a good many news-bearers of a similar stamp? Are not the loving, the gentle, the self-sacrificing such ?— in a word, the Christ-like, who, if they do not carry letters about, are themselves living epistles " known and read of all men " ?

One of the low districts through which Solomon Flint had to pass daily embraced the dirty court in which Abel Bones dwelt. Anticipating a very different fate for it, no doubt, the builder of this region had named it Archangel Court.

As he passed rapidly through it Solomon observed a phenomenon by no means unusual in London and elsewhere, namely, a very small girl taking charge of an uncommonly large baby. Urgent though his duties were, Solomon would have been more than human if he had not stopped to observe the little girl attempt the apparently impossible feat of lifting the frolicsome mass of fat which was obviously in a rebellious state of mind. Solomon had occasionally seen the little girl in his rounds, but never before in possession of a baby. She grasped him round the waist, which her little arms could barely encircle, and, making a mighty effort, got the rebel on his legs. A second heave placed him on her knees, and a third effort, worthy of a gymnast, threw him on her little bosom. She had to lean dangerously far back to keep him there, and being incapable of seeing before her, owing to the bulk of her burden, was compelled to direct her course by faith. She knew the court well, however, and was progressing favourably, when a loose stone tripped her and she fell. Not having far to fall, neither she nor the baby was the worse for it.

"Hallo, little woman!" said Solomon, assisting her to rise, " can't he walk ?"

SOLOMON AND TOTTIE—Page 132.

" Yes, sir ; but 'e won't," replied the little maid, turning up her pretty face, and shaking back her dishevelled hair.

The baby looked up and crowed gleefully, as though it understood her, and would, if able to speak, have said, " That's the exact truth,—' he won't !'"

" Come, I'll help you," said Solomon, carrying the baby to the mouth of the alley pointed out by the little girl. " Is he your brother ? "

" O no, sir ; I ain't got no brother. He b'longed to a neighbour who's just gone dead, an' mother she was fond o' the neighbour, an' promised to take care of the baby. So she gave 'im to me to nuss. An' oh ! you've no *h*idea, sir, what a *h*obstinate thing 'e is. I've 'ad 'im three days now."

Yes ; the child had had him three days, and an amazing experience it had been to her. During that brief period she had become a confirmed staggerer, being utterly incapable of *walking* with baby in her arms. During the same period she had become unquestionably entitled to the gold medals of the Lifeboat Institution and the Humane Society, having, with reckless courage, at the imminent risk of her life, and on innumerable occasions, saved that baby from death by drowning in washtubs and kennels, from mutilation by hot water, fire, and steam, and from sudden extinction by the wheels of cabs, carriages, and drays, while, at the same time,

she had established a fair claim to at least the
honorary diploma of the Royal College of Surgeons,
by her amazing practice in the treatment of bruises
and cuts, and the application of sticking-plaster.

"Have you got a father or mother, my dear?"
asked the letter-carrier.

"Yes, sir; I've got both of 'em. And oh! I'm
so miserable. I don't know what to do."

"Why, what's wrong with you?"

The child's eyes filled with tears as she told
how her father had gone off "on the spree;" how
her mother had gone out to seek him, promising to be back in time to relieve her of the baby
so as to let her keep an appointment she had
with a lady; and how the mother had never come
back, and didn't seem to be coming back; and how
the time for the engagement was already past, and
she feared the lady would think she was an ungrateful little liar, and she had no messenger to send
to her.

"Where does the lady live, and what's her name,
little woman?" asked Solomon.

"Her name is Miss Lillycrop, sir, and she lives
in Pimlico."

"Well, make your mind easy, little woman. It's
a curious coincidence that I happen to know Miss
Lillycrop. Her house lies rather far from my beat,
but I happen to have a messenger who does his

work both cheaply and quickly. I do a deal of work for him too, so, no doubt, he'll do a little for me. His name is Post-Office.—What is your's, my dear ?"

" Tottie Bones," replied the child, with the air of a full-grown woman. " An' please, sir, tell 'er I meant to go back to her at the end of three days, as I promised ; but I couldn't leave the 'ouse with baby inside, an' the fire, an' the kittle, with nobody to take care on 'em—could I, sir ?"

" Cer'nly not, little woman," returned the letter-carrier, with a solemn look at the overburdened creature who appealed to him. Giving her two-pence, and a kindly nod, Solomon Flint walked smartly away—with a reproving conscience—to make up for lost time.

That evening Mrs. Bones returned without her husband, but with an additional black eye, and other signs of bad treatment. She found the baby sound asleep, and Tottie in the same condition by his side, on the outside of the poor counterpane, with one arm round her charge, and her hair tumbled in confusion over him. She had evidently been herself overcome while in the act of putting the baby to sleep.

Mrs. Bones rushed to the bed, seized Tottie, clasped her tightly to her bosom, sat down on a stool, and began to rock herself to and fro.

The child, nothing loath to receive such treatment, awoke sufficiently to be able to throw her arms round her mother's neck, fondled her for a moment, and then sank again into slumber.

"Oh! God help me! God save my Abel from drink and bad men!" exclaimed the poor woman, in a voice of suppressed agony.

It seemed as if her prayer had been heard, for at that moment the door opened and a tall thin man entered. He was the man who had accosted George Aspel on his first visit to that region.

"You've not found him, I fear?" he said kindly, as he drew a stool near to Mrs. Bones and sat down, while Tottie, who had been reawakened by his entrance, began to bustle about the room with something of the guilty feeling of a sentry who has been found sleeping at his post.

"Yes, Mr. Sterling; thank you kindly for the interest you take in 'im. I found 'im at the old place, but 'e knocked me down an' went out, an' I've not been able to find 'im since."

"Well, take comfort, Molly," said the city missionary, for such he was; "I've just seen him taken up by the police and carried to the station as drunk and incapable. That, you know, will not bring him to very great trouble, and I have good reason to believe it will be the means of saving him from much worse."

He glanced at the little girl as he spoke.

"Tottie, dear," said Mrs. Bones, "you go out for a minute or two; I want to speak with Mr. Sterling."

"Yes, mother, and I'll run round to the bank; I've got twopence more to put in," said Tottie as she went out.

"Your lesson has not been lost, sir," said the poor woman, with a faint smile; "Tottie has a good bit o' money in the penny savings-bank now. She draws some of it out every time Abel brings us to the last gasp, but we don't let 'im know w'ere it comes from. To be sure, 'e don't much care. She's a dear child is Tottie."

"Thank the Lord for *that*, Molly. He is already answering our prayers," said Mr. Sterling. "Just trust Him, keep up heart, and persevere; we're *sure* to win at last."

When Tottie Bones left the dark and dirty den that was the only home she had ever known, she ran lightly out into the neighbouring street, and, threading her way among people and vehicles, entered an alley, ascended a stair, and found herself in a room which bore some resemblance to an empty schoolroom. At one corner there was a desk, at which stood a young man at work on a business-looking book. Before him were several children of various ages and sizes, but all having

one characteristic in common—the aspect of extreme poverty. The young man was a gratuitous
servant of the public, and the place was, for the
hour at least, a penny savings-bank.

It was one of those admirable institutions, which
are now numerous in our land, and which derive
their authority from Him who said, " Gather up the
fragments that remain, that nothing be lost."
Noble work was being done there, not so much
because of the mere pence which were saved from
the grog and tobacco shops, as because of the habits
of thrift which were being formed, as well as the
encouragement of that spirit of thoughtful economy,
which, like the spirit of temperance, is one of the
handmaids of religion.

" Please, sir," said Tottie to the penny banker,
" I wants to pay in tuppence."

She handed over her bank-book with the money.
Receiving the former back, she stared at the mysterious figures with rapt attention.

" Please, sir, 'ow much do it come to *now* ?" she
asked.

" It 's eight and sevenpence, Tottie," replied the
amiable banker, with a smile.

" Thank you, sir," said Tottie, and hurried home
in a species of heavenly contemplation of the enormous sum she had accumulated.

When Solomon Flint returned home that night

he found Miss Lillycrop seated beside old Mrs.
Flint, shouting into her deafest ear. She desisted
when Solomon entered, and rose to greet him.

"I have come to see my niece, Mr. Flint; do you
expect her soon?"

The letter-carrier consulted his watch.

"It is past her time now, Miss Lillycrop; she can't
be long. Pray, sit down. You'll stay and 'ave a
cup of tea with us? Now, don't say no. We're
just goin' to 'ave it, and my old 'ooman delights in
company.—There now, sit down, an' don't go split-
tin' your lungs on *that* side of her next time you
chance to be alone with her. It's her deaf side. A
cannon would make no impression on that side,
except you was to fire it straight *into* her ear.—I've
got a message for you, Miss Lillycrop."

"A message for me?"

"Ay, from a beautiful angel with tumbled hair and
ragged clothes named Tottie Bones. Ain't it strange
how coincidences happen in this life! I goes an'
speaks to Tottie, which I never did before. Tottie
wants very bad to send a message to Miss Lillycrop.
I happens to know Miss Lillycrop, an' takes the
message, and on coming home finds Miss Lillycrop
here before me—and all on the same night—ain't
it odd?"

"It is very odd, Mr. Flint; and pray what was
the message?"

The letter-carrier, having first excused himself
for making arrangements for the evening meal
while he talked, hereupon related the circumstances
of his meeting with the child, and had only concluded when May Maylands came in, looking a
little fagged, but sunny and bright as usual.

Of course she added her persuasions to those of
her landlord, and Miss Lillycrop, being induced to
stay tea, was taken into May's private boudoir to
put off her bonnet.

While there the good lady inquired eagerly about
her cousin's health and work and companions ; asked
for her mother and brother, and chatted pleasantly
about her own work among the poor in the immediate neighbourhood of her dwelling.

"By the way," said she, "that reminds me that I
chanced to meet with that tall, handsome friend of
your brother's in very strange circumstances. Do
you know that he has become a shopman in the
bird-shop of my dear old friend Mr. Blurt, who is
very ill—has been ill, I should have said,—were
you aware of that ?"

"No," answered May, in a low tone.

"I thought he came to England by the invitation
of Sir Somebody Something, who had good prospects
for him.   Did not you ?"

"So I thought," said May, turning her face away
from the light.

"It is very strange," continued Miss Lillycrop, giving a few hasty touches to her cap and hair; "and do you know, I could not help thinking that there was something queer about his appearance? I can scarce tell what it was. It seemed to me like— like—but it is disagreeable even to think about such things in connection with one who is such a fine, clever, gentlemanly fellow—but—"

Fortunately for poor May, her friend was suddenly stopped by a shout from the outer room :—

"Hallo, ladies! how long are you goin' to be titivatin' yourselves? There ain't no company comin'. The sausages are on the table, and the old 'ooman 's gittin' so impatient that she 's beginnin' to abuse the cat."

This last remark was too true and sad to be passed over in silence. Old Mrs. Flint's age had induced a spirit of temporary oblivion as to surroundings, which made her act, especially to her favourite cat, in a manner that seemed unaccountable. It was impossible to conceive that cruelty could actuate one who all her life long had been a very pattern of tenderness to every living creature. When therefore she suddenly changed from stroking and fondling her cat to pulling its tail, tweaking its nose, slapping its face, and tossing it off her lap, it is only fair to suppose that her mind had ceased to be capable of two simultaneous thoughts, and that when it was powerfully fixed on sausages she was not aware of what her hands were doing to the cat.

"You'll excuse our homely arrangements, Miss Lillycrop," said Mr. Flint, as he helped his guest to the good things on the table. "I never could get over a tendency to a rough-and-ready sort o' feedin'. But you'll find the victuals good."

"Thank you, Mr. Flint. I am sure you must be very tired after the long walks you take. I can't think how postmen escape catching colds when they have such constant walking in all sorts of weather."

"It's the constancy as saves us, ma'am, but we don't escape altogether," said Flint, heaping large supplies on his grandmother's plate. "We often kitch colds, but they don't often do us damage."

This remark led Miss Lillycrop, who had a very inquiring mind, to induce Solomon Flint to speak about the Post-Office, and as that worthy man was enthusiastic in regard to everything connected with his profession, he willingly gratified his visitor.

"Now, I want to know," said Miss Lillycrop, after the conversation had run on for some time, and appetites began to abate,—"when you go about the poorer parts of the city in dark nights, if you are ever attacked, or have your letters stolen from you."

" Well, no, ma'am—never.   I can't, in all my long experience, call to mind sitch a thing happenin'— either to me or to any other letter-carrier.   The worst of people receives us kindly, 'cause, you see, we go among 'em to do 'em service.   I did indeed once hear of a letter being stolen, but the thief was not a man—he was a tame raven !"

" Oh, Solomon !" said May, with a laugh.   " Remember that Grannie hears you."

" No, she don't, but it's all the same if she did. Whatever I say about the Post-Office I can give chapter and verse for.   The way of it was this. The letter-carrier was a friend o' mine.   He was goin' his rounds at Kelvedon, in Essex, when a tame raven seized a money letter he had in his hand and flew away with it.   After circlin' round the town he alighted, and, before he could be prevented, tore the letter to pieces.   On puttin' the bits together the contents o' the letter was found to be a cheque for thirty pounds, and of course, when the particulars o' the strange case were made known the cheque was renewed !—There now," concluded Solomon, " if you don't believe that story, you 've only got to turn up the Postmaster-General's Report for 1862, and you 'll find it there on page 24."

" How curious !" said Miss Lillycrop.   " There 's another thing I want to know," she added, looking with deep interest into the countenance of her host, while that stalwart man continued to stow incredible quantities of sausages and crumpets into his capacious mouth. " Is it really true that people post letters without addresses ?"

" True, ma'am ? why, of course it 's true. Thousands of people do. The average number of letters posted without addresses is about eighty a day."

" How strange ! I wonder what causes this ? "

Miss Lillycrop gazed contemplatively into her teacup, and Solomon became suddenly aware that Grannie's plate was empty. Having replenished it, he ordered Dollops to bring more crumpets, and then turned to his guest.

" I 'll tell you what it is, ma'am, that causes this—it 's forgetfulness, or rather, what we call absence of mind. It 's my solemn belief, ma'am, that if our heads warn't screwed on pretty tight you 'd see some hundreds of people walkin' about London of a mornin' with nothin' whatever on their shoulders. Why, there was one man actually posted a cheque for £9, 15s. loose, in a pillar letter-box in Liverpool, without even an envelope on it. The owner was easily traced through the bank, but was unable to explain how the cheque got out of his possession or into the pillar.—Just listen to this, ma'am," he added, rising and taking down a pamphlet from a bookshelf, " this is last year's Report. Hear what it says :—

" ' Nearly 28,500 letters were posted this year without addresses. 757 of these letters were found to contain, in the aggregate, about £214 in cash and bank-notes, and about £9088 in bills of exchange, cheques, etc.'—Of course," said the letter-carrier, refreshing himself with a mouthful of tea, " the money and bills were returned to the senders, but it warn't possible to do the same with 52,856 postage-stamps which were found knocking about loose in the bottom of the mail-bags."

" How many ? " cried Miss Lillycrop, in amazement.

" Fifty-two thousand eight hundred and fifty-six," repeated Solomon with deliberation. " No doubt," he continued, " some of these stamps had bin carelessly stuck on the envelopes, and some of 'em p'r'aps had come out of busted letters which contained stamps sent in payment of small accounts. You 've no idea, ma'am, what a lot o' queer things get mixed up in the mail-bags out of bust letters and packages—all along of people puttin' things into flimsy covers not fit to hold 'em. Last year no fewer than 12,525 miscellaneous articles reached the Returned Letter Office (we used to call it the Dead Letter Office) without covers or addresses, and the number of inquiries dealt with in regard to these things and missing letters by that Office was over 91,000.

K

" We 're very partickler, Miss Lillycrop, in regard
to these things," continued Solomon, with a touch of
pride.   "We keep books in which every stray article,
unaddressed, is entered and described minutely, so
that when people come howlin' at us for our carelessness in non-delivery, we ask 'em to describe
their missing property, and in hundreds of cases
prove to them their own carelessness in makin' up
parcels by handin' the wrecks over to 'em ! "

" But what sort of things are they that break
loose ? " asked Miss Lillycrop.

" Oh, many sorts.   Anything may break loose if
it 's ill packed, and, as almost every sort of thing
passes through the post, it would be difficult to describe 'em all.   Here is a list, however, that may
give you an idea of what kind of things the public
sent through our mail-bags last year.   A packet
of pudding, a steam-gauge, a tin of cream, a bird's
wing, a musical box, packet of snowdrops, fruit,
sweets, shrimps, and sample potatoes ; a dormouse,
four white mice, two goldfinches, a lizard and a blind-
worm, all alive ; besides cutlery, medicines, varnish,
ointments, perfumery, articles of dress ; a stoat, a
squirrel, fish, leeches, frogs, beetles, caterpillars, and
vegetables.   Of course, many of these, such as live
animals, being prohibited articles, were stopped and
sent to the Returned Letter Office, but were restored,
on application, to the senders."

Observing Miss Lillycrop's surprised expression of face, the old woman's curiosity was roused. "What's he haverin' aboot, my dear?" she asked of May.

"About the many strange things that are sent through the post, Grannie."

"Ay, ay, likely enough," returned the old creature, shaking her head and administering an unintentional cuff to the poor cat; "folk write a heap o' lees noo-a-days, nae doot."

"You'd hardly believe it now," continued Solomon, turning the leaves of the Report, "but it's a fact that live snakes have frequently been sent through the post. No later than last year a snake about a yard long managed to get out of his box in one of the night mail sorting carriages on the London and North-Western Railway. After a good deal of confusion and interruption to the work, it was killed. Again, a small box was sent to the Returned Letter Office in Liverpool, which, when opened, was found to contain eight living snakes."

"Come now, Mr. Flint," said May, "you mustn't bore my cousin with the Post-Office. You know that when you once begin on that theme there is no stopping you."

"Very well, Miss May," returned the letter-carrier, with a modest smile, "let's draw round the fire and talk of something else.—Hallo, Dollops! clear away the dishes."

" But he doesn't bore me," protested Miss Lilly-crop, who had the happy knack of being intensely interested in whatever happened to interest her friends. " I like, of all things, to hear about the Post-Office. I had no idea it was such a wonderful in-stitution.—Do tell me more about it, Mr. Flint, and never mind May's saucy remarks."

Much gratified by this appeal, Solomon wheeled the old woman to her own corner of the fire, placed a stool under her feet, the cat on her knees, and patted her shoulder, all of which attentions she received with a kindly smile, and said that " Sol was a good laddie."

Meanwhile the rotund maid-of-all-work having, as it were, hurled the crockery into her den, and the circle round the fire having been completed, as well as augmented, by the sudden entrance of Phil Maylands, the " good laddie " re-opened fire.

" Yes, ma'am, as you well observe, it *is* a wonder-ful institution. More than that, it's a gigantic one, and it takes a big staff to do the duty too. In London alone the staff is 10,665. The entire staff of the kingdom is 13,763 postmasters, 10,000 clerks, and 21,000 letter-carriers, sorters, and messengers, —sum total, a trifle over 45,500. Then, the total number of Post-offices and receptacles for receiving letters throughout the kingdom is 25,000 odd. Before the introduction of the penny postage—

in the year 1840—there were only 4500! Then, again ——"

"O Mr. Flint! pray stop!" cried Miss Lillycrop, pressing her hands to her eyes; "I never *could* take in figures. At least I never could keep them in. They just go in here, and come out there (pointing to her two ears), and leave no impression whatever."

"You're not the only one that's troubled with that weakness, ma'am," said the gallant Solomon, "but if a few thousands puzzle you so much what will you make of this?—The total number of letters, post-cards, newspapers, etc., that passed through the Post-Offices of the kingdom last year was fourteen hundred and seventy-seven million eight hundred and twenty-eight thousand two hundred! What d'ye make o' that, ma'am?"

"Mr. Flint, I just make nothing of it at all," returned Miss Lillycrop, with a placid smile.

"Come, Phil," said May, laughing, "can *you* make nothing of it? You used to be good at arithmetic."

"Well, now," said Phil, "it don't take much knowledge of arithmetic to make something of that. George Aspel happened to be talking to me about that very sum not long ago. He said he had been told by a man at the Post-Office that it would take a man about a hundred and seventy years to count it. I tried the calculation, and found

he was right.   Then I made another calculation :
I put down the average length of an envelope at
four inches, and I found that if you were to lay
fourteen hundred and seventy-seven million letters
out in a straight line, end to end, the lot would
extend to above 93,244 miles, which is more than
three times the circumference of the world.   Moreover, this number is considerably more than the
population of the whole world, which, at the present time, is about 1444 millions, so that if the
British Post-Office were to distribute the 1477
millions of letters that pass through it in the year im-
partially, every man, woman, and child on the globe
would receive one letter, post-card, newspaper, or
book-packet, and leave thirty-three millions to spare!"

"Now, really, you *must* stop this," said May; "I
see that my cousin's colour is going with her efforts
to understand you.   Can't you give her something
more amusing to think of?"

"Oh, cer'nly," said Solomon, again turning with
alacrity to the Report.   "Would you like to hear
what some people think it's our dooty to attend to ?
I'll give you a letter or two received by our various
departments."

Here the letter-carrier began to read the following
letters, which we give from the same Report, some
being addressed to the " Chief of the Dead Office,"
others to the Postmaster-General, etc. :—

"*May* 18—.

"DEAR SIR,—I write to ask you for some information about finding out persons who are missing—I want to find out my mother and sisters who are in Melbourne in Australia i believe—if you would find out for me please let me know by return of post, and also your charge at the lowest, yours," etc.

"*Novr.* 8, 18—.

"SIR,—Not having received the live bullfinch mentioned by you as having arrived at the Returned Letter Office two days ago, having been posted as a letter contrary to the regulations of the Postal system, I now write to ask you to have the bird fed and forwarded at once to ——, and to apply for all fines and expenses to ——. If this is not done, and I do not receive the bird before the end of the week, I shall write to the Postmaster-General, who is a very intimate friend of my father's, and ask him to see that measures are taken against you for neglect.

"This is not an idle threat, so you will oblige by following the above instructions."

"WALES, *Nov.* 12, 18—.

"DEAR SIR,—I am taking the liberty of writeing you those few lines as I am given to understand that you do want men in New South Wales, and I am a Smith by Trade ; a single man. My age is 24 next birthday. I shood be verry thankful if you wood be so kind and send all the particulars by return."

"LONDON, Nov. 5, 18—.

" SIR,—i right to you and request of you sinsearly for to help me to find out my husband. i ham quite a stranger in London, only two months left Ireland —i can find know trace of my husband—your the only gentleman that I know that can help me to find him. thears is letters goes to him to —— in his name and thears is letters comes to him to the —— Post-Office for him.—Sir you may be sure that i ham low in spirit in a strange contry without a friend. I hope you will be so kind as not to forget me. Sir, I would never find —— for I would go astray, besides i have no money."

" So you see, ma'am," continued Solomon, closing the Report, "much though we do, more is expected of us. But although we can't exactly comply with such requests as these, we do a pretty stroke of business in other ways besides letter-distributin'. For instance, we are bankers on a considerable scale. Through our money-order agency the sum we transmitted last year was a trifle over £27,870,000, while the deposits in our Savings-Banks amounted to over £9,166,000. Then as to telegraphs : there were—But I forgot," said Solomon, checking himself, " Miss May is the proper authority on that subject.—How many words was it you sent last year ?"

"I won't tell you," said May, with a toss of her little head. "You have already driven my cousin distracted. She won't be able to walk home."

"My dear, I don't intend to walk home; I shall take a cab," said the mild little woman. "*Do* tell me something about your department."

"No, cousin, I won't."

"Sure, if ye don't, I will," said Phil.

"Well then, I will tell you a very little just to save you from Phil, who, if he once begins, will kill you with his calculations. But you can't appreciate what I say. Let me see. The total number of telegraphic messages forwarded by our offices in the United Kingdom during the last twelve months amounted to a little more than twenty-two millions."

"Dear me!" said Miss Lillycrop, with that look and tone which showed that if May had said twenty-two quintillions it would have had no greater effect.

"There, that's enough," said May, laughing. "I knew it was useless to tell you."

"Ah, May!" said Phil, "that's because you don't know how to tell her.—See here now, cousin Sarah. The average length of a message is thirty words. Well, that gives 660 millions of words. Now, a good average story-book of 400 pages contains about ninety-six thousand words. Divide the one by the other, and that gives you a magnificent library of 6875 volumes as the work done by the Postal Telegraphs every year. All these telegrams are kept for a certain period in case of inquiry, and then destroyed."

"Phil, I must put on my things and go," exclaimed Miss Lillycrop, rising. "I've had quite as much as I can stand."

"Just cap it all with this, ma'am, to keep you steady," interposed Solomon Flint ;— "the total revenue of the Post-Office for the year was six millions and forty-seven thousand pounds ; and the expenditure three millions nine hundred and ninety-one thousand. Now, you may consider yourself pretty well up in the affairs of the Post-Office."

The old 'ooman, awaking at this point with a start, hurled the cat under the grate, and May laughingly led Miss Lillycrop into her little boudoir.

CHAPTER XII.

IN WHICH A BOSOM FRIEND IS INTRODUCED, RURAL FELICITY IS
ENLARGED ON, AND DEEP PLANS ARE LAID.

A BOSOM friend is a pleasant possession. Miss
Lillycrop had one. She was a strong-minded woman.
We do not say this to her disparagement. A strong
mind is as admirable in woman as in man. It is
only when woman indicates the strength of her
mind by unfeminine self-assertion that we shrink
from her in alarm. Miss Lillycrop's bosom friend
was a warm-hearted, charitable, generous, hard-
featured, square-shouldered, deep-chested, large-
boned lady of middle age and quick temper. She
was also in what is styled comfortable circumstances,
and dwelt in a pretty suburban cottage. Her name
was Maria Stivergill.

"Come with me, child," said Miss Stivergill to
Miss Lillycrop one day, "and spend a week at The
Rosebud."

It must not be supposed that the good lady had
given this romantic name to her cottage. No, when

Miss Stivergill bought it, she found the name on the two gate-posts; found that all the tradespeople in the vicinity had imbibed it, and therefore quietly accepted it, as she did all the ordinary affairs of life.

" Impossible, dear Maria," said her friend, with a perplexed look, " I have so many engagements, at least so many duties, that—"

" Pooh !" interrupted Miss Stivergill.   " Put 'em off.   Fulfil 'em when you come back.   At all events," she continued, seeing that Miss Lillycrop still hesitated, " come for a night or two."

" But—"

" Come now, Lilly"—thus she styled her friend —" but give me no *buts*.   You know that you 've no good reason for refusing."

" Indeed I have," pleaded Miss Lillycrop ; " my little servant—"

" What, the infant who opened the door to me ?"

" Yes, Tottie Bones ; she is obliged to stay at nights with me just now, owing to her mother, poor thing, being under the necessity of shutting up her house while she goes to look after a drunken husband, who has forsaken her."

" Hah !" exclaimed Miss Stivergill, giving a nervous pull at her left glove, which produced a wide rent between the wrist and the thumb.   " I wonder why women marry !"

" Don't you think it's a sort of—of—unavoidable necessity ?" suggested Miss Lillycrop, with a faint smile.

"Not at all, my dear, not at all. I have avoided it. So have you. If I had my way, I'd put a stop to marriage altogether, and bring this miserabl-world to an abrupt close.—But littl

difficulty : we'll take her along with ι

"But, dear Maria—"

"Well, what further objections, Lilly ?"

"Tottie has charge of a baby, and—"

"What! one baby in charge of another ?"

"Indeed it is too true; and, you know, you couldn't stand a baby."

"Couldn't I ?" said Miss Stivergill sharply. "How d'you know that ? Let me see it."

Tottie being summoned with the baby, entered the room staggering with the rotund mountain of good-natured self-will entirely concealing her person, with exception of her feet and the pretty little coal-dusted arms with which she clasped it to her heaving breast.

"Ha! I suppose little Bones is behind it," said Miss Stivergill.—"Set the baby down, child, and let me see you."

Tottie obeyed. The baby, true to his principles, refused to stand. He sat down and stared at those around him in jovial defiance.

"What is your age, little Bones ?"

" Just turned six, m'm," replied Tottie, with a courtesy, which Miss Lillycrop had taught her with great pains.

" You're sixty-six, at the least, compared with male creatures of the same age," observed her interrogator.

"Thank you, m'm," replied Tottie, with another dip.

" Have you a bonnet and shawl, little Bones ?"

Tottie, in a state of considerable surprise, replied that she had.

" Go and put 'em on then, and get that thing also ready to go out."

Miss Stivergill pointed to the baby contemptuously, as it were, with her nose.

" He's a very good bybie "—so the child pronounced it—" on'y rather self-willed at times, m'm," said Tottie, going through the athletic feat of lifting her charge.

" Just so. True to your woman's nature. Always ready to apologise for the male monster that tyrannises over you. I suppose, now, you'd say that your drunken father was a good man ? "

Miss Stivergill repented of the speech instantly on seeing the tears start into Tottie's large eyes as she replied quickly—

" Indeed I would, m'm. Oh ! you've no notion 'ow kind father is w'en 'e 's not in liquor."

" There, there. Of course he is. I didn't mean to say he wasn't, little Bones. It's a curious fact

that many drun—, I mean people given to drink,
are kind and amiable.   It's a disease.   Go now,
and get your things on, and do you likewise, Lilly.
My cab is at the door.   Be quick."

In a few minutes the whole party descended to
the street.   Miss Stivergill locked the door with
her own hand, and put the key in her pocket.   As
she turned round, Tottie's tawdry bonnet had fallen
off in her efforts to raise the baby towards the out-
stretched hands of her mistress, while the cabman
stood looking on with amiable interest.

Catching up the bonnet, Miss Stivergill placed it
on the child's head, back to the front, twisted the
strings round her head and face—anyhow—lifted
her and her charge into the cab, and followed them.

"Where to, ma'am?" said the amiable cabman.

"Charing Cross,—you idiot."

"Yes, ma'am," replied the man, with a broad grin,
touching his hat and bestowing a wink on a passing
policeman as he mounted the box.

On their way to the station the good lady put
out her head and shouted "Stop!"

The maligned man obeyed.

"Stay here, Lilly, with the baby.—Jump out,
little Bones.   Come with me."

She took the child's bonnet off and flung it under
the cab, then grasped Tottie's hand and led her
into a shop.

" A hat," demanded the lady of the shopwoman.

" What kind of hat, ma'am ?"

" Any kind," replied Miss Stivergill, " suitable for this child—only see that it 's not a doll's hat.   Let it *fit* her."

The shopwoman produced a head-dress, which ᴛottie afterwards described as a billycock 'at with a feather in it.   The purchaser paid for it, thrust it firmly on the child's head, and returned to the cab.

A few minutes by rail conveyed them to a charmingly country-like suburb, with neat villas dotting the landscape, and a few picturesque old red brick cottages scattered about here and there.

Such a drive to such a scene, reader, may seem very commonplace to you, but what tongue can tell, or pen describe, what it was to Tottie Bones ?   That pretty little human flower had been born in the heart of London—in one of the dirtiest and most unsavoury parts of that heart.   Being the child of a dissolute man and a hard-working woman, who could not afford to go out excursioning, she had never seen a green field in her life.   She had never seen the Thames, or the Parks.   There are many such unfortunates in the vast city.   Of flowers— with the exception of cauliflowers — she knew nothing, save from what little she saw of them in broken pots in the dirty windows of her poor neighbourhood, and on the barrows and baskets of the people who hawked them about the city. There was a legend among the neighbours of Archangel Court that once upon a time—in some remote period of antiquity—a sunbeam had been in the habit of overtopping the forest of chimneys and penetrating the court below in the middle of each summer, but a large brick warehouse had been erected somewhere to the southward, and had effectually cut off the supply, so that sunshine was known to the very juvenile population only through the reflecting power of roofs and chimney-cans and gable windows. In regard to scents, it need scarcely be said that Tottie had had considerable experience of that class which it is impossible to term sweet.

Judge then, if you can, what must have been the feelings of this little town-sparrow when she suddenly rushed, at the rate of forty miles an hour, into the heavenly influences of fields and flowers, hedgerows and trees, farm-yards and village spires, horse-ponds, country inns, sheep, cattle, hay-carts, piggeries, and poultry.

Her eyes, always large and liquid, became great crystal globes of astonishment, as, forgetful of herself, and *almost* of baby, she sat with parted lips and heaving breast, gazing in rapt ecstasy from the carriage window.

L

Miss Stivergill and Miss Lillycrop, being sympathetic souls, gazed with almost equal interest on the child's animated face.

"She only wants wings and washing to make her an angel," whispered the former to the latter.

But if the sights she saw on the journey inflated Tottie's soul with joy, the glories of Rosebud Cottage almost exploded her. It was a marvellous cottage. Rosebushes surrounded it, ivy smothered it, leaving just enough of room for the windows to peep out, and a few of the old red bricks to show in harmony with the green. Creepers in great variety embraced it, and a picturesque clump of trees on a knoll behind sheltered it from the east wind. There was a farm-yard, which did not belong to itself, but was so close to it that a stranger could scarcely have told whether it formed part of the Rosebud domain or that of the neighbouring cottage. The day, too, was exceptionally fine. It was one of those still, calm, sunny, cloudless days, which induce healthy people sometimes to wish that earth might be their permanent home.

"Oh, bybie!" exclaimed Tottie Bones, when, having clambered to the top of the knoll, she sat down on a tree-root and gazed on the cottage and the farm-yard, where hens were scratching in the interest of active chickens, and cows were standing in blank felicity, and pigs were revelling in dirt and sunshine—"Oh, bybie! it's 'eaven upon earth, ain't it, darling?"

The darling evidently agreed with her for once, for, lying on his back in the long grass, he seized two handfuls of wild-flowers, kicked up his fat legs, and laughed aloud.

"That's right, darling. Ain't it fun? And *such* flowers too—oh! all for nothing, only got to pull 'em. Yes, roll away, darling, you can't dirty yourself 'ere. Come, I shall 'ave a roll too." With which remark Tottie plunged into the grass, seized the baby and tumbled him and herself about to such an extent that the billycock hat was much deteriorated and the feather damaged beyond recovery.

Inside the Rosebud the other two members of the party were also enjoying themselves, though not exactly in like manner. They revelled in tea and in the feast of reason.

"Where, and when, and why did you find that child?" asked Miss Stivergill.

Her friend related what she knew of Tottie's history.

"Strange!" remarked Miss Stivergill, but beyond that remark she gave no indication of the state of her mind.

"It is indeed strange," returned her friend, "but it is just another instance of the power of God's Word to rescue and preserve souls, even in the most

unfavourable circumstances. Tottie's mother is a
Christian, and all the energies of her vigorous
nature are concentrated on two points—the training
of her child in the fear of God, and the saving of her
husband from drink. She is a woman of strong
faith, and is quite convinced that her prayers will
be answered, because, she says, ' He who has
promised is faithful,' but I fear much that she
will not live to see it."

" Why so ?" demanded the other sharply.

" Because she has a bad affection of the lungs.
If she were under more favourable circumstances
she might recover."

" Pooh ! nonsense. People constantly recover
from what is called bad affection of the lungs. Can
nothing be done for her ?"

" Nothing," replied Miss Lillycrop ; " she will not
leave her husband or her home. If she dies—"

" Well, what then ?"

" Little Tottie must be rescued, you know, and I
have set my heart on doing it."

" You 'll do nothing of the sort," said Miss Stivergill firmly.

Miss Lillycrop looked surprised.

" No, you shan't rescue her," continued the good
lady, with still firmer emphasis ; " you 've got all
London at your feet, and there 's plenty more where
that one came from. Come, Lilly, you mustn't be

greedy. You may have the baby if you like, but you must leave little Bones to me."

Miss Lillycrop was making feeble resistance to this proposal when the subject of dispute suddenly appeared at the door with glaring eyes and a horrified expression of face. Baby was in her arms as usual, and both he and his nurse were drenched, besides being covered from head to foot with mud.

It needed little explanation to tell that in crossing a ditch on a single plank Tottie had stumbled and gone headlong into the water with baby in her arms. Fortunately neither was hurt, though both had been terribly frightened.

Miss Stivergill was equal to the occasion. Ordering two tubs half-full of warm water into the back kitchen, she stripped the unfortunates and put them therein, to the intense joy of baby, whose delight in a warm bath was only equalled by his pleasure in doing mischief. At first Miss Stivergill thought of burning the children's garments, and fitting them out afresh, but on the suggestion of her friend that their appearing at home with new clothes might create suspicion, and cause unpleasant inquiries, she refrained. When thoroughly cleaned, Tottie and baby were wrapped up in shawls and set down to a hearty tea in the parlour.

While this was being devoured, the two friends conversed of many things. Among others, Miss

Stivergill touched on the subject of her progenitors, and made some confidential references to her mother, which her friend received with becoming sympathy.

"Yes, my dear," said Miss Stivergill, in a tone of unwonted tenderness. "I don't mind telling you all about her, for you're a good soul, with a feeling heart. Her loss was a terrible loss to me, though it was great gain to her. Before her death we were separated for a time—only a short time,—but it proved to be a blessed separation, for the letters she wrote me sparkled with love and wit and playfulness, as though they had been set with pearls and rubies and diamonds. I shall show you my treasures before going to bed. I keep them in that box on the side-board, to be always handy. It is not large, but its contents are more precious to me than thousands of gold and silver."

She paused ; and then, observing that Tottie was staring at her, she advised her to make the most of her opportunity, and eat as much as possible.

"If you please, m'm, I can't eat any more," said Tottie.

"Can't eat more, child ?—try," urged the hospitable lady.

Tottie heaved a deep sigh and said that she couldn't eat another morsel if she were to try ever so much. As baby appeared to be in the same happy condition, and could with difficulty keep his eyes open, both children were sent to bed under the care of a maid, and Miss Stivergill, taking down her treasure-box, proceeded to read part of its contents to her bosom friend.

Little did good Miss Stivergill imagine that she had dug a mine that night under Rosebud Cottage, and that the match which was destined to light it was none other than her innocent *protégée*, little Bones.

Throwing herself into the receptive arms of her mother, two days after the events just described, Tottie poured the delight and amazement of her surcharged spirit into sympathetic ears. Unfortunately her glowing descriptions also reached unsympathetic ears. Mrs. Bones had happily recovered her husband, and brought him home, where he lay in his familiar corner, resting from his labours of iniquity. The unsympathetic ears belonged to Mr. Abel Bones.

When Tottie, however, in her discursive wandering began to talk of pearls, and rubies, and diamonds, and treasures worth thousands of gold and silver, in a box on the sideboard, the ears became suddenly sympathetic, and Mr. Bones raised himself on one elbow.

"Hush! darling," said Mrs. Bones, glancing uneasily at the dark corner.

Mr. Bones knew well that if his wife should caution Tottie not to tell him anything about Rosebud Cottage, he would be unable to get a word out of her. He therefore rose suddenly, staggered towards the child, and seized her hand.

"Come, Tot, you and I shall go out for a walk."

"Oh, Abel, don't. Dear Abel—"

But dear Abel was gone, and his wife, clasping her hands, looked helplessly and hopelessly round the room. Then a gleam of light seemed to come into her eyes. She looked up and went down on her knees.

Meanwhile Abel went into a public-house, and, calling for a pint of beer, bade his child drink, but Tottie declined. He swore with an oath that he'd compel her to drink, but suddenly changed his mind and drank it himself.

"Now, Tot, tell father all about your visit to Miss Stivergill. She's very rich—eh?"

"Oh! awfully," replied Tottie, who felt an irresistible drawing to her father when he condescended to speak to her in kindly tones.

"Keeps a carriage—eh?"

"No, nor a 'oss—not even a pony," returned the child.

"An' no man-servant about the house?"

"No—not as I seed."

"Not even a gardener, now?"

"No, only women—two of 'em, and very nice they was too. One fat and short, the other tall and thin. I liked the fat one best."

"Ha! blessin's on 'em both," said Mr. Bones, with a bland smile. "Come now, Tot, tell me all about the cottage—inside first, the rooms and winders, an' specially the box of treasure. Then we 'll come to the garden, an' so we 'll get out by degrees to the fields and flowers. Go ahead, Tot."

It need scarcely be said that Abel Bones soon possessed himself of all the information he required, after which he sent Tottie home to her mother, and went his way.

CHAPTER XIII.

MISS LILLYCROP GETS A SERIES OF SURPRISES.

WHAT a world this is for plots!   And there is no escaping them.   If we are not the originators of them, we are the victims—more or less.   If we don't originate them designedly we do so accidentally.

We have seen how Abel Bones set himself deliberately to hatch one plot.   Let us now turn to old Fred Blurt, and see how that invalid, with the help of his brother Enoch, unwittingly sowed the seeds of another.

"Dear Enoch," said Fred one day, turning on his pillow, " I should have died but for you."

"And Miss Lillycrop, Fred.   Don't be ungrateful. If Miss Lillycrop had not come to my assistance, it's little I could have done for you."

" Well, yes, I ought to have mentioned her in the same breath with yourself, Enoch, for she has been kind—very kind and patient.   Now, I want to know if that snake has come."

" Are you sure you 've recovered enough to attend to business ?" asked the brother.

" Yes, quite sure.   Besides, a snake is not business —it is pleasure.   I mean to send it to my old friend Balls, who has been long anxious to get a specimen. I had asked a friend long ago to procure one for me, and now that it has come I want you to pack it to go by post."

" By post !" echoed the brother.

" Yes, why not ?"

" Because I fear that live snakes are prohibited articles."

" Get the Post-Office Directory and see for yourself," said the invalid.

The enormous volume, full six inches thick, which records the abodes and places of business of all noteworthy Londoners, was fetched.

" Nothing about snakes here," said Enoch, running his eye over the paragraph referring to the articles in question,—" 'Glass bottles, leeches, game, fish' (but that refers to dead ones, I suppose) 'flesh, fruit, vegetables, or other perishable substances' (a snake ain't perishable, at least not during a brief post-journey)—'nor any bladder or other vessel containing liquid' (ha! that touches him: a snake contains blood, don't it?)—'or anything whatsoever which might by pressure or otherwise be rendered injurious to the contents of the mail-bags or to the officers of the Post-Office.'—Well, brother," continued Enoch, " I 'm not quite sure that it comes within the forbidden degrees, so we 'll give it the benefit of the doubt and pack it. How d' you propose doing it up ? In a letter?"

" No, I had a box made for it before I was taken ill. You 'll find it in the shop, on the upper shelf, beside the northern diver."

The little box was brought, and the snake, which had been temporarily consigned to an empty glass aquarium, was put into it.

" You 're sure he don't bite, Fred, and isn't poisonous ?"

" Quite sure."

" Then here goes—whew ! what a lively fellow he is !"

This was indeed true. The animal, upwards of a yard in length, somewhat resembled the eel in his efforts to elude the grasp of man, but Mr. Blurt fixed him, coiled him firmly down on his bed of straw and wadding, pressed a similar bed on the top of him to keep him quiet, and shut the lid.

" There ; I 've got him in all right. Now for the screws. He can't move easily, and even if he could he wouldn't make much noise."

The box was finally secured with a piece of string, a label with the address and the proper number of stamps was affixed, and then it was committed to

the care of George Aspel to post, in time for the
evening mail.

It was five minutes to six when Aspel ascended
the steps of St. Martin's-le-Grand.   The usual rush
was in progress.   There was a considerable crowd
in front of the letter-box.   Instead of pushing
through, George took advantage of his height,
stretched his long arm over the heads of the people,
and, with a good aim, pitched the box into the
postal jaws.

For a few seconds he stood still, meditating a call
on Phil Maylands.   But he was not now as eager to
meet his friend as he used to be.   He had begun a
course of dissipation, and, superior though he was
in years, physique, and knowledge to his friend, he
felt a new and uncomfortable sense of inferiority
when in the presence of the straightforward, steady
boy.

At seventeen a year adds much to the manhood
of a youth.   Phil's powers of perception had been
greatly quickened by his residence in London.
Although he regarded Aspel with as warm affection
as ever, he could not avoid seeing the change for
the worse in him, and a new feeling of deep anxiety
and profound but respectful pity filled his heart.
He prayed for him also, but did not quite believe
that his prayers would be heard, for as yet he did
not fully realise or comprehend the grand truths of

the religion in which his mother had faithfully trained him. He did not at that time understand, as he afterwards came to understand, that the prayer of faith—however weak and fluttering—is surely answered, whether we see the answer or not, and whether the answer be immediate or long delayed.

On one occasion, with feelings of timorous self-abasement, he ventured to remonstrate with his friend, but the effort was repelled. Possibly the thought of another reproof from Phil was the cause of Aspel's decision not to look him up on the present occasion.

As he descended the steps, a man as tall and powerful as himself met him and stared him in the face. Aspel fired up at once and returned the stare. It was Abel Bones, on his way to post a letter. The glare intensified, and for a moment it seemed as if the two giants were about to fight. A small street boy, observing the pair, was transfixed with ardent hope, but he was doomed to disappointment. Bones had clenched his right hand. If he had advanced another inch the blood of the sea-kings would have declared for war on the spot, regardless of consequences. But Bones was too old a bird thus to come within reach of his great enemy, the law. Besides, a deeper though not immediate plan of revenge flashed into his mind. Relaxing the hand and frown simultaneously, he held out the former.

"Come," he said, in a hearty tone, "I don't bear you no ill-will for the crack on the nut you gave me, and you've surely no occasion to bear ill-will to a man you floored so neatly. Shake hands."

The familiarity, not to say insolence, of this proposal, from one so much beneath him, would probably have induced the youth to turn aside with scorn, but the flattering reference to his pugilistic powers from one who was no mean antagonist softened his feelings.

"Well, I'm sure that I bear *you* no ill-will." he said, with a smile, extending his hand.

"Bah! chicken-livers," exclaimed the small boy, turning away in supreme contempt.

"And I assure you," continued Aspel, "I had no intention of doing you injury. But no doubt a stout fellow like you didn't let a knock-down blow interfere with his next day's work."

"His next day's work!" repeated Mr. Bones, with a chuckle. "It would be a queer blow as would interfere with *my* work. Why, guv'nor, I hain't got no work at all." Here he put on a very lugubrious expression. "P'r'aps you won't believe it, sir, but I do assure you that I haven't, in them hard times, had a full day's work for ever so long. And I haven't earned a rap this day, except the penny I got for postin' this here letter."

George Aspel, besides being, as we have said, a kind-hearted man, was unusually ignorant of the ways of the world, especially the world of London. He believed Abel Bones at once, and spoke in quite a softened, friendly tone as he replied—

"I'm sorry to hear that, and would gladly help you if I could, but, to tell you the truth, Mr. Bones, I'm not in flourishing circumstances myself. Still, I may perhaps think of some way of helping you. Post your letter, and I'll walk with you while we talk over it."

The man ran up the steps, posted his letter, which had missed the mail—though he did not appear to care for that—and returned.

Although we have spoken of this man as a confirmed drunkard, it must not be supposed that he had reached the lowest state of degradation. Like George Aspel, he had descended from a higher level in the social scale. Of course, his language proved that he had never been in the rank of a gentleman, but in manners and appearance he was much above the unhappy outcasts amongst whom he dwelt. Moreover, he had scarcely reached middle life, and was, or had been, a handsome man, so that, when he chose to dress decently and put on a sanctimonious look (which he could do with much facility), he seemed quite a respectable personage.

"Now, guv'nor, I'm at your sarvice," he said. "This is my way. Is it yours?"

"Yes—any way will do," continued Aspel. "Now let me hear about you. I owe you some sort of reparation for that blow. Have you dined?—will you eat?"

"Well, no; thank 'ee all the same, but I've no objection to driuk."

They chanced to be near a public-house as he spoke. It would be difficult in some thoroughfares of London to stop *without* chancing to be near a public-house!

They entered, and Aspel, resolving to treat the man handsomely, called for brandy and soda. It need scarcely be said that at that hour the brandy and soda was by no means the first of its kind that either of the men had imbibed that day. Over it they became extremely confidential and chatty. Mr. Bones was a lively and sensible fellow. It was noticeable, too, that his language improved and his demeanour became more respectful as the acquaintance progressed. After a time they rose. Aspel paid for the brandy and soda, and they left the place in company.

Leaving them, we shall return to St. Martin's-le-Grand, and follow the footsteps of no less a personage than Miss Lillycrop, for it so happened that that enthusiastic lady, having obtained permission to

M

view the interior of the Post-Office, had fixed on that
evening for her visit.   But we must go back a little
in time—to that period when the postal jaws were
about to open for the reception of the evening
mail.

Ever since Miss Lillycrop's visit to the abode of
Solomon Flint, she had felt an increasing desire to
see the inside and the working of that mighty
engine of State about which she had heard so much.
A permit had been procured for her, and her cousin,
May Maylands, being off duty at that hour, was
able to accompany her.

They were handed over to the care of a polite
and intelligent letter-sorter named Bright.   The
sorter seemed fully to appreciate and enter into Miss
Lillycrop's spirit of inquiry.   He led her and May
to the inside—the throat, as it were—of those postal
jaws, the exterior aspect of which we have already
described.   On the way thither they had to pass
through part of the great letter-sorting hall.   It
seemed to Miss Lillycrop's excited imagination as
if she had been suddenly plunged over head and
ears into a very ocean of letters.   From that moment
onwards, during her two hours' visit, she swam, as
it were, among snowy billows of literature.

" This is the receiving-box—the inside of it," said
Mr. Bright, as he led the way through a glass
door into a species of closet or compartment about

six feet by ten in dimension, or thereabouts, with a low roof.

"This way, ladies. Stand here, on one side. They are just going to open it."

The visitors saw in front of them a recess, divided by a partition, in which were two large baskets. A few letters were falling into these as they entered. Glancing upwards, they saw a long slit, through which a number of curious human eyes peeped for a moment, and disappeared, to be replaced by other eyes. Little spurts of letters came intermittently through the slit and fell into the baskets. These, when full, were seized by two attendants, dragged away, and replaced by empty ones.

Suddenly the upper lip of the slit, or postal mouth, rose.

"Oh, May, look!" exclaimed Miss Lillycrop eagerly.

Not only the eyes but the heads and shoulders of the moving public now became visible to those inside, while the intermittent spurts became gradually a continuous shower of letters. The full significance of the old superscription, "Haste, post haste, for thy life," now began to dawn on Miss Lillycrop. The hurry, mentioned elsewhere in our description of the outside view, increased as the minutes of grace flew by, and the visitors fairly laughed aloud when they saw the cataract of correspondence—the absolute waterfall, with, now and then, a bag or an entire bandboxful of letters, like a loosened boulder—that tumbled into the baskets below.

From this letter-fall Miss Lillycrop was led, speechless, by her cicerone, followed by May, to whom the scene was not quite new, and whose chief enjoyment of it consisted in observing her interested and excitable friend's surprise.

Mr. Bright led them back to the great sorting-room, where the energetic labour of hundreds of men and boys—facing, carrying, stamping, distributing, sorting, etc.—was going on full swing. Everywhere there was rapid work, but no hurry; busy and varied action, but no confusion; a hum of mingled voice and footfall, but no unnecessary noise. It was a splendid example of the power of orderly and united action. To Miss Lillycrop it conveyed the idea of hopeless and irretrievable confusion !

Mounting a staircase, Mr. Bright conducted the ladies to a gallery from which they had a bird's-eye view of the entire hall. It was, in truth, a series of rooms, connected with the great central apartment by archways. Through these—extending away in far perspective, so that the busy workers in the distance became like miniature men—could be seen rows on rows of facing and sorting tables, covered,

INSIDE THE LETTER-BOX—Page 180.

heaped up, and almost hidden, by the snows of the evening mail. Here the chaos of letters, books, papers, etc., was being reduced to order—the whole under the superintendence of a watchful gentleman, on a raised platform in the centre, who took good care that England should not only *expect*, but also be *assured*, that every man and boy did his duty.

Miss Lillycrop glanced at the clock opposite. It was a quarter to seven.

"Do you mean to tell me," she said, turning full on Mr. Bright, and pointing downwards, "that that ocean of letters will be gone, and these tables emptied by eight o'clock?"

"Indeed I do, ma'am; and more than what you see there, for the district bags have not all come in yet. By eight o'clock these tables will be as bare as the palm of my hand."

Mr. Bright extended a large and manly palm by way of emphasising his remark.

Miss Lillycrop was too polite to say, "That's a lie!" but she firmly, though mutely, declined to believe it.

"D' you observe the tables just below us, ma'am?"

He pointed to what might have been six large board-room tables, surrounded by boys and men as close as they could stand. As, however, the tables in question were covered more than a foot deep with letters, Miss Lillycrop only saw their legs.

"These are the facing tables," continued Mr. Bright. "All that the men and lads round 'em have got to do with the letters there is to arrange them for the stampers, with their backs and stamps all turned one way. We call that facing the letters. They have also to pick out and pitch into baskets, as you see, all book-packets, parcels, and news-papers that may have been posted by mistake in the letter-box."

While the sorter went on expounding matters, one of the tables had begun to show its wooden surface as its "faced" letters were being rapidly removed, but just then a man with a bag on his shoulder came up, sent a fresh cataract of letters on the blank spot, and re-covered it. Presently a stream of men with bags on their backs came in

"These are the district mails, ma'am," explained Mr. Bright; "during the last half-hour and more they have been hurrying towards us from all quar-ters of London ; the nearest being brought by men on foot, the more distant bags by vans. Some are still on their way ; all will concentrate here at last, in time for sorting."

The contents of these bags as they came in were shot out, and the facing-tables—all of which had begun to show symptoms of the flood going down and dry land appearing—were flooded and reflooded again and again to a greater depth than before.

"The mail will be late to-night," observed Miss Lillycrop, with an assured nod.

"O no, ma'am, it won't," replied Bright, with an easy smile, and May laughed as they returned to the hall to inspect the work in detail.

"Here, you see, we stamp the letters."

Mr. Bright stopped in front of a long table, at which was standing a row of stampers, who passed letters under the stamps with amazing rapidity. Each man or youth grasped a stamp, which was connected with a machine on a sort of universal joint. It was a miniature printing-machine, with a little inking-roller, which was moved over the types each time by the mere process of stamping, so the stamper had only to pass the letters under the die with the one hand and stamp with the other as fast as he could. The rate varied, of course, considerably. Nervous and anxious stampers illustrated more or less the truth of the proverb, "The more hurry the less speed," while quiet, steady hands made good progress. They stamped on the average from 100 to 150 letters in the minute, each man.

"You see, ma'am," remarked Mr. Bright, "it's the way all the world over : cool-headed men who know their powers always get on best. The stamping-machine is a great improvement on the old system, where you had to strike the inker first, and then the letter. It just doubled the action and the time.

We have another ingeniously contrived stamp in the office. It might not occur to you that stamping parcels and other articles of irregular shape is rather difficult, owing to the stamper not striking flatly on them. To obviate this, one of our own men invented a stamp with an indiarubber neck, so that, no matter how irregular the surface of the article may be, the face of the stamp is forced flat upon it by one blow."

"When stamped," continued Mr. Bright, moving on, "the letters are taken by boys, as you see, to the sorters. You observe that each sorter has a compartment or frame before him, with separate divisions in it for the great towns only, such as Manchester, Liverpool, Birmingham, Brighton, etc. Now, you know"—here he stopped and assumed an impressive explanatory tone—"you couldn't expect any single man to sort the letters for every town and village in the kingdom—could you, ma'am?"

Miss Lillycrop admitted that she could not indulge such an expectation, and further expressed her belief that any man who could must be little better than a lunatic.

"But every man you see here," continued Mr. Bright, "has batch after batch of letters put before him, which may contain letters from anywhere to everywhere. So, you see, we subdivide the work. The sorters you are now looking at sort the letters

for the large towns into separate sections, and all
the rest into divisions representing the various parts
of the country, such as northern, southern, etc.
The letters are then collected by the boys you see
going up and down the hall."

"I don't see them," interrupted Miss Lillycrop.

"There, that's a northern division boy who has
just backed against you, ma'am."

The boy referred to turned, apologised, and gathering the letters for the northern division from the
sorter at their elbow, moved on to gather more from
others.

"The division letters," continued Bright, "are
then conveyed to other sorters, who subdivide them
into roads, and then the final sorting takes place
for the various towns. We have a staff of about a
thousand sorters, assistant sorters, and boy sorters in
this (Inland) office alone, who have been, or are
being, carefully trained for the work. Some are
smart, and some of course are slow. They are tested
occasionally. When a sorter is tested he is given a
pack of five hundred cards—dummies—to represent
letters. A good man will sort these in thirteen or
fifteen minutes. There are always sure to be a few
mis-sorts, even in *our* well-regulated family—that
is, letters sorted to the wrong sections or divisions.
Forty mis-sorts in the five hundred is considered
very bad work."

"But what if a sorter does not happen to know the division to which any particular letter belongs ?" asked Miss Lillycrop.

"He ought to know," replied her guide, "because all the sorters have to undergo a strict examination once a year as to their knowledge of towns and villages throughout England."

"Indeed! but," persisted Miss Lillycrop, "what does he do with a letter if he chances to forget ?"

"Why, he must get other sorters to help him."

"And what happens if he finds a letter so badly addressed that he cannot read it ?"

"Sends it to the blind division; we shall come to that presently," said Mr. Bright. "Meanwhile we shall visit the hospital. I need scarcely explain to you that the hospital is the place to which wounded letters and packages are taken to be healed. Here it is."

The party now stood beside a table, at which several clerks—we might almost say surgeons— were at work, busy with sealing-wax and string.

The patients were a wondrous lot, and told eloquently of human carelessness. Here were found letters containing articles that no envelope of mere paper could be expected to hold—such as bunches of heavy keys, articles of jewellery, etc., which had already more than half escaped from their covers. There were also frail card-board boxes, so squeezed and burst that their contents were protruding, and parcels containing worsted and articles of wearing apparel, which had been so carelessly put up as to have come undone in the mail-bags. All these things were being re-tied, re-folded, patched up here and there with sealing-wax, or put into new covers, by the postal surgeons, and done with as much care, too, as though the damage had been caused by the Post-Office rather than by carelessness in the public.

But among these invalided articles were a few whose condition accidentally revealed attempts to contravene the postal laws. One letter which had burst completely open revealed a pill-box inside, with "Dinner Pills" on the outside. On examination, the pills turned out to be two sixpences wrapped up in a scrap of paper, on which was written—"Thought you had no money to get a stamp with, so sent you some." It is contrary to regulations to send coin by post without registering the letter. The unfortunate receiver would have to pay eightpence, as a registration fee, for this shilling!

While the party was looking at the hospital work another case was discovered. A book packet came open and revealed a letter inside. But still further, the letter was found to contain sixpence in silver, sent to defray postage when the book should be returned. Here was a double sin! No letter, or writing of the nature of a letter, is allowed to go by book post,

and coin may not be sent unregistered.   In this
case the book would be forwarded at letter-rate, and
the 8d. registration fee would be charged for the
coin—the whole amounting to 6s. 6d.

"If the public would only attend," observed Mr.
Bright, in commenting on these facts, "to the
regulations laid down for their guidance by the
Post-Office—as detailed in our Directories and
Postal Guides—such errors would seldom occur, for
I believe that things of this sort are the result of
ignorance rather than dishonesty."

"Now, ma'am," he continued, " we come to the
blind officers."

There were several of those gentlemen, whose
title, we presume, was satirically expressive of the
extraordinary sharpness of their eyes and intellects.
They were seated at a table, engaged in examining
addresses so illegible, so crabbed, so incomplete, and
so ineffably ridiculous, that no man of ordinary
mental capacity could make head or tail of them.
All the principal London and Provincial Directories,
Guides, and Gazetteers were ranged in front of the
blind officers, to assist them in their arduous labours,
and by the aid of these, and their own extensive
knowledge of men and places, they managed to
dispose of letters for which a stranger would think
it impossible to find owners.

"What would you make of that address, now?"

said Mr. Bright, presenting a letter to Miss Lillycrop for inspection.

"It looks like Cop—Cup—no—it begins with a C at all events.—What think you of it, May?" said the puzzled lady.

"It seems to me something like Captain Troller of Rittler Bunch," said May, laughing. "It is quite illegible."

"Not *quite*," said one of the blind officers, with a smile. "It is—Comptroller of the Returned Letter Branch. Some one making inquiries, no doubt, after a lost letter addressed as badly as this one."

Having looked at a few more of the letters that were then passing under examination, Mr. Bright showed them a book in which were copied fac-similes of addresses which had passed through the post. Some of these were pictorial—embracing quaint devices and caricatures, most of them in ink, and some in colours, all of which had been traced by a gentleman in the office with great skill. One that struck May as being very original was the representation of an artist painting the portrait of the Queen. Her Majesty was depicted as sitting for her portrait, and the canvas on the easel before which the artist stood was made the exact size of the postage-stamp.

While the ladies were examining this book of literary curiosities, Mr. Bright took occasion to comment with pardonable pride on the working of the Post-Office.

"You see, ma'am," he said, "we do our best for the public—though many of 'em have no idea of it. We don't send letters to the Returned Letter Branch till we've tried, as you see, to get the correct addresses, and until two separate letter-carriers have attempted to deliver them. After leaving the letter-carriers' hands, the address of every undelivered letter, and the indorsement it bears, are carefully examined by a superior officer, who is held responsible for discovering any wrong treatment it may have undergone, and for having recourse to any further available means of finding the owner. It is considered better that the sender of a letter should know as soon as possible of its non-delivery, than that it should travel about with little prospect of its owner being found. We therefore send it to the Returned Branch without further delay, where it is carefully examined by a superior officer, to see that it has actually been presented as addressed, and that the reasons assigned for its non-delivery are sufficient. In doubtful cases the Directories and other books of reference in the branch are consulted, and should it be found that there has been any oversight or neglect, the letter is immediately reissued. After all has been done that can be to deliver such letters, they are opened, and returned the same day to the senders. If valuables are enclosed, the address and contents are recorded in case of inquiry. When senders fail to give their addresses, sometimes these are discovered by bills of exchange, cheques, or money-orders, which happen to be enclosed. When addresses of senders can be discovered by information on the outside of covers, the letters are returned without passing through the Returned Letter Branch, and are not opened. When all efforts have failed, and the letters do not contain property, they are not preserved."

"Do many letters come into the Returned Letter Offices in this way?" asked Miss Lillycrop.

"Ay; over the whole kingdom, including the letters sent direct to the senders last year, there were above four millions eight hundred thousand, and of these we managed to return nine-tenths to the writers, or re-issued them to corrected addresses."

"Oh, indeed!" said Miss Lillycrop, utterly bewildered.

"A large proportion of the letters passing through this office," said Mr. Bright, "consists of circulars. An account of these was once taken, and the number was found to be nearly twenty millions a year, and of these circulars it was ascertained that —"

"Stop! pray, sir, stop!" exclaimed Miss Lillycrop, pressing her hand to her forehead; "I am lost in admiration of your amazing memory, but I—J

have no head for figures.   Indeed, what I have
already heard and seen in this place has produced
such confusion in my poor brain that I cannot perceive any difference whatever between millions,
billions, and trillions ! "

"Well, come, we will continue our round," said
Mr. Bright, laughing.

Now, while all this was going on in the hall,
there was a restive creature inside of a box which
did not relish its confinement.   This was Mr. Fred
Blurt's snake.

That sagacious animal discovered that there was
a knot in the side of his pine-wood box.   Now, knots
are sometimes loose.   Whether the snake found this
out, and wrought at the knot intentionally, or forced
it out accidentally during its struggles, we cannot
tell, but certain it is that it got it out somehow,
made its escape, and glided away into the darkest
corner it could find.

Meanwhile its box was treated after the manner
of parcels, and put safely into one of the mail-bags.

As the mass of letters began to diminish in bulk
the snake began to feel uncomfortably exposed.   At
the same time Miss Lillycrop, with that wicked
delight in evil prophecy which is peculiar to mankind, began to feel comfortably exultant.

"You see I was right !" she said to her guide,
glancing at the clock, which now indicated ten

minutes to eight; "the confusion is almost as great as ever."

"We shall see," replied Mr. Bright, quietly, as he led the way back to the gallery.

From this point it could be seen, even by un-practised eyes, that, although the confusion of letters all over the place was still considerable, there were huge gaps on the sorting-tables everywhere, while the facing-tables were of course empty. There was a push and energy also which had not prevailed at first. Men seemed as though they really were in considerable haste. Letters were being bundled up and tied with string and thrust into bags, and the bags sealed with a degree of celerity that transfixed Miss Lillycrop and silenced her. A few minutes more and the tables were cleared. Another minute, and the bags were being carried out. Thirty red vans outside gaped to receive them. Eight o'clock struck, whips cracked, wheels rattled, the eight o'clock mail was gone, and there was not a single letter left in the great sorting-room of St. Martin's-le-Grand!

"I was right, you see," said Mr. Bright.

"You were right," responded Miss Lillycrop.

They descended and crossed the now unencum-bered floor. The snake took it into its mottled head at that moment to do the same. Miss Lillycrop saw it, shrieked, sprang to get out of its way, fell, and sprained her ankle!

N

There was a rush of sorters, letter-carriers, boy-sorters, and messengers; the snake was captured, and Miss Lillycrop was tenderly borne from the General Post-Office in a state of mental amazement and physical collapse.

CHAPTER XIV.

FORMATION OF THE PEGAWAY LITERARY ASSOCIATION
AND OTHER MATTERS.

CLOSE to the residence of Solomon Flint there
was a small outhouse or shed, which formed part of
the letter-carrier's domain, but was too small to be
sub-let as a dwelling, and too inconveniently situated
in a back court to be used as an apartment. It was
therefore devoted to the reception of lumber. But
Solomon, not being a rich man, did not possess
much lumber. The shed was therefore comparatively empty.

When Philip Maylands came to reside with
Solomon, he was allowed to use this shed as a
workroom.

Phil was by nature a universal genius—a Jack-of-
all-trades—and formed an exception to that rule
about being master of none, which is asserted, though
not proved, by the proverb, for he became master of
more than one trade in the course of his career.
Solomon owned a few tools, so that carpentry was

naturally his first attempt, and he very soon became
proficient in that.   Then, having discovered an old
clock among the lumber of the shed, he took to
examining and cleaning its interior of an evening
after his work at the Post-Office was done.   As
his mechanical powers developed, his genius for invention expanded, and soon he left the beaten
tracks of knowledge and wandered into the less
trodden regions of fancy.

In all this Phil had an admirer and sympathiser
in his sister May ; but May's engagements, both in
and out of the sphere of her telegraphic labours,
were numerous, so that the boy would have had to
pursue his labours in solitude if it had not been for his
friend Peter Pax, whose admiration for him knew no
bounds, and who, if he could, would have followed
Phil like his shadow.   As often as the little fellow
could manage to do so, he visited his friend in the
shed, which they named Pegaway Hall.   There he
sometimes assisted Phil, but more frequently held
him in conversation, and commented in a free and
easy way on his work,—for his admiration of Phil
was not sufficient to restrain his innate insolence.

One evening Phil Maylands was seated at his
table, busy with the works of an old watch.   Little
Pax sat on the table swinging his legs.   He had
brought a pipe with him, and would have smoked,
but Phil sternly forbade it.

"It's bad enough for men to fumigate their mouths," he said, with a smile on his lip and a frown in his eye, "but when I see a thing like you trying to make yourself look manly by smoking, I can't help thinking of a monkey putting on the boots and helmet of a Guardsman. The boots and helmet look grand, no doubt, but that makes the monkey seem all the more ridiculous. Your pipe suggests manhood, Pax, but you look much more like a monkey than a man when it's in your mouth."

"How severe you are to-night, Phil!" returned Pax, putting the pipe, however, in his pocket; "where did you graduate, now—at Cambridge or Oxford? Because w'en my eldest boy is big enough I'd like to send 'im w'ere he'd acquire sitch an amazin' flow of eloquence."

Phil continued to rub the works of the watch, but made no reply.

"I say, Phil," observed the little fellow, after a thoughtful pause.

"Well?"

"Don't it strike you, sometimes, that this is a queer sort of world?"

"Yes, I've often thought that, and it has struck me, too, that you are one of the queerest fish in it."

"Come, Phil, don't be cheeky. I'm in a sedate frame of mind to-night, an' want to have a talk in a philosophical sort o' way of things in general."

"Well, Pax, go ahead. I happen to have been reading a good deal about things in general of late, so perhaps between us we may grind something out of a talk."

"Just so ; them's my ideas precisely. There's nothin'," said Pax, thrusting both hands deeper into his trousers pockets, and swinging his legs more vigorously—"nothin' like a free an' easy chat for developin' the mental powers. But I say, what a fellow you are for goin' ahead ! Seems to me that you're always either workin' at queer contrivances or readin'."

"You forget, Pax, that I sometimes carry tele-graphic messages."

"Ha ! true, then you and I are bound together by the cords of a common dooty—p'r'aps I should say an *un*common dooty, all things considered."

"Among other things," returned Phil, "I have found out by reading that there are two kinds of men in the world, the men who push and strive and strike out new ideas, and the men who jog along easy, on the let-be-for-let-be principle, and who grow very much like cabbages."

"You're right there, Phil—an' yet cabbages ain't bad vegetables in their way," remarked Pax, with a contemplative cast of his eyes to the ceiling.

"Well," continued Phil gravely, " I shouldn't like to be a cabbage."

"W'ich means," said the other, "that you'd rather be one o' the fellows who push an' strive an' strike out noo ideas."

Phil admitted that such were his thoughts and aspirations.

"Now, Pax," he said, laying down the tool with which he had been working, and looking earnestly into his little friend's face, "something has been simmering in my mind for a considerable time past."

"You'd better let it out then, Phil, for fear it should bu'st you," suggested Pax.

"Come, now, stop chaffing for a little and listen, because I want your help," said Phil.

There was something in Phil's look and manner when he was in earnest which effectually quelled the levity of his little admirer. The appeal to him for aid, also, had a sedative effect. As Phil went on, Pax became quite as serious as himself. This power of Pax to suddenly discard levity, and become interested, was indeed one of the qualities which rendered him powerfully attractive to his friend.

"The fact is," continued Phil, "I have set my heart on forming a literary association among the telegraph boys."

"A what?"

"A literary association. That is, an association of those boys among us who want to read, and study, and discuss, and become knowing and wise."

The daring aspirations suggested by this proposition were too much for little Pax. He remained silent—open mouthed and eyed—while Phil went on quietly to expound his plans.

"There is a capital library, as you know, at the Post-Office, which is free to all of us, though many of us make little use of it—more's the pity,—so that we don't require a library of our own, though we may come to that, too, some day, who knows? Sure it wouldn't be the first time that great things had come out of small beginnings, if all I have read be true. But it's not only books we would be after. What we want, Pax, is to be organised—made a body of. When we've got that done we shall soon put soul into the body,—what with debates, an' readings, an' lectures, an' maybe a soirée now and then, with music and speeches, to say nothing of tea an' cakes."

As Phil Maylands warmed with his subject his friend became excited. He ceased to chaff and raise objections, and finally began to see the matter through Phil's rose-coloured glasses.

"Capital," he exclaimed heartily. "It'll do, Phil. It'll work—like everything else you put your hand to. But"—here his chubby little visage elongated—"how about funds? Nothin' in this world gets along without funds; an' then we've no place to meet in."

" We must content ourselves with funds of humour to begin with," returned Phil, resuming his work on the watch. "As for a meeting-room, wouldn't this do? Pegaway Hall is not a bad place, and quite enough room in it when the lumber's cleared out o' the way. Then, as to members, we would only admit those who showed a strong desire to join us."

"Just so—who showed literary tastes, like you an' me," suggested Pax.

"Exactly so," said Phil, "for, you see, I don't want to have our society flourished about in the eyes of people as a public Post-Office affair. We must make it private and very select."

"Yes, *uncommon* select," echoed Pax.

"It would never do, you know," continued the other, "to let in every shallow young snipe that wanted to have a lark, and make game of the affair. We will make our rules very stringent."

"Of course," murmured Pax, with a solemn look, "*tremendously* stringent. For first offences of any kind—a sousin' with dirty water. For second offences —a woppin' and a fine. For third—dismissal, with ears and noses chopped off, or such other mutilation as a committee of the house may invent. But, Phil, who d'yee think would be suitable men to make members of?"

"Well, let me see," said Phil, again laying down his tools, and looking at the floor with a thoughtful air, "there 's Long Poker, he 's a long-legged, good-hearted fellow—fond o' the newspapers."

" Yes," put in Pax, " Poker 'll do for one. He 'd be a capital member. Long and thin as a literary c'racter ought to be, and pliable too. We could make a'most anything of him, except a fire-screen or a tablecloth. Then there's Big Jack—he 's got strong sedate habits."

" Too fond of punning," objected Phil.

" A little punishment in the mutilation way would stop that," said Pax.

" And there 's Jim Brown," rejoined Phil. " He 's a steady, enthusiastic fellow; and little Grigs, he 's about as impudent as yourself, Pax. Strange, isn't it, that it 's chiefly little fellows who are impudent?"

" Wouldn't it be strange if it were otherwise?" retorted Pax, with an injured look. " As we can't knock people down with our fists, aren't we justified in knockin' 'em down with our tongues?"

" Then," continued Phil, " there 's George Granger and Macnab—"

" Ah! ain't he the boy for argufyin' too?" interrupted Pax, "and he 'll meet his match in Sandy Tod. And there 's Tom Blunter—"

" And Jim Scroggins—"

" An' Limp Letherby—"

" An' Fat Collins—"

" An' Bobby Sprat. Oh!" exclaimed Pax, with a

glowing countenance, "we've got lots o' first-rate
men among the message-boys, though there *are*
some uncommon bad 'uns.   But we'll have none
except true-blues in *our* literary association."

The society thus planned was soon called into
being, for Philip Maylands was one of those determined characters who carry their plans into execution with vigour and despatch.   His first move was
to seek counsel of Mr. Sterling, a city missionary—
the same who had directed George Aspel to the
abode of Abel Bones on the night of that youth's
visit to Archangel Court,—with whom he had
become acquainted on one of his visits to Miss
Lillycrop.   That good lady was a staunch ally and
able assistant of many city missionaries, and did
much service in the way of bringing them into
acquaintance with people who she thought might
be helpful to them, or get help from them.   A
mutual liking had sprung up between Mr. Antony
Sterling and Phil on that occasion, which had
ripened into friendship.

"You'll help us at our first meeting, won't you?"
asked Phil, after they had talked the matter over.

"Yes, if you wish it," replied Mr. Sterling.   "But
I won't come at the beginning.   I'll drop in towards
the close, and won't say much.   You'd best begin
the work by yourselves.   I'll come to your aid
whenever you seem to require it.   But have a care

how you start, Phil.   Whatever the other members
may do, remember that you, as the originator of the
association, are bound to lay the foundations with
the blessing of God."

Phil did not neglect this all-important point, and,
having obtained permission from Solomon Flint to
use the shed, the society was soon auspiciously
commenced with a lively debate, in Pegaway Hall,
as to the best method of conducting its own affairs.
On this occasion Philip Maylands proved himself
to be an able organiser.   Long Poker showed that
he had not dabbled in newspapers without fishing
up and retaining a vast amount of miscellaneous
knowledge.   Jim Brown roused the meeting to a
pitch of enthusiasm almost equal to his own.   Little
Grigs made stinging remarks all round, and chaffed
little Pax with evident delight.   Macnab disputed
with everybody.   Sandy Tod argued and objected
more or less to everything, while Tom Blunter, Jim
Scroggins, Limp Letherby, Fat Collins, and Bobby
Sprat, lent more or less effectual fire to the debate.
Big Jack did not speak much.   He preferred, as he
said, to form a large audience, but, if he might be
permitted to offer an opinion, would suggest that
less talk and more action might facilitate the
despatch of business, and that they ought to try to
emulate the House of Commons by allowing a little
common sense to mingle with their discussions.

As for Peter Pax, he assumed the *rôle* of peace-maker-general. When the debaters seemed to be getting too warm, he rose to order; and, in a calm dignified manner, commented on the conduct of the disputants with such ineffable insolence as to draw down their wrath on his devoted head—to the great delight of the other members. Thus he threw oil on the troubled waters, and, generally, kept the meeting lively.

Finally, the laws of the Pegaway Literary Association were fixed, the plan of meetings was arranged, and the whole thing fairly started.

The society worked well for a time, but after the various members had done their best, as Pax said, to keep the pot boiling, it was felt and suggested that they should seek a little aid from without. A reading or a lecture was proposed, seconded, and carried. Then came the question who should be asked to read or lecture. Macnab proposed that their chairman should endeavour to procure a lecturer, and report to next meeting. Sandy Tod objected, and proposed a committee to consider the subject. Phil Maylands said he had anticipated the demand, and had already secured the promise of a lecturer—if the members chose to accept him.

"Name! name!" cried several voices.

"Our excellent landlord, Solomon Flint," said Phil. "You all know his admirable powers of memory, and his profound knowledge of men and things ('At least if you don't, you ought to,' from Pax), and you may be sure he'll give us something good."

"And proverbial," added little Grigs.

"Ay, Flint will certainly strike fire out of whatever he tackles," said Big Jack.

("Order!" from Pax.)

"When is he to give it?" asked one.

"Won't fix the time just yet," said Phil.

"What's his subject?" asked another.

"Can't say; not yet decided."

With this uncertainty as to time and subject the association was obliged to rest content, and thereafter the meeting was dissolved.

We are grieved to be obliged to state that the society thus hopefully commenced came to a premature close at an early period of its career, owing to circumstances over which its members had no control.

Some time before that sad event occurred, however, Solomon Flint delivered his discourse, and as some of the events of that memorable evening had special bearing on the issues of our tale, we shall recur to it in a succeeding chapter.

CHAPTER XV.

GEORGE ASPEL RECEIVES VARIOUS VISITORS AT THE ORNITHO-
LOGICAL SHOP, AND IS CALLED TO VIGOROUS ACTION.

As long as a man retains a scrap of self-respect, and struggles, from any motive whatever, against his evil tendencies, his journey to destruction ¹ comparatively slow ; but when once h(despair, assumes that he has tried ¹ and throws the reins on the neck of his passions, his descent into the dark abyss is terribly rapid.

For a time George Aspel was buoyed up by hope. He hoped that May Maylands might yet come to regard him with favour, though she studiously avoided giving him ground for such hope. He also continued, though faintly, to hope that Sir James Clubley might still think of fulfilling his promises, and, in pursuance of that hope, frequently inquired whether any letters had been left for him at the hotel where he first put up on arriving in London. But when both of these hopes forsook him, and he found himself in what he deemed the ridiculous position of shopman to a bird-stuffer, without an influential friend in the great city, or the slightest prospect of improving his condition, he gave way to despair.

Before quite giving way, however, he made several attempts to obtain work more suited to his tastes and acquirements, in which efforts he was heartily seconded by Mr. Enoch Blurt; but Enoch was about as unknown in London as himself, so that their united efforts failed.

In these circumstances the ambitious youth began to regard himself as a martyr to misfortune, and resolved to enjoy himself as he best might. With a view to this he spent his evenings in places of amusement, with companions whose example and influence helped to drag him down and increase his tendency to drink.

This tendency was in part hereditary. His father had been a confirmed drinker. Although well aware of this, he did not believe in his own fallibility. Few young men of his stamp do. Other men might give way to it, but there was no fear of him. He admitted that he could, and sometimes did, take a stiff glass of grog—but what then? It did him no harm. He was not a slave to it. He could give it up and do without it if he chose— although, it is to be remarked, he had never made the trial, and only assumed this power. To be rather "screwed" now and then was, he admitted, somewhat discreditable ; but he wasn't worse than many others, and it didn't occur often. Thus he reasoned, half-justifying himself in a thoroughly selfish, sinful course; growling at his "bad luck," and charging the guilt of his sin, which he said he couldn't help, on Fate—in other words, on God.

It never occurred to George Aspel that the true way to get out of his troubles was to commit his way to his Maker ; to accept the position assigned him ; to do the work of a faithful servant therein ; to get connected with good society through the medium of churches and young men's Christian associations, and to spend a few years in establishing a character for trustworthiness, capacity, vigour, and intelligence, which would secure his advancement in life. At least, if such thoughts did occur to him, he refused to entertain them, and resolved to fling care to the dogs and defy fortune.

Of course, it soon became apparent to his employer that there was a great change for the worse in the youth, whom he not only admired for his frank bearing and strapping appearance, but loved as his deliverer from death. Delicacy of feeling, however, prevented Mr. Blurt from alluding to dissipations at which he could only guess.

Poverty and distress bring about strange companionships. When Aspel first arrived in London he

o

would have scouted the idea of his having anything whatever to do with such a man as Abel Bones, but he had not proceeded far in his downward course when that disreputable character became, if not a companion, at least an acquaintance.

This state of things was brought about primarily by the patronage which Aspel had extended to the "poor worthless fellow" whom he had so unceremoniously knocked down.   But the poor worthless fellow, although born in a lower rank of life, was quite equal to him in natural mental power, and much superior in cunning and villainy.   Mr. Bones had also a bold, reckless air and nature, which were attractive to this descendant of the sea-kings. Moreover, he possessed a power of mingling flattery with humbug in a way that made his victim fall rather easily into his toils.

Revenge, as we have said, lay at the bottom of Abel Bones' desire to become better acquainted with Aspel, but profit soon took the place of revenge. Mr. Bones earned his livelihood chiefly by appropriating what belonged to other people.   He was not particular as to what he took, or how he took it, but on the whole preferred easy work (like most people) and large profit.   Being a man of bold, ambitious views, he had often thought of forgery, but a neglected education stood in the way of that. Being also a man of resource, he did not doubt that this, like many other difficulties, would ere long succumb to his perseverance. While in this frame of mind it occurred to him that he might make a tool of his new acquaintance and would-be patron. At the same time he had penetration enough to perceive that his intended tool was a dangerous instrument, highly-tempered and sharp-set, with a will of its own, not yet quite demoralised, and not by any means to be played with.

It might be tedious to trace the steps and winding ways by which Abel Bones led his victim from one piece of impropriety to another—always concealing his real character, and playing the *rôle* of an unfortunate man, willing to work, but unable to find employment—until he almost had him in his toils.

"It's of no use your dancing attendance on me any longer, Bones," said Aspel one day, as the former appeared at the door of the ornithological shop. "I have all the will to help you, but I have not the power. My friends have failed me, and I can do no more than keep my own soul in my body. You must look to some one else with more influence than I possess."

"That's a bad job, sir," returned Bones, with a downcast look. "I've bin down at the docks all day, an' earned only enough to get a plate of bacon and beans. Surely there's somethin' wrong when a cove that's willin' to work must starve; and there's my wife and child starvin' too. Seems to me that a cove is justified in stealin' in the circumstances."

He cast a sidelong glance at Aspel. It was the first time he had ventured to suggest dishonest intentions. If they should be taken ill, he could turn it off as a jest; if taken well, he could proceed.

"I'm very sorry for you, Bones," said Aspel, not noticing the hint, "very sorry, but what can I do? I have not a copper left beyond what I absolutely require."

"Well, sir, I know that you can do nothing, but now that my wife and child are actually starvin', I really don't see the sin of helpin' myself to a loaf at the nearest baker's, and giving him leg-bail for it."

"Nothing justifies stealing," said Aspel.

"D'ee think not, sir?" said Bones. "If you saw your wife now, supposin' you had one, at the pint of death with hunger, an' you saw a loaf lyin' as didn't belong to you, would you let her die?"

Aspel thought of May Maylands.

"I don't know," he replied, "what I should *do*. All that I say is, that stealing is unjustifiable."

The argument was stopped at this point by the entrance of a small telegraph message-boy.

Bones was startled by his sudden entrance.

"Well, good-night, sir, we'll talk that matter over some other time," he said quickly, pulling his wideawake well over his face as he went out, and giving the message-boy a prolonged stare.

The boy paid no regard to him, but, turning to Aspel, introduced himself as Peter Pax.

" What! the comrade-in-arms of my friend Phil Maylands?" asked Aspel.

" The same, at your service," replied the small messenger; " an' if you are the friend he talks to me so much about, as goes by the name of George Aspel, an' is descended in a direct line from the old sea-kings, I'm proud to make your acquaintance."

Aspel laughed at the consummate self-possession of the boy, and shaking hands with him heartily as a comrade of their common friend Phil, bade him take a seat, which he immediately did on the counter.

" You're surrounded by pleasant company here," observed Pax, gazing intently at the pelican of the wilderness.

" Well, yes ; but it's rather silent company," said Aspel.

" Did that fellow, now," continued Pax, pointing to the owl, " die of surprise ?"

" Perhaps he did, but I wasn't present at his death," returned the other.

" Well, now, I do like this sort o' thing."

Little Pax said this with such genuine feeling, and looked round him with such obvious interest, that Aspel, with some surprise, asked him why he liked it.

" Why ? because from my earliest years I always was fond of animals. No matter what sort they wos, I liked 'em all—birds an' beasts an' fishes, flyers and creepers, an' squeakers and flutterers," said the boy, clasping both hands over one knee, and rocking himself to and fro on the counter, while he gazed into the owl's face with the air of one whose mind is rambling far away into the remote past.

" Once on a time," he continued, sadly, " I dwelt in the country. I was born in the country. I 'm a sort o' country gentleman by nature, so to speak, and would have bin revellin' in the country to this day if a perwerse fate hadn't driven me into the town—a very perwerse fate indeed."

" Indeed ?" said Aspel, unable to restrain a laugh at his visitor's old-fashioned ways, " what sort of fate was it ? "

" A perwerse one, didn't I tell you ?"

" Yes, but wherein consisted its perversity ? How did it act, you know ?"

" Ah, its perwersity consisted in drivin' me into town in a market-cart," said Pax. " You must know that my perwerse fate was a uncle. He was a big brute. I don't mean to speak of 'im disrespectfully. I merely give 'im his proper name. He was a market-gardener and kept cows—also a pump.

He had a wife and child—a little girl. Ah! a sweet child it was."

"Indeed," said Aspel, as the boy relapsed into a silent contemplative gaze at the pelican.

"Yes," resumed Pax, with a sigh, "it *was* a child, that was. Her name was Mariar, but we called 'er Merry. Her father's name—the Brute's, you know —was Blackadder, and a blacker adder don't wriggle its slimy way through filthy slums nowhere—supposin' him to be yet unscragged, for he was uncommon hard on his wife—that's my Aunt Georgie. *Her* name was Georgianna. I wonder how it is that people *never* give people their right names! Well, Mr. Aspel, you must know I was nuss to baby. An amytoor nuss I was—got no pay for it, but a considerable allowance o' kicks from the Brute, who wasn't fond o' me, as I'd done 'im a mortal injury, somehow, by being his defunct brother's orphan child. You understand?"

George Aspel having professed a thorough comprehension of these family relationships, little Pax went on.

"Well then, bein' nuss to Merry, I used to take 'er out long walks in the fields among the flowers, an' I was used to catch butterflies and beetles for 'er, an' brought 'em home an' stuck pins through 'em an' made c'lections; an' oh, I *did* like to scuttle about the green lanes an' chase the cows, an' roll on

the grass in the sunshine with Merry, an' tear an
bu'st my trousers, for w'ich I got spanked by the
Brute, but didn't care a rap, because that brought
me double allowance o' coddlin' from Aunt Georgie.
One day the Brute drove me into town in the
market-cart; set me down in the middle of a street,
and drove away, an' I haven't seen him, nor Aunt
Georgie, nor Merry from that day to this."

"Dear me!" exclaimed George Aspel, rather
shocked at this sudden and unexpected termination
of the narrative ; "do you mean to say—"

"It strikes me," interrupted Pax, looking pointedly
at the door, "that you've got another visitor."

Aspel turned and saw the dishevelled curls and
pretty face of Tottie Bones in the doorway.

"Please, sir," she said, entering, "I didn't like to
interrupt you, but Miss Lillycrop sent me to say
that there was a strange smell of singein' in the
'ouse, an' would Mr. Aspel be so kind as to come
and try to find out where it was, as she didn't
understand such things."

"Smell of singeing, child!" exclaimed Aspel,
rising at once and putting on his coat and hat.
"Did you search for the cause, especially about
your kitchen fireplace ?"

"O yes, sir," exclaimed Tottie, "an' we couldn't
see no cause at all—only the flue seemed to be
'otter than usual.   We looked all over the 'ouse too,

but couldn't see nothink—but we could feel a most drefful smell."

Desiring Mrs. Murridge to call Mr. Blurt to attend to the shop, George Aspel hurried out.

"Don't try to keep up with us," said Aspel to Tottie ; "I must run.   It may be fire !"

"Oh ! please, sir, don't leave me behind," pleaded the child.

"All right—we won't ; kitch hold of my hand ; give the other to Mr. Aspel," said Peter Pax.

Holding on to her two friends, Tottie was swept along the streets at a rate which she had never before experienced—at least not as a foot-passenger, —and in a few minutes they were in Miss Lilly-crop's dwelling.

That excellent lady was in a state of dreadful perturbation, as well she might be, for the house was filled with a thin smoke of very peculiar odour.

Few persons except the initiated are fully alive to the immense importance of checking fire at its commencement.   The smoke, although not dense enough to attract the attention of people outside, was sufficiently so to make those inside commence an anxious search, when they should have sent at once for the fire-engine.

Three families occupied the tenement.   Miss Lillycrop's portion was at the top.   A dealer in oils and stores of a miscellaneous and unsavoury kind occupied the basement.

George Aspel at once suspected and made for this point, followed by Miss Lillycrop, who bade Tottie remain in her kitchen, with the intention of keeping her at once out of danger and out of the way.

"There's certainly fire somewhere, Pax; run, call the engines out," said Aspel, descending three steps at a time.

Pax took the last six steps at a bound, and rushed along the street, overturning in his flight two boys bigger than himself, and a wheelbarrow.

The owner of the cellars was absent and his door locked. Where was the key? No one knew, but George Aspel knew of a key that had done some service in times past. He retreated a few steps, and, rushing at the door with all his weight and momentum, dashed it in with a tremendous crash, and went headlong into the cellar, from out of which came belching flames and smoke. Re-issuing instantly therefrom with singed hair and glaring eyes, he found Miss Lillycrop lying on her back in a faint, where the fire and smoke had floored her. To gather her up and dash into the street was the work of a moment. Scarcely less rapid was the rush of the fire, which, having been richly fed and long pent up in the cellar, now dashed up the staircases like a giant refreshed,

Meanwhile little Pax ran headlong into a police-man, and was collared and throttled.

"Now then, young 'un!"

"Fire! station!" gasped Pax.

"All right, this way—just round the corner," said the man in blue, releasing his captive, and running along with him; but the man in blue was stout, middle-aged, and heavy. Pax outran him, saw the red lamp, found the fire-station door open, and leaped through with a yell of "*Fire!*" that nearly split his little lungs.

The personification of calmness in the form of a fireman rose and demanded "Where?"

Before Pax could gasp the address, two other personifications of calmness, who had been snoring on trestle-beds, dressed and booted, when he entered, now moved swiftly out, axed and helmeted. There was a clattering of hoofs outside. The double doors flew open, and the red engine rolled out almost of its own accord. More brass helmets were seen flashing outside.

"Are you sure of the address, youngster?" asked one of the imperturbable firemen, settling his chin-strap more comfortably.

"Are you sure o' your own grandmother?" said Pax.

"You're cheeky," replied the man, with a smile.

"You make haste," retorted Pax; "three minutes

allowed to get under weigh.   Two and a half gone already.   Two-and-six fine if late, besides a—"

The whip cracked, and Pax, leaping forward, seized the side of the engine.   Six brass helmets bounded into the air, and their owners settled on their seats, as the horses made that momentary pause and semi-rear which often precedes a dashing start.   The man whom he had been insulting held out a hand; Pax seized it, and was next moment in a terrestrial heaven, while calmness personified sauntered into the back office to make a note of the circumstance, and resume his pipe.

Oh! it was a brief but maddening ride.   To ex- perience such a magnificent rush seemed to Pax worth living for.   It was not more than half-a-mile ; but in that brief space there were three corners to turn like zigzag lightning, which they did chiefly on the two near wheels, and there were carts, vans, cabs, drays, apple-stalls, children, dogs, and cats innumerable.   To have run over or upset these would have been small gratification to the com- paratively tender spirit of Pax, but to *shave* them ; to graze the apple-stalls ; to just scrape a lamp-post with your heart in your mouth ; to hear the tremendous roar of the firemen ; to see the abject terror of some people, the excitement of others, the obedient " skedaddling " of all, while the sparks from the pump-boiler trailed behind, and the two

bull's-eyes glared ahead, so that the engine resembled some awful monster rushing through thick
and thin, and waving in triumph its fiery tail—ah!
words are but feeble exponents of thought: it was
excruciating ecstasy! To have been born for this
one burst, and died, would have been better than
never to have been born at all,—in the estimation
of the enthusiastic Peter Pax!

A few minutes after George Aspel had borne
the fainting Miss Lillycrop from the house the
engine arrived. Some of the men swarmed into
the house, and dived to the basement, as if fire
and smoke were their natural food. Others got
the engine to work in a few seconds, but already
the flames had rushed into the lower rooms and
passages and licked away the windows. The thick
stream of water had just begun to descend on the
fire, when another engine came rattling to the field,
and its brazen-headed warriors leaped down to join
the battle.

"Oh!" groaned Miss Lillycrop at that moment,
recovering in Aspel's arms. "Oh! Tottie—
To-o-o-o-tie's in the kitchen!"

Little Pax heard and understood. In one
moment he bounded through the blazing doorway
and up the smoking stair.

Just then the fire-escape came into view, towering up against the black sky.

" Hold her, some one !" cried Aspel, dropping his poor burden into the ready arms of a policeman.

" The boy's lost !" he exclaimed, leaping after Pax.

Aspel was a practised diver. Many a time had he tried his powers under the Atlantic waves on the west of Ireland. He drew one long breath, and was in the attic kitchen before it was expended. Here he found little Pax and Tottie on the floor. The former had fallen, suffocated, in the act of hauling the latter along by the hair of the head. Aspel did not see them. He stumbled over them, grasped both in his strong arms, and bore them to the staircase. It was by that time a roaring furnace. His power of retaining breath was exhausted. In desperation he turned sharp to the right, and dashed in Miss Lillycrop's drawing-room door, just as the fire-escape performed the same feat on one of the windows. The gush of air drove back the smoke for one moment. Gasping and reeling to the window, Aspel hurled the children into the bag of the escape. He retained sufficient power to plunge in head first after them and ram them down its throat. All three arrived at the bottom in a state of insensibility.

In this state they were borne to a neighbouring house, and soon restored to consciousness.

The firemen battled there during the greater part

of that night, and finally gained the victory ; but, before this happy consummation was attained, poor Miss Lillycrop's home was gutted and her little property reduced to ashes.

In these circumstances she and her little maid found a friend in need in Miss Stivergill, and an asylum in Rosebud Cottage.

CHAPTER XVI.

BEGINS WITH JUVENILE FLIRTATION, AND ENDS WITH CANINE CREMATION.

THE disreputable nature of the wind which blows good to nobody has been so frequently referred to and commented on by writers in general that it merits only passing notice here. The particular breeze which fanned the flames that consumed the property that belonged to Miss Lillycrop, and drove that lady to a charming retreat in the country, thereby rescuing her from a trying existence in town, also blew small Peter Pax in the same direction.

"Boy," said Miss Stivergill in stern tones, on the occasion of her first visit to the hospital in which Pax was laid up for a short time after his adventure, "you 're a good boy. I like you. The first of your sex I ever said that to."

"Thank you, ma'am. I hope I shan't be the last," returned Pax languidly, for he was still weak from the effects of the partial roasting and suffocation he had undergone.

"Miss Lillycrop desired me to come and see you," resumed Miss Stivergill. "She has told me how bravely you tried to rescue poor little Bones, who—"

"Not much hurt, I hope?" asked the boy eagerly.

"No, very little—scarcely at all, I'm glad to say. Those inexplicable creatures called firemen, who seem to me what you may call fire-fiends of a good-natured and recklessly hilarious type, say that her having fallen down with her nose close to the ground, where there is usually a free current of air, saved her. At all events she *is* saved, and quite well."

"I hope I didn't haul much of the hair out of her poor head?" said Pax.

"Apparently not, if one may judge from the very large quantity that remains," replied his visitor.

"You see, ma'am, in neck-or-nothin' scrimmages o' that sort," continued Pax, in the off-hand tone of one much experienced in such scrimmages, "one can't well stop to pick and choose; besides, I couldn't see well, d'ee see? an' her hair came first to hand, you know, an' was convenient. It's well for both on us, however, that that six foot odd o' magnificence came to the rescue in time. I like 'im, I do, an' shall owe 'im a good turn for savin' little Bones.—What was her other name, did you say, ma'am?"

"I didn't mention any other name, but I believe

P

it is Tottie.—Now, little Peter, when the doctor gives you leave to be moved, you are to come to me to recruit your health in the country."

"Thank you, ma'am. You're too good," said Pax, becoming languid again. "Pray give my best respects to Tottie and Miss Lillycrop."

"So small, and so pretty, and such a wise little thing," murmured Miss Stivergill, unaware, apparently, that she soliloquised aloud.

"So big, and so ugly, and such a good-hearted stoopid old thing!" murmured Pax; but it is only just to add that he was too polite to allow the murmur to be heard.

"Good-bye, little Peter, till we meet again," said Miss Stivergill, turning away abruptly.

"Farewell, ma'am," said Pax, "farewell; and if for ever—"

He stopped, because his visitor was gone.

According to this arrangement, Pax found himself, not many days after, revelling in the enjoyment of what he styled "tooral-ooral" felicity—among cows and hay, sunshine and milk, buttercups and cream, green meadows and blue skies,—free as a butterfly from telegraphic messagery and other postal cares. He was allowed to ramble about at will, and, as little Bones was supposed to be slightly invalided by her late semi-suffocation, she was frequently allowed by her indulgent mistress to accompany him.

Seated on a stile one day, Pax drew Tottie out as to her early life, and afterwards gave an account of his own in exchange.

"How strange," said Tottie, "that you and I should both have had bybies to nuss w'en we was young, ain't it?"

"It is, Tot—very remarkable. And we've had a sad fate, both of us, in havin' bin wrenched from our babbies. But the wrench couldn't have bin so bad in your case as in mine, of course, for your babby was nobody to you, whereas mine was a full cousin, an' such a dear one too. Oh, Tot, you've no notion what splendid games we used to have, an' such c'lections of things I used to make for 'er! Of course she was too young to understand it, you know, for she could neither walk nor speak, and I don't think could understand, though she crowed sometimes as if she did. My! how she crowed! —But what's the matter, Tot?"

Tottie was pouting.

"I don't like your bybie at all—not one bit," she said emphatically.

"Not like my babby!" exclaimed Pax.

"No, I don't, 'cause it isn't 'alf so good as mine."

"Well," returned Pax, with a smile, "I was took from mine. I didn't forsake it like you."

"I *didn't* forsake it," cried Tottie, with flashing eyes, and shaking her thick curls indignantly—

which latter, by the way, since her coming under the stern influence of Miss Stivergill, had been disentangled, and hung about her like a golden glory.—" I left it to go to service, and mother takes care of it till I return home.   I won't speak to you any more.   I hate *your* bybie, and I *adore* mine !"

So saying, little Bones jumped up and ran away. Small Pax made no attempt to stop her or to follow. He was too much taken aback by the sudden burst of passion to be able for more than a prolonged whistle, followed by a still more prolonged stare. Thereafter he sauntered away slowly, ruminating, perhaps, on the fickle character of woman, even in her undeveloped stages.

Tottie climbed hastily over a stile and turned into a green lane, where she meant to give full vent to her feelings in a satisfactory cry, when she was met face to face by Mr. Abel Bones.

" Why, father !" she exclaimed, running to her sire with a look of joyful surprise, for occasional bad treatment had failed to dry up the bottomless well of love in her little heart.

" Hush ! Tottie ; there—take my hand, an' don't kick up such a row.   You needn't look so scared at seein' me here.   I 'm fond o' the country, you know, an' I 've come out to 'ave a little walk and a little talk with you.—Who was that you was talkin' with just now ?"

Tottie told him.

"Stoppin' here, I s'pose?"

"Yes. He's bin here for some time, but goes away soon—now that he's better. It was him as saved my life—at least him and Mr. Aspel, you know."

"No, I don't know, Tot. Let's hear all about it," replied Mr. Bones, with a look of unwonted gravity.

Tottie went off at once into a glowing account of the fire and the rescue, to which her father listened with profound attention, not unmingled with surprise. Then he reverted to the aspect of the surrounding country.

"It's a pretty place you live in here, Tot, an' a nice house. It's there the lady lives, I suppose, who has the strange fancy to keep her wealth in a box on the side-board? Well, it *is* curious, but there's no accountin' for the fancies o' the rich, Tot. An' you say she keeps no men-servants about her? Well, that's wise, for men are dangerous characters for women to 'ave about 'em. She's quite right. There's a dear little dog too, she keeps, I'm told. Is that the only one she owns?"

"Yes, it's the only one, and such a darlin' it is, and *so* fond of me!" exclaimed Tottie.

"Ah, yes, wery small, but wery noisy an' vicious," remarked Mr. Bones, with a sudden scowl, which fortunately his daughter did not see.

"O no, father; little Floppart ain't vicious, though it *is* awful noisy w'en it chooses."

"Well, Tot, I'd give a good deal to see that dear little Floppart, and make friends with it. D'you think you could manage to get it to follow you here?"

"Oh, easily. I'll run an' fetch it; but p'r'aps you had better come to the house. I know they'd like to see you, for they're *so* kind to me."

Mr. Bones laughed sarcastically, and expressed his belief that they wouldn't like to see him at all.

Just at that moment Miss Stivergill came round the turn of the lane and confronted them.

"Well, little Bones, whom have you here?" asked the lady, with a stern look at Mr. Bones.

"Please, ma'am, it's father. He 'appened to be in this neighbourhood, and came to see me."

"Your father!" exclaimed Miss Stivergill, with a look of surprise. "Indeed!"

"Yes, ma'am," said Bones, politely taking off his hat and looking her coolly in the face. "I 'ope it's no offence, but I came a bit out o' my way to see 'er. She says you've bin' wery kind to her."

"Well, she says the truth. I mean to be kind to her," returned Miss Stivergill, as sternly as before. —"Take your father to the cottage, child, and tell them to give him a glass of beer. If you see Miss Lillycrop, tell her I've gone to the village, and won't be back for an hour." So saying, Miss Stivergill walked down the lane with masculine strides, leaving Tottie pleased, and her father smiling.

"I don't want no beer, Tot," said the latter. "But you go to the cottage and fetch me that dear little dog. I want to see it; and don't forget the lady's message to Miss Lillycrop—but be sure you don't say I'm waitin' for you. Don't mention me to nobody. D'ee understand?"

Poor Tottie, with a slight and undefined misgiving at her heart, professed to understand, and went off.

In a few minutes she returned with the little dog —a lively poodle—which at first showed violent and unmistakable objections to being friendly with Mr. Bones. But a scrap of meat, which that worthy had brought in his pocket, and a few soothing words, soon modified the objection.

Presently Mr. Bones pulled a small muzzle from his pocket.

"D'you think, now, that Floppart would let you put it on 'er, Tot?"

Tot was sure she would, and soon had the muzzle on.

"That's right; now, hold 'er fast a moment— just a—there— !"

He sprang at and caught the dog by the throat, choked a snarling yelp in the bud, and held it fast.

" Dear, dear, how wild it has got all of a sudden !
W'y, it must be ill—p'r'aps mad.   It's well you put
that muzzle on, Tot."

While he spoke Abel Bones thrust the dog into
one of the capacious pockets of his coat.

" Now, Tot," he said, somewhat sternly, " I durstn't
let this dog go.   It wants a doctor very bad.   You
go back to the 'ouse and tell 'em a man said so.
You needn't say what man ; call me a philanthropist
if you choose, an' tell 'em I'll send it back w'en it
recovers.   But you needn't tell 'em anything until
you're axed, you know—it might get me into trouble,
d'ee see, an' say to Miss Stivergill it wasn't your
father as took the dog, but another man."

He leaped over a low part of the hedge and was
gone, leaving poor Tottie in a state of bewildered
anxiety on the other side.

Under the influence of fear Tottie told the lies
her father had bid her tell, and thereafter dwelt at
Rosebud Cottage with an evil conscience and a
heavy heart.

Having gained the high-road, Mr. Bones sauntered
easily to the railway station, took a third-class
ticket for Charing Cross, and in due time found himself passing along the Strand.   In the course of that
journey poor little Floppart lay on its back in the
bottom of its captor's pocket, with a finger and
thumb gently pressing her windpipe.   Whenever

she became restive, the finger and thumb tightened, and this with such unvarying regularity that she soon came to understand the advantage of lying still. She did, however, make sundry attempts to escape—once very violently, when the guard was opening the carriage-door to let Mr. Bones enter, and again almost as violently at Charing Cross, when Mr. Bones got out. Indeed, the dog had wellnigh got off, and was restored to its former place and position with difficulty.

Turning into Chancery Lane, and crossing over to Holborn, Abel Bones continued his way to Newgate, where, appropriately enough, he stopped and gazed grimly up at the massive walls.

" Don't be in a 'urry," said a very small boy, with dirt and daring in equal proportions on his face, " it 'll wait for you."

Mr. Bones made a tremendous demonstration of an intention to rush at the boy, who precipitately fled, and the former passed quietly on.

At St. Martin's-le-Grand he paused again.

"Strange," he muttered, " there seems to be some sort o' fate as links me wi' that Post-Office. It was here I began my London life as a porter, and lost my situation because the Postmaster-General couldn't see the propriety of my opening letters that contained coin and postage-stamps and fi'-pun' notes, which was quite unreasonable, for I had a special

talent that way, and even the clargy tell us that
our talents was given us to be used.   It wasn't far
from here where I sot my little nephy down, that
time I got rid of him, and it was goin' up these wery
steps I met with the man I'm tryin' my best to
bring to grief, an' that same man wants to marry
one of the girls in the Post-Office, and now, I find,
has saved my Tot from bein' burnt alive !   Wery
odd !   It was here, too, that—"

Floppart at this moment turned the flow of his
meditations by making a final and desperate struggle
to be free.   She shot out of his pocket and dropped
with a bursting yell on the pavement.   Recovering
her feet before Bones recovered from his surprise,
she fled.   Thought is quick as the lightning-flash.
Bones knew that dogs find their way home mysteri-
ously from any distance.   He knew himself to be
unable to run down Floppart.   He saw his schemes
thwarted.   He adopted a mean device, shouted
" Mad dog !" and rushed after it.   A small errand-
boy shrieked with glee, flung his basket at it, and
followed up the chase.   Floppart took round by St.
Paul's Churchyard.   However sane she might have
been at starting, it is certain that she was mad with
terror in five minutes.   She threaded her way among
wheels and legs at full speed in perfect safety.   It
was afterwards estimated that seventeen cabmen,
four gentlemen, two apple-women, three and-twenty

errand-boys—more or less,—and one policeman, flung umbrellas, sticks, baskets, and various missiles at her, with the effect of damaging innumerable shins and overturning many individuals, but without hurting a hair of Floppart's body during her wild but brief career. Bones did not wish to recapture her. He wished her dead, and for that end loudly reiterated the calumny as to madness. Floppart circled round the grand cathedral erected by Wren, and got into Cheapside. Here, doubling like a hare, she careered round the statue of Peel and went blindly back to St. Martin's-le-Grand, as if to add yet another link to the chain of fate which bound her arch-pursuer to the General Post-Office. By way of completing the chain, she turned in at the gate, rushed to the rear of the building, dashed in at an open door, and skurried along a passage. Here the crowd was stayed, but the policeman followed heroically. The passage was cut short by a glass door, but a narrow staircase descended to the left. "Any port in a storm" is a proverb as well known among dogs as men. Down went Floppart to the basement of the building, invading the sanctity of the letter-carriers' kitchen or *salle-à-manger*. A dozen stalwart postmen leaped from their meals to rush at the intruder. In the midst of the confusion the policeman's truncheon was seen to sway aloft. Next instant the vaulted roof rang with a

terrible cry, which truth compels us to state was
Floppart's dying yell.

None of those who had begun the chase were in
at the death—save the policeman,—not even Abel
Bones, for that worthy did not by any means court
publicity. Besides, he felt pretty sure that his end
was gained. He remembered, no doubt, the rule of
the Office, that no letters or other things that have
been posted can be returned to the sender, and,
having seen the dog safely posted, he went home
with a relieved mind.

Meanwhile the policeman took the remains of
poor Floppart by the tail, holding it at arm's-length
for fear of the deadly poison supposed to be on its
lips, and left the kitchen by a long passage. The
men of the Post-Office returned to their food and
their duties. Those who manage the details of her
Majesty's mails cannot afford to waste time when on
duty. The policeman, left to himself, lost himself
in the labyrinth of the basement. He made his way
at last into the warm and agreeable room in which
are kept the boilers that drive the engine that works
the lifts. He was accosted by a stalwart stoker,
whose appearance and air were as genial as the
atmosphere of his apartment.

"Hallo!" said he, "what 'ave you got there?"

"A mad dog," answered the policeman.—"I say,
stoker, have you any ashpit where I could bury him?"

"Couldn't allow 'im burial in our ashpit," replied the stoker, with a decided shake of the head ; "altogether out of the question."

The policeman looked at the dead dog and at the stoker with a perplexed air.

"I say, look here," he said, "couldn't we—ah— don't you think that we might—"

He paused, and cast a furtive glance at the furnaces.

"What! you don't mean—cremate 'im ?"

The policeman nodded.

"Well, now, I don't know that it's actooally against the rules of the G.P.O.," replied the stoker, with a meditative frown, "but it seems to me a raither unconstitootional proceedin'. It's out o' the way of our usual line of business, but—"

"That's right," said the policeman, as the stoker, who was an obliging man, took up a great shovel and flung open the furnace-door.

A terrific glare of intense heat and light shot out, appearing as if desirous of licking the stoker and policeman into its dreadful embrace.

"I don't half like it," said the stoker, glancing in ; "the Postmaster-General might object, you know."

"Not a bit of it, he's too much of a gentleman to object—come," said the policeman encouragingly.

The stoker held up the shovel. The body of Floppart was put thereon, after the removal of its collar.   There was one good swing of the shovel, followed by a heave, and the little dog fell into the heart of the fiery furnace.   The stoker shut the great iron door with a clang, and looked at the police-man solemnly.   The policeman returned the look, thanked him, and retired.   In less probably than three minutes Floppart's body was reduced to its gaseous elements, vomited forth from the furnace chimney, and finally dissipated by the winds of heaven.

Thus did this, the first recorded and authentic case of cremation in the United Kingdom, emanate— as many a new, advantageous, and national measure has emanated before—from the prolific womb of the General Post-Office.

CHAPTER XVII.

TOTTIE AND MRS. BONES IN DIFFICULTY.

THE descent of George Aspel became very rapid in
course of time. As he lost self-respect he became reckless and, as a natural consequence, more dissipated.
Remonstrances from his friend Mr. Blurt, which
were repelled at first with haughty disdain, came to
be received with sullen indifference. He had nothing to say for himself in reply, because, in point
of fact, there was nothing in his case to justify his
taking so gloomy and despairing a view of life.
Many men, he knew, were at his age out of
employment, and many more had been crossed
in love. He was too proud to condescend to false
reasoning with his lips, though he encouraged it in
his heart. He knew quite well that drink and bad
companionship were ruining him, and off-hand, open-
hearted fellow though he was said to be, he was mean
enough, as we have already said, to growlingly
charge his condition and his sins on Fate.

At last he resolved to give up the business that

was so distasteful to him.   Unable to give a satisfactory reason for so doing, or to say what he meant
to attempt next, and unwilling or ashamed to incur
the remonstrances and rebut the arguments of his
patron, the bold descendant of the sea-kings adopted
that cowardly method of departure called taking
French leave.   Like some little schoolboy, he ran
away !   In other words, he disappeared, and left no
trace behind him.

Deep was Mr. Enoch Blurt's regret, for he loved
the youth sincerely, and made many fruitless efforts
to find him—for lost in London means lost indeed !
He even employed a detective, but the grave man
in grey—who looked like no class of man in particular, and seemed to have no particular business
in hand, and who talked with Mr. Blurt, at their
first meeting, in a quiet, sensible, easy way, as
though he had been one of his oldest friends—could
find no clew to him, for the good reason that Mr.
Bones had taken special care to entice Aspel into
a distant locality, under pretence of putting him in
the way of finding semi-nautical employment about
the docks.   Moreover, he managed to make Aspel
drunk, and arranged with boon companions to strip
him, while in that condition, of his garments, and
re-clothe him in the seedy garb peculiar to those
gentlemen who live by their wits.

"Very strange," muttered Aspel, on recovering

sufficiently to be led by his friend towards Arch-angel Court,—"very strange that I did not feel the scoundrels robbing me. I must have slept very soundly."

"Yes, you slep' wery sound, and they're a bad lot, and uncommon sharp in that neighbourhood. It's quite celebrated. I tried to get you away, but you was as obstinate as a mule, an' kep' on singing about some sort o' coves o' the old times that must have bin bigger blackguards than we 'ave about us now-a days, though the song calls 'em glorious."

"Well, well," said Aspel, shrinking under the public gaze as he passed through the streets, "don't talk about that. Couldn't you get into some by-lanes, where there are not so many people? I don't like to be seen, even by strangers, in this disreputable guise. I wish the sun didn't shine so brightly. Come, push on, man."

"W'y, sir," said Bones, becoming a little more respectful in spite of himself, "you've no need to be ashamed of your appearance. There's not 'alf a dozen people in a mile walk in London as would look twice at you whatever appearance you cut— so long as it was only disreputable."

"Never mind—push on," said Aspel sternly; "I *am* ashamed whether I have need to be or not. I'm a fool. I'm more—I'm a brute. I tell you what it is, Bones, I'm determined to turn over a new leaf.

Q

I 'll write to Mr. Blurt and tell him where I am, for, of course, I can't return to him in such clothes as these, and—and—I 'll give up drink."

Bones met this remark with an unexpected and bitter laugh.

" What d' you mean ?" demanded Aspel, turning fiercely upon him.

" I mean," replied Bones, returning his stare with the utmost coolness, " that you *can't* give up drink, if you was to try ever so much.   You 're too far gone in it.   I 've tried it myself, many a time, and failed, though I 've about as strong a will as your own— maybe stronger."

" We shall see," returned Aspel, as they moved on again and turned into the lane which led to the wretched abode of Bones.

" Bring me pen, ink, and paper !" he exclaimed, on entering the room, with a grand air—for a pint of ale, recently taken, had begun to operate.

Bones, falling in with his friend's humour, rummaged about until he found the stump of a quill, a penny inkbottle, and a dirty sheet of paper.   These he placed on a rickety table, and Aspel wrote a scrawly note, in which he gave himself very bad names, and begged Mr. Blurt to come and see him, as he had got into a scrape, and could by no means see his way out of it.   Having folded the note very badly, he rose with the intention of going out to post it, but his friend offered to post it for him.

Accepting the offer, he handed him the note and flung himself down in a heap on the straw mattress in the dark corner, where he had first become acquainted with Bones. In a few seconds he was in a deep lethargic slumber.

"What a wretched spectacle!" exclaimed Bones, touching him with his toe, and, in bitter mockery, quoting the words that Aspel had once used regarding himself.

He turned to leave the room, and was met by Mrs. Bones.

"There's a friend o' yours in the corner, Molly. Don't disturb him. I'm goin' to post a letter for him, and will be back directly."

Bones went out, posted the letter in the common sewer, and returned home.

During the brief interval of his absence Tottie had come in—on a visit after her prolonged sojourn in the country. She was strangling her mother with a kiss when he entered.

"Oh, mother! I'm *so* happy, and *so* sorry!" she exclaimed, laughing and sobbing at once.

Tottie was obviously torn by conflicting emotions.

"Take your time, darling," said Mrs. Bones, smoothing the child's hair with her red toil-worn hand.

"Ay, take it easy, Tot," said her father, with a meaning glance, that sent a chill to the child's heart, while he sat down on a stool and began to fill his pipe. "What's it all about?"

"Oh! it's the beautiful country I've been in. Mother, you can't think—the green fields and the trees, and, oh! the flowers, and no bricks—almost no houses—and—But did you know"—her grief recurred here—"that Mr. Aspel 'as bin lost? an' I've been tellin' *such* lies! We came in to town, Miss Lillycrop an' me, and we've heard about Mr. Aspel from old Mr. Blurt, who's tryin' to find him out with 'vertisements in the papers an' detectives an' a message-boy they call Phil, who's a friend of Mr. Aspel, an' also of Peter."

"Who's Peter?" asked Mrs. Bones.

"Ah, who's Peter?" echoed Mr. Bones, with a somewhat sly glance under his brows.

"He's a message-boy, and such a dear fellow," replied Tottie. "I don't know his other name, he didn't mention it, and they only call him little Peter, but he saved me from the fire; at least he tried—"

"Saved you from the fire!" exclaimed Mrs. Bones in amazement.

"Yes; didn't Miss Lillycrop tell you?" asked Tottie in no less surprise.

Now it is but justice to Miss Lillycrop to say that even in the midst of her perturbation after the

fire she sought to inform Mrs. Bones of her child's
safety, and sent her a note, which failed to reach her,
owing to her being away at the time on one of her
prolonged absences from home, and the neighbour to
whose care it had been committed had forgotten all
about it.   As Mrs. Bones read no newspapers and
took no interest in fires, she knew nothing about
the one that had so nearly swallowed up Tottie.

"Come, tell us all about it, Tot.   You mentioned
it to me, but we couldn't go into details at the time,"
said her father, puffing a vigorous cloud of smoke
into the chimney.

Nothing loath, the child gave her parents an account of the event, which was as glowing as the fire
itself.   As she dwelt with peculiar delight on the
brave rescue effected by Aspel at the extreme peril
of his life, conscience took Abel Bones by surprise
and gave him a twinge.

At that moment the sleeper in the corner heaved
a deep sigh and turned round towards the light.
Mrs. Bones and the child recognised him at once,
and half rose.

"Keep still!" said Bones, in a low savage growl,
which was but too familiar to his poor wife and
child.   "Now, look here," he continued in the same
voice, laying down his pipe,—"if either of you two
tell man, woman, or child w'ere George Aspel is,
it'll be the death of you both, and of him too."

"Oh, Abel! Don't be hard on us," pleaded his wife. "You would—no, you *can't* mean to do 'im harm!"

"No, I won't hurt him," said Bones, "but you must both give me your word that you'll make no mention of him or his whereabouts to any one till I give you leave."

They were obliged to promise, and Bones, knowing from experience that he could trust them, was satisfied.

"But you'll make a promise to me too, Abel, won't you, dear?" said Mrs. Bones; "you'll promise not to do 'im harm of any kind—not to tempt 'im?"

"Yes, Molly, I promise that."

Mrs. Bones knew, by some peculiarity in the tone of her husband's voice, that he meant what he said, and was also satisfied.

"Now, Molly," said Bones, with a smile, "I want you to write a letter for me, so get another sheet of paper, if you can; Mr. Aspel used up my last one."

A sheet was procured from a neighbouring tobacconist. Mrs. Bones always acted as her husband's amanuensis (although he wrote very much better than she did), either because he was lazy, or because he entertained some fear of his handwriting being recognised by his enemies the police! Squaring her elbows, and with her head very much on one side—almost reposing on the left arm—Mrs. Bones produced a series of hieroglyphics which might have been made by a fly half drowned in ink attempting to recover itself on the paper.   The letter ran as follows :—

"Deer bil i am agoin to doo it on mundy the 15th tother cove wont wurk besides Iv chaningd my mind about him.   dont fale."

"What 's the address, Abel ? ' asked Mrs. Bones.

" Willum Stiggs," replied her husband.

"So—i—g—s," said Mrs. Bones, writing very slowly, " Rosebud Cottage."

" What !" exclaimed the man fiercely, as he started up.

" Oh, I declare !" said Mrs. Bones, with a laugh, "if that place that Tottie's been tellin' us of ain't runnin' in my 'ead.   But I 've not writ it, Abel, I only said it."

" Well, then, don't say it again," growled Bones, with a suspicious glance at his wife ; " write number 6 Little Alley, Birmingham."

"So—numr sx littlaly bringinghum," said Mrs. Bones, completing her task with a sigh.

When Bones went out to post this curious epistle, his wife took Tottie on her knee, and, embracing her, rocked to and fro, uttering a moaning sound. The child expressed anxiety, and tried to comfort her.

"Come what's the use o' strivin' against it?" she exclaimed suddenly. "She's sure to come to know it in the end, and I need advice from some one—if it was even from a child."

Tottie listened with suspense and some anxiety.

"You've often told me, mother, that the best advice comes from God. So has Miss Lillycrop."

Mrs. Bones clasped the child still closer, and uttered a short, fervent cry for help.

"Tottie," she said, "listen—you're old enough to understand, I think. Your father is a bad man —at least, I won't say he's altogether bad, but— but, he's not good."

Tottie quite understood that, but said that she was fond of him notwithstanding.

"Fond of 'im, child!" cried Mrs. Bones, "that's the difficulty. I'm so fond of 'im that I want to save him, but I don't know how."

Hereupon the poor woman explained her difficulties. She had heard her husband murmuring in his sleep something about committing a burglary, and the words Rosebud Cottage had more than once escaped his lips.

"Now, Tottie dear," said Mrs. Bones firmly, " when I heard you tell all about that Rosebud Cottage, an' the treasure Miss Stiffinthegills—"

" Stivergill, mother."

" Well, Stivergill. It ain't a pretty name, which-

ever way you put it. When I heard of the treasure
she's so foolish as to keep on her sideboard, I felt
sure that your father had made up his mind to rob
Miss Stivergill—with the help of that bad man Bill
Stiggs—all the more w'en I see how your father
jumped w'en I mentioned Rosebud Cottage. Now,
Tottie, we *must* save your father. If he had only
got me to post his letter, I could easily have
damaged the address so as no one could read it. As
it is, I've writ it so bad that I don't believe there's
a man in the Post-Office could make it out. This
is the first time, Tottie, that your father has made
up his mind to break into a 'ouse, but when he do
make up his mind to a thing he's sure to go through
with it. He must be stopped, Tottie, somehow—
must be stopped—but I don't see how."

Tottie, who was greatly impressed with the
anxious determination of her mother, and therefore
with the heinous nature of her father's intended sin,
gave her entire mind to this subject, and, after talking it over, and looking at it in all lights, came to
the conclusion that she could not see her way out
of the difficulty at all.

While the two sat gazing on the ground with
dejected countenances, a gleam of light seemed to
shoot from Tottie's eyes.

"Oh! I've got it!" she cried, looking brightly
up. "Peter!"

"What! the boy you met at Rosebud Cottage?" asked Mrs. Bones.

"Yes. He's *such* a nice boy, and you've no idea, mother, what a inventor he is. He could invent anythink, I do believe—if he tried, and I'm sure he'll think of some way to help us."

Mrs. Bones was not nearly so hopeful as her daughter in regard to Peter, but as she could think of nothing herself, it was agreed that Tottie should go at once to the Post-Office and inquire after Peter. She did so, and returned crestfallen with the news that Peter was away on a holiday until the following Monday.

"Why, that's the 15th," said Mrs. Bones anxiously. "You must see him that day, Tottie dear, though I fear it will be too late. How did you find him out? There must be many Peters among the telegraph boys."

"To be sure there are, but there are not many Peters who have helped to save a little girl from a fire, you know," said Tottie, with a knowing look. 'They knew who I wanted at once, and his other name is such a funny one; it is Pax—"

"What?" exclaimed Mrs. Bones, with a sudden look of surprise.

"Pax, mother; Peter Pax."

Whatever Mrs. Bones might have replied to this

was checked by the entrance of her husband. She
cautioned Tottie, in earnest, hurried tones, to say
nothing about Rosebud Cottage unless asked, and
especially to make no mention whatever of the
name of Pax.

CHAPTER XVIII.

BUSINESS INTERFERED WITH IN A REMARKABLE MANNER.

The modest estimate which Mrs. Bones had formed of her penmanship turned out to be erroneous, and her opinion that there was not a man in the Post-Office able to read it was ill-founded. She was evidently ignorant of the powers and intelligence of the Blind Division.

To make this more plain we will follow the letter. You and I, reader, will post ourselves, as it were, and pass through the General Post-Office unstamped. At a few minutes to six P.M. the mouth is wide enough to admit us bodily. Mr. Bones has just put in his epistle and walked away with the air of a man who feels that he has committed himself, and is "in for it." He might have posted it at an office or a pillar nearer home, but he has an idea, founded no doubt on experience, that people, especially policemen, are apt to watch his movements and prefers a longish walk to the General.

There! we take a header and descend with the cataract into the basket. On emerging in the great sorting-room, somehow, we catch sight of the Bones epistle at once. There is no mistaking it. We should know its dirty appearance and awry folding —not to mention bad writing—among ten thousand. Having been turned with its stamp in the right direction at the facing-tables and passed under the stamping machines without notice, it comes at last to one of the sorters, and effectually, though briefly, stops him. His rapid distributive hand comes to a dead pause. He looks hard at the letter, frowns, turns it upside down, turns his head a little on one side, can make nothing of it, puts it on one side, and continues his work.

But at the Blind Division, to which it is speedily conveyed, our letter proves a mere trifle. It is nothing to the hieroglyphics which sometimes come under the observation of the blind officers. One of these officers gazes at it shrewdly for a few seconds. "William Stiggs, I think," he says, appealing to a comrade. "Yes," replies the comrade, "number six little lady—no—aly—oh, Little Alley, Bring—Bringing—ah, Birmingham!"

Just so—the thing is made out almost as quickly as though it had been written in copperplate, and the letter, redirected in red ink, finds its way into the Birmingham mail-bag.

So far so good, but there is many a slip 'twixt the cup and the lip, and other elements were more successful than bad writing in preventing Mr. William Stiggs from receiving that letter.

When the mail-bag containing it was put into the Travelling Post-Office van, Mr. Bright passed in after it. Our energetic sorter was in charge of the van that night, and went to work at once. The letters to be dropped at the early stages of the journey had to be commenced even before the starting of the train. The letter did not turn up at first. The officials, of whom there were six in the van, had littered their sorting-table and arranged many of the letters, and the limited mail was flying north at full speed before the Bones epistle found its appropriate pigeon-hole—for it must be understood that the vans of the Travelling Post-Office—the P.T.O., as it is familiarly called by its friends—are fitted up on one side with a long narrow table, above which are numerous pigeon-holes, arranged somewhat like those of the sorting-tables in the non-travelling Post-Offices. There is a suggestive difference, however, in the former. Their edges are padded to prevent the sorters' knuckles and noses from being damaged in the event of violent jolting. The sides and ends of the vans are padded all round to mini-mise their injuries in the event of an accident. Beyond this padding, however, there are no luxuries

—no couches or chairs; only a few things like bicycle saddles attached to the tables, astride which the sorters sit in front of their respective pigeon-holes. On the other side of the van are the pegs on which to hang the mail-bags, a lamp and wax for sealing the same, and the apparatus for lowering and lifting the net which catches the bags.

Everything connected with railways must needs be uncommonly strong, as the weight of materials, coupled with high speed, subjects all the parts of a carriage to extremely violent shocks. Hence the bag-catching affair is a powerful iron frame with rope netting, the moving of which, although aided by a pulley and heavy weight, tries the strength of a strong man.

Nimbly worked the sorters, as they swept by town and field, village, tunnel, bridge, and meadow, —for time may not be wasted when space between towns is being diminished at the rate of forty or fifty miles an hour, and chaos has to be reduced to order. The registered-letter clerk sat in one corner in front of a set of special pigeon-holes, with a sliding cover, which could be pulled over all like a blind and locked if the clerk should have occasion to quit his post for a moment. While some were sorting, others were bagging and sealing the letters. Presently the junior sorter, whose special duty it is to manipulate the net, became aware that a bag-exchanging station drew near. His eyes might have assured him of this, but officers of the Travelling Post-Office become so expert with their ears as to know stations by the peculiarity of the respective sounds connected with them—caused, it might be, by the noise of tunnels, cuttings, bridges, or even slighter influences.

Going quietly to the apparatus above referred to, the junior sorter looked out at the window and lowered the net, which, instead of lying flat against the van, now projected upwards of three feet from it. As he did so something flashed about his feet. He leaped aside and gave a shout. Fearful live creatures were sometimes sent by post, he knew, and serpents had been known before that to take an airing ir Post-Office vans as well as in the great sorting-room of St. Martin's-le-Grand ! A snake had only a short time before been observed at large on the floor of one of the night mail sorting carriages on the London and North-Western Railway, which, after a good deal of confusion and interruption to the work, was killed. This flashed into his mind, but the moment was critical, and the junior sorter had no time to indulge in private little weaknesses. Duty required prompt action.

About a hundred yards from the approaching station, a mail-bag hung suspended from a massive wooden frame. The bag weighed nearly eighty pounds. It was fitted so exactly in its place, with reference to the approaching train, that its neck was caught to a nicety in a fork, which swept it with extreme violence off its hook, and laid it in the net. This process, reversed, had been at the same moment performed on the bag given out by the train. To prevent the receiving and delivering apparatus from causing mutual destruction in passing each other, the former is affixed to the upper, the latter to the lower, part of the van. There was a rather severe jerk. The junior sorter exerted his powers, raised the net, and hauled in the bag, while the train with undiminished speed went thundering on.

" What was that I saw on the floor ? " asked the junior sorter, looking anxiously round as he set the mail-bags down.

" Only two white mice," replied Bright, who was busy in front of his pigeon-holes. " They nibbled themselves out of a parcel under my very nose. I made a grab at 'em, but they were too quick for me."

" Isn't it strange," observed the registered-letter clerk, sealing one of the bags which had just been made up, " that people *will* break the law by sending live animals through the post ?"

" More strange, it seems to me," returned Bright, as he tied up a bundle of letters, " that the people who do it can't pack 'em properly."

R

"There's the next station," said the junior sorter, proceeding once more to the net.

"Whew!" shrieked the steam-whistle, as the train went crashing towards the station. Bright looked out. The frame and its mail-bags were all right and ready. The net was lowered. Another moment and the mail-bags were swept into the van, while the out-going bags were swept off the projecting arm into the fixed net of the station. The train went through the station with a shriek and a roar. There was a bridge just beyond. The junior sorter forgot to haul up the net, which caught some object close to the bridge—no one knew what or how. No one ever does on such occasions! The result was that the whole apparatus was demolished; the side of the van was torn out, and Mr. Bright and the junior sorter, who were leaning against it at the time, were sent, in a shower of woodwork, burst bags, and letters, into the air. The rest of the van did not leave the rails, and the train shot out of sight in a few seconds, like a giant war-rocket, leaving wreck and ruin behind!

There are many miraculous escapes in this world. Mr. Bright and the junior sorter illustrated this truth by rising unhurt from the débris of their recent labours, and began sadly to collect the scattered mails. These however were not, like their guardians, undamaged. There were several fatal cases, and among these was the Bones epistle. That important document had been caught by a mass of timber and buried beyond recovery in the ballast of the line.

But why pursue this painful subject further? It is sufficient to say that although the scattered mails were carefully collected, re-sorted, and, finally, as far as possible, delivered, the letter with which we have specially to do never reached its destination. Indeed, it never more saw the light of day, but remained in the hole where it had been buried, and thus it came to pass that Mr. William Stiggs failed to make his appearance on the appointed night of the 15th, and Abel Bones was constrained to venture on his deed of darkness alone.

On the appointed night, however, Tottie did not fail to do her best to frustrate her father's plans. After a solemn, and last, consultation with her mother, she left her home with fluttering heart and dry tongue, and made for the General Post-Office.

CHAPTER XIX.

DEEP-LAID PLANS FOR CHECKMATING MR. BONES.

Now it chanced that the Post-Office Message-boys'
Literary Association had fixed to hold its first grand
soirée on the night of the 15th.

It was a great occasion. Of course it was held in
Pegaway Hall, the shed in rear of Solomon Flint's
dwelling. There were long planks on trestles for
tables, and school forms to match. There were slabs
of indigestible cake, buns in abundance, and tea,
with milk and sugar mixed, in illimitable quantities.
There were paper flowers, and illuminated texts and
proverbs round the walls, the whole being lighted
up by two magnificent paraffin lamps, which also
served to perfume the hall agreeably to such of the
members and guests as happened to be fond of bad
smells.

On this particular evening invitations had been
issued to several friends of the members of the Association, among whom were Mr. Enoch Blurt and

Mr. Sterling the missionary.   No ladies were invited.
A spirited discussion had taken place on this point
some nights before the soirée, on which occasion the
bashful Poker opposed the motion " that invitations
should be issued to ladies," on the ground that, being
himself of a susceptible nature, the presence of the
fair sex would tend to distract his attention from the
business on hand.   Big Jack also opposed it, as he
thought it wasn't fair to the fair sex to invite them
to a meeting of boys, but Big Jack was immediately
called to order, and reminded that the Society was
composed of young men, and that it was unmanly
—not to say unmannerly—to make puns on the
ladies.   To this sentiment little Grigs shouted
" Hear ! hear !' in deafening tones, and begged leave
to support the motion.   This he did in an eloquent
but much interrupted speech, which was finally cut
short by Macnab insisting that the time of the
Society should not be taken up with an irrelevant
commentary on ladies by little Grigs ; whereupon
Sandy Tod objected to interruptions in general—
except when made by himself—and was going on to
enlarge on the inestimable blessing of free discussion when he was in turn called to order.   Then
Blunter and Scroggins, and Fat Collins and Bobby
Sprat, started simultaneously to their feet, but were
put down by Peter Pax, who rose; and, with a calm
dignified wave of his hand, remarked that as the

question before the meeting was whether ladies
should or should not be invited to the soirée, the
simplest plan would be to put it to the vote.   On
this being done, it was found that the meeting was
equally divided, whereupon the chairman—Phil
Maylands—gave his casting vote in favour of the
amendment, and thus the ladies were excluded from
the soirée amid mingled groans and cheers.

But although the fair sex were debarred from
joining in the festivities, they were represented on
the eventful evening in question by a Mrs. Square,
an angular washerwoman with only one eye (but
that was a piercingly black one), who dwelt in the
same court, and who consented to act the double
part of tea-maker and doorkeeper for that occasion.
As most of the decorations and wreaths had been
made and hung up by May Maylands and two of
her telegraphic friends, there was a pervading influence of woman about Pegaway Hall, in spite of
Phil's ungallant and un-Irish vote.

When Tottie Bones arrived at the General Post-
Office in search of Peter Pax, she was directed to
Pegaway Hall by those members of the staff whose
duties prevented their attendance at the commencement of the soirée.

Finding the hall with difficulty, she was met and
stopped by the uncompromising and one-eyed stare
of Mrs. Square.

"Please, ma'am, is Mr. Peter Pax here?" asked Tottie.

"Yes, he is, but he's engaged."

Tottie could not doubt the truth of this, for through the half open door of the hall she saw and heard the little secretary on his little legs addressing the house.

"Please may I wait till he's done?" asked Tottie.

"You may, if you keep quiet, but I doubt if he'll 'ave time to see you even w'en he *is* done," said the one-eyed one, fiercely.—"D'you like buns or cake best?"

Tottie was much surprised by the question, but stated at once her decided preference for cake.

"Look here," said Mrs. Square, removing a towel from a large basket.

Tottie looked, and saw that the basket was three-quarters full of buns and cakes.

"That," said the washerwoman, "is their leavin's. One on 'em called it the debree of the feast, though what that means is best known to hisself. For one hour by the clock these literairies went at it, tooth an' nail, but they failed to get through with all that was purwided, though they stuffed themselves to their muzzles.—There, 'elp yourself."

Tottie selected a moderate slab of the indigestible cake, and sat down on a stool to eat it with as much patience as she could muster in the circumstances.

Peter Pax's remarks, whatever else they might have been considered, possessed the virtue of brevity. He soon sat down amid much applause, and Mr. Sterling rose to speak.

At this point Tottie, who had cast many anxious glances at a small clock which hung in the outer porch or vestibule of the hall, entreated Mrs. Square to tell Pax that he was wanted very much indeed.

" I durstn't," said Mrs. Square ; it 's as much as my sitooation 's worth. I was told by Mr. Maylands, the chairman, to allow of no interruptions nor anythink of the kind."

" But please, ma'am," pleaded Tottie, with such an earnest face that the woman was touched, " it 's a matter of—of—life an' death—at least it *may* be so. Oh ! do-o-o-o tell 'im he 's wanted—by Tottie Bones. Only say Tottie Bones, that 'll be *sure* to bring 'im out."

" Well—I never !" exclaimed Mrs. Square, sticking her fists in her waist and leaning her head to one side in critical scrutiny of her small petitioner. "You do seem cock-sure o' your powers. H'm ! p'r'aps you 're not far out neither. Well, I'll try it on, though it *may* cost me a deal of abuse. You sit there an' see that cats don't get at the wittles for the cats in this court are a sharper set than or'nar."

Mrs. Square entered the hall, and begged one of the members near the door to pass up a message—as quietly as possible—to the effect that Mr. Pax was wanted.

This was immediately done by the member shouting, irreverently, that the secretary's mother "'ad come to take 'im 'ome."

"Order, order! Put 'im out!" from several of the members.

"Any'ow, 'e's wanted by some one on very partikler business," growled the irreverent member, and the secretary made his way to the door.

"W'y, Tottie!" exclaimed Pax, taking both the child's hands patronisingly in his, "what brings you here?"

With a furtive glance at Mrs. Square, Tottie said, "Oh! please, I want to speak about something very partikler."

"Indeed! come out to the court then," said little Pax, leading the way; "you'll be able to air the subject better there, whatever it is, and the cats won't object. Sorry I can't take you into the hall, little 'un, but ladies ain't admitted."

When the child, with eager haste, stated the object of her visit, and wound up her discourse with the earnest remark that her father *must* be stopped, and *mustn't* be took, her small counsellor looked as perplexed and anxious as herself. Wrinkling up his smooth brow, he expressed the belief that it was a difficult world to deal with, and he had had some trouble already in finding out how to manage it.

"You see, Tot," he said, "this is a great evenin with the literary message-boys. Not that I care a rap for that, but I've unfortunately got to move a vote of thanks to our lecturer to-night, and say somethin' about the lecture, which I couldn't do, you know, unless I remained to hear it. To be sure, I might get some one else to take my place, but I'm not easily spared, for half the fun o' the evenin' would be lost if they hadn't got me to make game of and air their chaff upon. Still, as you say, your dad must have his little game stopped. He must be a great blackg— I beg pardon, Tot, I mean that he must be a great disregarder of the rights of man—woman, as it happens, in this case. However, as you said, with equal truth, he must not be took, for if he was, he'd probably be hanged, and I couldn't bear to think of your father bein' scragged. Let me see. When did you say he meant to start?"

"He said to mother that he'd leave at nine, and might 'ave to be out all night."

"At nine—eh? That would just give 'im time

to get to Charing Cross to catch the 9.30 train. Solomon Flint's lecture will be over about eight. I could polish 'im off in ten minutes or so, and 'ave plenty of time to catch the same train. Yes, that will do. But how am I to know your father, Tot, for you know I haven't yet had the pleasure of makin' his acquaintance?"

"Oh, you *can't* mistake him," replied the child confidently. "He's a big, tall, 'andsome man, with a 'ook nose an' a great cut on the bridge of it all down 'is left cheek. You'll be sure to know 'im. But how will you stop 'im?"

"That is more than I can tell at present, my dear," replied Pax, with a careworn look, "but I'll hatch a plot of some sort durin' the lecture. —Let me see," he added, with sudden animation, glancing at the limited portion of sky that roofed the court, "I might howl 'im down! That's not a bad idea. Yellin' is a powerful influence w'en brought properly to bear. D' you mind waitin' in the porch till the lecture's over?"

"O no! I can wait as long as ever you please, if you'll only try to save father," was Tottie's piteous response.

"Well, then, go into the porch and sit by the door, so that you can hear and see what's goin' on. Don't be afraid of the one-eyed fair one who guards the portals. She's not as bad as she looks; only take care that you don't tread on her toes; she can't stand *that.*"

Tottie promised to be careful in this respect, and expressed a belief that she was too light to hurt Mrs. Square, even if she did tread on her toes accidentally.

" You 're wrong, Tottie," returned Pax ; " most females of your tender years are apt to jump at wrong conclusions. As you live longer you 'll find out that some people's toes are so sensitive that they can't bear a feather's weight on 'em. W'y, there 's a member of our Society who riles up directly if you even look at his toes. We keep that member's feet in hot water pretty continuously, we do.—There now, I 'll be too late if I keep on talkin' like this. You 'll not feel tired of the lecture, for Solomon's sure to be interesting, whatever his subject may be. I don't know what it is—he hasn't told us yet. You 'll soon hear it if you listen."

Pax re-entered the hall, and Tottie sat down by the door beside Mrs. Square, just as Solomon Flint rose to his legs amid thunders of applause.

CHAPTER XX.

THE POST OF THE OLDEN TIME.

WHEN the applause had subsided Solomon Flint caused a slight feeling of depression in the meeting by stating that the subject which he meant to bring before them that evening was a historical view of the Post-Office. Most of those present felt that they had had more than enough of the Post-Office thrust on their attention every day of their lives, and the irreverent member ventured to call out " Shop," but he was instantly and indignantly called to order.

When, however, Solomon went on to state his firm belief that a particular branch of the Post-Office began in the immediate neighbourhood of the Garden of Eden, and that Adam was the first Post-master-General, the depression gave way to interest, not unmingled with curiosity.

" You see, my young friends," continued the lecturer, " our information with regard to the origin of the Post-Office is slight. The same may be said as

to the origin of a'most everythink. Taking the
little information that we do possess, and applying
to it the reasoning power which was given to us for
the purpose of investigatin' an' discoverin' truth, I
come to the following conclusions :—

"Adam was a tiller of the ground. There can
be no doubt about that. Judging from analogy, we
have the best ground for supposing that while Adam
was digging in the fields Eve was at home preparing
the dinner, and otherwise attending to the domestic
arrangements of the house, or hut, or hovel, or cave.
Dinner being ready, Eve would naturally send little
Cain or Abel to fetch their father, and thus, you see,
the branch of boy-messengers began. (Applause,
mingled with laughter and cheers.)

"Of course," continued Solomon, "it may be objected—for some people can always object—(Hear,
hear)—that these were not *Post-Office* messengers,
but, my young friends, it is well known that the
greater includes the less. As mankind is involved
in Adam, and the oak is embedded in the acorn, so
it may be maintained that the first faint germ of
the Boy-Messenger Branch of the Post-Office was
included in Cain and Abel.

"Passing, however, from what I may style this
Post-Office germ, over many centuries, during which
the records of postal history are few and faint and
far between, we come down to more modern times—

say five or six hundred years ago—and what do
we find? (Here Solomon became solemn.) We
find next to nothink! Absolutely next to nothink!
The Boy-Messenger Department had indeed developed amazingly, insomuch that, whereas there
were only two to begin with, there were in the 15th
century no fewer than innumerable millions of 'em
in every region and land and clime to which the
'uman family had penetrated, but no section of them
had as yet prefixed the word 'Telegraph' to their
name, and as to postal arrangements, w'y, they were
simply disgraceful. Just think, now, up to the century of which I speak—the fifteenth—there was no
regular Post-Office in this country. Letters were
conveyed by common carriers at the rate, probably,
of three or four miles an hour. Flesh and blood
couldn't stand that, you know, so about the close of
the century, places, or 'posts,' were established in
some parts of the country, where horses could be
hired by travellers, and letters might be conveyed.
The post-boys of those days evidently required
spurring as well as their horses, for letters of the
period have been preserved with the words '*Haste,
post haste*' on their backs. Sometimes the writers
seem to have been in a particularly desperate hurry.
One letter, written by a great man of the period, had
on the back of it the words, 'In haste; post haste,
for thy life, for thy life, for thy life;' and it is

believed that this was no idle caution, but a threat which was apt to be carried out if the post-boy loitered on the way."

It may be remarked that Solomon's language became more refined as he proceeded, but lapsed into a free-and-easy style whenever he became jocular.

"The first horse-posts," continued the lecturer, "were established for military purposes—the convenience of the public being deemed quite a secondary matter. Continental nations were in advance of England in postal arrangements, and in the first quarter of the sixteenth century (1514) the foreign merchants residing in London were so greatly inconvenienced by the want of regular letter conveyance, that they set up a Post-Office of their own from London to its outports, and appointed their own Postmaster, but, quarrelling among themselves, they referred their dispute to Government. James I. established a Post-Office for letters to foreign countries, for the benefit of English merchants, but it was not till the year 1635—in the reign of Charles I.—that a Post-Office for inland letters was established. It was ordained that the Postmaster of England for foreign parts 'should settle a running post or two to run night and day between Edinburgh and London, to go thither and come back again in six days, and to take with them all such letters as shall be directed to any post-town in or near that road.

" In 1640 the Post-Office was placed under the
care and superintendence of the Principal Secretary
of State, and became one of the settled institutions
of the country.

" Here, then, we have what may be considered the
birth of the Post-Office, which is now pretty nigh
two centuries and a half old.   And what a wonderful difference there is between this infant Post-Office
and the man!   *Then*, six days; *now*, less than a
dozen hours, between the capitals of England and
Scotland—to say nothing of other things.   But, my
lads, we must not turn up our noses at the day of
small things."

" Hear, hear," cried little Grigs, who approved
the sentiment.

" Lay it to heart then, Grigs," said Peter Pax,
who referred to the fact that little Grigs's nose
was turned up so powerfully by nature that it could
not help turning up at things small and great. alike.

Laughter and great applause were mingled with
cries of " Order," which Solomon subdued by holding
up his hand.

" At the same time," continued the lecturer,
" bye-posts were set agoing to connect the main line
with large towns, such as Hull, Lincoln, Chester,
etc.   These bye-posts were farmed out to private
individuals, and the rates fixed at 2d. a single letter
to any place under 80 miles; 4d. up to 140 miles;

6d. to any more distant place in England ; and 8d. to Scotland.

" From that date forward the infant began to grow —sometimes slowly, sometimes quickly, now and then by spurts—just like other infants, and a horribly spoiled and mismanaged baby it was at first. Those who see it now,—in the prime of its manhood, wielding its giant strength with such ease, accomplishing all but miraculous work with so great speed, regularity, and certainty, and with so little fuss,—can hardly believe what a cross-grained little stupid thing it was in those early days, or what tremendous difficulties it had to contend with.

" In the first place, the roads in the land were few, and most of them inconceivably bad, besides which they were infested by highwaymen, who often took a fancy to rummage the mail-bags and scatter their contents.   The post in those days was slow, but not sure. Then it experienced some trouble from other infants, of the same family, who claimed a right to share its privileges.   Among these was a Post-Office established by the Common Council of London in direct rivalry to the Parliamentary child.   This resulted in a great deal of squabbling and pamphleteering, also in many valuable improvements—for it is well known that opposition is the life of trade.   The Council of State, however, came to the conclusion that, in an affair so thoroughly national, the office

of Postmaster and the management of the Post-
Office ought to rest in the sole power and disposal
of Parliament; the City posts were peremptorily
suppressed; opposition babies were quietly—no
doubt righteously—murdered; and from that date
the carrying of letters has remained the exclusive
privilege of the Crown. But considerable and
violent opposition was made to this monopoly.
This is a world of opposition, my young friends"—the
lecturer was pathetic here—"and I have no doubt
whatever that it was meant to be a world of opposition "—the lecturer was energetic here, and drew an
emphatic " Hear, hear," from the Scotch members.
" Why, it is only by opposition that questions are
ventilated and truth is established !

" No doubt every member of this ancient and
literary Society is well acquainted with the name
of Hill—(great cheering)—Sir Rowland Hill, who
in the year 1840 succeeded in getting introduced
to the nation one of the greatest boons with which
it has been blessed—namely, the Penny Post. (Renewed cheering.) Well, it is a curious and interesting fact that in the middle of the seventeenth
century—more than two hundred years ago—a
namesake of Sir Rowland (whether an ancestor or
not I cannot tell), a Mr. John Hill, wrote a pamphlet
in which monopoly was condemned and a penny
post suggested. The title of the pamphlet was

' John Hill's Penny Post ; or, A Vindication of every Englishman in carrying Merchants' or any other Men's Letters against any restraints of Farmers of such Employment.' So, you see, in regard to the Penny Post, the coming event cast its shadow about two hundred years in advance.

" The Creeping Era may be the title assigned to this period of Post-Office history. Little was expected of the Post-Office, and not much was done. Nevertheless, considering the difficulties in its way, our infant progressed wonderfully. Its revenue in 1649 was £5000. Gradually it got upon its legs. Then it monopolised post-horses and began to run. Waxing bolder, it also monopolised packet-boats and went to sea. Like all bold and energetic children, it had numerous falls, and experienced many troubles in its progress. Nevertheless its heart was kept up by the steady increase of its revenue, which amounted to £76,000 in 1687. During the following seventy-eight years the increase was twofold, and during the next ninety years (to 1854) it was tenfold.

" It was hard times with the Post-Office officials about the beginning of last century.

" During what we may call the Post-boy Era, the officials were maltreated by robbers on shore and by privateers (next thing to pirates) at sea. In fact they were compelled to become men of war.

And the troubles and anxieties of the Postmaster-Generals were proportionately great. The latter had to fit out the mail-packets as ships of war, build new ships, and sell old ones, provide stores and ammunition for the same, engage captains and crews, and attend to their disputes, mutinies, and shortcomings. They had also to correspond with the deputy-postmasters all over the country about all sorts of matters—chiefly their arrears and carelessness or neglect of duty—besides foreign correspondence. What the latter involved may be partly gathered from lists of the articles sent by post at that time. Among other things, we find reference to 'fifteen couple of hounds going to the King of the Romans with a free pass.' A certain 'Dr. Crichton, carrying with him a cow and divers other necessaries,' is mentioned as having been posted! also 'two servant-maids going as laundresses to my Lord Ambassador Methuen,' and 'a deal case with four flitches of bacon for Mr. Pennington of Rotterdam.' The captains of the mail-packets ought to have worn coats of mail, for they had orders to run while they could, to fight when they could not run, and to throw the mails overboard when fighting failed !

"Of course, it is to be hoped, this rule was not strictly enforced when doctors and females formed part of the mails !

"In one case a certain James Vickers, captain of

the mail-packet 'Grace Dogger,' lay in Dublin Bay waiting till the tide should enable him to get over the bar. A French privateer chanced to be on the look-out in these waters, and pounced upon James Vickers, who was either unable or unwilling to fight. The French captain stripped the 'Grace Dogger'—as the chronicler writes—'of rigging, sails, spars, yards, and all furniture wherewith she had been provided for due accommodation of passengers, leaving not so much as a spoone, or a naile, or a hooke to hang anything on.' Having thus made a clean sweep of her valuables, and having no use for the hull, the Frenchman ransomed the 'Grace Dogger' to poor J. V. for fifty guineas, which the Post-Office had to pay !

"But our mail-packets were not always thus easily or summarily mastered. Sometimes they fought and conquered, but, whatever happened, the result was invariably productive of expense, because wounded men had to be cared for and cured or pensioned. Thus one Edward James had a donation of £5, because 'a musket shot had grazed the tibia of his left leg.' What the *tibia* may be, my young friends, is best known to the doctors—I have not taken the trouble to inquire! (Hear, hear, and applause.) Then another got £12 'because a shot had divided his frontal muscles and fractured his skull;' while a third received a yearly pension of £6, 13s. 4d. 'on account of a shot in the hinder part of the head, whereby a large division of scalp was made.' Observe what significance there is in that fourpence! Don't it speak eloquently of the strict justice of the Post-Office authorities of those days? Don't it tell of tender solicitude on their part thus to gauge the value of gunshot wounds? Might it not be said that the men were carefully rated when wounded? One Postmaster-General writes to an agent at Falmouth in regard to rates: 'Each arm or leg amputated above the elbow or knee is £8 per annum; below the knee, 20 nobles. Loss of sight of one eye, £4; of pupil of the eye, £5; of sight of both eyes, £12; of pupils of both eyes, £14.' Our well-known exactitude began to crop up, you see, even in those days.

"The post-boys—who in many instances were grey-headed men—also gave the authorities much trouble, many of them being addicted to strong drink, and not a few to dilatory habits and dishonesty. One of them was at one time caught in the act of breaking the laws. At that period the bye-posts were farmed, but the post-boys, regardless of farmers' rights, often carried letters and brought back answers on their own account—receiving and keeping the hire, so that neither the Post-Office nor the farmer got the benefit. The particular boy referred to was convicted and committed to prison, but as he could not get bail—having neither friends nor money—he begged to be whipped instead ! His petition was granted, and he was accordingly whipped to his heart's content—or, as the chronicler has it, he was whipped 'to the purpose.'

" Many men of great power and energy contributed to the advance of the Post-Office in those times. I won't burden your minds with many of their names however. One of them, William Dockwra, started a penny post in London for letters and small parcels in 1683. Twenty-three years later an attempt was made to start a halfpenny post in London, but that was suppressed.

" Soon after that a great man arose named Ralph Allen. He obtained a lease of the cross posts from Government for life at £6000 a year. By his wisdom and energy he introduced vast improvements in the postal system, besides making a profit of £12,000 a year, which he lived to enjoy for forty-four years, spending much of his fortune in charity and in the exercise of hospitality to men of learning and genius.

"About the middle of last century—the eighteenth —the Post-Office, although greatly increased in efficiency, was an insignificant affair compared with that of the present day. It was bound to pay into the Exchequer £700 a week. In Ireland and Scotland improvements also went on apace, but not so rapidly as in England, as might have been expected, considering the mountainous nature of these countries. In Scotland the first modern stage-coach was introduced in 1776. The same year a penny post was started in Edinburgh by a certain Peter Williamson of Aberdeen, who was a keeper of a coffee-stall in the Parliament House, and his experiment was so successful that he had to employ four carriers to deliver and collect letters. These men rang a bell on their rounds and wore a uniform. Others soon entered into competition, but the Post-Office authorities came forward, took the local penny post in hand, and pensioned Williamson off.

"It was not till the end of the century that the Post-Office made one of its greatest and most notable strides.

"The Mail-coach Era followed that of the post-boys, and was introduced by Mr. John Palmer, manager of the Bath theatre. The post-boys had become so unbearably slow and corrupt that people had taken to sending valuable letters in brown paper parcels by the coaches, which had now begun to run between most of the great towns. Palmer, who afterwards became Controller-General of the Post-Office, proposed that mail-bags should be sent by passenger-coaches with trusty and armed guards. His advice, after some opposition, was acted on, and thus the mails came to travel six miles an hour, instead of three or four—the result being an immediate increase of correspondence, despite an increase of postage. Rapidity, security, regularity, economy, are the great requisites in a healthy postal system. Here, then, was an advance in at least two of these. The advance was slight, it is true, but once more, I repeat, we ought not to turn up our noses at the day of small things. (Little Grigs was going to repeat "Hear! hear!" but thought better of it and checked himself.) Of course there was opposition to the stage-coaches. There always is and will be opposition to everything in a world of mixed good and evil. (The Scotsman here thought of repeating "Hear! hear!" but refrained.) One pamphleteer denounced them as the 'greatest evil that had happened of late years in these kingdoms,—mischievous to the public, prejudicial to trade, and destructive to lands. Those who travel in these coaches contract an idle habit of body, become weary and listless when they had rode a few miles, and were unable to travel on horseback, and not able to endure frost, snow, or rain, or to lodge in the fields.' Opposition for ever! So it ever is. So it was when foot-runners gave place to horsemen; so it was when horseflesh succumbed to steam. So it will be when electro-galvanic aerial locomotives take the place—. (The remainder of the sentence was lost in laughter and rapturous applause.) But roads were still intolerably bad. Stage-coach travelling was a serious business. Men made their wills before setting out on a journey. The journey between Edinburgh and London was advertised to last ten days in summer, and twelve in winter, and that, too, in a so-called 'flying machine on steel springs.' But, to return :—Our infant, having now become a sturdy youth, advanced somewhat more rapidly. In 1792 a money-order office was set on foot for the first time. It had been originally undertaken by some post-office clerks on their own account, but was little used until the introduction of the penny postage. Great reforms were made in many departments. Among them was an Act passed to authorise the sending of letter-bags by private ships. This originated the ship-letter system, by which letters are now conveyed to every part of the world visited by private ships.

" Another mighty influence for good was the introduction (about 1818) of macadamised roads, which brought travelling up to the point of ten miles an hour. So also was the opening for use in 1829 of St. Martin's-le-Grand—a *grand* event this, in every sense of the word. (Here a member objected to punning, and was immediately hooted out of countenance.)

" With mail-coaches, macadamised roads, security, ten miles an hour, and a vastly increased revenue, the Post-Office seemed to have reached the highest heights of prosperity. The heights from which we now look down upon these things ought to make us humble in our estimate of the future! We have far surpassed the wildest dreams of those days, but there were some points of picturesque interest in which we can never surpass them. Ah! boys," said Solomon, looking up with a gleam of enthusiasm in his eyes, " I mind the old mail-coaches well. They had for a long time before I knew them reached their best days. It was about the year 1820 that most of the post-roads had been macadamised, and the service had reached its highest state of efficiency. In 1836 there were fifty four-horse mails in England, thirty in Ireland, and ten in Scotland, besides forty-nine two-horse mails in England. Those who have not seen the starting of the mail-coaches from the General Post-Office can never understand the magnificence and excitement of that scene. The coaches were clean, trim, elegant, and glittering; the blood-horses were the finest that could be procured, groomed to per-fection, and full of fire ; the drivers and guards were tried and trusty men of mettle, in bright scarlet costume—some of the former being lords, baronets, and even parsons ! It was a gay and stirring sight when the insides and outsides were seated, when the drivers seized their reins, and the bugles sounded, the whips cracked, the impatient steeds reared, plunged, or sprang away, and the Royal Mails flew from the yard of St. Martin's-le-Grand towards every corner of the Kingdom.

" Their progress, too, was a sort of royal progress— a triumphal march. Wherever they had to pass, crowds of people waited for them in subdued excitement, hailed them with delight, and waved them on with cheers, for they were almost the only means of distributing news; and when a great victory, such as Trafalgar, Vittoria, or Waterloo had to be announced, the mail-coaches—dressed in flowers and ribbons, with guards shouting the news to eager crowds as they passed through hamlet, village, and town—swept like a thrill of electric fire throughout the land. News *was* news in those days! You didn't get it at all till you got it altogether, and then you got it like a thunderbolt. There was no dribbling of advance telegrams; no daily papers to spread the news (or lies), and contradict 'em next day, in the same columns with commentaries or prophetic remarks on what might or should have been, but wasn't, until news got tied up into a hopeless entanglement, so that when it was at last cleared up you 'd been worried out of half your interest in it! Yes, my lads, although I would not wish to see the return of those stirring days, I 'm free to assert that the world lost something good, and that it was not all clear gain when the old four-in-hand Royal Mail coaches drove out of the present into the past, and left the Iron Horse in possession of the field.

"But nothing can arrest the hand of Time. When mail-coaches were at their best, and a new Great North Road was being laid out by Telford, the celebrated engineer, another celebrated engineer, named Stephenson, was creating strange commotion among the coal-pits of the North. The iron horse was beginning to snort. Soon he began to shriek and claw the rails. Despite the usual opposition, he succeeded in asserting himself, and, in the words of a disconsolate old mail-coach guard, 'men began to make a gridiron of old England.' The romance of the road had faded away. No more for the old guard were there to be the exciting bustle of the start, the glorious rush out of the smoky town into the bright country; the crash through hamlet and village; the wayside changings; the rough crossing of snow-drifted moorlands; the occasional breakdowns; the difficulties and dangers; the hospitable inns; the fireside gossipings. The old guard's day was over, and a new act in the drama of human progress had begun.

" The Railway Era may be said to have commenced

about the time of the opening of the Liverpool and
Manchester line in 1830, though the railway system developed slowly during the first few years.
Men did not believe in it, and many suggestions were
made to accelerate the speed of mails in other ways.
One writer proposed balloons. Another—Professor
Babbage—suggested a series of high pillars with
wires stretched thereon, along which letter-bags
might be drawn. He even hinted that such pillars
and wires might come to be 'made available for a
species of *telegraphic communication* yet more rapid'
—a hint which is peculiarly interesting when we
consider that it was given long prior to the time of
the electric telegraph. But the Iron Horse rode
roughshod over all other plans, and finally became
the recognised and effective method of conveyance.

"During this half-century of the mail-coach
period many improvements and alterations had
been made in the working of the Post-Office.

"Among other things, the mails to India were
despatched for the first time by the 'overland
route'—the Mediterranean, Suez, and the Red Sea
—in 1835. A line of communication was subse-
quently extended to China and Australia. In the
following year the reduction of the stamp-duty on
newspapers to one penny led to a great increase in
that branch of the service.

"But now approached the time for the greatest

reform of all—that reduction of postage of which I
have already spoken—namely, the uniform rate of
one penny for all inland letters not exceeding a
certain weight.

"The average postage of a letter in 1837 was
$8\frac{3}{4}$d. Owing to the heavy rates the net proceeds
of the Department had remained stationary for
nearly twenty years. To mend this state of matters,
Sir Rowland Hill fought his long and famous fight.
the particulars of which I may not enter on just
now, but which culminated in victory in 1840,
when the Penny Post was established throughout the
kingdom. Sir Rowland still (1879) lives to witness
the thorough success of his daring and beneficent
innovation! It is impossible to form a just estimate of the value of cheap postage to the nation,
—I may say, to the world. Trade has been
increased, correspondence extended, intelligence
deepened, and mental activity stimulated.

"The immediate result of the change was to
raise the number of letters passing through the post
from seventy-six millions in 1839 to one hundred
and sixty-nine millions in 1840. Another result
was the entire cessation of the illicit smuggling of
letters. Despite penal laws, some carriers had been
doing as large a business in illegal conveyance of
letters as the Post-Office itself! One seizure made,
of a single bag in the warehouse of a well-known

London carrier, revealed eleven hundred such
letters! The horrified head of the firm hastened
to the Postmaster-General, and offered immediate
payment of £500 to escape the penalties incurred.
The money was accepted, and the letters were all
passed through the Post-Office the same night!

"Sir Rowland—then Mr.—Hill had said that the
Post-Office was 'capable of performing a distinguished part in the great work of national education.'
His prophetic words have been more than justified.
People who never wrote letters before write them
now. Those who wrote only a few letters now
write hundreds. Only grave and important subjects
were formerly treated of by letter, now we send the
most trifling as well as the most weighty matters
by the penny post in such floods that there is scarce
room to receive the correspondence, but liberal men
and measures have been equal to the emergency.
One objector to cheap rates prophesied that their
adoption would cause the very walls of the General
Post-Office to burst. Well, it has seemed as if his
prophecy were about to come true, especially on
recent Christmas eves, but it is not yet fulfilled, for
the old place has a tough skin, and won't burst up
for a considerable time to come. (Great applause.)

"Financially, too," continued Solomon, "the
Penny Post reform was an immense success,
though at first it showed a tendency to hang fire.

T

The business of the Money Order Office was enormously increased, as the convenience of that important department became obvious to the public, and trade was so greatly improved that many tradesmen, at the end of the first three years, took the trouble to write to the Post-Office to tell how their business had increased since the introduction of the change.   In short, the Penny Post would require a lecture to itself.   I will therefore dismiss it with the remark that it is one of the greatest blessings of modern times, and that the nation owes an everlasting debt of gratitude to its author.

" With decreased rates came the other great requisites,—increased speed and security ; and now, as you all know, the work of the Post-Office, in all its wide ramifications, goes on with the uniform regularity of a good chronometer from year to year.

"To the special duty of letter-carrying the Post-Office has now added the carriage of books and patterns, and a Savings Bank as well as a Money Order department ; but if I were to enlarge on the details of all this it would become necessary to order coffee and buns for the whole Society of literary message-boys, and make up our beds on the floor of Pegaway Hall—(Hear ! hear ! applause, and cries of ' Go on !')—to avoid which I shall bring my discourse to a close, with a humble apology for having detained you so long."

CHAPTER XXI.

TELLS OF A SERIES OF TERRIBLE SURPRISES.

" WELL, what did you think of that, old girl?" asked Peter Pax of Tottie, on issuing from the Literary Message-Boys' Hall, after having performed his duties there.

" It was wonderful. I 'ad no idear that the Post-Office was so old or so grand a' institootion—But please don't forget father," said Tottie, with an anxious look at the battered clock.

" I don't forget 'im, Tot. I've been thinkin' about 'im the whole time, an' I've made up my mind what to do. The only thing I ain't sure of is whether I shouldn't take my friend Phil Maylands into partnership."

" Oh, please, don't," pleaded Tottie ; " I shouldn't like 'im to know about father."

" Well, the less he knows about 'im the better. P'r'aps you 're right. I'll do it alone, so you cut away home. I'll go to have my personal appearance

improved, and then off to Charing Cross.   Lots of
time, Tottie.   Don't be anxious.   Try if you can
trust me.   I'm small, no doubt, but I'm tough.
—Good-night."

When Abel Bones seated himself that night in a
third-class carriage at Charing Cross, and placed a
neat little black hand-bag, in which he carried his
housebreaking tools, on the floor between his feet,
a small negro boy entered the carriage behind him,
and, sitting down directly opposite, stared at him as
if lost in unutterable amazement.

Mr. Bones took no notice of the boy at first, but
became annoyed at last by the pertinacity of his
attention.

"Well, you chunk of ebony," he said, "how
much are you paid a week for starin'?"

"No pound no shillin's an' nopence, massa, and
find myself," replied the negro so promptly that
Bones smiled in spite of himself.   Being, however,
in no mood for conversation, he looked out at the
window and let the boy stare to his heart's
content.

On drawing up to the platform of the station for
Rosebud Cottage, Mr. Bones seemed to become
anxious, stretched his head out at the carriage
window, and muttered to himself.   On getting out,
he looked round with a disappointed air.

"Failed me!" he growled, with an anathema

on some one unknown. "Well, I'll do it alone,"
he muttered, between his teeth.

"O no! you won't, my fine fellow," thought the
negro boy; "I'll help you to do it, and make you do
it badly, if you do it at all.—May I carry your bag,
massa?" he added, aloud.

Mr. Bones replied with a savage kick, which the
boy eluded nimbly, and ran with a look of mock
horror behind a railway van. Here he put both
hands to his sides, and indulged in a chuckle so
hearty—though subdued—that an ordinary cat, to
say nothing of a Cheshire one, might have joined
him from sheer sympathy.

"O the brute!" he gasped, on partially recovering, "and Tottie!—Tottie!! why she's—" Again
this eccentric boy went off into subdued convulsions,
in which state he was discovered by a porter, and
chased off the premises.

During the remainder of that night the " chunk
of ebony " followed Mr. Bones like his shadow.
When he went down to the small public-house of
the hamlet to moisten his throat with a glass of
beer, the negro boy waited for him behind a
hay-stack; when he left the public-house, and
took his way towards Rosebud Cottage, the boy
walked a little behind him—not far behind, for the
night was dark. When, on consulting his watch,
with the aid of a match, Bones found that his time

for action had not arrived and sat down by the side of a hedge to meditate, the chunk crept through a hole in the same hedge, crawled close up like a panther, lay down in the grass on the other side, and listened.   But he heard nothing, for the burglar kept his thoughts, whatever they might have been, to himself.   The hour was too still, the night too dark, the scene too ghostly for mutterings.   Peering through the hedge, which was high and thick, the boy could see the red glow of Mr. Bones's pipe.

Suddenly it occurred to Pax that now was a favourable opportunity to test his plan.   The hedge between him and his victim was impassable to any one larger than himself; on his side the ground sloped towards a plantation, in which he could easily find refuge if necessary.   There was no wind. Not a leaf stirred.   The silence was profound— broken only by the puffing of the burglar's lips. Little Pax was quick to conceive and act.   Suddenly he opened his mouth to its widest, took aim where he thought the ear of Bones must be, and uttered a short, sharp, appalling yell, compared to which a shriek of martyrdom must have been as no- thing.

That the effect on Bones was tremendous was evinced by the squib-like action of his pipe, as it flew into the air, and the stumbling clatter of his feet, as he rushed blindly from the spot.   Little

Pax rolled on the grass in indescribable ecstasies for a few seconds, then crept through the hole, and followed his victim.

But Bones was no coward. He had only been taken by surprise, and soon stopped. Still, he was sufficiently superstitious to look frequently over his shoulder as he walked in the direction of Miss Stivergill's Cottage.

Pax was by that time on familiar ground. Fearing that Bones was not to be scared from his purpose by one fright, he made a détour, got ahead of him, and prepared to receive him near the old well of an adjoining farm, which stood close by the road. When the burglar's footsteps became audible, he braced himself up. As Bones drew near Pax almost burst his little chest with an inhalation. When Bones was within three feet of him, he gave vent to such a skirl that the burglar's reason was again upset. He bounded away, but suddenly recovered self-possession, and, turning round, dashed at the old well, where Pax had prematurely begun to enjoy himself.

To jump to his feet and run like the wind was the work of a moment. Bones followed furiously. Rage lent him for the moment unwonted power. He kept well up for some distance, growling fiercely as he ran, but the lithe limbs and sound lungs of the boy were too much for him. He soon fell

behind, and finally stopped, while Pax ran on until
out of breath.

Believing that he had now rid himself of some mischievous boy of the neighbourhood, the burglar turned
back to transact his business at Rosebud Cottage.

Peter Pax also turned in the same direction.
He felt that things were now beginning to look
serious.   To thwart Mr. Bones in his little game,
by giving information as to his intentions, would
have been easy, but then that would have involved
his being "took," which was not to be thought of.
At the same time, it was evident that he was no
longer to be scared by yells.

Somewhat depressed by his failure, Pax hastened
towards the cottage as fast as he could, resolved to
give his enemy a last stunning reception in the
garden, even although, by so doing, he would probably scare Miss Stivergill and her household out
of their wits.

He reached the garden some minutes before
Bones, and clambered over the wall.   While in the
very act of doing so, he felt himself seized by the
throat and nearly strangled.

"Now then, young 'un," growled a deep voice,
which was not that of Bones, "what little game may
you be up to?"

"Ease your grip and I'll tell you," gasped Pax.

It was the constable of the district who had

caught him. That faithful guardian of the night, having been roused by the unwonted yells, and having heard Pax's footsteps, had followed him up.

"I'm not a burglar, sir," pleaded Pax, not well knowing what to say. Suddenly he opened his mouth in desperation, intending to give one final yell, which might scare Bones from his impending fate, but it was nipped in the bud by the policeman's strong hand.

"Ha! you'd give your pal a signal, would you?" he said, in a gruff whisper. "Come now, keep quiet if you don't want to be choked. You can't save 'im, so you'd better give in."

Poor Pax now saw that nothing more could be done. He therefore made a virtue of necessity, and revealed as much of the object of his mission as he deemed prudent. The man believed him, and, on his promising to keep perfectly still, released him from his deadly grip.

While the policeman and the boy lay thus biding their time in the shrubbery, Bones got over the wall and quietly inspected the premises.

"I'll let him begin, and take him in the act," whispered the policeman.

"But he's an awful big, strong, determined feller," said Pax.

"So am I," returned the policeman, with a smile, which was lost in the dark.

Now it so happened that Miss Lillycrop, who had
been spending that day with Miss Stivergill, had
been induced to spend the night also with her
friend.   Of course these two had much to talk
about—ladies generally have in such circumstances
—and they were later than usual in going to bed.
Mr. Bones was therefore, much against his will,
obliged to delay the execution of his plans.   Little
dreaming that two admirers lay in ambush about
fifty yards off, he retired to a dark corner behind a
bit of old wall, and there, appropriately screened
by a laurel bush, lit his pipe and enjoyed himself.

"My dear," said Miss Stivergill to her friend
about midnight, "we must go to bed.   Do you go
up to my room ; I 'll follow after looking round."

It was the nightly practice of this lady to go over
her premises from cellar to garret, to make quite
sure that the servant had fastened every bolt and
bar and lock.   She began with the cellars.   Finding
everything right there, she went to the dining-room
windows.

"Ha! the gipsy !—unbolted, and the shutters
open !" exclaimed Miss Stivergill, fastening the bolt.

"H'm !   The old fool," thought the burglar, observing her tall square figure while thus engaged,
"might as well bolt the door of Newgate with a steel
pen.   Cottage window-gear is meant for show, not
for service, old girl."

" I look round regularly every night," observed Miss Stivergill, entering her bedroom, in which Miss Lillycrop usually occupied a chair bed when on a visit to The Rosebud. "You've no idea how careless servants are ('Haven't I, just?' thought her friend), and although I have no personal fear of burglars, I deem it advisable to interpose some impediments to their entrance."

"But what would you do if they did get in?" asked Miss Lillycrop, in some anxiety, for she had a very strong personal fear of burglars.

"Oh! I have several little plans for their reception," replied the lady, with a quiet smile. There's a bell in the corner there, which was meant for the parish church, but was thought to be a little too small. I bought it, had a handle affixed to it, as you see, and should ring it at an open window if the house were attempted.

"But they might rush in at the door and stop you—kill you even!" suggested the other, with a shudder.

"Have you not observed," said Miss Stivergill, "that I lock my door on the inside? Besides, I have other little appliances which I shall explain to you in the morning, for I scorn to be dependent on a man-servant for protection. There's a revolver in that drawer beside you"—Miss Lillycrop shrank from the drawer in question—"but I would only use it in the last extremity, for I am not fond of taking human life. Indeed, I would decline to do so even to save my own, but I should have no objection to maim. Injuries about the legs or feet might do burglars spiritual as well as physical good in the long-run, besides being beneficial to society.—Now, my dear, good-night."

Miss Stivergill extinguished the candle as violently as she would have maimed a burglar, and poor Miss Lillycrop's heart leapt as she was suddenly plunged into total darkness—for she was naturally timid, and could not help it.

For some time both ladies lay perfectly still; the hostess enjoying that placid period which precedes slumber; the guest quaking with fear caused by the thoughts that the recent conversation had raised.

Presently Miss Lillycrop raised herself on one elbow, and glared in the direction of her friend's bed so awfully that her eyes all but shone in the dark.

"Did you hear THAT, dear?" she asked, in a low whisper.

"Of course I did," replied Miss Stivergill aloud. "Hush! listen."

They listened and heard "that" again. There could be no doubt about it—a curious scratching sound at the dining-room window immediately below theirs.

"Rats," said Miss Stivergill in a low voice.

"Oh! I *do* hope so," whispered Miss Lillycrop. She entertained an inexpressible loathing of rats, but compared with burglars they were as bosom friends whom she would have welcomed with a glad shudder.

In a few minutes the scratching ceased and a bolt or spring snapped. The wildest of rats never made a sound like that! Miss Lillycrop sat bolt up in her bed, transfixed with horror, and could dimly see her friend spring from her couch and dart across the room like a ghostly phantom.

"Lilly, if you scream," said Miss Stivergill, in a voice so low and stern that it caused her blood to curdle, "I'll do something awful to you.—Get up!"

The command was peremptory. Miss Lillycrop obeyed.

"Here, catch hold of the bell-handle—so. Your other hand—there—keep the tongue fast in it, and don't ring till I give the word."

Miss Lillycrop was perfect in her docility.

A large tin tea-tray hung at the side of Miss Stivergill's bed. Beside it was a round ball with a handle to it. Miss Lillycrop had wondered what these were there for. She soon found out.

Miss Stivergill put the dressing-table a little to one side, and placed a ewer of water on it.

At that moment the dining-room window was heard to open slowly but distinctly.

Miss Stivergill threw up the bedroom window.

The marrow in Miss Lillycrop's spine froze.

Mr. Bones started and looked up in surprise. He received a deluge of water on his face, and at the same moment a ewer burst in atoms on the gravel at his feet — for Miss Stivergill did nothing by halves. But Bones was surprise-proof by that time; besides, the coveted treasure was on the side-board—almost within his grasp. He was too bold a villain to be frightened by women, and he knew that sleeping country-folk are not quickly roused to succour the inmates of a lonely cottage. Darting into the room, he tumbled over chairs, tables, work-boxes, fire-irons, and coal-scuttle.

"Ring!" said Miss Stivergill sharply. At the same moment she seized the tea-tray in her left hand and belaboured it furiously with the drumstick.

"Ring out at the window!" shouted Miss Stivergill.

Miss Lillycrop did so until her spinal marrow thawed.

The noise was worse than appalling. Little Pax, unable to express his conflicting emotions in any other way, yelled with agonising delight. Even the hardened spirit of Bones trembled with mingled feelings of alarm and surprise. He found and grasped the coveted box, and leaped out of the window with a bound. It is highly probable that he would have got clear off but for the involuntary action of Miss Lillycrop. As that lady's marrow waxed warm she dashed the great bell against the window-sill with such fervour that it flew from her grasp and descended full on the burglar's cranium, just as he leaped into the arms of the policeman, and both fell heavily to the ground. The guardian of the night immediately jumped up uninjured, but Bones lay prone on the green sward—stunned by the bell.

"That's well done, anyhow, an' saved me a world o' trouble," said the constable, looking up at the window as he held the burglar down, though there was little necessity for that. "You couldn't shy me over a bit of rope, could you, ma'am?"

Miss Stivergill, to whom nothing seemed difficult, and who had by that time stopped her share in the noise, went into a cupboard and fetched thence a coil of rope.

"I meant it to be used in the event of fire," she said quietly to her friend, who had thrown herself flat on her bed, "but it will serve other purposes as well.—There, policeman."

She threw it down, and when Bones recovered consciousness he found himself securely tied and seated in a chair in the Rosebud kitchen—the policeman looking at him with interest, and the domestics with alarm. Miss Stivergill regarded him with calm severity.

"Now he's quite safe, ma'am, but I can't venture to take 'im to the station alone. If you'll kindly consent to keep an eye on him, ma'am, till I run down for a comrade, I'll be greatly obleeged. There's no fear of his wrigglin' out o' that, ma'am; you may make your mind easy."

"My mind is quite easy, policeman; you may go. I shall watch him."

When the man had left, Miss Stivergill ordered the servants to leave the kitchen. Little Pax, who had discreetly kept out of range of the burglar's eye, went with them, a good deal depressed in spirit, for his mission had failed. The burglary had not, indeed, been accomplished, but—"father" was "took."

When Miss Stivergill was left alone with the burglar she gazed at him for some time in silence.

"Man," she said at length, "you are little Bones's father."

"If you means Tottie, ma'am, I is," replied Bones, with a look and tone which were not amiable.

"I have a strong feeling of regard for your child, though not a scrap of pity for yourself," said Miss Stivergill, with a frown.

Mr. Bones muttered something to the effect that he returned the compliment with interest.

"For Tottie's sake I should be sorry to see you transported," continued the lady, "therefore I mean to let you off. Moreover, bad as you are, I believe you are not so bad as many people would think you. Therefore I'm going to trust you."

Bones looked inquiringly and with some suspicion at his captor. He evidently thought there was a touch of insanity about her. This was confirmed when Miss Stivergill, seizing a carving-knife from the dresser, advanced with masculine strides towards him. He made a desperate effort to burst his bonds, but they were too scientifically arranged for that. "Don't fear," said the lady, severing the cord that bound the burglar's wrists, and putting the knife in his hands. "Now," she added, "you know how to cut yourself free, no doubt."

"Well, you *are* a trump!" exclaimed Bones, rapidly touching his bonds at salient points with the keen edge.

In a few seconds he was free.

"Now, go away," said Miss Stivergill, "and don't let me see you here again."

Bones looked with admiration at his deliverer, but could only find words to repeat that she *was* a trump, and vanished through the back-door just as a band of men, with pitchforks, rakes, spades, and lanterns, came clamouring in at the front garden gate from the neighbouring farm.

"What is it?" exclaimed the farmer.

"Only a burglar," answered Miss Stivergill.

"Where is he?" chorussed everybody.

"That's best known to himself," replied the lady, who, in order to give the fugitive time, went into a minute and slow account of the whole affair—excepting, of course, her connivance at the escape—to the great edification of her audience, among whom the one who seemed to derive the chief enjoyment was a black boy. He endeavoured to screen himself behind the labourers, and was obviously unable to restrain his glee.

"But what's come of 'im, ma'am?" asked the farmer impatiently.

"Escaped!" answered Miss Stivergill.

"Escaped!" echoed everybody, looking furtively round, as though they suppos'd he had only escaped under the dresser or into the keyhole.

"Escaped!" repeated the policeman, who entered at the moment with two comrades; "impossible! I tied 'im so that no efforts of his own could avail 'im. Somebody *must* 'ave 'elped 'im."

"The carving-knife helped him," said Miss Stivergill, with a look of dignity.—"Perhaps, instead of speculating how he escaped, policeman, it would be better to pursue him. He can't be very far off, as it is not twenty minutes since he cut himself free."

In a state of utter bewilderment the policeman rushed out of the cottage, followed by his comrades and the agriculturists. Peter Pax essayed to go with them, but was restrained by an iron grip on his collar. Pulling him back, Miss Stivergill dragged her captive into a parlour and shut the door.

"Come now, little Pax," she said, setting the boy in a chair in front of her, "you needn't try to deceive *me*. I'd know you among a thousand in any disguise. If you were to blacken your face with coal-tar an inch thick your impertinence would shine through. You know that the burglar is little Bones's father; you've a pretty good guess that I let him off. You have come here for some purpose in connection with him. Come—out with it, and make a clean breast."

Little Pax did make a clean breast then and there, was washed white, supped and slept at The Rosebud, returned to town next day by the first train, and had soon the pleasure of informing Tottie that the intended burglary had been frustrated, and that her father wasn't "took" after all.

CHAPTER XXII.

SHOWS HOW ONE THING LEADS TO ANOTHER, AND SO ON.

IT is a mere truism to state that many a chain of grave and far-reaching events is set in motion by some insignificant trifle. The touching of a trigger by a child explodes a gun which extinguishes a valuable life, and perhaps throws a whole neighbourhood into difficulties. The lighting of a match may cause a conflagration which shall "bring down" an extensive firm, some of whose dependants, in the retail trade, will go down along with it, and cause widespreading distress, if not ruin, among a whole army of greengrocers, buttermen, and other small fry.

The howling of a bad baby was the comparatively insignificant event which set going a certain number of wheels, whose teeth worked into the cogs which revolved in connection with our tale.

The howling referred to awoke a certain contractor near Pimlico with a start, and caused him to rise off what is popularly known as the " wrong side." Being an angry man, the contractor called the baby bad names, and would have whipped it had it been his own. Going to his office before breakfast with the effects of the howl strong upon him, he met a humble labourer there with a surly " Well, what do you want ?"

The labourer wanted work. The contractor had no work to give him. The labourer pleaded that his wife and children were starving. The contractor didn't care a pinch of snuff for his wife or children, and bade him be off. The labourer urged that the times were very hard, and he would be thankful for any sort of job, no matter how small. He endeavoured to work on the contractor's feelings by referring to the premature death, by starvation, of his pet parrot, which had been for years in the family, and a marvellous speaker, having been taught by his mate Bill. The said Bill was also out of work, and waiting for him outside. He too would be thankful for a job—anything would do, and they would be willing to work for next to nothing. The contractor still professed utter indifference to the labourer's woes, but the incident of the parrot had evidently touched a cord which could not be affected by human suffering. After a few minutes' consideration he said there *was* a small job—a pump at the corner of a certain street not far off had to be taken down, to make way for contemplated alterations. It was not necessary to take it down just then, but as the labourers were so hard up for a job they were at liberty to undertake that one.

Thus two wheels were set in motion, and the result was that the old pump at the corner of Purr Street was uprooted and laid low by these labourers, one of whom looked into the lower end of the pump and said " Hallo !"

His companion Bill echoed the "Hallo !" and added " What 's up ?"

" W'y, if there ain't somethink queer inside of the old pump," said the labourer, going down on both knees in order to look more earnestly into it. " I do b'lieve it 's letters. Some double-extra stoopids 'ave bin an' posted 'em in the pump."

He pulled out handfuls of letters as he spoke, some of which, from their appearance, must have lain there for years, while others were quite fresh !

A passing letter-carrier took charge of these letters, and conveyed them to the Post-Office, where the machinery of the department was set in motion on them. They were examined, faced, sorted, and distributed. Among them was the letter which George Aspel had committed to the care of Tottie Bones at the time of his first arrival in London, and thus it came to pass that the energies of Sir James Clubley, Baronet, were roused into action.

" Dear me ! how strange !" said Sir James to himself, on reading the letter. " This unaccountable
silence is explained at last. Poor fellow, I have
judged him hastily. Come ! I 'll go find him out."

But this resolve was more easily made than carried into effect. At the hotel from which the letter
had been dated nothing was known of the missing
youth except that he had departed long long ago,
leaving as his future address the name of a bird-
stuffer, which name had unfortunately been mislaid
—not lost. Oh no—only mislaid ! On further
inquiry, however, there was a certain undersized,
plain-looking, and rather despised chamber-maid
who retained a lively and grateful recollection of
Mr. Aspel, in consequence of his having given her
an unexpectedly large tip at parting, coupled with
a few slight but kindly made inquiries as to her
welfare, which seemed to imply that he regarded her
as a human being. She remembered distinctly his
telling her one evening that if any one should call
for him in his absence he was to be found at the
residence of a lady in Cat Street, Pimlico, but for
the life of her she couldn't remember the number,
though she thought it must have been number nine,
for she remembered having connected it in her mind
with the well-known lives of a cat.

" Cat Street ! Strange name—very !" said Sir
James. " Are you sure it was Cat Street ?"

" Well, I ain't quite sure, sir," replied the little plain one, with an inquiring frown at the chandelier, " but I know it 'ad somethink to do with cats. P'r'aps it was Mew Street ; but I 'm *quite* sure it was Pimlico."

" And the lady's name ?"

" Well, sir, I ain't sure of that neither.   It was somethink queer, I know, but then there 's a-many queer names in London—ain't there, sir ?"

Sir James admitted that there were, and advised her to reflect on a few of them.

The little plain one did reflect—with the aid ot the chandelier—and came to the sudden conviction that the lady's name had to do with flowers.   " Not roses—no, nor yet violets," she said, with an air of intense mental application, for the maiden's memory was largely dependent on association of ideas ; " it might 'ave been marigolds, though it don't seem likely.   Stay, was it water-l—   Oh ! it was lilies !   Yes, I 'ave it now : Miss Lilies-somethink."

" Think again, now," said the Baronet, "everything depends on the ' something,' for Miss Lilies is not so extravagantly queer as you seem to think her name was."

" That 's true, sir," said the perplexed maid, with a last appealing gaze at the chandelier, and beginning with the first letter of the alphabet—Miss

Lilies A—Lilies B—Lilies C—, etc., until she came to K. "That's it now. I 'ave it *almost*. It 'ad to do with lots of lilies, I 'm quite sure—quantities, it must 'ave been."

On Sir James suggesting that quantities did not begin with a K the little plain one's feelings were slightly hurt, and she declined to go any further into the question. Sir James was therefore obliged to rest content with what he had learned, and continued his search in Pimlico. There he spent several hours in playing, with small shopkeepers and policemen, a game somewhat analogous to that which is usually commenced with the words "Is it animal, vege-table, or mineral?" The result was that eventually he reached No. 9 Purr Street, and found himself in the presence of Miss Lillycrop.

That lady, however, damped his rising hopes by saying that she did not know where George Aspel was to be found, and that he had suddenly dis-appeared—to her intense regret—from the bird-warehouse in which he had held a situation. It belonged to the brothers Blurt, whose address she gave to her visitor.

Little Tottie Bones, who had heard the conversa-tion through the open parlour door, could have told where Aspel was to be found, but the promise made to her father sealed her lips ; besides, particular inquiries after any one were so suggestive to her of policemen, and being "took," that she had a double motive to silence.

Mr. Enoch Blurt could throw no light on the subject, but he could, and did, add to Sir James's increasing knowledge of the youth's reported dissipation, and sympathised with him strongly in his desire to find out Aspel's whereabouts. Moreover, he directed him to the General Post-Office, where a youth named Maylands, a letter-sorter—who had formerly been a telegraph message-boy,—and an intimate friend of Aspel, was to be found, and might be able to give some information about him, though he (Mr. Blurt) feared not.

Phil Maylands could only say that he had never ceased to make inquiries after his friend, but hitherto without success, and that he meant to continue his inquiries until he should find him.

Sir James Clubley therefore returned in a state of dejection to the sympathetic Miss Lillycrop, who gave him a note of introduction to a detective—the grave man in grey,—a particular friend and ally of her own, with whom she had scraped acquaintance during one of her many pilgrimages of love and mercy among the poor.

To the man in grey Sir James committed his case, and left him to work it out.

Now, the way of a detective is a mysterious way. Far be it from us to presume to point it out, or

elucidate or expound it in any degree. We can
only give a vague, incomplete, it may be even
incorrect, view of what the man in grey did and
achieved, nevertheless we are bound to record what
we know as to this officer's proceedings, inasmuch
as they have to do with the thread of our narrative.

It may be that other motives, besides those connected with George Aspel, induced the man in
grey to visit the General Post-Office, but we do
not certainly know. It is quite possible that a
whole host of subsidiary and incidental cases on
hand might have induced him to take up the Post-
Office like a huge stone, wherewith to knock down
innumerable birds at one and the same throw; we
cannot tell. The brain of a detective must be essen-
tially different from the brains of ordinary men.
His powers of perception—we might add, of con-
ception, reception, deception, and particularly of
interception—are marvellous. They are altogether
too high for us. How then can we be expected to
explain why it was that, on arriving at the Post-
Office, the man in grey, instead of asking eagerly
for George Aspel at the Inquiry Office, or the Returned Letter Office, or the *poste restante*, as any
sane man would have done, began to put careless
and apparently unmeaning questions about little
dogs, and to manifest a desire to be shown the chief

points of interest in the basement of St. Martin's-le-Grand ?

In the gratifying of his desires the man in grey experienced no difficulty. The staff of the Post-Office is unvaryingly polite and obliging to the public. An order was procured, and he soon found himself with a guide traversing the mysterious regions underneath the splendid new building where the great work of postal telegraphy is carried on.

While his conductor led him through the labyrinthine passages in which a stranger would infallibly have lost his way, he explained the various objects of interest—especially pointing out the racks where thousands on thousands of old telegrams are kept, for a short time, for reference in case of dispute, and then destroyed. He found the man in grey so intelligent and sympathetic that he quite took a fancy to him.

"Do you happen to remember," asked the detective, in a quiet way, during a pause in his companion's remarks, "anything about a mad dog taking refuge in this basement some time ago—a small poodle I think it was—which disappeared in some mysterious way ?"

The conductor had heard a rumour of such an event, but had been ill and off duty at the time, and could give him no details.

"This," said he, opening a door, "is the Battery Room, where the electricity is generated for the instruments above.—Allow me to introduce you to the Battery Inspector."

The man in grey bowed to the Inspector, who was a tall, powerful man, quite fit, apparently, to take charge of a battery of horse artillery if need were.

"A singular place," remarked the detective, looking sharply round the large room, whose dimensions were partially concealed, however, by the rows of shelving which completely filled it from floor to ceiling.

"Somewhat curious," assented the Inspector; "you see our batteries require a good deal of shelving. All put together, there is in this room about three miles of shelving, completely filled, as you see, with about 22,000 cells or jars. The electricity is generated in these jars. They contain carbon and zinc plates in a solution of bichromate of potash and sulphuric acid and water. We fill them up once every two weeks, and renew the plates occasionally. There is a deal of sulphate of copper used up here, sir, in creating electricity— about six tons in the year. Pure copper accumulates on the plates in the operation, but the zinc wears away."

The detective expressed real astonishment and

interest in all this, and much more that the Inspector told him.

"Poisonous stuff in your jars, I should fancy?" he inquired.

"Rather," replied the Inspector.

"Does your door ever stand open?" asked the detective.

"Sometimes," said the other, with a look of slight surprise.

"You never received a visit down here from a mad dog, did you?" asked the man in grey.

"Never!"

"I only ask the question," continued the other, in a careless tone, "because I once read in the newspapers of a poodle being chased into the Post-Office and never heard of again. It occurred to me that poison might account for it.—A curious-looking thing here; what is it?"

He had come to a part of the Battery Room where there was a large frame or case of dark wood, the surface of which was covered with innumerable brass knobs or buttons, which were coupled together by wires.

"That is our Battery Test-Box," explained the Inspector. "There are four thousand wires connected with it—two thousand going to the instruments up-stairs, and two thousand connected with the battery jars. When I complete the circuit by connecting any couple of these buttons, the influence of the current is at once perceived."

He took a piece of charcoal, as he spoke, and brought it into contact with two of the knobs. The result was to convert the coal instantly into an intense electric light of dazzling beauty. The point of an ordinary lead pencil applied in the same way became equally brilliant.

" That must be a powerful battery," remarked the detective.

The Inspector smilingly took two handles from a neighbouring shelf and held them out to his visitor.

" Lay hold of these," he said, " and you will feel its powers."

The detective did as directed, and received a shock which caused him to fling down the handles with great promptitude and violence. He was too self-possessed a man, however, to seem put out.

" Strong !" he said, with a short laugh ; " remarkably strong and effective."

" Yes," assented the Inspector, " it *is* pretty powerful, and it requires to be so, for it does heavy work and travels a considerable distance. The greater the distance, you know, the greater the power required to do the work and transmit the messages. This is the battery that fires two signal-guns every day at one o'clock—one at Newcastle, the other at South Shields, and supplies Greenwich time to all our principal stations over a radius of three hundred miles.—I sent the contents of one hundred and twenty jars through you just now!"

"That's curious and interesting; I may even say it is suggestive," returned the detective, in a meditative tone. "Double that number of jars, now, applied to the locks of street doors at night and the fastenings of windows would give a powerful surprise to burglars."

" Ah, no doubt, and also to belated friends," said the Inspector, "not to mention the effect on servant-maids in the morning when people forgot to disconnect the wires."

The man in grey admitted the truth of the observation, and, thanking the Battery Inspector for his kind attentions, bade him a cordial adieu. Continuing his investigation of the basement, he came to the three huge fifty-horse-power engines, whose duty it is to suck the air from the pneumatic telegraph tubes in the great hall above. Here the detective became quite an engineer, asked with much interest and intelligence about governors, pistons, escape-valves, actions, etc., and wound up with a proposition.

"Suppose, now," he said, "that a little dog were to come suddenly into this room and dash about in a miscellaneous sort of way, could it by any means manage to become entangled in your machinery and get so demolished as never more to be seen or heard of?"

The engineer looked at his questioner with a somewhat amused expression. "No, sir, I don't think it could. No doubt it might kill itself with much facility in various ways, for fifty horse-power, properly applied, would do for an elephant, much more a dog, but I don't believe that power to be sufficient to produce annihilation. There would have been remains of some sort."

From the engine-room our detective proceeded to the boiler-room and the various kitchens, and thence to the basement of the old building on the opposite side of the street, where he found a similarly perplexing labyrinth. He was taken in hand here by Mr. Bright, who chanced to be on duty, and led him first to the Stamp Department. There was much to draw him off his "canine" mania here. First he was introduced to the chief of the department, who gave him much interesting information about stamps in general.

Then he was conducted to another room, and shown the tables at which men were busy counting sheets of postage-stamps and putting them up in envelopes for all parts of the United Kingdom. The officer in charge told him that the weight of stamps sent out from that room averaged a little over three tons daily, and that the average value of the weekly issue was £150,000. Then he was led into a fireproof safe—a solid stone apartment— which was piled from floor to ceiling with sheets of postage-stamps of different values.   Those for letters ranged from one halfpenny to one pound, but those used for telegrams ran up to as much as five pounds sterling for a single stamp.   Taking down from a shelf a packet of these high-priced stamps, which was about the size of a thick octavo book, the official stated that it was worth £35,000.

"Yes, sir," he added, "this strong box of ours holds a deal of money.   You are at this moment in the presence of nearly two millions sterling !"

"A tidy little sum to retire upon.   Would build two thousand Board Schools at a thousand pounds each," said the detective, who was an adept at figures,—as at everything else.

Feeling that it would be ridiculous to inquire about mad dogs in the presence of two millions sterling, the man in grey suffered himself to be led through long passages and vaulted chambers, some of which latter were kitchens, where the men on duty had splendid fires, oceans of hot water, benches and tables, and liberty to cook the food either brought by themselves for the day or pro- cured from a caterer on the premises—for Post- Office officials when on duty may not leave the premises for any purpose whatever, *except* duty, and must sign books specifying to the minute when, where, and why, they come and go. In this basement also, as in the other, were long rows of numbered cupboards or large pigeon-holes with lockable doors, one of which was appropriated to each man for the safe depositing of his victuals and other private property.

Here, too, were whitewashed lavatories conveniently and plentifully distributed, with every appliance for cleanliness and comfort, including a large supply of fresh and good water. Of this, 49,000 gallons a day is supplied by an artesian well, and 39,000 gallons a day by the New River Company, in the new building. In the old building the 27,000 gallons consumed daily is supplied by the New River Company. It is, however, due to the 5900 human beings who labour in both buildings to state that at least 55,000 of these gallons are swallowed by steam-engines on the premises.

To all these things Mr. Bright directed attention with professional zeal, and the man in grey observed with much interest all that he saw and heard, until he came to the letter-carriers' kitchen, where several of the men were cooking food at the fire, while others were eating or chatting at the tables.

Happening to mention the dog here, he found that Mr. Bright was partially acquainted with the incident,

"It was down these stairs it ran," he said, "and was knocked on the head in this very room by the policeman. No one knows where he took the body to, but he went out at that door, in the direction, it is supposed, of the boiler-house."

The detective had at last got hold of a clew. He was what is styled, in a well-known game, "getting warm."

"Let us visit the boiler-house," he said.

Again, for the nonce, he became an engineer. Like Paul, he was all things to all men. He was very affable to the genial stoker, who was quite communicative about the boilers. After a time the detective referred to the dog, and the peculiar glance of the stoker at once showed him that his object was gained.

"A policeman brought it?" he asked quietly.

"Yes, a policeman brought it," said the stoker suspiciously.

The man in grey soon, however, removed his suspicions and induced him to become confidential. When he had obtained all the information that the stoker could give—in addition to poor Floppert's collar, which had no name on it, but was stamped with three stars on its inside—the detective ceased to make any further inquiries after mad dogs, and, with a disengaged mind, accompanied Mr. Bright through the remainder of the basement, where he

commented on the wise arrangement of having the
mail-bags made by convicts, and on the free library,
which he pronounced a magnificent institution, and
which contained about 2000 volumes, that were said
by the courteous librarian to be largely used by
the officials, as well as the various newspapers and
magazines, furnished gratuitously by their pro-
prietors.   He was also shown the " lifts," which
raised people—to say nothing of mails, etc.—from
the bottom to the top of the building, or *vice versa ;*
the small steam-engine which worked the same, and
the engineer of which—an old servant—was particularly impressive on the peculiar " governor " by
which his engine was regulated ; the array of letter
stampers, which were kept by their special guardian
in immaculate order and readiness ; the fire-hose,
which was also ready for instant service, and the
firemen, who were in constant attendance with a
telegraphic instrument at their special disposal,
connecting them with other parts of the building.
All this, and a great deal more which we have not
space to mention, the man in grey saw, admired,
and commented on, as well as on the general evidence of order, method, regularity, neatness, and
system which pervaded the whole place.

" You manage things well here," he said to his
conductor at parting.

" We do," responded Mr. Bright, with an approving nod; "and we had need to, for the daily despatch of Her Majesty's mails to all parts of the world is no child's play. Our motto is—or ought to be—' Security, Celerity, Punctuality, and Regularity.' We couldn't carry that out, sir, without good management.—Good-bye."

"Good-bye, and thank you," said the detective, leaving St. Martin's-le-Grand with his busy brain ruminating on a variety of subjects in a manner that no one but a detective could by any possibility understand.

CHAPTER XXIII.

THE TURNING-POINT.

As time advanced Philip Maylands' circumstances improved, for Phil belonged to that class of which it is sometimes said "they are sure to get on." He was thorough-going and trustworthy—two qualities these which the world cannot do without, and which, being always in demand, are never found begging.

Phil did not "set up" for anything. He assumed no airs of superior sanctity. He did not even aim at being better than others, though he did aim, daily, at being better than he was. In short, the lad, having been trained in ways of righteousness, and having the Word of God as his guide, advanced steadily and naturally along the narrow way that leads to life. Hence it came to pass in the course of time that he passed from the ranks of Out-door Boy Telegraph Messenger to that of Boy Sorter, with a wage of twelve shillings a week, which was raised to eighteen shillings. His hours of attendance at the Circulation Department were from 4.30

in the morning till 9 ; and from 4.30 in the evening till 8.   These suited him well, for he had ever been fond of rising with the lark while at home, and had no objection to rise before the lark in London.   The evening being free he devoted to study—for Phil was one of that by no means small class of youths who, in default of a College education, do their best to train themselves, by the aid of books and the occasional help of clergymen, philanthropists, and evening classes.

In all this Phil was greatly assisted by his sister May, who, although not much more highly educated than himself, was quick of perception, of an inquiring mind, and a sympathetic soul.   He was also somewhat assisted, and, at times, not a little retarded, by his ardent admirer Peter Pax, who joined him enthusiastically in his studies, but, being of a discursive and enterprising spirit, was prone to tempt him off the beaten paths of learning into the thickets of speculative philosophy.

One evening Pax was poring over a problem in Euclid with his friend in Pegaway Hall.

" Phil," he said uneasily, " drop your triangles a bit and listen.   Would you think it dishonest to keep a thing secret that ought to be known ?"

" That depends a good deal on what the secret is, and what I have got to do with it," replied Phil. " But why do you ask ?"

" Because I've been keeping a secret a long time
—much against my will—an' I can stand it no
longer. If I don't let it out, it'll bu'st me—besides,
I've got leave to tell it."

" Out with it, then, Pax ; for it's of no use trying
to keep down things that don't agree with you."

" Well, then," said Pax, " I know where George
Aspel is !"

Phil, who had somewhat unwillingly withdrawn
his mind from Euclid, turned instantly with an
eager look towards his little friend.

" Ah, I thought that would rouse you," said the
latter, with a look of unwonted earnestness on his
face. " You must know, Phil, that a long while ago—
just about the time of the burglary at Miss Stivergill's cottage—I made the amazin' discovery that
little Tottie Bones is Mariar—*alias* Merry,—the
little baby-cousin I was nuss to in the country long
ago, whom I've often spoke to you about, and from
whom I was torn when she had reached the tender
age of two or thereby. It follows, of course, that
Tottie's father—old Bones—is my uncle, *alias*
Blackadder, *alias* the Brute, of whom I have also
made mention, and who, it seems, came to London
to try his fortune in knavery after havin' failed in
the country. I saw him once, I believe, at old
Blurt's bird-shop, but did not recognise 'im at the
time, owin' to his hat bein' pulled well over his

eyes, though I rather think he must have recognised
me.   The second time I saw him was when Tottie
came to me for help and set me on his tracks, when
he was goin' to commit the burglary on Rosebud Cottage.   I 've told you all about that, but did not tell
you that the burglar was Tottie's father, as Tottie
had made me promise not to mention it to any
one.   I knew the rascal at once on seeing him in
the railway carriage, and could hardly help explodin'
in his face at the fun of the affair.   Of course he
didn't know me on account of my bein' as black in
the face as the King of Dahomey.—Well," continued
Pax, warming with his subject, " it also follows, as
a matter of course, that Mrs. Bones is my blessed
old aunt Georgie—now changed into Molly, on
account, no doubt, of the Brute's desire to avoid the
attentions of the police.   Now, as I 've a great
regard for aunt Georgie, and have lost a good deal
of my hatred of the Brute, and find myself fonder
than ever of Tottie—I beg her pardon, of Merry—
I 've been rather intimate — indeed, I may say,
pretty thick—with the Boneses ever since ; and as I
am no longer a burden to the Brute—can even help
'im a little—he don't abominate me as much as he
used to.   They 're wery poor—awful poor—are the
Boneses.   The Brute still keeps up a fiction of a
market-garden and a dairy—the latter bein' supplied by a cow and a pump—but it don't pay, and

the business in the city, whatever it may be, seems equally unprofitable, for their town house is not a desirable residence."

"This is all very interesting and strange, Pax, but what has it to do with George Aspel?" asked Phil. "You know I'm very anxious about him, and have long been hunting after him. Indeed, I wonder that you did not tell me about him before."

"How could I," said Pax, "when Tot—I mean Merry — no, I'll stick to Tottie : it comes more natural than the old name—told me not for worlds to mention it. Only now, after pressin' her and aunt Georgie wery hard, have I bin allowed to let it out, for poor Aspel himself don't want his whereabouts to be known."

"Surely !" exclaimed Phil, with a troubled, anxious air, "he has not become a criminal."

"No. Auntie assures me he has not, but he is sunk very low, drinks hard to drown his sorrow, and is ashamed to be seen. No wonder. You'd scarce know 'im, Phil, workin' like a coal-heaver, in a suit of dirty fustian, about the wharves—tryin' to keep out of sight. I've come across 'im once or twice, but pretended not to recognise 'im. Now, Phil," added little Pax, with deep earnestness in his face, as he laid his hand impressively on his friend's arm, "we must save these two men somehow—you and I."

"Yes, God helping us, we must," said Phil.

From that moment Philip Maylands and Peter Pax passed, as it were, into a more earnest sphere of life, a higher stage of manhood. The influence of a powerful motive, a settled purpose, and a great end, told on their characters to such an extent that they both seemed to have passed over the period of hobbledehoyhood at a bound, and become young men.

With the ardour of youth, they set out on their mission at once. That very night they went together to the wretched abode of Abel Bones, having previously, however, opened their hearts and minds to May Maylands, from whom, as they had expected, they received warm encouragement.

Little did these unsophisticated youths know what a torrent of anxiety, grief, fear, and hope their communication sent through the heart of poor May. The eager interest she manifested in their plans they regarded as the natural outcome of a kind heart towards an old friend and playfellow. So it was, but it was more than that!

The same evening George Aspel and Abel Bones were seated alone in their dismal abode in Archangel Court. There were tumblers and a pot of beer before them, but no food. Aspel sat with his elbows on the table, grasping the hair on his temples with both hands. The other sat with arms crossed, and his chin sunk on his chest, gazing gloomily but intently at his companion.

Remorse—that most awful of the ministers of vengeance—had begun to torment Abel Bones. When he saved Tottie from the fire, Aspel had himself unwittingly unlocked the door in the burglar's soul which let the vengeful minister in. Thereafter Miss Stivergill's illustration of mercy, *for the sake of another,* had set the unlocked door ajar, and the discovery that his ill-treated little nephew had nearly lost his life in the same cause, had pulled the door well back on its rusty hinges.

Having thus obtained free entrance, Remorse sat down and did its work with terrible power. Bones was a man of tremendous passions and powerful will. His soul revolted violently from the mean part he had been playing. Although he had not succeeded in drawing Aspel into the vortex of crime as regards human law, he had dragged him very low, and, especially, had fanned the flame of thirst for strong drink, which was the youth's chief—at least his most dangerous—enemy. His thirst was an inheritance from his forefathers, but the sin of giving way to it—of encouraging it at first when it had no power, and then of gratifying it as it gained strength, until it became a tyrant—was all his own. Aspel knew this, and the thought filled him with despair as he sat there with his now scarred and roughened fingers almost tearing out his hair, while his blood-shot eyes stared stonily at the blank wall opposite.

Bones continued to gaze at his companion, and to wish with all his heart that he had never met him. He had, some time before that, made up his mind to put no more temptation in the youth's way. He now went a step further— he resolved to attempt the task of getting him out of the scrapes into which he had dragged him. But he soon found that the will which had always been so powerful in the carrying out of evil was wofully weak in the unfamiliar effort to do good !

Still, Bones had made up his mind to try. With this end in view he proposed a walk in the street, the night being fine. Aspel sullenly consented. The better to talk the matter over, Bones proposed to retire to a quiet though not savoury nook by the river-side. Aspel objected, and proposed a public-house instead, as being more cheerful.

Just opposite that public-house there stood one of those grand institutions which are still in their infancy, but which, we are persuaded, will yet take a prominent part in the rescue of thousands of mankind from the curse of strong drink. It was a "public house without drink"—a coffee-tavern, where working men could find a cheap and wholesome meal, a cheerful, warm, and well-lit room wherein to chat and smoke, and the daily papers, without being obliged to swallow fire-water for the good of the house.

Bones looked at the coffee-house, and thought of suggesting it to his companion. He even willed to do so, but, alas! his will in this matter was as weak as the water which he mingled so sparingly with his grog. Shame, which never troubled him much when about to take a vicious course, suddenly became a giant, and the strong man became weak like a little child. He followed Aspel into the public-house, and the result of this first effort at reformation was that both men returned home drunk.

It seemed a bad beginning, but it *was* a beginning, and as such was not to be despised.

When Phil and Pax reached Archangel Court, a-glow with hope and good resolves, they found the subjects of their desires helplessly asleep in a corner of the miserable room, with Mrs. Bones preparing some warm and wholesome food against the period of their recovery.

It was a crushing blow to their new-born hopes. Poor little Pax had entertained sanguine expectations of the effect of an appeal from Phil, and lost heart completely. Phil was too much cast down by the sight of his friend to be able to say much, but he had a more robust spirit than his little friend, and besides, had strong faith in the power and willingness of God to use even weak and sinful instruments for the accomplishment of His purposes of mercy.

Afterwards, in talking over the subject with his friend Sterling, the city missionary, he spoke hopefully about Aspel, but said that he did not expect any good could be done until they got him out of his miserable position, and away from the society of Bones.

To his great surprise the missionary did not agree with him in this.

"Of course," he said, "it is desirable that Mr Aspel should be restored to his right position in society, and be removed from the bad influence of Bones, and we must use all legitimate means for those ends ; but we must not fall into the mistake of supposing that ' no good can be done ' by the Almighty to His sinful creatures even in the worst of circumstances. No relatives or friends solicited the Prodigal Son to leave the swine-troughs, or dragged him away. It was God who put it into his heart to say ' I will arise and go to my father.' It was God who gave him ' power to will and to do.' "

"Would you then advise that we should do nothing for him, and leave him entirely in the hands of God?" asked Phil, with an uncomfortable feeling of surprise.

"By no means," replied the missionary. " I only combat your idea that no good can be done to him if he is left in his present circumstances. But we are bound to use every influence we can bring to bear in his behalf, and we must pray that success may be granted to our efforts to bring him to the Saviour. Means must be used as if means could accomplish all, but means must not be depended on, for 'it is God who giveth us the victory.' The most appropriate and powerful means applied in the wisest manner to your friend would be utterly ineffective unless the Holy Spirit gave him a receptive heart. This is one of the most difficult lessons that you and I and all men have to learn, Phil—that God must be all in all, and man nothing whatever but a willing instrument. Even that mysterious willingness is not of ourselves, for 'it is God who maketh us both to will and to do of His good pleasure.' 'Without me,' says Jesus, 'ye can do nothing.' A rejecter of Jesus, therefore, is helpless for good, yet responsible."

"That is hard to understand," said Phil, with a perplexed look.

" The reverse of it is harder to understand, as you will find if you choose to take the trouble to think it out," replied the missionary.

Phil Maylands did take the trouble to think it out. One prominent trait in his character was an intense reverence for truth—any truth, every truth—a strong tendency to distinguish between truth and error in all things that chanced to come under his observation, but especially in those

Y

things which his mother had taught him, from earliest infancy, to regard as the most important of all.

Many a passer-by did Phil jostle on his way to the Post-Office that day, after his visit to the missionary, for it was the first time that his mind had been turned, earnestly at least, to the subject of God's sovereignty and man's responsibility.

"Too deep by far for boys," we hear some reader mutter. And yet that same reader, perchance, teaches her little ones to consider the great fact that God is One in Three!

No truth is too deep for boys and girls to consider, if they only approach it in a teachable, reverent spirit, and are brought to it by their teacher in a prayerful spirit. But fear not, reader. We do not mean to inflict on you a dissertation on the mysterious subject referred to. We merely state the fact that Phil Maylands met it at this period of his career, and, instead of shelving it—as perhaps too many do—as a too difficult subject, which might lie over to a more convenient season, tackled it with all the energy of his nature. He went first to his closet and his knees, and then to his Bible.

"To the law and to the testimony" used to be Mrs. Maylands' watchword in all her battles with Doubt. "To whom shall we go," she was wont to say, "if we go not to the Word of God?"

Phil therefore searched the Scripture. Not being a Greek scholar, he sought help of those who were learned—both personally and through books. Thus he got at correct renderings, and by means of dictionaries ascertained the exact meanings of words. By study he got at what some have styled the general spirit of Scripture, and by reading *both* sides of controverted points he ascertained the thoughts of various minds. In this way he at length became "fully persuaded in his own mind" that God's sovereignty and man's responsibility are facts taught in Scripture, and affirmed by human experience, and that they form a great unsolvable mystery—unsolvable at least by man in his present condition of existence.

This not only relieved his mind greatly, by convincing him that, the subject being bottomless, it was useless to try to get to the bottom of it, and wise to accept it "as a little child," but it led him also to consider that in the Bible there are two kinds of mysteries, or deep things—the one kind being solvable, the other unsolvable. He set himself, therefore, diligently to discover and separate the one kind from the other, with keen interest.

But this is by the way. Phil's greatest anxiety and care at that time was the salvation of his old friend and former idol, George Aspel.

CHAPTER XXIV.

PLANS AND COUNTER PLANS.

ONE evening Phil sat in the sorting-room of the
General Post-Office with his hand to his head—for
the eight o'clock mail was starting; his head, eyes,
and hands had been unusually active during the
past two hours, and when the last bundle of letters
dropped from his fingers into the mail-bags, head,
eyes, and hands were aching.

A row of scarlet vans was standing under a
platform, into which mail-bags, apparently innumerable, were being shot. As each of these vans
received its quota it rattled off to its particular
railway station, at the rate which used, in the olden
time, to be deemed the extreme limit of "haste,
haste, post haste." The yard began to empty when
eight o'clock struck. A few seconds later the last
of the scarlet vans drove off; and about forty tons
of letters, etc., were flying from the great centre to
the circumference of the kingdom.

Phil still sat pressing the aching fingers to the aching head and eyes, when he was roused by a touch on the shoulder. It was Peter Pax, who had also, by that time, worked his way upwards in the service.

"Tired, Phil?" asked Pax.

"A little, but it soon passes off," said Phil lightly, as he rose. "There's no breathing-time, you see, towards the close, and it's the pace that kills in everything."

"Are you going to Pegaway Hall to-night?" asked Pax, "because, if so, I'll go with you, bein', so to speak, in a stoodious humour myself."

"No, I'm not going to study to-night,—don't feel up to it. Besides, I want to visit Mr. Blurt. The book he lent me on Astronomy ought to be returned, and I want to borrow another.—Come, you'll go with me."

After exchanging some books at the library in the basement, which the man in grey had styled a "magnificent institootion," the two friends left the Post-Office together.

"Old Mr. Blurt is fond of you, Pax."

"That shows him to be a man of good taste," said Pax, "and his lending you and me as many books as we want proves him a man of good sense. D'you know, Phil, it has sometimes struck me that, what between our Post-Office library and the liberality of Mr. Blurt and a few other friends, you and I are rather lucky dogs in the way of literature."

"We are," assented Phil.

"And ought, somehow, to rise to somethin', some time or other," said Pax.

"We ought—and will," replied the other, with a laugh.

"But do you know," continued Pax, with a sigh, "I've at last given up all intention of aiming at the Postmaster-Generalship."

"Indeed, Pax!"

"Yes. It wouldn't suit me at all. You see I was born and bred in the country, and can't stand a city life. No; my soul—small though it be—is too large for London. The metropolis can't hold me, Phil. If I were condemned to live in London all my life, my spirit would infallibly bu'st its shell an' blow the bricks and mortar around me to atoms."

"That's strange now; it seems to me, Pax, that London is country and town in one. Just look at the Parks."

"Pooh! flat as a pancake. No ups and downs, no streams, no thickets, no wild-flowers worth mentioning—nothin' wild whatever 'cept the child'n," returned Pax, contemptuously.

"But look at the Serpentine, and the Thames, and—"

"Bah!" interrupted Pax, "would you compare the Thames with the clear, flowing, limpid—"

"Come now, Pax, don't become poetical, it isn't your forte; but listen while I talk of matters more important. You've sometimes heard me mention my mother, haven't you?"

"I have—with feelings of poetical reverence," answered Pax.

"Well, my mother has been writing of late in rather low spirits about her lonely condition in that wild place on the west coast of Ireland. Now, Mr. Blurt has been groaning much lately as to his having no female relative to whom he could trust his brother Fred. You know he is obliged to look after the shop, and to go out a good deal on business, during which times Mr. Fred is either left alone, or under the care of Mrs. Murridge, who, though faithful, is old and deaf and stupid. Miss Lillycrop would have been available once, but ever since the fire she has been appropriated—along with Tottie Bones—by that female Trojan Miss Stivergill, and dare not hint at leaving her. It's a good thing for her, no doubt, but it's unfortunate for Mr. Fred. Now, do you see anything in the mists of that statement?"

"Ah—yes—just so," said Pax; "Mr. Blurt wants help; mother wants cheerful society. A sick-room ain't the perfection of gaiety, no doubt, but it's better than the west coast of Ireland—at least as depicted by you. Yes, somethin' might come o' that."

"More may come of it than you think, Pax. You see I want to provide some sort of home for George Aspel to come to when we save him—for we're sure to save him at last. I feel certain of that," said Phil, with something in his tone that did not quite correspond to his words—"quite certain of that," he repeated, "God helping us. I mean to talk it over with May."

They turned, as he spoke, into the passage which led to Mr. Flint's abode.

May was at home, and she talked the matter over with Phil in the boudoir with the small window, and the near prospect of brick wall, and the photographs of the Maylands, and the embroidered text that was its occupant's sheet-anchor.

She at once fell in with his idea about getting their mother over to London, but when he mentioned his views about her furnishing a house so as to offer a home to his friend Aspel, she was apparently distressed, and yet seemed unable to explain her meaning or to state her objections clearly

"Oh! Phil, dear," she said at last, "don't plan and arrange too much. Let us try to walk so that we may be led by God, and not run in advance of Him."

Phil was perplexed and disappointed, for May not only appeared to throw cold water on his efforts, but seemed unwilling to give her personal aid in the rescue of her old playmate. He was wrong in this. In the circumstances, poor May could not with propriety bring personal influence to bear on Aspel, but she could and did pray for him with all the ardour of a young and believing heart.

"It's a very strange thing," continued Phil, "that George won't take assistance from any one. I know that he is in want—that he has not money enough to buy respectable clothes so as to be able to appear among his old friends, yet he will not take a sixpence from me—not even as a loan."

May did not answer. With her face hid in her hands she sat on the edge of her bed, weeping at the thought of her lover's fallen condition. Poor May! People said that telegraphic work was too hard for her, because her cheeks were losing the fresh bloom that she had brought from the west of Ireland, and the fingers with which she manipulated the keys so deftly were growing very thin. But sorrow had more to do with the change than the telegraph had.

"It must be pride," said her brother.

"Oh! Phil," she said, looking up, "don't you think that shame has more to do with it than pride?"

Phil stooped and kissed her.

"Sure it's that, no doubt, and I'm a beast entirely for suggesting pride."

"Supper! Hallo in there," shouted Mr. Flint, thundering at the door; "don't keep the old 'ooman waiting!"

Phil and May came forth at once, but the former would not remain to supper. He had to visit Mr. Blurt, he said, and might perhaps sup with him. Pax would go with him.

"Well, my lads, please yourselves," said Mr. Flint, wheeling the old woman to the table, on which smoked a plentiful supply of her favourite sausages.

"Let me take the cat off your lap, grannie," said May.

"Let the cat be, lassie; it's daein' nae ill. Are the callants gaein' oot?"

"Yes, grannie," said Phil, "we have business to attend to."

"Bizness!" exclaimed Mrs. Flint. "Weel, weel, they lay heavy burdens on 'ee at that Post-Office. Night an' day—night an' day. They've maist killed my Solomon. They've muckle to answer for."

In her indignation she clenched her fist and brought it down on her knee. Unfortunately the cat came between the fist and the knee. With its usual remonstrative mew it fled and found a place of rest and refuge in the coal-box.

"But it's not to the Post-Office we're goin', grannie," said Phil, laying his hand kindly on the old woman's shoulder.

"What o' that? what o' that?" she exclaimed somewhat testily at being corrected, "has that onything to dae wi' the argiment? If ye git yer feet wat, bairns, mind to chynge them; an' whatever ye dae—"

She stopped suddenly. One glance at her placid old countenance sufficed to show that she had retired to the previous century, from which nothing now could recall her except sausages. The youths therefore went out.

Meanwhile Mr. Enoch Blurt sat in his brother's back shop entertaining a visitor. The shop itself had, for a considerable time past, been put under the care of an overgrown boy, who might—by courtesy and a powerful stretch of truth—have been styled a young man.

Jiggs—he appeared to have no other name— was simply what men style a born idiot: not sufficiently so to be eligible for an asylum, but far enough gone to be next to useless. Mr. Blurt had picked him up somewhere, in a philanthropic way—no one ever knew how or where—during one of his many searches after George Aspel.

Poor Mr. Blurt was not happy in his selection of men or boys. Four of the latter whom he had engaged to attend the shop and learn the business had been dismissed for rough play with the specimens, or making free with the till when a few coppers chanced to be in it. They had failed, also, to learn the business; chiefly because there was no business to learn, and Mr. Enoch Blurt did not know how to teach it. When he came in contact with Jiggs, Mr. Blurt believed he had at last secured a prize, and confided that belief to Mrs. Murridge. So he had, as regards honesty. Jiggs was honest to the core, but as to other matters he was defective—to say the least. He could, however, put up and take down the shutters, call Mr. Blurt down-stairs if wanted— which he never was; and tell customers, when he was out, to call again—which he never did, as customers never darkened the door. Jiggs, how- ever, formed a sufficient scarecrow to street boys and thieves.

The visitor in the back shop—to whom we now return—was no less a personage than Miss Gentle, whose acquaintance Mr. Blurt had made on board the ill-fated mail steamer *Trident*. That lady had chanced, some weeks before, to pass the ornitho- logical shop, and, looking in, was struck dumb by the sight of the never-forgotten fellow-passenger who had made her a confidant. Recovering speech, she entered the shop and introduced herself. The introduction was needless. Mr. Blurt recognised her at once, dropped his paper, extended both hands, gave her a welcome that brought even Jiggs back to the verge of sanity, and had her into the back shop, whence he expelled Mrs. Murridge to some other and little-known region of the interior.

The interview was so agreeable that Mr. Blurt begged it might be repeated. It was repeated four times. The fifth time it was repeated by special arrangement in the evening, for the purpose of talking over a business matter.

"I fear, Miss Gentle," began Mr. Blurt, when his visitor was seated in the back shop, and Mrs. Murridge had been expelled to the rear as usual, and Jiggs had been left on guard in the front—"I fear that you may think it rude in me to make such a proposal, but I am driven to it by necessity, and—the fact is, I want you to become a nurse."

"A nurse, Mr. Blurt!"

"There, now, don't take offence. It's below your position, I dare say, but I have gathered from you that your circumstances are not—are not—not exactly luxurious, and,—in short, my poor brother Fred is a hopeless invalid. The doctors say he will never be able to leave his bed. Ah! if those diamonds I once spoke to you about had only been mine still, instead of adorning the caves of crabs and fishes, Miss Gentle, I would have had half-a-dozen of the best nurses in London for dear Fred. But the diamonds are gone ! I am a poor man, a very poor man, Miss Gentle, and I cannot afford a good nurse. At the same time, I cannot bear to think of Fred being, even for a brief period, at the mercy of cheap nurses, who, like other wares, are bad when cheap —although, of course, there may be a few good ones even among the cheap. What I cannot buy, therefore, I must beg ; and I have come to you, as one with a gentle and pitiful spirit, who may, per-haps, take an interest in my poor brother's case, and agree to help us."

Having said all this very fast, and with an expres-sion of eager anxiety, Mr. Blurt blew his nose, wiped his bald forehead, and, laying both hands on his knees, looked earnestly into his visitor's face.

"You are wrong, Mr. Blurt, in saying that the office of nurse is below my position. It is below the position of no one in the land. I may not be very competent to fill the office, but I am quite willing to try."

"My dear madam," exclaimed the delighted Mr. Blurt, "your goodness is—but I expected as much. I knew you would—. Of course," he said, inter-rupting himself, "all the menial work will be done

by Mrs. Murridge.   You will be only required to
fill, as it were, the part of a daughter—or—or a
sister—to my poor Fred.   As to salary : it will
be small, very small, I fear ; but there are a couple
of nice rooms in the house, which will be entirely
at your—"

"I quite understand," interrupted Miss Gentle,
with a smile.   "We won't talk of these details,
please, until you have had a trial of me, and see
whether I am worthy of a salary at all !"

"Miss Gentle," returned Mr. Blurt, with sudden
gravity, "your extreme kindness emboldens me
to put before you another matter of business, which
I trust you will take into consideration in a purely
business light.—I am getting old, madam."

Miss Gentle acknowledged the truth with a slight
bow.

"And you are—excuse me—not young, Miss
Gentle."

The lady acknowledged this truth with a slighter
bow.

"You would not object to regard me in the light
of a brother, would you ?"

Mr. Blurt took one of her hands in his, and looked
at her earnestly.

Miss Gentle looked at Mr. Blurt quite as earnestly, and replied that she had no objection whatever to that.

"Still further, Miss Gentle : if I were to presume to ask you to regard me in the light of a husband, would you object to that ?"

Miss Gentle looked down and said nothing, from which Mr. Blurt concluded that she did *not* object. She withdrew her hand suddenly, however, and blushed. There was a slight noise at the door. It was Jiggs, who, with an idiotical stare, asked if it was not time to put up the shutters !

The plan thus vexatiously interrupted was, however, ultimately carried into effect. Miss Gentle, regardless of poverty, the absence of prospects, and the certainty of domestic anxiety, agreed to wed Mr. Enoch Blurt and nurse his brother. In consideration of the paucity of funds, and the pressing nature of the case, she also agreed to dispense with a regular honeymoon, and to content herself with, as it were, a honey-star at home.

Of course, the event knocked poor Phil's little plans on the head for the time being, though it did not prevent his resolving to do his utmost to bring his mother to London.

CHAPTER XXV.

LIGHT SHINING IN DARK PLACES.

DOWN by the river-side, in an out-of-the-way and unsavoury neighbourhood, George Aspel and Abel Bones went one evening into a small eating-house to have supper after a day of toil at the docks. It was a temperance establishment. They went to it, however, not because of its temperance but its cheapness. After dining they adjourned to a neighbouring public-house to drink.

Bones had not yet got rid of his remorse, nor had he entirely given up desiring to undo what he had done for Aspel. But he found the effort to do good more difficult than he had anticipated. The edifice pulled down so ruthlessly was not, he found, to be rebuilt in a day. It is true, the work of demolition had not been all his own. If Aspel had not been previously addicted to careless living, such a man as Bones never could have had the smallest chance of influencing him. But Bones did not care to reason deeply. He knew that he had desired

z

and plotted the youth's downfall, and that downfall had been accomplished. Having fallen from such a height, and being naturally so proud and self-sufficient, Aspel was proportionally more difficult to move again in an upward direction.

Bones had tried once again to get him to go to the temperance public-house, and had succeeded. They had supped there once, and were more than pleased with the bright, cheerful aspect of the place, and its respectable and sober, yet jolly, frequenters. But the cup of coffee did not satisfy their depraved appetites. The struggle to overcome was too much for men of no principle. They were self-willed and reckless. Both said, "What's the use of trying?" and returned to their old haunts.

On the night in question, after supping, as we have said, they entered a public-house to drink. It was filled with a noisy crew, as well as with tobacco-smoke and spirituous fumes. They sat down at a retired table and looked round.

"God help me," muttered Aspel, in a low husky voice, "I've fallen *very* low!"

"Ay," responded Bones, almost savagely, "*very* low."

Aspel was too much depressed to regard the tone. The waiter stood beside them, expectant. "Two pints of beer," said Bones,—"*ginger*-beer," he added, quickly.

" Yessir."

The waiter would have said "Yessir" to an order for two pints of prussic acid, if that had been an article in his line. It was all one to him, so long as it was paid for. Men and women might drink and die; they might come and go; they might go and not come—others would come if they didn't,—but *he* would go on, like the brook, "for ever," supplying the terrible demand.

As the ginger-beer was being poured out the door opened, and a man with a pack on his back entered. Setting down the pack, he wiped his heated brow and looked round. He was a mild, benignant-looking man, with a thin face.

Opening his box, he said in a loud voice to the assembled company, " Who will buy a Bible for sixpence ?"

There was an immediate hush in the room. After a few seconds a half-drunk man, with a black eye, said—

" We don't want no Bibles 'ere. We 've got plenty of 'em at 'ome. Bibles is only for Sundays."

" Don't people die on Mondays and Saturdays ?" said the colporteur, for such he was. " It would be a bad job if we could only have the Bible on Sundays. God's Word says, 'To-day if ye will hear His voice, harden not your hearts.' 'Jesus

Christ is the same yesterday, to-day, and for ever.'
'*Now* is the accepted time, *now* is the day of
salvation.' It says the same on Tuesdays and
Wednesdays, and every day of the week."

"That's all right enough, old fellow," said another
man, "but a public is not the right place to bring
a Bible into."

Turning to this man the colporteur said quietly,
"Does not death come into public-houses? Don't
people die in public-houses? Surely it is right
to take the Word of God into any place where
death comes, for 'after death the judgment.' 'The
blood of Jesus Christ, God's Son, cleanseth us
from all sin.'"

"Come, come, that 'll do. We don't want none
of that here," said the landlord of the house.

"Very well, sir," said the man respectfully, "but
these gentlemen have not yet declined to hear me."

This was true, and one of the men now came
forward to look at the contents of the box.
Another joined him.

"Have you any book that 'll teach a man how
to get cured of drink?" asked one, who obviously
stood greatly in need of such a book.

"Yes, I have. Here it is—*The Author of the
Sinner's Friend;* it is a memoir of the man who
wrote a little book called *The Sinner's Friend*," said
the colporteur, producing a thin booklet in paper

cover, " but I'd recommend a Bible along with it, because the Bible tells of the sinner's *best* friend, Jesus, and remember that without Him you can do *nothing*. He is God, and it is 'God who giveth us the victory.' You can't do it by yourself, if you try ever so much."

The man bought the booklet and a Testament. Before he left the place that colporteur had sold a fourpenny and a twopenny Testament, and several other religious works, beside distributing tracts gratuitously all round.[1]

"That's what I call carryin' the war into the enemy's camp," remarked one of the company, as the colporteur thanked them and went away.

"Come, let's go," said Aspel, rising abruptly and draining his glass of ginger-beer.

Bones followed his example. They went out and overtook the colporteur.

"Are there many men going about like you?" asked Aspel.

"A good many," answered the colporteur. "We work upwards of sixty districts now. Last year we sold Bibles, Testaments, good books and periodicals, to the value of £6700, besides distributing more than 300,000 tracts, and speaking to many people the blessed Word of Life. It is true we have not

---

[1] See Report of "The Christian Colportage Association for England," 1879, p. 12.

yet done much in public-houses, but, as you saw just now, it is not an unhopeful field. That branch has been started only a short time ago, yet we have sold in public-houses above five hundred Bibles and Testaments, and over five thousand Christian books, besides distributing tracts."

"It's a queer sort o' work," said Bones. "Do you expect much good from it?"

The colporteur replied, with a look of enthusiasm, that he *did* expect much good, because much had already been done, and the promise of success was sure. He personally knew, and could name, sinners who had been converted to God through the instrumentality of colporteurs; men and women who had formerly lived solely for themselves had been brought to Jesus, and now lived for Him. Swearers had been changed to men of prayer and praise, and drunkards had become sober men—"

"Through that little book, I suppose?" asked Bones quickly.

"Not altogether, but partly by means of it."

"Have you another copy?" asked George Aspel.

The man at once produced the booklet, and Aspel purchased it.

"What do you mean," he said, "by its being only 'partly' the means of saving men from drink?"

"I mean that there is no Saviour from sin of any kind but Jesus Christ. The remedy pointed out in that little book is, I am told, a good and effective one, but without the Spirit of God no man has power to persevere in the application of the remedy. He will get wearied of the continuous effort; he will not avoid temptation; he will lose heart in the battle unless he has a higher motive than his own deliverance to urge him on. Why, sirs, what would you expect from the soldier who, in battle, thought of nothing but himself and his own safety, his own deliverance from the dangers around him? Is it not those men who boldly face the enemy with the love of Queen and country and comrades and duty strong in their breasts, who are most likely to conquer? In the matter of drink the man who trusts to remedies alone will surely fail, because the disease is moral as well as physical. The physical remedy will not cure the soul's disease, but the moral remedy—the acceptance of Jesus—will not only cure the soul, but will secure to us that spiritual influence which will enable us to 'persevere to the end' with the physical. Thus Jesus will save both soul and body—' it is God who giveth us the victory.'"

They parted from the colporteur at this point.

"What think you of that?" asked Bones.

"It is strange, if true—but I don't believe it," replied Aspel.

"Well now, it appears to me," rejoined Bones,

"that the man seems pretty sure of what he believes, and very reasonable in what he says, but I don't know enough about the subject to hold an opinion as to whether it's true or false."

It might have been well for Aspel if he had taken as modest a view of the matter as his companion, but he had been educated—that is to say, he had received an average elementary training at an ordinary school,—and on the strength of that, although he had never before given a serious thought to religion, and certainly nothing worthy of the name of study, he held himself competent to judge and to disbelieve!

While they walked towards the City, evening was spreading her grey mantle over the sky. The lamps had been lighted, and the enticing blaze from gin-palaces and beer-shops streamed frequently across their path.

At the corner of a narrow street they were arrested by the sound of music in quick time, and energetically sung.

"A penny gaff," remarked Bones, referring to a low music-hall; "what d'ee say to go in?"

Aspel was so depressed just then that he welcomed any sort of excitement, and willingly went.

"What's to pay?" he asked of the man at the door.

"Nothing; it's free."

"That's liberal anyhow," observed Bones, as they pushed in.

The room was crowded by people of the lowest order—men and women in tattered garments, and many of them with debauched looks. A tall thin man stood on the stage or platform. The singing ceased, and he advanced.

"Bah!" whispered Aspel, "it's a prayer-meeting. Let's be off."

"Stay," returned Bones. "I know the feller. He comes about our court sometimes. Let's hear what he's got to say."

"Friends," said Mr. Sterling, the city missionary, for it was he, "I hold in my hand the Word of God. There are messages in this Word—this Bible —for every man and woman in this room. I shall deliver only two of these messages to-night. If any of you want more of 'em you may come back to-morrow. Only two to-night. The first is, 'Though your sins be as scarlet they shall be as white as snow, though they be red like crimson they shall be as wool.' The other is, 'It is God who giveth us the victory.'"

Bones started and looked at his companion. It seemed as if the missionary had caught up and echoed the parting words of the colporteur.

Mr. Sterling had a keen, earnest look, and a naturally eloquent as well as persuasive tongue.

Though comparatively uneducated, he was deeply
read in the Book which it was his life's work to
expound, and an undercurrent of intense feeling
seemed to carry him along—and his hearers along
with him—as he spoke. He did not shout or ges-
ticulate : that made him all the more impressive.
He did not speak of himself or his own feelings :
that enabled his hearers to give undistracted attention to the message he had to deliver. He did not
energise. On the contrary, it seemed as if he had
some difficulty in restraining the superabundant
energy that burned within him ; and as people
usually stand more or less in awe of that which
they do not fully understand, they gave him credit,
perhaps, for more power than he really possessed.
At all events, not a sound was heard, save now and
then a suppressed sob, as he preached Christ cruci-
fied to guilty sinners, and urged home the two
"messages" with all the force of unstudied language, but well-considered and aptly put illustration and anecdote.

At one part of his discourse he spoke, with bated
breath, of the unrepentant sinner's awful danger,
comparing it to the condition of a little child who
should stand in a blazing house, with escape by the
staircase cut off, and no one to deliver—a simile
which brought instantly to Bones's mind his little
Tottie and the fire, and the rescue by the man he

had resolved to ruin—ay, whom he *had* ruined, to all appearance.

"But there *is* a Deliverer in this case," continued the preacher. "'Jesus Christ came to seek and to save the *lost;*' to pluck us all as brands from the burning; to save us from the fire of sin, of impurity, of drink! Oh, friends, will you not accept the Saviour—"

"Yes! yes!" shouted Bones, in an irresistible burst of feeling, "I *do* accept Him!"

Every eye was turned at once on the speaker, who stood looking fixedly upwards, as though unaware of the sensation he had created. The interruption, however, was only momentary.

"Thanks be to God!" said the preacher. "There is joy among the angels of heaven over one sinner that repenteth."

Then, not wishing to allow attention to be diverted from his message, he continued his discourse with such fervour that the people soon forgot the interrupter, and Bones forgot them and himself and his friend, in contemplation of the "Great Salvation."

When the meeting was over he hurried out into the open air. Aspel followed, but lost him in the crowd. After searching a few minutes without success, he returned to Archangel Court without him.

The proud youth was partly subdued, though not overcome. He had heard things that night which he had never heard before, as well as many things which, though heard before, had never made such an impression as then. Lighting the remnant of the candle in the pint bottle, he pulled out the little book which he had purchased, and began to read, and ever as he read there seemed to start up the words, " It is God who giveth us the victory." At last he came to the page on which the prescription for drunkards is printed in detail. He read it with much interest and some hope, though, of course, being ignorant of medicine, it conveyed no light to his mind.

" I 'll try it at all events," he muttered in a somewhat desponding tone ; " but I 've tried before now to break off the accursed habit without success, and have my doubts of this, for—"

He paused, for the words, " It is God that giveth us the victory," leaped again to his mind with tenfold power.

Just then there arose a noise of voices in the court. Presently the sound of many footsteps was heard in the passage. The shuffling feet stopped at the door, and some one knocked loudly.

With a strange foreboding at his heart, Aspel leaped up and opened it.

Four men entered, bearing a stretcher. They

placed it gently on the low truckle-bed in the corner, and, removing the cover, revealed the mangled and bloody but still breathing form of Abel Bones.

"He seemed to be a bit unhinged in his mind," said one of the men in reply to Aspel's inquiring look—"was seen goin' recklessly across the road, and got run over. We would 'ave took 'im to the hospital, but he preferred to be brought here."

"All right, George," said Bones in a low voice, "I'll be better in a little. It was an accident. Send 'em away, an' try if you can find my old girl and Tottie.—It is strange," he continued faintly, as Aspel bent over him, "that the lady I wanted to rob set me free, for Tottie's sake; and the boy I cast adrift in London risked his life for Tottie; and the man I tried to ruin saved her; and the man I have often cursed from my door has brought me at last to the Sinner's Friend. Strange! very strange!"

CHAPTER XXVI.

TELLS OF A SHAM FIGHT AND A REAL BATTLE.

THERE are periods in the busy round of labour at the great heart in St. Martin's-le-Grand when some members of the community cease work for a time and go off to enjoy a holiday.

Such periods do not occur to all simultaneously, else would the great postal work of the kingdom come to a dead-lock. They are distributed so that the action of the heart never flags, even when large drafts are made on the working staff, as when a whole battalion of the employés goes out for a field-day in the garb of Volunteers.

There are between eight and nine hundred men of the Post Office, who, not content with carrying Her Majesty's mails, voluntarily carry Her Majesty's rifles. These go through the drudgery and drill of military service at odd hours, as they find time, and on high occasions they march out to the martial strains of fife and drum.

On one such occasion the Post-Office battalion (better known as the 49th Middlesex) took part in a sham fight, which Phil Maylands and Peter Pax (who chanced to have holidays at the time) went out to see. They did not take part in it, not being Volunteers, but they took pride in it, as worthy, right-spirited men of the Post could not fail to do.

The 49th Middlesex distinguished themselves on that occasion. Their appearance as they marched on to the battle-ground—some distance out of London—bore creditable comparison with the best corps in the service. So said Pax; and Pax was a good judge, being naturally critical.

When the fight began, and the rattling musketry, to say nothing of booming artillery, created such a smoke that no unmilitary person could make head or tail of anything, the 49th Middlesex took advantage of a hollow, and executed a flank movement that would have done credit to the 42d Highlanders, and even drew forth an approving nod and smile from the reviewing officer, who with his cocked-hatted staff witnessed the movement from an eminence which was swept by a devastating cross-fire from every part of the field.

When the artillery were ordered to another eminence to check the movement and dislodge them from the hollow, the gallant 49th stood their ground

in the face of a fire that would have swept that
hollow as with the besom of destruction.   They also
replied with a continuous discharge that would, in
five minutes, have immolated every man and horse
on the eminence.

When, afterwards, a body of cavalry was sent to
teach the gallant 49th a lesson, and came thundering down on them like a wolf on the fold, or an
avalanche on a Swiss hamlet, they formed square
with mathematical precision, received them with a
withering fire that ought to have emptied every
saddle, and, with the bayonet's point, turned them
trooping off to the right and left, discomfited.

When, finally, inflated with the pride of victory,
they began to re-form line too soon, and were caught
in the act by the returning cavalry, they flung
themselves into rallying squares, which, bristling
with bayonets like porcupines of steel, kept up
such an incessant roar of musketry that the spot
on which they stood became, as it were, a heart or
core of furious firing, in the midst of a field that
was already hotly engaged all round.   We do not
vouch for the correctness of this account of the
battle.   We received it from Pax, and give it for
what it is worth.

Oh ! it was, as Phil Maylands said, " a glorious
day entirely for the 49th Middlesex, that same
Queen's Birthday," for there was all the pomp and

circumstance of war, all the smoke and excitation, all the glitter of bright sunshine on accoutrements, the flash of sword and bayonet, and the smoke and fire of battle, without the bloodshed and the loss of life!

No doubt there were drawbacks. Where is the human family, however well regulated, that claims exemption from such? There were some of the warriors on that bloodless battle-field who had no more idea of the art of war than the leg of a telescope has of astronomy. There were many who did not know which were friends and which were foes. Many more there were who did not care! Some of the Volunteer officers (though not many), depending too much on their sergeants to keep them right, drove these sergeants nearly mad. Others there were, who, depending too much on their own genius, drove their colonels frantic; but by far the greater number, both of officers and men, knew their work and did it well.

Yes, it was indeed a glorious day entirely, that same Queen's Birthday, for all arms of the service, especially for the 49th Middlesex; and when that gallant body of men marched from the field of glory, with drums beating and fifes shrieking, little Pax could scarcely contain himself for joy, and wished with all his heart that he were drum-major of the corps, that he might find vent for his feelings in the bursting of the big drum.

"Now," said Phil, when they had seen the last of the Volunteers off the field, "what shall you and I do?"

"Ah! true, that is the question," returned Pax; "what are we to do? Our holidays are before us. The day is far spent; the evening is at hand. We. can't bivouac here, that is plain. What say you, Phil, to walking over to Miss Stivergill's? I have a general invite from that lady to spend any holidays I have to dispose of at Rosebud Cottage. It is not more than two miles from where we stand."

"D'ye think she'd extend her invite to me?" asked Phil dubiously.

"Think!" exclaimed Pax, "I am *sure* of it. Why, that respectable old lady owns a heart that might have been enshrined in a casket of beauty. She's a trump—a regular brick."

"Come, Pax, be respectful."

"Ain't I respectful, you Irish noodle? My language mayn't be choice, indeed, but you can't find fault with the sentiment. Come along, before it gets darker. Any friend of mine will be welcome; besides, I half expect to find your sister there, and we shall be sure to see Miss Lillycrop and my sweet little cousin Tottie, who has been promoted to the condition of ladies'-maid and companion."

"Ah, poor Tottie!" said Phil, " her father's illness has told heavily on her"

"That's true," returned Pax, as every vestige of fun vanished from his expressive face and was replaced by sympathy, "but I've good news for her to-night. Since her last visit her father has improved, and the doctor says he may yet recover. The fresh air of the new house has done him good."

Pax referred here to a new residence in a more airy neighbourhood, to which Bones had been removed through the kindness and liberality of Miss Stivergill, whose respect for the male sex had, curiously enough, increased from the date of the burglary. With characteristic energy she had removed Bones, with his wife and a few household goods, to a better dwelling near the river, but this turned out to be damp, and Bones became worse in it. She therefore instituted another prompt removal to a more decidedly salubrious quarter. Here Bones improved a little in health. But the poor man's injury was of a serious nature. Ribs had been broken, and the lungs pierced. A constitution debilitated by previous dissipation could not easily withstand the shock. His life trembled in the balance.

The change, however, in the man's spirit was marvellous. It had not been the result of sudden calamity or of prolonged suffering. Before his accident, while in full vigour and in the midst of his sins, the drops which melted him had begun to fall like dew. The night when his eyes were opened to see Jesus was but the culminating of God's work of mercy. From that night he spoke little, but the little he said was to express thankfulness. He cared not to reason. He would not answer questions that were sometimes foolishly put to him, but he listened to the Word of God, read by his poor yet rejoicing wife, with eager, thirsting looks. When told that he was in danger he merely smiled.

"Georgie," he whispered—for he had reverted to the old original name of his wife, which, with his proper name of Blackadder, he had changed on coming to London—"Georgie, I wish I might live for your sake and His, but it'll be better to go. We're on the same road at last, Georgie, and shall meet again."

Aspel marked the change and marvelled. He could not understand it at all. But he came to understand it ere long. He had followed Bones in his changes of abode, because he had formed a strange liking for the man, but he refused to associate in any way with his former friends. They occasionally visited the sick man, but if Aspel chanced to be with him at the time he invariably went out by the back-door as they entered by the front. He refused even to see Phil Maylands, but met Pax, and seemed not to mind him. At all events he took

no notice of him.   Whether his conduct was owing
to pride, shame, or recklessness, none could tell.

The changes of residence we have referred to had
the effect of throwing off the scent a certain gentleman who had been tracking out Abel Bones with
the perseverance, though not the success, of a blood-
hound.

The man in grey, after losing, or rather coming
to the end, of his clew at the Post-Office furnace,
recovered it by some magical powers known best to
himself and his compeers, and tracked his victim to
Archangel Court, but here he lost the scent again,
and seemed to be finally baffled.   It was well for
Bones that it so fell out, because in his weak state
it would probably have gone hard with him had he
believed that the police were still on his tracks.   As
it was, he progressed slowly but favourably, and with
this good news Pax and his friend hurried to Rosebud Cottage.

What an unmitigated blessing a holiday is to
those who work hard !   Ah ! ye lazy ones of
earth, if ye gain something by unbounded leisure
ye lose much.   Stay—we will not preach on that
text.   It needs not !

To return : Phil and Pax found Tottie and May
at The Rosebud as they had anticipated—the latter
being free for a time on sick-leave—and the four
went in for a holiday, as Pax put it, neck and crop.

It may occur to some that there was somewhat
of incongruity in the companionship of Tottie and
May, but the difference between the poor man's
daughter who had been raised to comparative afflu-
ence, and the gentleman's daughter who had been
brought down to comparative poverty, was not so
great as one might suppose. It must be remembered that Tottie had started life with a God-fearing
mother, and that of itself secured her from much
contamination in the midst of abounding evil,
while it surrounded her with a rich influence for
good. Then, latterly, she had been mentally,
morally, and physically trained by Miss Lillycrop, who was a perfect pattern of propriety
delicacy, good sense, and good taste. She first
read to her pupil, and then made the pupil read
to her. Miss Lillycrop's range of reading was
wide and choice. Thus Tottie, who was naturally
refined and intelligent, in time became more so by
education. She had grown wonderfully too, and
had acquired a certain sedateness of demeanour,
which was all the more captivating that it was an
utterly false index to her character, for Tottie's spirit
was as wildly exuberant as that of the wildest
denizen of Archangel Court.

In like manner Pax had been greatly improved
by his association with Phil Maylands. The vigorous strength of Phil's mind had unconsciously

exercised a softening influence on his little admirer.
We have said that they studied and read together.
Hence Pax was learned beyond his years and station.
The fitness therefore of the four to associate plea-
santly has, we think, been clearly made out.

Pax, at all events, had not a shadow of a doubt
on that point, especially when the four lay down
under the shadow of a spreading oak to examine
the butterflies and moths they had captured in the
fields.

"What babies we are," said Phil, "to go after
butterflies in this fashion!"

"Speak for yourself," retorted Pax; "I consider
myself an entomologist gathering specimens. Call
'em specimens, Phil; that makes a world of difference.—Oh, Tot! what a splendid one you have got
there! It reminds me so of the time when I used
to carry you about the fields on my back, and call
you Merry. Don't you remember?"

"No," said Tottie, "I don't."

"And *won't* you let me call you Merry?" pleaded
Pax.

"No, I won't. I don't believe you ever carried
me on your back, or that my name was Merry."

"What an unbeliever!" exclaimed Pax.

"You can't deny that you are merry to-day, Tot,"
said May.

Tot did not deny it, but, so to speak, admitted it

by starting up and giving sudden chase to a remarkably bright butterfly that passed at the moment.

"And don't you remember," resumed Pax, when she returned and sat down again by his side, "the day when we caught the enormous spider, which I kept in a glass box, where it spun a net and caught the flies I pushed into the box for it to feed on? No? Nor the black beetle we found fighting with another beetle, which, I tried to impress on you, was its grandmother, and you laughed heartily as if you really understood what I said, though you didn't. You remember that, surely? No? Well, well—these joys were thrown away on you, for you remember nothing."

"O yes, I do remember something," cried Tottie. "I remember when you fell into the horse-pond, and came out dripping, and covered from head to foot with mud and weeds!"

She followed up this remark with a merry laugh, which was suddenly checked by a shrill and terrible cry from the neighbouring field.

In order to account for this cry, we must state that Miss Lillycrop, desirous of acquiring an appetite for dinner by means of a short walk, left Rosebud Cottage and made for the dell, in which she expected to meet May Maylands and her companions. Taking a short cut, she crossed a field. Short cuts are frequently dangerous. It proved so in the present instance. The field she had invaded was the private preserve of an old bull with a sour temper.

Beholding a female, he lowered his horrid head, cocked his tail, and made at her. This it was that drew from poor Miss Lillycrop a yell such as she had not uttered since the days of infancy.

Phil Maylands was swift to act at all times of emergency. He vaulted the fence of the field, and rushed at Miss Lillycrop as if he himself had been a bull of Bashan, and meant to try his hand at tossing her. Not an idea had Phil as to what he meant to do. All he knew was that he had to rush to the rescue ! Between Phil and the bull the poor lady seemed to stand a bad chance.

Not a whit less active or prompt was Peter Pax, but Peter had apparently more of method in his madness than Phil, for he wrenched up a stout stake in his passage over the fence.

" Lie down ! lie down ! O lie down !" shouted Phil in agony, for he saw that the brute was quickly overtaking its victim.

Poor Miss Lillycrop was beyond all power of self-control. She could only fly. Fortunately a hole in the field came to her rescue. She put her foot into it and fell flat down. The bull passed right over her, and came face to face with Phil, as it pulled up, partly in surprise, no doubt, at the sudden disappearance of Miss Lillycrop and at the sudden appearance of a new foe. Before it recovered from its surprise little Pax brought the paling down on its nose with such a whack that it absolutely sneezed —or something like it—then, roaring, rushed at Pax.

As if he had been a trained matadore, Pax leaped aside, and brought the paling down again on the bull's head with a smash that knocked it all to splinters.

"Don't dodge it," shouted Phil, "draw it away from her!"

Pax understood at once. Tempting the bull to charge him again, he ran off to the other side of the field like a greyhound, followed by the foaming enemy.

Meanwhile Phil essayed to lift Miss Lillycrop, who had swooned, on his shoulders. Fortunately she was light. Still, it was no easy matter to get her limp form into his arms. With a desperate effort he got her on his knee; with an inelegant hitch he sent her across his shoulder, where she hung like a limp bolster, as he made for the fence. May and Tottie stood there rooted to the earth in horror. To walk on uneven ground with such a burden was bad enough, but Phil had to run. How he did it he never could tell, but he reached the fence at last, and shot Miss Lillycrop over into the arms of her friends, and all three were sent headlong down into a thick bush.

Phil turned at once to run to the aid of Pax, but there was no occasion to do so. That youth had reached and leaped the fence like an acrobat, and was now standing on the other side of it making faces at the bull, calling it names, and insulting it with speeches of the most refined insolence, by way of relieving his feelings and expressing his satisfaction.

CHAPTER XXVII.

THE GREATEST BATTLE OF ALL.

TIME advanced apace, and wrought many of those innumerable changes in the fortunes of the human race for which Time is famous.

Among other things it brought Sir James Clubley to the bird-shop of Messrs. Blurt one Christmas eve.

"My dear sir," said Sir James to Mr. Enoch in the back shop, through the half-closed door of which the owl could be seen gazing solemnly at the pelican of the wilderness, "I have called to ask whether you happen to have heard anything of young Aspel of late?"

"Nothing whatever," replied Mr. Blurt, with a sad shake of his head. "Since Bones died—the man, you know, with whom he lived—he has removed to some new abode, and no one ever hears or sees anything of him, except Mrs. Bones. He visits her occasionally (as I believe you are aware), but refuses to give her his address. She says, however, that he has given up drink—that the dying words of her husband had affected him very deeply. God grant it may be so, for I love the youth."

"I join in your prayer, Mr. Blurt," said Sir James, who was slightly, though perhaps unconsciously, pompous in his manner. ."My acquaintance with him has been slight—in fact only two letters have passed between us—but I entertained a strong regard for his father, who in schoolboy days saved my life. In after years he acquired that passion for spirits which his son seems to have inherited, and, giving up all his old friends, went to live on a remote farm in the west of Ireland."

Sir James spoke slowly and low, as if reflectively, with his eyes fixed on the ground.

"In one of the letters to which I have referred," he continued, looking up, "young Aspel admitted that he had fallen, and expressed regret in a few words, which were evidently sincere, but he firmly, though quite politely, declined assistance, and wound up with brief yet hearty thanks for what he called my kind intentions, and especially for my expressions of regard for his late father, who, he said, had been worthy of my highest esteem."

" He's a strange character ;—but how did you,

manage to get a letter conveyed to him ?" asked
Mr. Blurt.

"Through Mrs. Bones.   You are aware, I think,
that a considerable time ago I set a detective to
find out his whereabouts—"

"How strange !   So did I," said Mr. Blurt.

"Indeed !" exclaimed Sir James.   "Well, this
man happened by a strange coincidence to be
engaged in unravelling a mystery about a lost
little dog, which after many failures led him to
the discovery of Abel Bones as being a burglar who
was wanted.   Poor Bones happened at the time of
his visit to be called before a higher tribunal.   He
was dying.   Aspel was at his bedside, and the
detective easily recognised him as the youth of
whom he had been so long in search.   I sent my
letter by the detective to Mrs. Bones, who gave it
to Aspel.   His reply came, of course, through the
ordinary channel—the post."

"And what do you now propose doing ?" asked
Mr. Blurt.

"I think of going to see Philip Maylands, who,
I am given to understand by Miss Lillycrop, was
once an intimate friend of Aspel.   D' you happen
to know his address ?"

"Yes, he lives with his mother now, but it's of
no use your going to his home to-night.   You are
aware that this is Christmas eve, and all the officials

of the Post-Office will be unusually busy. They often work night and day at this season."

"Then I will go direct to the General Post-Office. Perhaps I shall be able to exchange a few words with him there," said Sir James, rising.

At that moment there burst upon the ears of the visitor a peculiar squall, which seemed to call forth a bland and beaming smile on the glad countenance of Mr. Blurt. Sir James looked at him inquiringly.

"My babe, Sir James," said Mr. Blurt, with ill-concealed pride; "since last I had the pleasure of seeing you I have been married. Ah! Sir James, 'it is not good for man to be alone.' That is a truth with which I was but feebly impressed until I came to understand the blessedness of the wedded state. Words cannot—"

He was cut short by a sudden crash of something overhead, and a bump, followed by a squall of unwonted vehemence. The squall was simultaneous with the ringing of a handbell, and was followed by the cry of a soft entreating voice roused to excitation.

"Oh! Nockie dear"—thus the former Miss Gentle named her spouse,—"come here, quick—oh! *do* be quick! Baby's fallen and Fred's ringing."

The truth of this was corroborated by another furious ring by the invalid, which mingled with the recurring squalls, and was increased by the

noisy and pertinacious clatter of the cracked bell
that announced the opening of the shop-door.

"Zounds! Mrs. Murridge, mind the shop!—
Good-bye, Sir James. Excuse—. Coming, dear!"

Mr. Blurt, glaring as he clutched his scant
side locks, dashed up-stairs with the agility of a
school-boy.

Sir James Clubley, who was a bachelor, left the
place with a quiet smile, and proceeded, at what we
may style a reflective pace, towards the City.

But Sir James might have saved himself the
trouble. It was, as we have said, Christmas eve,
and he might as well have demanded audience of a
soldier in the heat of battle as of a Post-Office
official on that trying night of the year.

In modern times the tendency of the human race
(the British part of it at least) to indulge in social
intercourse by letter and otherwise at the Christmas
season has been on the increase, and, since the introduction of cheap postage, it has created a pressure
on the Post-Office which has taxed its powers very
considerably. The advent of halfpenny post-cards,
and especially the invention of Christmas-card and
packet correspondence, with the various facilities
which have of late years been afforded to the
public by the Department, have created such a
mass of intercommunication throughout the kingdom, that Christmas has now to be regularly pre-

pared for as a great field-day, or rather a grand campaign extending over several days. Well-planned arrangements have to be made beforehand. Contingencies and possibilities have to be weighed and considered. All the forces of the Department have to be called out, or rather called in. Provisions—actual food, of exceptional kind and quantity—have to be provided, and every man, boy, nerve, muscle, eye, hand, brain, and spirit, has to be taxed to the very uttermost to prevent defeat.

On the particular year of which we write, symptoms of the coming struggle began to be felt before Christmas eve. On the morning of the 23d, the enemy—if we may so style the letters—began to come in like a flood, and the whole of that day the duty was most pressing, although the reserve forces had been called into action. On the morning of the 24th the strain was so severe that few men could be allowed to leave the Office, though some of them had been at work for eighteen hours. During the whole of the 24th the flood was at its height. Every available man in the other branches whose services could be utilised was pressed into the service of the Circulation Department at St. Martin's-le-Grand.

The great mouth under the portico was fed with a right royal feast that day—worthy of the Christmas season! The subsidiary mouths elsewhere

were fed with similar liberality. Through these,
letters, cards, packets, parcels, poured, rushed,
leaped, roared into the great sorting-hall. Floods
is a feeble word ; a Highland spate is but a wishy-
washy figure wherewith to represent the deluge.
A bee-hive, an ant-hill, were weak comparisons.
Nearly two thousand men energised—body, soul,
and spirit—in that hall that Christmas-tide, and an
aggregate of fifteen thousand eight hundred and
seventy-nine hours' work was accomplished by them.
They faced, stamped, sorted, carried, bundled, tied,
bagged, and sealed without a moment's intermission
for two days and two nights continuously. It was
a great, a tremendous battle ! The easy-going
public outside knew and cared little or nothing
about the conflict which themselves had caused.
Letters were heaped on the tables and strewed on
the floors. Letters were carried in baskets, in bags,
in sacks, and poured out like water. The men
and boys absolutely swam in letters. Eager activity—but no blind haste—was characteristic of the
gallant two thousand. They felt that the honour
of Her Majesty's mails depended on their devotion,
and that was, no doubt, dearer to them than life !
So the first day wore on, and the warriors stood
their ground and kept the enemy at bay.

As the evening of the 24th drew on apace, and the
ordinary pressure of the evening mail began to be

added to the extraordinary pressure of the day, the real tug of war began! The demand for extra service throughout the country began to exercise a reflex influence on the great centre. Mails came from the country in some instances with the letters unsorted, thus increasing the difficulties of the situation. The struggle was all the more severe that preparations for the night despatch were begun with a jaded force, some of the men having already been twenty-six and twenty-eight hours at work. Moreover, frost and fog prevailed at the time, and that not only delayed trains and the arrival of mails, but penetrated the building so that the labour was performed in a depressing atmosphere. To meet the emergency, at least in part, the despatch of the usual eight o'clock mail was delayed for that night fifty minutes. As in actual war an hour's delay may be fraught with tremendous issues for good or ill, so this brief postal delay permitted the despatch of an enormous amount of correspondence that would have otherwise been left over to the following day.

Usually the despatch of the evening mail leaves the vast sorting-hall in serene repose, with clean and empty tables; but on the night of this great battle—which has to be re-fought every Christmas —the embarrassment did not cease with the despatch of the evening mail. Correspondence continued to flow on in as great a volume as before.

Squads of the warriors, however, withdrew at intervals from the fight, to refresh themselves in the various kitchens of the basement.

As we have said elsewhere, the members of the Post-Office provide their own food, and there are caterers on the premises who enable them to do so without leaving the Office while on duty. But on this occasion extra and substantial food—meat, bread, tea, coffee, and cocoa—were provided by the Department at its own cost, besides which the men were liberally and deservedly remunerated for the whole severe and extra duty.

It chanced that Phil Maylands and Peter Pax retired from the battle about the same time, and met in the sorters' kitchen.

"Well, old fellow," said Phil, who was calm and steady but looking fagged, to Pax, who was dishevelled about the head and dress and somewhat roused by the exciting as well as fatiguing nature of the work,—"Well, old fellow ; tough work, isn't it ?"

"Tough ?   It's glorious !" said Pax, seating himself enthusiastically at the table ; " I'm proud of my country—proud of the G. P. O.—proud . . . . I say, is that beef that I see before me ?   Hand me a dagger —no, a knife will do.   You cut it, Phil, and help me first, 'cause I'm little."

While Phil was cutting the meat Pax rested

his head on the table, and was asleep almost instantly.

"Hallo, Pax! rouse yourself!" cried Phil, giving his comrade a hearty slap on the shoulder; "up, lad, and eat—the battle still rages; no rest allowed till victory is ours."

His little friend set to work at once, and the food and coffee soon banished drowsiness. A number of men were similarly engaged around him. But they did not feast long. Like giants refreshed, they returned to the scene of combat, while others took their places.

And what a scene it was! Despite all that had been done, the hall might be described as waist-deep in letters! The fever had not yet abated. It seemed as if the whole world had concentrated its literary produce into one mighty avalanche on St. Martin's-le-Grand!

The midnight mails worked off some of this, but a large portion of it still remained to be disposed of on Christmas-day, together with what the mails brought in on that morning, but the officers worked so well that between nine and ten on Christmas morning all were allowed to go home, with the exception of twenty-six, who volunteered to remain.

Thus the battle was fought and won; the tables were cleared; the fever was subdued; and the pulse of the Post-Office was reduced to its normal condition.

Think on these things, reader, when next you read the little card that wishes you "a merry Christmas!"

Some of the facts and results connected with this great battle are worth recording. The number of *extra* bags and sacks received at the chief office altogether on that occasion was 1401. The number of extra bags despatched was 2269; all of them were crammed full to their mouths, and the aggregate weight of these extra mails was 197 tons.

To convey these from the chief office 176 extra vans were used, and 75 extra carts. As nearly as could be estimated, the number of extra letters and packets was not less than four millions. There was a vast increase, also, in the registered correspondence—to the extent of thirty-one thousand in excess of the ordinary numbers.

During these three days some of the men did nearly thirty hours' extra duty, *besides* performing their ordinary work. The continuous attendance at the office of some of them varied from forty to forty-eight hours, and the total increase to the revenue on that auspicious but trying occasion was estimated to be about twenty thousand pounds sterling!

Phil Maylands and Peter Pax were among those who had volunteered to remain after the press of work was over; and it was not till the afternoon of Christmas-day that they finally, and simultaneously, plunged into their beds and oblivion.

CHAPTER XXVIII.

THE STORMING OF ROCKY COTTAGE AND OTHER MATTERS.

YEARS flew by. The daily routine at St. Martin's-le-Grand went on; the mails departed and came in with unvarying regularity; in the working of the vast machine good men and boys rose to the surface, and bad ones went down. Among the former were Phil Maylands and Peter Pax.

The latter, in course of time, rose to the rank of Inspector, in which condition he gradually developed a pretty pair of brown whiskers and a wonderful capacity for the performance of duty. He also rose to the altitude of five feet six inches, at which point he stuck fast, and continued the process of increase laterally. Pax, however, could not become reconciled to city life. He did his work cheerfully and with all his might, because it was his nature so to do, but he buoyed up his spirits—so he was wont to say—by fixing his eye on the Postmaster-Generalship and a suburban villa on the Thames.

His friend Phil, on the contrary, was quite pleased with city life, and devoted himself with such untiring energy to his work, and to his own education, that he came ere long to be noted as the youth who knew everything. Faults he had, undoubtedly, and his firm, severe way of expressing his opinions raised him a few enemies in the Post-Office, but he attained at last to the condition of being so useful and so trustworthy as to make men feel that he was almost indispensable. They felt as if they could not get on without him.

When man or boy comes to this point, success is inevitable. Phil soon became a favourite with the heads of departments. The Chief of the Post-Office himself at last came to hear of him, and, finding that he was more than capable of passing the requisite examinations, he raised him from the ranks and made him a clerk in the Savings-Bank Department.

Having attained to this position, with a good salary for a single man, and a prospect of a steady rise, Phil set about the accomplishment of the darling wish of his heart. He obtained leave of absence, went over to the west of Ireland, and took Rocky Cottage by storm.

"Mother dear," he said, almost before he had

sat down, " I 'm promoted. I 'm rich—comparatively. I've taken a house—a small house—at Nottinghill, and your room in it is ready for you; so pack up at once, for we leave this to-morrow afternoon."

" You jest, Phil."

" I 'm in earnest, mother."

"But it is impossible," said the good lady, looking anxiously round; " I cannot pack up on so short notice. And the furniture—"

" It's all arranged, mother," said Phil, stroking the curls of a strapping boy who no longer went by the name of Baby, but was familiarly known as Jim. "Being aware of your desire to get rid of the furniture, I have arranged with a man in Howlin' Cove to take it at a valuation. He comes out to value it this evening, so you've nothing to do but pack up your trunks. With the aid of Madge and Jim we 'll manage that in no time."

"Sure we 'll do it in less than no time !" cried Jim, who was a true son of Erin.

" You see, mother," continued Phil, "my leave extends only to four days. I have therefore ordered a coach—a sort of Noah's Ark—the biggest thing I could hire at the Cove—to take you and all your belongings to the railway to-morrow evening. We 'll travel all night, and so get to London on Thursday. May expects you.

May and I have settled it all, so you needn't look thunderstruck. If I hadn't known for certain that you'd be glad to come and live with us I would not have arranged it at all. If I had not known equally well that your fluttering bird of a heart would have been totally upset at the prospect, I would have consulted you beforehand. As it is, the die is cast. Your fate is fixed. Nothing can reverse the decrees that have gone forth, so it's as well to make your mind easy and go to work."

Mrs. Maylands wisely submitted. Three days afterwards she found herself in London, in a very small but charming cottage in an out-of-the-way corner of Nottinghill.

It was a perfect *bijou* of a cottage; very small—only two stories—with ceilings that a tall man could touch, and a trellis-work porch at the front door, and a little garden all to itself, and an ivy wall that shut out the curious public, but did not interfere with the sky, a patch of which gleamed through between two great palatial residences hard by, like a benignant eye.

"This is our new home, mother, and we have got it at such a low rent from Sir James Clubley, our landlord, that your income, coupled with May's salary and mine, will enable us easily to make the two ends meet, if we manage economically."

As he spoke, Phil seized the poker, and, with an

utter disregard of the high price of coal, caused the fire to roar joyously up the chimney.

It was a brilliant winter day. White gems sparkled on the branches of the trees, and Jim was already commencing that course of romping which had, up to that date, strewn his path through life with wreck and ruin. Madge was investigating the capabilities of cupboards and larders, under the care of a small maid-of-all-work.

" May won't be home till after dark," said Phil " She could not get away from duty to meet us. I shall telegraph to her that we have arrived, and that I shall meet her under the portico of the Post-Office and fetch her home this evening."

" It is an amazing thing that telegraph ! To think that one can send messages and make appointments so quickly !" remarked Mrs. Maylands.

" Why, mother," said Phil, with a laugh, " that is nothing to what can be—and is—done with it every day. I have a friend in the City who does a great part of his business with India by telegraph. The charge is four shillings and sixpence a word, and if a word has more than ten letters it is charged as two words. A registered address also costs a guinea, so, you see, telegraphic correspondence with India is expensive. Business men have therefore fallen on the plan of writing out lists of words, each of which means a longish sentence. This plan is so thoroughly carried out that books like thick dictionaries are now printed and regularly used.—What would you think, now, of '*Obstinate Kangaroo*' for a message ?"

"I would think it nonsense, Phil."

"Nevertheless, mother, it covers sense. A Quebec timber-merchant telegraphed these identical words the other day to a friend of mine, and when the friend turned up the words 'obstinate kangaroo' in his corresponding code, he found the translation to be, 'Demand is improving for Ohio or Michigan white oak (planks), 16 inches and upwards.'"

"You *don't* say so !" exclaimed Mrs. Maylands, raising both hands and eyebrows.

"Yes I do, mother, and in my City friend's code the word '*Blazing*' means '*Quality is approved,*' while '*Blissful*' signifies 'What is the smallest quantity you require ?'"

"Do you mean, Phil," asked the widow, with a perplexed look, "that if I were a man of business, and wanted to ask a customer in India *what was the smallest quantity of a thing he required*, I should have to telegraph only the word '*Blissful*'?"

"Only that, mother. A blissful state of brevity to have come to, isn't it ? And some of the telegraph clerks fall into queer mistakes, too, owing to their ignorance. One of the rules is that the words sent must be *bona fide* words—not a mere unmeaning arrangement of letters. My City friend told me that on three different occasions telegrams of his were refused, because the words were not known, yet each of them was taken from the Bible! One of the telegrams was, ' *Blastus unholy.*' "

" Oh, Phil, how *can* you !" exclaimed Mrs. May-lands, with a shocked look.

" Well, mother, what's wrong in that ?"

" You know very well, Phil, that ' Blast us ' is not in the Bible at all, and that it is a very awful species of slang swearing."

" So the telegraph clerk thought," returned Phil, " but when my City friend pointed out that Blastus was ' the king's chamberlain ' they were obliged to let the telegram go. ' *Blastus*' stands for ' *superior quality,*' and ' *unholy* ' for ' *Offer is open for three days from time of despatch of telegram.*' Using the same code, if a merchant wants to ask a Calcutta friend the question—' *How is the coming crop as regards extent and appearance ?*' he merely telegraphs the word ' *Hamlet.*' If he wishes to say ' *Bills of lading go forward by this mail, Invoices will follow,*' he has only to telegraph ' *Heretic.*' For the most part the compilers of these codes seem to have used the words arbitrarily, for the word ' *Ellwood*' has no visible connection with the words ' *Blue Velvet,*' which it represents ; neither is there connection between ' *Doves*' and ' *French Brandy,*' nor between

'*Collapse*' and '*Scotch Coals*,' though there does seem to have been a gleam of significance when they fixed on '*Downward*' to represent '*Irish Whisky*.' "

"That's true, Phil, there was a touch of sense there, if not sarcasm," said the widow heartily, for she was an abhorrer of strong drink !

"Then, mother, think of the saving of time accomplished by the telegraph. In days not long past, if a merchant in India wished to transact business with another in New York he had to write a letter which took months to make the voyage out, and his correspondent had to write a reply which took about the same time to return. Now, not long ago the head of an Indian house wanted a ship-load of something (I forget what) from New York. He telegraphed a few unconnected words to my City friend in London. If there had been no obstruction of any kind the message could have been flashed from Bombay to London in a few seconds ; as it was, it made the journey in three hours. My friend, who received it in the forenoon, telegraphed to New York, transacted the business, received a reply from New York, and telegraphed back to Bombay that the order was given and in process of execution before five P.M. on the same day. Thus a commercial transaction between India and America, *via* England, involving, perhaps, thousands of pounds, was completed at the cost of a few pounds between breakfast

and dinner.   In other words, Bombay aroused New
York to action by means of a flash of electricity
within twenty-four hours."

"Phil," remarked Mrs. Maylands, with a sigh,
"don't you think that man has now made almost
all the discoveries that it is possible to make?"

"Why, no, mother, I think he is only on the
threshold of discovery yet.   The thought has sometimes come into my mind with tremendous power,
that as God is infinite, and His knowledge infinite,
there is, as it were, a necessity that we shall go on
learning something new for ever!—But that is too
deep a subject to enter on just now," said Phil,
rising, "for I must go and send off my telegram
to May—she will be anxious to hear about you,
poor girl.   You must not be troubled when you see
how the roses have faded from her cheeks.   She is
in good enough health, but I fear the telegraph
service is too heavy for her, and the City air is not
so bracing as that of the west of Ireland."

Mrs. Maylands was quite prepared for the change
referred to, for she knew, what Phil did not know,
that it was neither the telegraph nor the City that
had robbed May of the bloom of youth and health.

CHAPTER XXIX.

DESCRIBES AN INTERVIEW AND A RECONTRE.

ONE frosty winter afternoon Sir James Clubley sat in his chambers, having finished dinner, and toasted his toes while he sipped his wine and glanced languidly over the *Times*.

Sir James was a lazy, good-natured man, in what is sometimes styled easy circumstances. Being lazy, and having nothing to do, he did nothing— nothing, that is, in the way of work. He found the world enjoyable, and enjoyed it. He never ran to excess—in truth he never ran at all, either literally or figuratively, but always ate, drank, slept, read, and amused himself in moderation. In politics, being nothing in particular, he was wont to say he was a Liberal-Conservative, if anything, as that happy medium, in which truth is said, though not proved, to lie, enabled him to agree with anybody. Everybody liked him, except perhaps a few fiery zealots who seemed uncertain

2 c

whether to regard him with indignation, pity, or contempt. It mattered not to which feeling the zealots leaned, Sir James smiled on them all alike.

"That foolish fellow is going to be late," he muttered, glancing over his paper at the clock on the chimney-piece.

The foolish fellow referred to was George Aspel. Sir James had at last discovered and had an interview with him. He had offered to aid him in any way that lay in his power, but Aspel had firmly though gratefully declined aid in any form.

Sir James liked the youth, and had begged him, by letter, to call on him, for the purpose of chatting over a particular piece of business, had appointed an hour, and now awaited his arrival.

The muttered remark had just passed Sir James's lips when there came a tap at the door, and Aspel stood before him.

But how changed from what he was when we last saw him, reader! His aspect might have forcibly recalled the words, "was lost and is found."

His tall, broad frame stood erect again as of old, but the proud bearing of the head was gone. There was the same fearless look in his bright blue eye, but the slightly self-satisfied curl of the lip was not there. He looked as strong and well as when,

on the Irish cliffs, he had longed for the free, wild
life of the sea-kings, but he did not look so youth-
ful ; yet the touch of sadness that now rested at
times on his countenance gave him a far more
regal air,—though he knew it not,—than he ever
possessed before.   He was dressed in a simple suit
of dark grey.

"Glad to see you, Aspel; thought you were
going to fail me. Sit down. Now, come, I hope
you have considered my proposal favourably.—The
piece of business I asked you to come about is
nothing more than to offer you again that situation,
and to press it on you. It would just suit a man
of your powers.—What ! No ?"

The Baronet frowned, for George Aspel had
smiled slightly and shaken his head as he sat
down.

"Forgive me, Sir James, if I seem to regard your
kind proposals with indifference.   Indeed, I am
sincerely grateful, especially for the motive that
actuates you—I mean regard for my dear father's
memory—"

"How do you know, sir," interrupted Sir James
testily, "that this is my only motive ?"

"I did not say it was your only motive, Sir
James. I cannot doubt, from your many expressions of kindness, that personal regard for myself
influences you ; but I may not accept the situation

you offer me—bright with future prospects though it be—because I feel strongly that God has called me to another sphere of action. I have now been for a considerable time, and hope to be as long as I live, a missionary to the poor."

"What! A city missionary? One of those fellows who go about in seedy black garments with long lugubrious faces!" exclaimed Sir James in amazement.

"Some of them do indeed wear seedy black garments," replied Aspel, "under some strange hallucination, I suppose, that it is their duty to appear like clergymen, and I admit that they would look infinitely more respectable in sober and economical grey tweeds; but you must have seen bad specimens of the class of men if you think their faces long and lugubrious. I know many of them whose faces are round and jovial, and whose spirits correspond to their faces. No doubt they are sometimes sad. Your own face would lengthen a little, Sir James, if you went where they go, and saw what they sometimes see."

"I dare say you are right. Well, but have you seriously joined this body of men?"

"Not officially. I—I—hesitate to offer myself, because—that is to say, I am a sort of free-lance just now."

"But, my young friend," returned Sir James

slowly, " I understand that city missionaries preach, and usually have a considerable training in theology; now, it is not very long ago since you were a—excuse me—I—I shrink from hurting your feelings, but—"

" A drunkard, Sir James," said Aspel, looking down and blushing crimson. "State the naked truth. I admit it, with humiliation and sorrow; but, to the everlasting praise of God, I can say that Jesus Christ has saved me from drink. Surely, that being the case, I am in some degree fitted to speak of the Great Remedy—the Good Physician—to the thousands who are perishing in this city from the effects of drink, even though I be not deeply versed in theology. To save men and women from what I have suffered, by exhorting and inducing them to come to the Saviour is all my aim—it is now my chief ambition."

Sir James looked inquiringly at the fire and shook his head. He was evidently not convinced.

" There is truth in what you say, Aspel, but by taking this course you sacrifice your prospects entirely—at least in this life."

" On the contrary, Sir James, I expect, by taking this course, to gain all that in this life is worth living for."

" Ah ! I see, you have become religiously mad," said Sir James, with a perplexed look; "well,

Aspel, you must take your own way, for I am aware that it is useless to reason with madmen ; yet I cannot help expressing my regret that a young fellow of your powers should settle down into a moping, melancholy, would-be reformer of drunkards."

To this Aspel replied with a laugh.

"Why, Sir James," he said, "do I look very moping or melancholy ? If so, my looks must belie my spirit, for I feel very much the reverse, and from past experience—which is now considerable—I expect to have a great deal of rejoicing in my work, for it does not all consist in painful strivings with unrepentant men and women. Occasionally men in our position know something of that inexpressible joy which results from a grateful glance of the eye or a strong squeeze of the hand from some one whom we have helped to pluck from the very edge of hell. It is true, I do not expect to make much money in my profession, but my Master promises me sufficient, and a man needs no more. But even if much money were essential, there is no doubt that I should get it, for the silver and gold of this world are in the hands of my Father."

" Where do you work ?" asked Sir James abruptly.

"Chiefly in the neighbourhood of Archangel Court. It was there I fell and sinned ; it was there my Saviour rescued me : it is there I feel bound to labour."

"Very well, I won't press this matter further," said the Baronet, rising; "but remember, if you ever get into a better frame of mind, I shall be happy to see you."

Profound and various were the thoughts of the reformed drunkard that afternoon as he left his friend's abode and walked slowly towards the City. There was a strange feeling of sadness in his heart which he could not account for. It was not caused by the sacrifice of worldly good he had just made, for that had cost him no effort. The desire to rescue the perishing had been infused so strongly into his soul that he had become quite regardless of mere temporal advancement. Neither had he been unfaithful, as far as he could remember, in the recent conversation—at least not in words. The hopes and joys which he had truly referred to ought to have been as strong as ever within him, nevertheless his spirit was much depressed. He began to think of the position from which he had fallen, and of the great amount of good he might have done for Christ in a higher sphere of society—but this thought he repelled as a recurrence of pride.

As he came to St. Martin's-le-Grand he stopped, and, forgetting the bustling crowd of people, busses, cabs, and carts by which he was surrounded, allowed his mind to wander into the past. It was on the broad steps of the Post-Office that he had been first

led astray by the man who wished to compass his
ruin, but who was eventually made the willing instrument in bringing about his salvation. He
thought of the scowling look and clenched fist of
poor Bones as he had stood there, long ago, under
the grand portico. He thought of the same man on
his sick-bed, with clasped hands and glittering eyes,
thanking God that he had been brought to the gates
of death by an accident, that his eyes and heart
had been opened to see and accept Jesus, and that
he had still power left to urge his friend (George
Aspel) to come to Jesus, the sinner's Refuge. He
thought also of the burglar's death, and of the fading
away of his poor wife, who followed him to the
grave within the year. He thought of the orphan
Tottie, who had been adopted and educated by Miss
Stivergill, and was by that time as pretty a specimen of budding womanhood as any one could desire
to see, with the strong will and courage of her
father, and the self-sacrificing, trusting, gentleness
of her mother. But above and beyond and under-
lying all these thoughts, his mind kept playing
incessantly round a fair form which he knew was
somewhere engaged at that moment in the building
at his side, manipulating a three-keyed instrument
with delicate fingers which he longed to grasp.

Ah! it is all very well for a man to resolve to
tear an idol from his heart; it is quite another

thing to do it.   George Aspel had long ago given
up all hope of winning May Maylands.   He not
only felt that one who had fallen so low as he,
and shown such a character for instability, had no
right to expect any girl to trust her happiness to
him ; but he also felt convinced that May had no
real love for him, and that it would be unmanly to
push his suit, even although he was now delivered
from the power of his great enemy.   He determined, therefore, to banish her as much as possible
from his mind, and, in furtherance of his purpose,
had conscientiously kept out of her way and out of
the way of all his former friends.

Heaving a little sigh as he dismissed her, for the
ten-thousandth time, from his mind, he was turning his back on the Post-Office—that precious
casket which contained so rich but unattainable a
jewel—when he remembered that he had a letter in
his pocket to post.

Turning back, he sprang up the steps.   The
great mouth was not yet wide open.   The evening
feeding-hour had not arrived, and the lips were only
in their normal condition—slightly parted.   Having
contributed his morsel to the insatiable giant, Aspel
turned away, and found himself face to face with
Phil Maylands.

It was not by any means their first meeting since
the recovery of Aspel, but, as we have said, the

latter had kept out of the way of old friends, and Phil was only partially excepted from the rule.

" The very man I wanted to see !" cried Phil, with gleaming eyes, as he seized his friend's hand. " I've got mother over to London at last. She's longing to see you. Come out with me this evening—do. But I'm in sudden perplexity : I've just been sent for to do some extra duty. It won't take me half an hour.-—You're not engaged, are you ?"

" Well, no—not particularly."

" Then you'll do me a favour, I'm sure you will. You'll mount guard here for half an hour, won't you ? I had appointed to meet May here this evening to take her home, and when she comes she'll not know why I have failed her unless you—"

" My dear Phil, I would stay with all my heart," said Aspel hastily, " but—but—the fact is—I've not seen May for a long time, and—"

" Why, what on earth has *that* to do with it ?" asked Phil, in some surprise.

" You are right," returned Aspel, with a deprecating smile, " that has nothing to do with it. My wits are wool-gathering, Phil. Go : I will mount guard."

Phil was gone in a moment, and Aspel leaned his head on his arm against one of the pillars of the portico. He had scarcely breathed a prayer for guidance when May approached. She stopped abruptly, flushed slightly, and hesitated a moment, then, advancing with the hearty air of an old playmate, she frankly held out her hand.

This was enough for Aspel. He had been depressed before; he was in the depths of despair now. If May had only shown confusion, or shyness, or anything but free-and-easy goodwill, hope might have revived, but he was evidently nothing more to her than the old playmate. Hope therefore died, and with its death there came over Aspel the calm subdued air of a crushed but resigned man. He observed her somewhat worn face and his heart melted. He resolved to act a brother's part to her.

"I'm so glad to meet you at last, May!" he said, returning the kindly grasp of the hand with interest, but quite in a brotherly way.

"You might have seen me long ago. Why did you not come? We would all have been so glad to see you."

May blushed decidedly as she made this reply, but the shades of evening were falling. Moreover, the pillar near to which they stood threw a deep shadow over them, and Aspel did not observe it. He therefore continued—in a quiet, brotherly way—

"Ah! May, it is cruel of you to ask that. You know that I have been unfit—"

"Nay, I did not mean *that*," interrupted May, with eager anxiety; "I meant that since—since—lately, you know—why did you not come?"

"True, May, I might have come *lately*—praise be to God!—but, but—why should I not speak out? It's all over now. You know the love I once bore you, May, which you told me I must not speak of, and which I have tried to cure with all the energy of my heart, for I do not want to lose you as a sister—an old playmate at least—though I may not have you as—But, as I said, it's all over now. I promise never again to intrude this subject on you. Let me rather tell you of the glorious work in which I am at present engaged."

He stopped, for, in spite of his efforts to be brotherly, there was a sense of sinking at his heart which slightly embittered his tone.

"Is true love, then, so easily cured?"

May looked up in his face as she asked the question. There was something in the look and in the tone which caused George Aspel's heart to beat like a sledge-hammer. He stooped down, and, looking into her eyes,—still in a brotherly way, said—

"Is it possible, May, that you could trifle with my feelings?"

"No, it is not possible," she answered promptly.

"Oh! May," continued Aspel, in a low, earnest

one ; "if I could only dare to think,—to believe,—
to hope, that—"

"Forgive me, May, I'm so sorry," cried her
brother Phil, as he sprang up the steps ; "I did my
best to hurry through with it. I'm afraid I've
kept you and George waiting very long."

"Not at all," replied May, with unquestionable
truth.

"If you could have only kept us waiting five
minutes longer!" thought Aspel, but he only said—
"Come along, Phil, I'll go home with you to
night."

The evening was fine—frosty and clear.

"Shall we walk to Nottinghill?" asked Phil.
"It's a longish tramp for you, May, but that's the
very thing you want."

May agreed that it was a desirable thing in every
point of view, and George Aspel did not object.

As they walked along, the latter began to wonder
whether a new experiment had been made lately in
the way of paving the streets with indiarubber. As
for May, she returned such ridiculous answers to
the simplest questions, that Phil became almost
anxious about her, and finally settled it in his
own mind that her labours in the telegraph
department of the General Post-Office must be
brought to a close as soon as possible.

"You see, mother," he said that night, after Aspel

had left the cottage and May had gone to her room, "it will never do to let her kill herself over the telegraph instrument. She's too delicately formed for such work. We must find something better suited to her."

"Yes, Phil, we must find something better suited to her.—Good-night," replied Mrs. Maylands.

There was a twinkle in the widow's eye as she said this that sorely puzzled Phil, and kept him in confused meditation that night, until the confusion became worse confounded and he fell into an untroubled slumber.

CHAPTER XXX.

THE LAST.

SITTING alone in the breakfast parlour of The Rosebud, one morning in June, Miss Stivergill read the following paragraph in her newspaper :—

"GALLANT RESCUE.—Yesterday forenoon a lady and her daughter, accompanied by a gentleman, went to the landing-wharf at Blackfriars with the intention of going on board a steamer. There were some disorderly men on the wharf, and a good deal of crowding at the time. As the steamer approached, one of the half-drunk men staggered violently against the daughter above referred to, and thrust her into the river, which was running rapidly at the time, the tide being three-quarters ebb. The gentleman, who happened to have turned towards the mother at the moment, heard a scream and plunge. He looked quickly back and missed the young lady. Being a tall powerful man, he dashed the crowd aside, hurled the drunk man—no doubt inadvertently—into the river, sprang over his head, as he was falling, with a magnificent bound, and reached the water so near to the young lady that a few powerful strokes enabled him to grasp and support her. Observing that the unfortunate cause of the whole affair was rolling helplessly past him with the tide, he made a vigorous stroke or two with his disengaged arm, and succeeded in grasping him by the nape of the neck, and holding him at arm's-length, despite his struggles, until a boat rescued them all. We believe that the gentleman who effected this double rescue is named Aspel, and that he is a city missionary. We have also been informed that the young lady is engaged to her gallant deliverer, and that the wedding has been fixed to come off this week."

Laying down the paper, Miss Stivergill lifted up her eyes and hands, pursed her mouth, and gave vent to a most unladylike whistle! She had barely terminated this musical performance, and recovered the serenity of her aspect, when Miss Lillycrop burst in upon her with unwonted haste and excitement.

"My darling Maria!" she exclaimed, breathlessly, flinging her bonnet on a chair and seizing both the hands of her friend, "I am *so* glad you're at home. It's *such* an age since I saw you! I came out by the early train on purpose to tell you. I hardly know where to begin. Oh! I'm *so* glad!—"

"You're not going to be married?" interrupted Miss Stivergill, whose stern calmness deepened as her friend's excitement increased.

"Married? oh no! Ridiculous! but I think I'm going deranged."

"That is impossible," returned Miss Stivergill. "You have been deranged ever since I knew you. If there is any change in your condition it can only be an access of the malady. Besides, there is no particular cause for joy in that. Have you no more interesting news to give me?"

"More interesting news!" echoed Miss Lilly-crop, sitting down on her bonnet, "of course I have. Now, just listen: Peter Pax—of the firm of Blurt, Pax, Jiggs, and Company, Antiquarians, Bird-Stuffers, Mechanists, Stamp-Collectors, and I don't know what else besides, to the Queen—is going to be married to—whom do you think?"

"The Queen of Sheba," replied Miss Stivergill, folding her hands on her lap with a placid smile.

"To—Tottie Bones!" said Miss Lillycrop, with an excited movement that ground some of her bonnet to straw-powder.

Miss Stivergill did not raise her eyes or whistle at this. She merely put her head a little on one side and smiled.

"I knew it, my dear—at least I felt sure it would come to this, though it is sooner than I expected.   It is not written anywhere, I believe, that a boy may not marry a baby, nevertheless—"

" But she's not a baby," broke in Miss Lillycrop. "Tottie is seventeen now, and Pax is twenty-four. But this is not the half of what I have to tell you. Ever since Pax was taken into partnership by Mr. Enoch Blurt the business has prospered, as you are aware, and our active little friend has added all kinds of branches to it—such as the preparation and sale of entomological, and ichthyological, and other -ological specimens, and the mechanical parts of toy-engines ; and that lad Jiggs has turned out such a splendid expounder of all these things, that the shop has become a sort of terrestrial heaven for boys.   And dear old Fred Blurt has begun to recover under the influence of success, so that he is now able to get out frequently in a wheel-chair. But the strangest news of all is that Mister Enoch Blurt got a new baby—a girl—and recovered his diamonds on the self-same day !"

" Indeed !" said Miss Stivergill, beginning to be influenced by these surprising revelations.

" Yes, and it's a curious evidence of the energetic and successful way in which things are managed by our admirable Post-Office—"

" What ! the union of a new baby with recovered diamonds ? "

" No, no, Maria, how stupid you are !   I refer, of

course, to the diamonds. Have you not seen reference made to them in the papers?"

"No. I've seen or heard nothing about it."

"Indeed! I'm surprised. Well, that hearty old letter-carrier, Solomon Flint, sent that ridiculously stout creature whom he calls Dollops to me with the last Report of the Postmaster-General, with the corner of page eleven turned down, for he knew I was interested in anything that might affect the Blurts. But here it is. I brought it to read to you. Listen: 'On the occasion of the wreck of the *Trident* in Howlin' Cove, on the west of Ireland, many years ago, strenuous efforts were made by divers to recover the Cape of Good Hope mails, and, it will be recollected, they were partially successful, but a portion which contained diamonds could not be found. Diving operations were, however, resumed quite recently, and with most satisfactory results. One of the registered-letter bags was found. It had been so completely imbedded in sand, and covered by a heavy portion of the wreck, that the contents were not altogether destroyed, notwithstanding the long period of their immersion. On being opened in the Chief Office in London, the bag was found to contain several large packets of diamonds, the addresses on which had been partially obliterated, besides about seven pounds weight of loose diamonds, which, having escaped from their covers, were mixed with the pulp in the bottom of the bag. Every possible endeavour was used by the officers of the Department to discover the rightful owners of those packets which were nearly intact, and with such success that they were all, with very little delay, duly delivered. The remaining diamonds were valued by an experienced broker, and sold— the amount realised being about £19,000. After very great trouble, and much correspondence, the whole of the persons for whom the loose diamonds were intended were, it is believed, ascertained, and this sum proved sufficient to satisfy the several claimants to such an extent that not a single complaint was heard.' "

" How strange ! Why did you not tell me of this before, Lilly ?"

" Because Mr. Blurt resolved to keep it secret until he was quite sure there was no mistake about the matter. Now that he has received the value of his diamonds he has told all his friends. Moreover, he has resolved to take a house in the suburbs, so that Fred may have fresh country air, fresh milk, and fresh eggs. Peter Pax, too, talks of doing the same thing, being bent, so he says, on devoting himself to the entomological department of his business, in order that he may renew his youth by hunting butterflies and beetles with Tottie."

" It never rains but it pours," said Miss Stiver-

gill. "Surprises don't come singly, it appears.—
Have you read *that ?*" She handed her friend the
newspaper which recounted the "gallant rescue."

Miss Lillycrop's countenance was a study which
cannot be described. The same may be said of her
bonnet. When she came to the name of Aspel her
eyeballs became circular, and her eyebrows apparently attempted to reach the roots of her hair.

"Maria dear !" she cried, with a little shriek,
"this only reminds me that I have still more
news to tell. You remember Sir James Clubley ?
Well, he is dead, and he has left the whole of
his property to George Aspel ! It seems that Sir
James went one night, secretly, as it were, to some
low locality where Aspel was preaching to poor
people, and was so affected by what he heard and
saw that he came forward at the close, signed the
pledge along with a number of rough and dirty
men, and then and there became a total abstainer.
This, I am told, occurred a considerable time ago,
and he has been a helper of the Temperance cause
ever since. Sir James had no near relatives. To
the few distant ones he possessed he left legacies,
and in his will stated that he left the rest of his
fortune—which, although not large, is considerable
—to George Aspel, in the firm belief that by so
doing he was leaving it to further the cause of
Christianity and Temperance."

"Come, now, don't stop there," observed Miss Stivergill calmly, "go on to tell me that Phil Maylands has also had a fortune left him, or become Postmaster-General and got married, or is going to be."

"Well, I can't exactly tell you that," returned Miss Lillycrop, "but I can tell you that he has had a rise in the Post-Office Savings Bank, with an increase of salary, and that May declines to marry Aspel unless he agrees to live with her mother in the cottage at Nottinghill. Of course Aspel has consented—all the more that it is conveniently situated near to a station whence he can easily reach the field of his missionary labours."

"Does he intend to continue these now that he is rich?" asked Miss Stivergill.

"How can you ask such a question?" replied her friend, with a slightly offended look. "Aspel is not a man to be easily moved from his purpose. He says he will labour in the good cause, and devote health and means to it as long as God permits."

"Good!" exclaimed Miss Stivergill with a satisfied nod.—"Now, Lilly," she added, with the decision of tone and manner peculiar to her, "I mean to make some arrangements. The farmer next to me has a very pretty villa, as you are aware, on the brow of the hill that overlooks the whole country in the direction of London. It is at present to let. Mr. Blurt must take it. Beside it stands a cottage just large enough for a new-married couple. I had already rented that cottage for a poor friend. He, however, knows nothing about the matter. I will therefore have him put somewhere else, and sub-let the cottage to Mr. and Mrs. Pax. Lastly, you shall give up your insane notion of living alone, come here, with all your belongings, and take up your abode with me for ever."

"That's a long time, dear Maria," said Miss Lilly-crop, with a little smile.

"Not *too* long, by any means, Lilly. Now, clear that rubbish off the chair—it's well got rid of, I never liked the shape—go, put yourself to rights, use one of my bonnets, and come out for a walk. To-morrow you shall go into town and arrange with Pax and Blurt about the villa and the cottage to the best of your ability. It's of no use attempting to resist me, Lilly—tell them that—for in this affair I have made up my mind that my will shall be law"

.   .   .   .

Reader, what more need we add—except that Miss Stivergill's will did eventually become law, because it happened to correspond with the wishes of all concerned. It is due, also, to Solomon Flint to record that after his long life of faithful service in the Post-Office he retired on a small but comfortable pension, and joined the "Rosebud Colony," as Pax styled it, taking his grandmother along with him. That remarkable piece of antiquity, when last seen by a credible witness, was basking in the sunshine under a rustic porch covered with honeysuckle, more wrinkled, more dried-up, more tough, more amiable—especially to her cat—and more steeped in the previous century than ever. Mr. Bright, the energetic sorter, who visits Solomon whenever his postal duties will allow, expresses his belief that the old lady will live to see them all out, and Mr. Bright's opinion carries weight with it; besides which, Phil Maylands and May Aspel with her husband are more than half inclined to agree with him. Time will show!

Pegaway Hall still exists, but its glory has departed, for although Mrs. Square still keeps her one watchful eye upon its closed door, its walls and rafters no longer resound with the eloquence, wit, and wisdom of Boy Telegraph Messengers, although these important servants of the Queen still continue—with their friends the letter-carriers—to tramp the kingdom " post-haste," in ceaseless, benignant activity, distributing right and left with impartial justice the varied contents of Her Majesty's Mails.

THE END.

PRINTED BY T. AND A. CONSTABLE, PRINTERS TO HER MAJESTY,
AT THE EDINBURGH UNIVERSITY PRESS.

www.ingramcontent.com/pod-product-compliance
Lightning Source LLC
Chambersburg PA
CBHW030947110726
47900CB00004B/1168